To Angi

Enjoy the book

Counterplay

S.A. Van

INFINITY
PUBLISHING

Copyright © 2012 by S.A. Van

ISBN 978-0-7414-7337-0 Paperback
ISBN 978-0-7414-7338-7 eBook
Library of Congress Control Number: 2012932198

Printed in the United States of America

Published April 2012

INFINITY PUBLISHING
1094 New DeHaven Street, Suite 100
West Conshohocken, PA 19428-2713
Toll-free (877) BUY BOOK
Local Phone (610) 941-9999
Fax (610) 941-9959
Info@buybooksontheweb.com
www.buybooksontheweb.com

Acknowledgments

For countless hours and helping me breathe life into my characters and their story, I want to express my sincere thanks to my very good friend Kim Wilson.

To my editing team of Marta Ficke, Alicia Muncey, Joan Murphy, Kathy Nerlinger, Shannon Peters, Karen Roth and Nancy Wilson, I appreciate your special insights and the time you spent with red pens hovering over the pages.

To Eric Peters for his valuable help with launching my author's website, and providing my official book-signing pen.

To authors Lynn Kellan and Glen Goleburn for their helpful insights into the world of publishing, I appreciate your guidance and good wishes.

To my husband Steve and daughter Caitlin, for their patience and understanding when I needed to spend time with my new *family-in-print* foregoing dinner prep and the ironing pile.

And to my friends at TS, who inspire me daily with their creativity, dedication and their sense of humor.

For the real JR,
Keep your chin up
and
your heart open

"...for every action
there is a reaction
and
for every play
there is a
counterplay."

Prologue

September 1980
New York City

Sylvia's entire body was drenched in sweat, yet she couldn't stop shaking. The sheet and pillow she was lying on were damp from her body's moisture. She could feel her clothes clinging to her. It was an eerie feeling; her skin was chilled like she was freezing, but her face felt so warm. How her body could be experiencing two distinct temperatures at the same time was such a mystery to her. Was her mind playing games with her as she drifted in and out of sanity?

Mason left an hour ago, not bothering to return to the bedroom to check on her. Thank God, or he would have noticed the terror on her face. She had overheard his phone conversation. He had made little effort to conceal it. Was Mason bragging...about stealing artifacts...and *killing* someone?

Was she going to be next?

Sylvia gripped the sheet so tightly she almost tore it in half. Rolling to her side, she attempted to get out of bed. Her legs shook uncontrollably; she had to steady herself a couple of times before she was able to stand. She walked on her tiptoes, so afraid Mason might come back any moment. She opened her bedroom door slowly, cringing as it gave a slight creak. Peering around the door to her empty living room, she was finally able to breathe.

She was alone and safe...for now.

Sylvia headed straight for her living room window. Separating the blinds ever so carefully, she glanced down at the street below. Nothing out of the ordinary for a late Tuesday evening. Traffic and pedestrians were fading into the dark as the time approached midnight. Her section of the city was beginning to put itself to bed.

Sylvia assumed it wasn't the case for Mason Hamilton, her demanding lover and boss at Hamilton-Knox, the world-renowned museum foundation which sponsored large-scale art exhibits.

When Mason left her apartment in Tribeca, he was in a rush. God knows who Mason was meeting at this late hour or where he was even headed. Sylvia dared to speculate. Mason had gotten himself mixed up with thieves and murderers. She needed to get the hell away from him.

Or maybe Mason was just going home to his pretty, rich wife of three months.

Sylvia shook her head; she really didn't give a damn about what he was doing at the moment. The bastard. He had quickly maneuvered himself into her bed, claiming another victory for his inflated ego. She had been so stupid...to let him.

Sylvia cursed the day she met Mason Hamilton. Now, she needed to find a way to disentangle herself from him once and for all. There was no way she could stay in New York and pretend like nothing had happened...not after what she had just heard. His sadistic tone had scared the daylights out of her. Mason was turning into a monster right in front of her eyes, or her ears to be exact.

Turning away from her front window, she gazed around the living room. At one point, she had heard Mason grunting as he moved a piece of furniture. But why? What was he doing? Was he hiding something?

Sylvia noticed the carpet indentations by her antique bookshelf. It hadn't been returned to its original location. The two left legs had been re-positioned. Mason had moved her bookshelf for a reason.

Yes, she remembered now. Mason had ordered someone to pick up a package at her apartment when she was at work the next morning.

What could possibly be worth hiding in her apartment of all places? She had a right to know. It was her apartment after all, except for the fact Mason had bought it for her.

Sylvia turned off all the lights except for the small crystal lamp on her bed stand. Only the soft, filtered light from the moon coming in through the blinds lit a pathway.

Moving the bookshelf took quite an effort. Sylvia felt the muscles in her back straining as she pulled the left side towards her. Finally, she was able to wedge her arm far enough back to reach behind. Her fingers came in contact with a small bundle, wrapped in a soft cloth. After a few tugs, Sylvia successfully yanked it free.

The darkness limited her ability to see exact details on the covering. The silky cloth appeared to be very old, and it smelled musty.

Peeling back the corners of the cloth, Sylvia noticed five small objects individually wrapped in yellowed newspaper. When she started to unravel the first piece, the newspaper fell into pieces. The date on the paper was from 1932 – almost 50 years ago! No wonder the paper was so brittle.

"What did you find, Mason?" Sylvia said to herself.

Gently pushing the paper fragments away, she was surprised to reveal a small elephant figurine. It had to be solid gold. It weighed so heavy in her hand. Setting it aside, she quickly unwrapped the other four. A tiger, a monkey, a giraffe and a lion.

Sylvia was bewildered.

"Was this actually worth killing for?"

Whatever these small objects were, Sylvia had no doubt they were probably worth a fortune; otherwise Mason wouldn't have taken such a risk to keep them hidden.

He had killed for these figurines; what else was he capable of?

Mason spent weeks at a time, travelling abroad in Europe. He always said it was for international business arrangements, but now she wondered. He rarely discussed the details of his trips. Mason had made it perfectly clear…Sylvia had no business interfering in matters which did not concern her.

But this did *concern* her.

He had hidden this bundle of gold animals in her apartment and he was planning on…

Sylvia shuddered as she remembered what he had said. It was all coming back to her. Initially, she had been in shock and couldn't possibly have heard correctly.

But now…she recalled Mason's exact words.

He was planning on killing her.

Sylvia debated her options. Should she call the police? Not a good idea. Mason would deny any allegations of wrong-doing and surround himself with his high-paid attorneys. There would be no one attesting to the fact she was his lover or he had even come to her apartment. Mason was careful to hide his tracks, always taking the back stairs.

Should she take a chance and call the museum to see if there were any artifacts missing from its inventory? Probably not. Mason would find a way to accuse Sylvia of stealing the figurines.

"What in the hell am I going to do?"

Leaning against the bookshelf, Sylvia closed her eyes, which were beginning to tear. She needed a third option...an option to ensure her safety until she felt confident enough to beat Mason at his own game.

There was only one possible solution.

"I have to leave...*now*."

Sylvia reached for one of her magazines in the rack by the sofa. She tore pieces of paper and wrapped each of the gold animals separately, then covered them with the old cloth. Shoving the bookshelf back as far as she could, she hurried to the bedroom to pack some clothes.

Sylvia had a renewed sense of determination. She would be long gone before Mason figured out what she had done.

Sylvia waited until the security guard took his break, then she descended the stairs to the underground garage. As the owner of the apartment building, Mason informed the security team he did not want any video monitors in the garage, lobby and elevators. No tracking devices which could be used against him.

"What an ass."

Sylvia chuckled to herself, realizing Mason's obsession with anonymity was now working to her advantage. Racing to her car, she slipped out into the night totally unnoticed.

As she passed familiar shops and restaurants, Sylvia took one last look. She wouldn't be coming back to New York any time soon. She needed to disappear where Mason couldn't reach her. The days of Mason controlling every aspect of her life were over.

There was someone else to consider.

Her baby. Sylvia sighed as her hand moved to rest on her stomach. She only found out she was pregnant a few days ago. At first she had been so happy, so naïve. Playfully thinking about colors for a nursery, toys to put on shelves, names to pick out for a boy or girl. Then she caught herself.

Who was she kidding?

Mason wouldn't want the child; he was married to a rich socialite. An illegitimate child would tarnish his precious image. No, he would make the problem go away…

One way or another…

Sylvia tried to push those horrible thoughts out of her mind. She turned up the radio as she drove south of the city. Fortunately, there was light traffic and she cleared the New Jersey state line in a short time.

Stopping at the first rest stop along the Jersey turnpike, she called the one person she knew she could rely on for anything…her best friend Lois Green.

"Lois, thank God! I need your help! Something has gone very…*very* wrong!"

"Can you get to my house? Quickly?"

"Yes, I'll be there as soon as I can."

"I'll be waiting."

Lois Green was Sylvia's closest friend ever since they had been at Syracuse together. Even after graduation, they kept in touch, checking in with each other almost every weekend.

Now, Lois was shocked to hear her friend's voice in such dramatic overtones, but she knew better than to ask too many questions. Especially over the phone.

As soon as she hung up with Sylvia, Lois made a few other quick calls. To Candace Light in Virginia, Mary Fortenni in South Carolina and Gail Tremont in Massachusetts.

College roommates, forever friends.

Sylvia would need their help, too. Lois was certain.

"You look like hell," Lois muttered as Sylvia entered her small apartment, just outside of Atlantic City.

"You have no idea."

Dressed all in black with tousled hair and streaked make-up from her tears, Sylvia looked entirely different from the last time Lois had seen her.

Working at the Hamilton-Knox museum foundation had provided Sylvia with a nice little income, not to mention the lavish gifts from her mysterious boyfriend. Lois had never seen Sylvia wearing anything that didn't have a designer label.

Yet here she was, standing in Lois' apartment looking like a wrecked train.

"What the hell happened to you?"

Sylvia's eyes darted around the living room.

"Relax. We're clear."

"I've got a complication. Actually, more than one. I need your help."

Sylvia threw herself into a big overstuffed armchair. Lois had simple tastes, yet her comfortable, little apartment was the only place Sylvia felt entirely at home.

"I overheard Mason giving an order to kill someone."

Lois did a double-take. Sylvia was in way over her head.

"Are you sure? You didn't hear the conversation out of context?"

Sylvia shook her head. It had been very clear to her what Mason was implying.

Lois paced the floor.

"I knew you were getting in too deep. Thank God you had the sense to get out of there."

Sylvia looked away, not wanting to meet Lois' eyes.

"What else aren't you telling me?"

Sylvia bit her lip. "I want you to hide something for me." Sylvia dug inside her overnight bag, and pulled out the cloth bundle. She unwrapped the gold elephant and handed it to Lois.

"What is this? My God, is it solid gold?"

"I think so. They look very old. It must be some type of treasure. Stolen for sure. Why else would Mason feel the need to hide them in my apartment?"

"Not sure. But something is going on. If Mason Hamilton is interested in them, they're probably worth quite a bit. What do you want to do?"

Sylvia sat back and let the warm chair envelop her. What she wanted to do, and what she had to do were two different things.

"I need you to hide them for me. Mason will track me down once he knows I outsmarted him. I can't stay here. I'll put you in danger. I need to get away from here...*fast*."

Lois thought for a moment. A temporary fix on a long-term problem, but it was the best she could come up with.

"Until we get a handle on this, you can stay in my aunt's beach house in Stone Harbor. No one will find you there. It's deserted most of the year anyway."

Sylvia sighed in relief. At least she'd have some breathing room until she could figure out her next move.

"I might be there for several months. Is that ok?"

Lois gave her a friend a curious glance.

"I'm pregnant."

"Are you sure?"

Sylvia nodded. "I can't let Mason know about the baby. He will hunt us down. I've got to protect my child."

Lois sat down on the floor and rubbed her forehead.

"Ok, I'll think of something. Right now, we'll get you to my aunt's beach house. I've already called the others. Don't worry. We'll protect you and your baby."

"I was foolish. I actually believed…"

Lois took her friend's hand.

"We'll take care of this. You know we will. Friends till the end."

Sylvia tried to smile. She squeezed Lois' hand letting her know with an unspoken gesture she would readily return the favor if there was ever a need.

Chapter 1

Jenna Reed leaned back in her squeaky desk chair and ran her fingers through her long, silky brown hair. Finding a rubber band in the top drawer of her desk, she promptly pulled her hair into a ponytail. She needed to get her hair off her neck.

As one of the youngest teachers on staff at the Myers-Mill Academy, north Wilmington's most prestigious college prep school, she could easily pass as one of the students.

With her slender shape and trendy style, it was very common for a parent to mistake her for a student, making some crass remark that she was skipping class as she crossed the main lobby on her free period. Youthful appearance seemed more of a detriment than a compliment when you taught high school. The students wanted to be your best friends to get brownie points. The parents questioned your ability to teach their children when you looked slightly older than the student population.

But she took it in stride.

Teaching was an honorable profession and very rewarding at times. Looking into the faces of students who *finally* got the meaning of a Shakespeare play made her happy, even if it had taken all year. Helping struggling writers perfect essays after multiple revisions, she knew they would be grateful once they got to college.

She was helping to shape a few young minds. So if she had to endure the occasional smart-ass remarks and glares due to parent misconceptions about her teaching abilities, so be it.

She was teaching the students, not the parents. *Thank God.*

Besides, she was gaining valuable experience at the prestigious, private school level. And she had her summers off. Which was awesome.

The entire summer to relax at her favorite beach town – Cape May, New Jersey.

In a few short hours, summer vacation would begin.

Life was good and getting better.

Almost.

Her trip to *Exit Zero* - the lowest point on the Jersey shore, couldn't come fast enough. The school's air conditioning system had the audacity to cut out in her wing of the building. Maintenance wouldn't have it fixed in time for the last day of classes. The best they could do, the foreman offered, was to provide oscillating fans.

A nice idea, but impractical. The fans only succeeded in blowing hot air in everyone's faces. This was especially irritating to the teenage girls who were trying to maintain their rock star looks for the sake of impressing their male counterparts, most of whom could care less.

It had been a long, hot morning.

Jenna's students were miserable, she was miserable, and everyone was counting the seconds until they could get the hell out of the front doors.

It was so cruel for the school administrators to require the students and faculty to come back for a half day when everyone was in summer-mode anyway. What was the purpose of a half-day? Finals were done and graded, lockers had been cleaned out and the students were doing nothing but signing yearbooks. Everyone was bitching and moaning.

What a *lovely* end to the school year.

Even the teaching staff couldn't figure out the logic of the half-day requirement. Probably thought up by someone in the administrative offices who wanted to stick it to the people who had off all summer. *Whatever.* Jenna could see the end of the tunnel now as each minute ticked away.

She had made it through her first two teaching periods. Now third period was free. Jenna popped open a can of Diet Pepsi, took a sip, and then began to clean out her desk. She found a couple of Peppermint Patties, which would be her reward if she finished her task on time. Diet soda and candy, what a wonderful, wacky combination so many people relied on to get through the day.

Jenna bent down to unplug her phone charger from the multi-strip under her desk. Hearing a knock on her doorframe, she rose up too suddenly, hitting her head on the edge of the desk.

"Idiot!"

"Are you referring to yourself, or did you just insult me?"

Jenna's best friend and co-worker Kelly McBride came bounding into her classroom and laughed.

Jenna just shrugged her shoulders and rubbed the spot on her head which had caused a few stars.

"No comment."

Kelly threw herself into the chair next to Jenna's desk, and brushed a strand of sweaty hair out of her face.

"Please tell me you were saying a prayer while you were down on your knees? I'm about ready to crucify the Registrar right this very moment!"

Kelly picked up two of Jenna's candies, unwrapped them, and then stuck them both in her mouth.

"You know you look like a squirrel. Very *professional*."

"Thank you so much," Kelly said with her mouth full.

Jenna couldn't help but laugh.

"Drowning your sorrows in my melted candies will not change the fact you procrastinated. Why did you log in your grades at the last minute like everyone else? Now the system has probably reached its limit of users, am I right?"

"Yes, *All-Knowing One,* you're right."

Kelly pouted between swallows.

"I know, I should have been proactive like you and put the grades in the first time the system was open. But…I don't know, putting things off till the last minute, well…you know me."

"Yes, I certainly do."

Jenna tried to stifle another laugh.

"I'm sure you'll be able to get back online in about an hour or so. Grades aren't due until 5pm today. You have several hours to get them done."

Kelly rolled her eyes. "Great. Just where I want to spend the start of my summer vacation. Stuck here…in the heat."

Jenna just had to rub it in. She checked her watch for effect.

"By the time you get done, I'll probably be at the shore."

"I could say something right now but we have impression-able young people wandering the halls, and I'm sure none of them have ever heard those words before."

"Wanna bet? With the a/c off today, I've been hearing quite a few choice words."

Kelly nodded her head and pushed a wayward strand out of her face. She picked up a file folder from Jenna's desk and fanned herself.

"Please tell me it's cooler by the ocean."

"Should be with the ocean breezes. Speaking of Cape May, when are you coming down? I think my brother Austin is coming next week, but he hasn't given me an exact arrival date. Austin isn't the "exact" type; everything he does is spur of the moment."

Jenna gestured to her brother's picture on the windowsill.

Kelly walked over and picked up the frame.

"Oh, he's so cute. When did you say he's coming down?"

Jenna was the one to roll her eyes this time.

Kelly could charm the pants off of anyone with her runner's body and long, wavy blond hair. She looked like she belonged on a runway instead of in a history classroom. Training for marathons, Kelly had the body every thirty-something wanted, male and female. Men seemed to flock to her, but she dated only for amusement, not commitment.

"You're kidding me, right? Austin? Kelly, he's twenty-five! *Twenty-five*! You are almost five years older. You know what twenty-five year old guys want, and it's not conversation."

Jenna grabbed the picture away from Kelly.

"Speaking from experience? You know, if you get them young, you can train them."

Kelly leaned against the windowsill and grinned.

"I have no desire to train anyone."

Jenna stood up and started packing one of her boxes with an increased sense of urgency.

Without thinking, Kelly hit a nerve which both of them instantly realized.

"I'm sorry, Jenna, I didn't mean to bring up...God, sometimes I don't think."

"Don't worry about it."

"New subject...tell me about Cape May. I've only been to the Hamptons. When I moved down here last August, I didn't have time to check out the local beaches."

Jenna tried to shrug off Kelly's comment about the men in her life, or lack thereof. She knew her friend hadn't meant to upset her. It certainly wasn't Kelly's fault Jenna was destined for bad relationships.

Her recent break-up occurred the week before Valentine's Day after five months of hot and heavy dating. Perfect timing. The guy didn't even have to send roses, which was usually a red flag another break-up was imminent. Even the school's receptionist had been cautioned not to accept any flower deliveries for Jenna Reed. Stupid flowers, what were they good for anyway?

It was so ironic. Jenna couldn't seem to hold down a relationship for more than a few months, and her best friend, who looked like a super-model, didn't want to keep relationships for more than a few days or weeks.

Life just isn't fair.

Which prompted the promise Jenna made to herself - to swear off men for the summer. She needed a break. She had no desire to take up with some seasonal lifeguard or tourist staying in town for a couple of weeks, then to have to break it off and start fresh again in the fall. A couple of months, men-free sounded like a good plan. No hassles, no heartbreaks.

"Well....Cape May is a lot of fun."

"What type of fun are we talking? Bars, pool parties, working on a tan-kind of fun, I hope! I'm up for a new adventure!"

"Well, Cape May does offer entertainment for the over-21 crowd, but there is so much more to do down there. Trolley tours, trendy restaurants, walks along the beach at sunrise, an outdoor mall. You will love it as much as I do, I promise."

"Sounds great – I can't wait!"

"I'll email you directions to our beach house. It's a great location. It's on North Street in the quiet section of town, and just a short walk to the beach and the mall. We've never had a problem with renters being too loud. Hope that won't be too boring for you."

"Oh, I wouldn't mind being bored for a few days. I have to visit my father in New York next week and believe me, I'll be ready for a change of scenery whether it's boring or not."

Kelly groaned as she took a seat in one of the student chairs.

"I'm not looking forward to spending time with the Old Man. He's, well...let's just say, we're not very close. It's only when he beckons me that I put in a personal appearance. I'd rather stay down here far away from him. We don't communicate too well. It's our family curse..."

Kelly drifted off and stared out the window.

"I'm sorry about you and your father."

"Don't be, Jenna, he's not worth it. I should be able to drive down either next Thursday or Friday. How's that?"

"Perfect! That will give me some time to get the house ready. It's been closed up since last summer, when...."

Jenna's voice cracked. It had been almost a year since her family had been together at the beach house. The wounds she thought were closing, had just re-surfaced.

Losing both parents to an auto accident the week before Christmas had stymied Jenna and Austin for months. Dealing with such sudden loss had slammed them both very hard. They had survived...barely...clinging to each other and their friends for desperate support.

It had all been so senseless.

Lois and Jim Reed were driving to meet Jenna and Austin in Philadelphia for dinner and last-minute Christmas shopping. After dinner at Romanelli's, they all planned to go back to Austin's apartment a few blocks away to help him trim his tree.

Lois and Jim never made it to the restaurant. Driving from Chadds Ford to Philadelphia usually took extra time during rush hour, but that evening with a thin layer of snow on the ground, Jenna and Austin just figured their parents were being extra careful on the wet roads.

After an hour had passed, Jenna finally gave up trying to reach them by cell. She told Austin to go back to his apartment and she would drive down to their parents' home. Her father's car was in the garage but there was no sign of her mother's car in the driveway.

Something wasn't right. Her parents were still not answering their cell phones.

Within the hour, Austin drove down from Philadelphia. As he was pulling into his parents' driveway, a police car pulled up alongside the curb. The officer inquired if this was the Reed house and Austin felt his stomach lurch.

His worst fears were confirmed. Lois and Jim's car had veered off the road into an embankment, causing an explosion. Both were killed instantly.

By the skids on the road, the police determined the car had lost control or was diverted to the embankment by another vehicle. No witnesses had come forth and due to the weather conditions which had intensified, the Crime Scene Unit could only make their best educated guess.

Part of a family unit one day and orphans the next.

Jenna and Austin clung to each other for support. They were all that was left of the Reed family.

Now, Jenna shook her head to push back the painful memories. It was time she got on with her life. Her parents would have wanted that. *If you move on, you will never fall back,* her mother would always say.

Her mother was right. She needed to focus on the positive moments of life. Like her summer vacation...spending time with her brother and her friends.

Jenna waved as Kelly left to return to her own classroom. Two hours to go. She could make it.

Cape May was calling her home.

Chapter 2

Jenna's road trip to Cape May was uneventful on a Thursday afternoon. She had timed it just about right.

Turning left on Perry Street, she rounded a couple more blocks. As she neared the intersection of North and Congress, her hands gripped the wheel. Pushing through the sudden impact of grief, she pulled her car into the driveway. She sat frozen in her seat.

Jenna laid her head on the steering wheel. The entire drive down she had filled her head with thoughts of what she wanted to do this summer. Never focusing once on the fact her parents would not be there to greet her.

Mom and Dad would want me to be here.

She sat motionless for a few minutes, just staring at the two-story cottage-style house. Heartfelt family memories were beckoning her, but a deep-rooted loneliness was keeping her at bay.

Even after the passing of her grandparents, the original owners of the beach house, Jenna's family had continued the tradition of the annual shore trips. Her parents' best friends and neighbors, George and Teresa Maylor, loved to visit them in Cape May every August. When the house next door came on the market two years ago, the Maylors didn't hesitate to buy it.

The Maylors also became the owners of Molly's Pancake House, where Jenna and Austin had worked part-time every summer since they turned sixteen.

Jenna finally worked up enough stamina to start unloading her car. It took her several trips to carry her suitcase and several boxes up the flight of stairs through the side entrance which led to the kitchen. She finally finished, drenched in sweat.

Where was Austin when she needed him?

Did she even need to ask?

Since she was the first to arrive, the cleaning and airing out the house was left to her. He would just saunter in like he always did, carefree and lackadaisical.

Austin was the perpetual beach bum. Why he just didn't live at the beach house, Jenna never knew. He fit the casual lifestyle better than anyone.

Jenna laughed, remembering Kelly's comments about Austin's picture. Kelly had no idea. But she was sure her friend would be able to size Austin up in five minutes or less.

"Kelly, you are certainly in for a treat!" Jenna said to herself in between bouts of laughter.

After a quick water break, Jenna started on her tasks.

She cleaned the bathrooms, made up the beds, put away her food items and opened up all the windows.

Her stomach growled. Time to refuel.

Jenna knew exactly what she wanted.

Jake's Pizza. Hands down.

She was very discerning when it came to pizza. Her mouth watered just thinking about sinking her teeth into the homemade crust and fresh vegetables.

Jake's was busy year-round. Families owning beach properties would continue to come down well into the fall and even a few weekends in the winter and spring, especially if *MAC*, the Mid-Atlantic Center for the Arts and Humanities, was sponsoring a themed weekend such as their annual tribute to Sherlock Holmes or Christmas in Victorian Cape May. With several restaurants closed after September, Jake's always had a steady stream of traffic.

The beach and pizza, *two of life's perfect pleasures*, Jenna mused after she placed her phone order. She headed out the door, not wanting to waste a single moment. The pizza she had waited all year for would be ready in twenty minutes!

Jake's was packed with people waiting for their take-out orders. Jenna grabbed one of the last chairs at a table just inside the front door. The aroma of the pizzas baking wafted her way. She inhaled and smiled. Her summer vacation was off to a good start.

Jenna glanced up from looking at the menu. Her bubbly friend Lacey had just walked in the door. Lacey was the editor of the Cape May Gazette, the local paper. She and Jenna had remained good friends since childhood and kept in touch on a regular basis, even though Jenna usually only saw Lacey in the summer.

Lacey's auburn ringlets bounced when she ran over to give her friend a big hug.

"I missed you! How are you?"

"I'm good, Lacey. How are you doing?"

"Really, Jen? Are you doing ok?"

Lacey had helped Jenna get through the days following her parents' double funeral service with sincere companionship... and a couple bottles of Grey Goose. The morning after their indulgence, both Jenna and Lacey swore off vodka forever as they tended to their migraine headaches.

"I will be. I couldn't stay away. I need to be here. A change of scenery and some relaxation time is exactly what I'm hoping for."

"Bad break-up...again?"

"Yeah, you could say that. Actually... *don't* say that."

Lacey slid into the seat opposite Jenna and folded her arms. Enough said.

"Remind me not to get involved with anyone anytime soon. I decided to swear off men for the summer. A little personal promise. I do not need any more baggage right now."

"So you say. Don't make promises to yourself we both know you won't keep."

"I really mean it this time."

"Uh-huh. The first gorgeous guy who winks your way, girlfriend, I am so not holding you back. You're going to lose your heart again, so don't try and deny it. Just let it happen...and relax. If you have to throw a few fish back in the sea, so be it. One gone is one step closer to the one you're meant to be with."

"Thank you, *Dr. Phil*."

But Lacey was right, and Jenna knew it. She was a sucker for the cute guys who made her heart melt.

Lacey changed the subject. Sipping on her iced tea, she was glad for once Jake's was busy.

"So, friend from the North, I have a proposition for you."

"A proposition? You know, where I live, most people just say *favor*."

"Proposition...favor, whatever you want to call it. I'm in a little bind."

"Why do I have the distinct feeling I'm going to regret this?"

Jenna glanced up at the digital order board. Regrettably, her pizza order was still three orders away. She had no choice but to listen to Lacey's plea.

"Hear me out now. This is right up your alley. Actually, you may be *thanking* me."

Jenna looked at Lacey with wary eyes.

"The town council is hosting a book signing this Saturday for a visiting author who's also a history buff. Anyway, he's on a book tour and has agreed to present a lecture related to his new book, *Pirates on the East Coast.*"

Lacey made a face which made Jenna chuckle.

"I know, right? At first, I thought, great, this will be a yawner. Then I saw the author's picture...and let's just say...wow!"

"Twenty-eight?" The cashier called. Jenna's number.

Thank God, Jenna thought to herself. Now she could make a quick exit using the excuse her pizza was getting cold.

"Can I say 'no' now and get it over with?"

Jenna gripped her pizza box. She desperately wanted to get on her way, but Lacey was wound up as usual.

"Girl, you will thank me for this - he's a hottie!"

"Then why don't *you* just do the interview?"

"Wish I could, believe me. But you know how my Saturdays are – proofreading, making sure the ads get posted correctly, deadlines up to the...can't spare even one hour. We can't have a visiting author in town and not write this up for the paper. The managing committee would have my head!"

What was the point in delaying the inevitable, Jenna thought. She knew full well Lacey had *girlfriend fix-up* on the brain.

"Lacey, I know where this is headed."

"Jen, come on. You've done interviews for me before; you know the drill. What questions to ask, what you can't ask, yadda yadda. I doubt it would take more than fifteen or twenty minutes tops. *Please*...you would really be helping me."

Jenna sighed. It was useless. Lacey would win; she always did.

"Ok. Just let me know time and place."

"You're the best friend...*ever*. I'll text you."

Lacey jumped up to retrieve her pizza box from the counter.

"I want details..."

"It's just an interview."

"Uh-huh. Wait till you see him!"

As she walked back, Jenna refused to entertain the thought of thinking about the handsome author. She would do the interview, email Lacey her notes and be done with it.

Simple as that.

Right.

Jenna charged up the side steps and slid into a chair at the kitchen table. But before she took a bite of her pizza, she paused.

Could she actually make it through the entire summer without falling for someone?

Time would tell.

Chapter 3

The Promenade, Cape May's version of a boardwalk without the boards, was already bustling with a crowd of people. As Jenna neared Convention Hall, she saw a long line of mostly female fans curved around the front of the massive building.

"Great," Jenna muttered under her breath.

Lacey was going to owe her big time for this.

Flashing her Gazette ID, Jenna pushed her way through.

"Jenna Reed, from the Gazette. I'm here to interview Dr. Chase Garrett."

Ms. Sarah Fermont, the office manager, waved Jenna around the counter. Flustered, the short, stocky woman with the spiky silver hair and purple glasses had reached her patience limit. No one could have prepared her for the ruckus taking place around her small desk.

"Wait outside the conference room. Through the doors to your left. Knock on the door at precisely one o'clock. Not a minute earlier."

"Thank you."

Jenna rolled her eyes. What in the world was going on? It was like a literary rock concert. Photographers hanging around, police trying to hold back the crowd inside and out, Convention Hall employees looking like they were ready to pull their hair out. This was insane.

Who was this guy? She had never heard of Dr. Chase Garrett or his book. Jenna only read mystery novels and couldn't imagine anyone getting excited about reading a hyped-up documentary. It most certainly had to be boring...almost like a textbook. But still, the enthusiastic crowds were proving her wrong.

"This is too crazy," she said in a hushed tone.

Jenna checked her watch and fidgeted with her bracelet. Five more minutes and she was leaving.

The weather was perfect for an afternoon on the beach. She didn't want to waste a good beach day trying to fight for the attention of some unknown author...even if he was good-looking.

Jenna leaned against the door jamb and closed her eyes.

What in the hell did I get myself into?

As if to provide a divine answer, the door to the conference room swung wide open, knocking Jenna off-balance.

"Hey, I am so sorry. I didn't realize you'd be standing so close to the door."

Jenna didn't respond immediately. She was too busy staring. Sparkling brown eyes. Sandy brown hair cut just right. A smile curving onto lips that were...

Stop it right now. You're here to do a job, not flirt with the first guy who looks your way.

Probably a local. The cute guy locking eyes with her was dressed in a two-button Hollister shirt, khaki shorts and flip flops. She had no business getting mixed up with a local. Nothing good could come out of it. She lived two hours away. Two much commuting time.

"Hi."

Jenna finally realized she was blushing even though it was too late. Maybe he hadn't noticed.

"Hey, I am sorry."

"What?"

He had noticed. He was smiling. At her.

Oh, God, here we go again.

Jenna was tongue-tied.

"Getting a little crazy out there. A few people must have read the book."

"The book?"

Jenna's mind had gone completely blank.

"Yeah...actually...did you come for an autograph, too?"

He's flashing those gorgeous eyes at me again. God help me...

"No...no...not an autograph."

She couldn't help herself. She was fixated on his face. His stance. Everything about him.

Jenna caught herself.

Oh, no, he couldn't be...

Jenna squeezed her eyes shut to erase the onset of her pestering emotions.

"How about a picture then?"

Jenna shook herself out of her trance.

"Excuse me?"

The guy with the dreamy eyes leaned against the wall and folded his arms.

"Well, if you're not here for an autograph, I just assumed you wanted a picture."

"Of what?" She didn't get it.

"Most fans want an autograph or a picture, but you don't seem to want either. Makes me a little curious, that's all."

Jenna laughed nervously. "I'm not a fan."

"Well, I was hoping I could change your mind."

Unexpectedly, the door was yanked open and an older man appeared. He was dressed more formally in perfectly creased slacks, a long sleeve white shirt and a burgundy tie.

"Chase, stop fooling around and get back in here. That reporter from the paper will be here any minute, and I don't want to do the interview for you...I only do them *online* for you."

Jenna darted glances between the two men. Her suspicions had been correct.

"Pardon me, Miss, I didn't realize the exact nature of my son's distraction."

"Be right there, Dad. I'm being summoned. Nice to meet you. I'm Chase Garrett, by the way."

Jenna nodded with a grin and stretched out her hand.

"I'm Jenna Reed, and I'm *that reporter* from the Gazette."

Chase's expression turned to downright embarrassment, and then he laughed.

"Well, then, Jenna Reed from the Gazette, let's do our interview."

Holding the door open, he gestured for Jenna to take a seat.

"Dad, this is Jenna Reed, from the Gazette. Guess it was perfect timing."

Lloyd Garrett smiled and shook Jenna's hand.

"Perfect timing it is. I need another cup of coffee anyway. Nice to meet you, Miss Reed."

Chase took a seat across the table from Jenna. There was no way he wanted this interview to end any time soon. Jenna Reed had captivated him in just a few minutes.

"Dr. Garrett..."

"Chase. Dr. Garrett sounds so formal, don't you think? I prefer Chase."

"Ok. Chase. I have a few questions for you that I've…"

Chase couldn't wait any longer.

"Actually, can I start by asking you a question? Will you have dinner with me tonight?"

"What?"

"Dinner. The meal after lunch. But if you'd prefer lunch, we could leave right now and I…"

Jenna held her hand up. She couldn't believe this.

"I came here to interview you."

"We could make it a dinner interview."

Jenna shook her head. Not going to happen. She had no intention of breaking the promise she had made to herself…this soon anyway.

"No…thanks. I really need to get this interview done…*now*."

"So you already have dinner plans?"

Jenna pursed her lips. Lacey was right. Chase Garrett was handsome…and she did need to eat.

What are you thinking? Stop this while you still can…

Jenna got back on target.

"I have a few questions I've listed in my notebook."

"Ask away…but my offer still stands."

Chase leaned back in his chair. God, she was beautiful! He couldn't stop staring at her, but he didn't want to make her nervous. He diverted his eyes to the table instead.

"Well, I…," Jenna stammered. This was going to be harder than she realized. How could she concentrate now?

"Oh, the hell with this."

Jenna slammed her notebook shut.

Chase looked up, amused.

"Let's just improvise."

"My thoughts exactly. We could improvise *over lunch*."

Jenna managed a smile. He got her.

"Ok," she nodded. "But don't you have to meet your adoring fans soon?"

"I guess it would upset a few people if I snuck out. Dad probably wouldn't be able to hold them off for much longer. Guess we'll have to make it dinner."

Jenna got up to leave. *One meal.* It wasn't like she was making any sort of commitment.

"Ok, dinner. Where are you staying?"

"The Marquis de Lafayette on Beach Avenue."

"Oh, The Marq. Yes, that is one of the nicest hotels in Cape May, and you have a view of the ocean. I'll meet you in the lobby at six. We can eat there or take a walk and find another restaurant."

Chase clapped his hands. "You can be my tour guide."

Jenna shook her head.

"Dinner. Interview. That's all."

"For *now*."

Before Jenna could answer, Chase breezed past her on his way to the main hall.

So much for making promises to herself.

*****

Jenna walked briskly back to the beach house, so glad to get out of the craziness which had surrounded Chase Garrett when he stepped into the main hall to greet his fans. She was dumbstruck as people pushed and shoved until security finally stepped in to control the situation.

It was totally chaotic. High-strung female fans jockeying for position as their fingers flew across their cell phones. No doubt updating their Facebook pages. She wondered how many *likes* Dr. Chase Garrett was getting today.

God knows, she was ready to *like him*...

Jenna was willing to bet most of Chase's female fans couldn't even tell her what his book was about. The majority were bikini-clad and reeked of perfume.

Photo-op time, to be sure.

Exit opportunity. Jenna didn't hesitate.

She envisioned the crowd dispersing after Chase made his way back to his hotel. Perhaps some of his fans would follow him, hoping for a rendezvous, to talk about...what, the inspiration for the book?

Not exactly.

Actually, she had no desire to talk about the book, either. When Chase locked eyes with her, Jenna felt herself losing control.

She had done it again.

She was no better than one of his groupies. Was she that desperate for attention...for another boyfriend?

Snap out of it, Reed.

Enough temptation. He wasn't staying and she wasn't playing.

One dinner. One page of questions. End of story.

Right.

Why was she having trouble convincing herself?

She could do this; she could have dinner with Dr. Chase Garrett...Chase...and not fall for him.

As long as she didn't fall prey to his dazzling eyes.

Maybe a walk on the beach was just what she needed to put herself back on track. She was headed into familiar territory and she needed to be cautious.

No need to chalk up another defeat.

She would nip this in the bud before *anything* got started.

Jenna ran upstairs to change. Passing the door to her parents' room, she paused. It seemed strange to open a door to their room, knowing her parents would never be here again. But her hand was on the doorknob before she had a chance to reconsider.

The old wooden door made an eerie sound when Jenna pushed it open. Stepping inside, she instantly felt their presence.

Everything was exactly the same as it was when they had left at the end of last summer. The same pictures on the walls, the little collection of seashells her mother kept on her dresser and the closet door was still partially open with their summer clothes inside.

It was like she had stepped back in time.

The bed was stripped of linens as her mother always did the morning they were leaving. Her mother had left sheets, pillowcases, and bedspreads neatly folded in a plastic tub on top of the mattress. One of her mother's routines which seemed endless, until something happened destroying the familiar rhythm.

Jenna shivered. The rhythm was gone.

She felt an overwhelming desire to leave immediately. To run down the steps and out the front door. Maybe it was too soon to come back to the beach house. Her parents had only been gone six months.

Jenna felt like she was being pushed away. Memories of running into her parents' bedroom with her brother Austin when they were much younger were now screaming at her to leave and never come back.

In her haste to leave the room, Jenna bumped against a picture frame hanging just inside the door. The picture flew off its hanger and fell to the floor. Glass fragments scattered in different directions.

"Why am I so clumsy?"

Jenna bent down to pick up the photograph.

Smiling, she ran her fingers over her mother's favorite picture. Taken at sunset while her family sat in front of the lifeguard rowboat, the background of the sun descending into the ocean was breathtaking. No wonder her mother had loved it.

Jenna stared at the picture, remembering every detail of the time it was taken. She promised herself she would take it tomorrow to Dellas, the local general store on the Washington Street Mall, to get another frame. But as she held the picture, she noticed it felt heavier than most photo paper.

Turning it over, Jenna was surprised to find an envelope taped to the back of the picture. The tape was flimsy now, barely holding the envelope against the photo.

Jenna easily detached it, and flipped the envelope over.

The postmark was almost thirty years ago. The return address was listed as Candace Light in Manassas, Virginia.

Why on earth would her mother have hidden a letter behind a picture…from thirty years ago?

Curiosity tempted her.

Opening the envelope, she drew out the contents – a letter and a picture of an infant. On the back of the picture was written "Billy, 3 months."

Jenna was baffled. She had no relatives named Billy. None of her parents' friends had children with that name. Maybe reading the letter would shed some light on the child's identity.

Dear Lois,

I hope this finds you well. I wanted to give you an update on Billy. He's growing so big at 3 months! Sylvia would have been so proud of him. He is the most beautiful child I have ever seen! His blue eyes are so inquisitive and they seem to follow me everywhere. The staff at my office has been wonderful about giving him check-ups for free, and giving me pointers on how to be a new "aunt". He is such a joy to be around – he rarely ever cries and seems to be happy because he is always smiling.

I just wish I could keep him longer. My job is becoming more detailed now that I have received a promotion to Office Manager. I now have to be in charge of four other medical assistants and one medical transcriber. This requires longer hours and sometimes working on the weekends. Not a very good arrangement for my "aunt" duties, I'm afraid. So, as much as I would love to have Billy stay with me and keep my part of our commitment, I think it would be best if we all met again and tried to come up with another plan. Do you really think Sylvia will be coming back for him? We haven't heard from her in months. I have a bad feeling something has happened. Maybe she isn't coming back...ever. Where does that leave us and Billy?

Please call or write to me when you have a moment. I tried to call you a few times, but got your answering machine. Letters have always worked for me. I pray you are well and I will hear from you soon,

Your friend,
Candace

Jenna read the letter twice. She still couldn't believe her mother had something to do with a plan involving a baby boy, obviously abandoned by his mother.

Why didn't you tell me about this, Mom?

Who was Candace Light? Not one of her mother's current friends. Perhaps one of her mother's friends from college? Jenna couldn't remember. Her mother had told her tales of her college days but Jenna didn't recall exact names.

Too many thoughts were running through her head, not to mention the newest distraction named Chase Garrett.

So much for her uncomplicated, peaceful summer.

Jenna put the letter back in the envelope.

What was she going to do now?

Maybe she should just put the letter on her parents' dresser and forget it. If her mother hadn't felt the need to share the letter with her, then why was she wasting her time now with a mystery which didn't need to be solved?

Or did it?

She needed to know more.

Jenna booted up her laptop and Googled Candace Light in Virginia. There was one listing in Manassas. Too coincidental. It had to be the same person.

Jenna checked the address on the web search with the one on the envelope. An exact match. So far, so good.

The internet search also provided a telephone number. It was worth a shot. Jenna jotted down the number, and then picked up her cell phone.

What was she doing?

Solving a mystery. She couldn't help it. It was just like one of her favorite mystery novels. She was drawn in until the very last page.

Maybe she was meant to find the letter.

Maybe this was just plain crazy.

The child in the picture would be a thirty-year old man now. He obviously had his own life which didn't involve the Reed family. Her mother never felt the need to mention him.

"Why do I have to know?" Jenna asked herself.

The letter was older than she was. It didn't concern her. She had no business contacting the woman in Virginia. What would she say to her anyway?

Jenna threw the envelope on top of the dresser and took one step towards the door. She stopped and looked back.

She couldn't let it go. She knew that now.

Jenna *wanted* an answer. She couldn't rationalize it, but yet she had such a strong compulsion to find the truth.

The truth her mother had kept hidden.

But why?

There had to be a very good reason her mother had felt the need to secretly hide a letter and a picture away from everyone's view, and in the beach house, of all places?

When her mother had officially inherited the beach house upon the death of Jenna's grandparents, she wanted everything to remain the same, replacing only a few worn out pieces of furniture.

The only picture her mother had insisted upon hanging was the exact one Jenna had broken.

"What was going on, Mom?" Jenna's words echoed in the empty room.

Too many questions were coming to the surface and not enough answers. Maybe Candace Light could fill in the blanks.

Jenna took a deep breath and dialed the number listed on the internet.

"Candace, pick up the phone...*please*."

After four rings, Jenna was ready to give up. Maybe this was just a wild goose chase after all. The envelope was dated thirty years ago. Candace Light could have moved, or even died.

Jenna's finger hovered above the end call button when voicemail picked up. Her heart skipped a beat as the automated message directed callers to leave a message. Jenna immediately hung up.

"I can't do this."

Jenna sat down on the mattress and stared at her cell, then at the broken pieces of glass.

A new thought entered her mind. Maybe her mother *knew* she would find the letter.

Jenna was re-energized now. She dialed the number again with determination. When the voicemail picked up, she was ready to leave a message.

"This message is for Candace Light. I'm Jenna Reed, Lois Green Reed's daughter. I found a letter in my parents' beach house written by you to my mother. I'd really like to talk to you about it. Please call me at (302) 555-1015. Thank you."

Jenna was proud of herself. She had taken the first step.

But where would those steps lead?

Time passed very slowly those first few minutes after Jenna placed the call. She sat on the bed and waited. After twenty minutes, Jenna slipped her cell back into her pocket.

Maybe Candace Light wouldn't call her back at all. Maybe this was just a complete waste of time.

Or maybe this was the beginning of a mystery her mother didn't have *time* to tell her about.

Reality checked back in as Jenna looked at her watch.

She had a dinner date in a few hours. But first she wanted to stop by and see Teresa and George Maylor, who lived next door.

Jenna cleaned up the mess on the floor, and then headed over to visit her parents' best friends.

She was greeted warmly as usual by Teresa Maylor, the woman she considered to be her second mom.

"Glad to see you haven't forgotten us old folks."

"Teresa, you're not old."

"I don't know, Jenna, some days..." Teresa gave Jenna a big hug. Having no children of her own, Teresa always felt close to Jenna and Austin.

"I'll take one of those," George said as he rounded the corner.

He gave Jenna a big bear hug, then let out a loud whistle.

"You get prettier every time I see you."

"You have a biased opinion, George. You've been telling me that ever since I've been coming down to the shore."

"I know a pretty girl when I see one. Now, take this woman for example..."

George squeezed Teresa around the waist.

"Don't think a little flattery is going to get you out of cleaning the grill."

"Ok, ok. I'm on it."

George started to leave as Teresa just waved her hands in the air.

Jenna laughed. The Maylors were always the same. Kidding each other all the time. A nice couple. No wonder her parents had thought very highly of them.

"Hey, Teresa, I want to show you something."

Jenna pulled the letter out of her back pocket.

Before Jenna could continue, Teresa stared in surprise.

"Where did you get that?"

Jenna was startled by Teresa's tone.

"I...found it in my parents' bedroom. I knocked a frame off the wall. The envelope was taped to the back of the photo. Teresa, it's the weirdest thing, but I think my Mom *wanted* me to find this. I mean, at first, I was mad that she had hidden it, but now, I think she knew I would find it."

Teresa was still glaring at the envelope with a concerned look when George peered over her shoulder. Obviously, he hadn't gone too far into the kitchen and had overhead their conversation.

"What's in the letter? Do you want us to read it?"

"George, mind your own business. If Jenna wanted us to read it, she would ask us. Now, go clean the grill before I run over to Swain's and buy a new one!"

"Yes, dear."

George took off for the kitchen again, this time slamming the back door on his way out to the patio.

Teresa made sure George was out of earshot.

"Did you read the letter?"

Jenna nodded.

"I think it might be from one of Mom's college friends, but I'm not sure. There is a picture of a little boy inside. My mother never spoke about him. But for some reason, I want to find out how my mother was involved."

Teresa gave Jenna another hug and whispered in her ear, "We need to talk ...alone. I'll stop by sometime tomorrow or the next day when George is at the restaurant."

"Ok. Listen, Teresa, I'd love to stay but I have...well, I have a dinner date."

"Good for you. Have a good time. I'll talk to you later."

Teresa waved goodbye as she watched Jenna leave. Then she quickly hit the speed dial on her cell phone. A familiar voice answered on the second ring.

"She found the letter."

"Well, it was inevitable. Lois knew she would. Now, she's going to track down Candace."

"Do you want me to stall her?"

Silence on the line. It was making Teresa nervous.

"Well?"

"I'm thinking."

"Well can you think a little faster? George might come back inside any minute."

"Let her go. I'm not worried. Candace knows what to tell Jenna. She's known for quite some time."

"Ok. I hope you know what you're doing.

"So do I."

Teresa peered out her kitchen window which faced the Reeds' house. Poor Jenna had no idea what she was getting involved with...*or with whom.*

God help her...if she ever found out.

*****

What a day, Jenna thought as she walked past her phone charging on the side table. Her message light was blinking.

"You have two voicemail messages. Message one."

The cell beeped as Jenna held her breath.

"Hey, Jenna, it's Chase. Listen, I know we had plans for dinner, and God knows I don't want to cancel. But my dad lined up a private book signing without telling me, and I really can't get out of it. I would love to have breakfast with you tomorrow morning. How is eight? Can you meet me in the lobby? Send me a text. Thanks for understanding. I can't wait to see you again."

Jenna leaned against the bedroom door and closed her eyes. Was this an omen? Maybe she had placed a curse on herself after making that solemn vow about swearing off men.

"Message number two."

"Miss Reed, this is Candace Light. I'm glad you called. I heard of your parents' passing, and I am deeply sorry for your loss. If you wish to talk, I would like to do so in person. Please call me tomorrow and I will provide directions. Good night."

Jenna stared at her cell in total amazement.

Tomorrow…?

Chapter 4

The breakfast at Aleathea's had been perfect. Sitting on the outside deck enjoying the morning breeze had made the ambiance even better.

"Good choice."

Chase sipped his coffee and gazed over at Jenna.

"About me or the restaurant?"

Chase laughed. "Both, but you take precedence. Thanks for recommending this place for breakfast. The pecan stuffed French toast was amazing. Your omelet looked good, too. I was going to ask for a bite, but I didn't think that was first-date appropriate."

"I wouldn't have given it to you anyway. No one takes my western omelet away. I might get feisty with you."

"Really? I'm up for the challenge. Be feisty all you want."

Chase reached over and snuck a piece of omelet away from Jenna's plate as he surprised her with a kiss on the cheek. He popped the egg piece in his mouth trying not to laugh.

"Sneaky move. I'll remember that one."

"The kiss or the stealth maneuver with my fork?"

"Both, but I'll give the kiss precedence."

Jenna smiled as the waitress filled their mugs again with steaming coffee.

Although she was still on the cautious side of any new relationship, Jenna was determined to just let the moment speak for itself. She was having a nice time…with a nice man.

After breakfast, Chase tugged on Jenna's hand as they headed towards the beach. He was fascinated to see a few early morning surfers were already hitting the surf with their boogie boards.

"Can you do that?"

"Not quite." Jenna shrugged as she shook her head.

Chase and Jenna watched an agile girl ride her board for a long distance before crashing into the crescent as it rolled ashore.

"You surprise me, Jenna Reed. I thought with you being a beach-babe and all that, riding the surf would come naturally to you."

"Not in a million years. I mean, riding the board, not the part about being a beach-babe. I'll have to let you be the judge of that once I put on my bikini."

She smiled and shot Chase a wink.

"I'll cancel my book tour right now. There's no way I'm going to miss out on that!"

Chase enthusiastically grabbed Jenna's hand and raced along the concrete walkway.

"Why are you in such a hurry?"

Jenna was trying hard to keep up with him.

Chase stopped and spun around.

"I thought if we ran back to your beach house right now, you'd slip into your bikini. But I have no idea where I'm going. I just thought I would start running and you could push me in the right direction eventually."

Jenna wasn't sure if it was his compliment or the grabbing of her hand that unnerved her the most.

She was fueling his interest with her little inferences. This had to stop. *Right now.* Flirting was only going to get her into trouble.

Jenna let go of Chase's hand.

"We're not going back to my beach house."

"Ok. I get the message."

"Good."

"You know, you haven't asked me too many questions. Where's your notebook by the way? Don't you have to take notes for the interview you're doing for the Gazette?"

He was changing the subject.

Thank goodness.

"I think I can remember your answers. Besides, it's just a small article. No one will probably read it anyway."

"Thanks for that. And I was starting to feel so good about myself."

Chase frowned.

"Got you."

Chase shook his head and smiled. She was teasing him now. He was back on her good side.

"No, you most certainly did not. I knew you were kidding me."

"Liar."

Jenna snickered. At least she was having fun. Innocent fun at this point. But would it stay that way?

Chase pulled Jenna down one of the side streets.

"You know, I could get a better feel for Cape May if I had my own personal tour guide. Of course, it might take *all day*. I'm sure you wouldn't want me to miss any of the highlights."

"The whole day?"

What am I getting myself into?

"Please, Jenna. Spend the day with me. I want to leave Cape May with good memories."

"The book signing at Convention Hall wasn't enough?"

Jenna stifled a laugh.

"Don't go there. You have no idea. One girl tried to rip off my shirt at the same time another one wanted me to sign her..."

"We are a wild bunch here in Cape May. I'm holding myself back as we speak."

Chase wasted no time to respond. He grabbed Jenna around the waist and kissed her firmly until her arms wound around his neck.

"Don't hold back," Chase whispered as he leaned in for another kiss.

Jenna found herself falling into Chase's arms before her brain could tell her to stop. For some insane reason, she felt such a natural tendency to hold onto him.

When he pulled back, Jenna saw hope in Chase's eyes.

Or was it a reflection of her own?

"Nice."

Jenna blushed.

"Very nice."

"How about that tour now?"

Chase reached for Jenna's hand and held his breath.

How could she say no? Why not spend the entire day with a handsome man who kissed like...

"Jenna?"

"Sorry. Guess I zoned out for a moment. Let's go. If you want a tour of Cape May, then we have to start at the Washington Street Mall. We can check out some shops then catch a trolley tour. How's that sound?"

"As long as you're with me, I'll go anywhere."

"You're easy to please, Chase Garrett."

"I'm all yours."
Jenna hesitated in responding, but then gave Chase a smile.
"For today."
"For today," he repeated.
And longer. There was no way Jenna Reed was getting off
this easy. He planned on being in her life for quite some time.

*****

After a morning and afternoon in Chase's company, Jenna
felt a multitude of emotions. Happy to have found someone she
felt comfortable around, sad because he would be leaving soon for
the next leg of his book tour, nervous she had kissed him back so
forcefully, and hesitant she was treading into dangerous waters
again.

No wonder her head was spinning.

She and Chase walked up and down the Mall, stopping at
several unique shops. Fralingers for salt water taffy, the Cape
May Popcorn Factory for caramel corn, Love the Cook for a
seafood cookbook for his Dad, the Great White Shark for t-shirts
and rope bracelets, and Laura's for fudge samples.

Shopping for several hours worked up their appetites.

"Where can we get a burger?" Chase asked as his stomach
growled for the second time.

"Can't beat the Mug. They have the best burgers in town."

Jenna steered Chase towards the Ugly Mug restaurant. He
was immediately fascinated by all the mugs hanging from the
ceiling.

"Why are the mugs facing in different directions?"

"Well, if the mug is facing away from the ocean, then the
owner is alive. The mugs which have been turned towards the
ocean are in memory of the owners who have passed on."

Chase seemed interested with all of the town trivia, especially when Jenna suggested they take the afternoon trolley tour
which highlighted more sights including the Physick Estate, the
Southern Mansion and Elaine's, the home of the Haunted Dinner
Theater.

The more time they spent together, the more comfortable
Jenna felt. Chase was so easy-going; she didn't mind spending the

entire day with him. In fact, the day was going by way too quick-ly.

"Have dinner with me."

Chase caught Jenna off-guard, just as they stepped off the trolley.

"Dinner?"

She had promised to give him one day…which technically wasn't over until…

What was the harm? It would probably be the last time she saw Chase anyway.

He'd forget her as soon as the next female reporter flashed a pair of sexy eyes at him.

Maybe not. Chase didn't seem like the usual type she had dated in the past. He was kind, considerate, fun. He was making all possible efforts to keep her interested which is more than she could say for her past couple of boyfriends.

"Ok," Jenna said before she realized what was happening. "But I need to freshen up. Can you give me a couple of hours?"

She needed some breathing room.

"Two hours. I'll meet you right here."

As Jenna walked the last block towards her beach house, it finally dawned on her what she had forgotten to do.

Candace Light.

Oh, God, she had forgotten to call her!

Jenna picked up her pace. As she hurried up the side steps, she couldn't believe how distracted she had been all day.

"Please be home," Jenna prayed as she dialed Candace's number.

Once again, it went to voicemail.

Phone tag…*great, just great.*

Jenna left another message. She tossed her cell on the dining room table in frustration. Her phone vibrated within seconds.

She wasn't expecting a return call so fast.

"Ms. Light, thank you for returning my call."

Jenna was breathless with anticipation.

"You're Lois' daughter?"

"Yes."

"I see…well, I would like to speak with you in person. Would it be possible for you to drive to Virginia? I live just outside of D.C."

Jenna remembered Candace's voicemail message. A road trip? She could do that. She *wanted* to do that.

"Yes, I'd be happy to drive down to see you."

"Call me again when you're on your way. We can meet at a restaurant. I'll speak to you soon."

Candace hung up before Jenna could even say good-bye.

"How strange," Jenna murmured.

A chill ran up her back.

Why was Candace so anxious to get off the phone?

She would know soon enough. She was heading for Virginia in the morning.

*****

Jenna was a few minutes late meeting Chase at the kiosk on the mall.

"I'm sorry I'm late. Just needed to make a phone call. I'm all yours now."

Wrong choice of words. Jenna regretted the moment they flowed from her mouth.

"I meant…"

"You don't need to explain. But I am glad you're all mine, even if it's just for tonight."

Jenna felt her face getting warm.

Was she blushing again?

They needed to keep walking. Maybe the sea breezes would cool off her face.

"Let's walk down to Godmother's. Just a few blocks off the mall. They have great Italian food. It's one of my favorite places to eat."

"Lead the way."

Jenna kept her hands inside the pockets of her hoodie, knowing full well Chase would try to hold hands with her again. As much as she enjoyed his company, she knew they had to say good-bye. He was leaving for Norfolk, the next stop on his book tour, and she was driving to Manassas.

It dawned on her unexpectedly…they were both going to Virginia.

Was fate intervening?

"Are you purposely ignoring me?"

Chase nudged Jenna as she walked.

She hadn't responded to a word he said ever since they left the Mall.

"I'm sorry."

"Am I that boring?"

"No, not at all. In fact, you're the first guy I've dated in a long time I wish I could spend more time with. But you have to leave on your book tour and I have other plans as well."

"I don't have to leave...*tonight*."

Jenna shook her head.

"But I have to say good-bye *tonight* after dinner. Come on, we're almost at the restaurant."

Chase lagged two steps behind. Jenna had made up her mind. *Tonight* she was pushing him away.

But not if he could help it.

Dinner at Godmother's was nothing short of amazing. The atmosphere of a small Italian restaurant combined with mouth-watering homemade pasta dishes was just the distraction Jenna and Chase needed. It delayed the touchy subject both of them wanted to avoid.

But as they leisurely walked back towards the Mall, Jenna stopped at the corner of North and Congress.

"This is where I say good-bye. This is my beach house."

Chase looked up at the house with the grayish-blue shutters.

"Nice."

Both Chase and Jenna started to laugh nervously.

"Being cautious?"

"You might say that. Look, Chase," Jenna began as she turned to face him. "I think you're great, and I've really had a nice time, but I'm not looking for another relationship right now."

"Neither was I until I met you. Jenna, I don't want to leave here thinking I'll never see you again. Please don't go in yet."

Chase leaned in for a kiss, but Jenna stopped him by pressing her hands against his chest.

No, no, no. Stop this before it goes any further.

The little voice in the back of her head had woken up just in time.

Jenna kissed Chase lightly on the cheek.

"Good-bye, Chase Garrett. Thank you for making the past two days...*very* nice."

Before she got to the top of the stairs, Chase got her attention again.

"We could always get together in Virginia."

Why had she told Chase about the letter and her plans to travel to Manassas?

Maybe it was the wine clouding her good sense...or maybe she just needed to share her excitement with someone.

Either way, Jenna now regretted the decision.

"I don't know, Chase. I might be very busy."

"I'll text you my hotel information anyway. You already have my cell number. Just in case...."

She had to give him credit. Chase was trying, more than any of the men she had dated. It was a refreshing change, but the timing couldn't have been worse.

"Good-night, Chase."

"Well thanks again for the past couple of days. I'm glad I met you, Jenna Reed. My offer still stands. I'll keep my cell with me and my fingers crossed."

Chase gave Jenna a final smile then turned to walk away. He just needed to try harder.

Jenna needed him, whether she realized it or not.

*****

Jenna paused as her hand reached for the doorknob.

Why was the screen door open?

She felt sure she had checked both doors before she left to meet Chase. As she cautiously poked her head inside, she saw her brother Austin getting a bag of frozen peas out of the freezer.

Her laid-back brother had decided to come to the shore after all.

"I wasn't expecting you so soon."

When Austin turned to face her, Jenna stifled a scream.

His face had been beaten. One eye was swollen shut. A long gash by his left sideburn was dripping droplets of blood down his chin. Jenna had no idea how Austin could have possibly driven down from his apartment in Philadelphia after taking such a pounding.

"My God, Austin, what happened to you? How did you get here?"

Before he could respond, Austin pulled Jenna into the living room and sat down next to her on the sofa. Ignoring her past couple of questions, Austin just glared at his sister.

"I've been calling your cell for the past hour, where have you been?"

"Austin, I had no idea you were trying to reach me. I guess I had my cell turned off. We just got back from Godmother's."

"We?"

"I met a guy a couple days ago. A visiting author. Lacey asked me to do an interview which turned into a tour of the town and dinner. I guess I just forgot to turn my phone back on."

Jenna leaned in to get a better look at Austin's bruises and open wound.

"You need a doctor. This is bad."

Austin grimaced as he held the frozen pack of peas to his head.

"No doctor."

"You are such a baby. Don't be an idiot. You might need stitches. You want to tell me who did this to you?"

"Not really, but I guess you *need to know*."

Jenna shot a puzzled look in Austin's direction.

"What?"

"I was attacked outside of my apartment early this morning in case… *you care*."

Jenna carefully removed the bag of peas and looked at the cut.

"Of course I care. You're my brother…why wouldn't I care? You're not making any sense."

Austin moaned until Jenna put the frozen bag back against his forehead.

"This looks bad, Austin. I really think you should go to the emergency clinic."

"No way. I'm not sitting there for the next couple of hours so some nurse can put a bandage on me and give me a few pain pills."

Jenna shrugged her shoulders. He could be so stubborn at times.

"What did you get mixed up in this time, Austin?"

Austin started to laugh but it hurt too much.

"Well now, that's the funny part. I should ask you the same thing, Sis. What the hell is going on with you?"

"I have no idea what you're talking about."

"Really? I got jumped outside of my apartment when I came in from a late night party. This scary dude with a snake tat on his arm tells me to get the "treasure" *from you* before we both end up dead. Then he shoves this card in my hand and tells me to call the number when we have it. Oh, and he also said we have two days to call, or we'll suffer the consequences."

Austin pulled the card from his jeans' pocket and thrust it into Jenna's hand.

"Then I got my ass kicked before he shoved me down on the bed and held a gun to my head. I guess I passed out because the next thing I knew, it was morning. I high-tailed it out of there so fast it's a wonder some cop didn't pick me up."

Jenna couldn't even begin to respond.

"So, once again, Sis, what crazy-ass mess are *you* mixed up in?"

Jenna stared at the card which only contained a phone number on one side.

"I have no idea what this means."

"Well, you better think hard, because in two days we both need to have an answer."

Austin just about made it to the guest room on the first floor. He was too tired to climb the steps to his own bedroom.

Jenna suddenly felt a chill running up and down her arms. She never felt so cold on a summer's day. It was frightening. She followed Austin to the bedroom and leaned against the door.

"Maybe the guy who attacked you was looking for someone else."

"That's what I thought. I kept telling him I didn't know anything about a *treasure*. But he wouldn't back off. When he said your name, it threw me off-guard and I got defensive. That's when he clipped me with the back of his gun."

Jenna slowly sank to the edge of the bed.

"Austin, don't go to sleep. If you have a concussion, you need to stay awake...at least for a little while longer."

She was talking to herself. Austin had drifted off.

Jenna shut the bedroom door and returned to the living room.

What in the hell was going on?

A mystery, an attack, a treasure?
Her peaceful summer had just flown out the window.

*****

"I'm awake," Austin groaned as he sat against the head-board.

"We need to go to the police and report this attack, Austin. I really think you need some medical attention; that cut looks bad."

Taking the washcloth Jenna offered him, Austin shook his head slightly.

"No police and no doctors."

"Please think about this. We need help."

"The man who attacked me was very specific. Any cops involved, and neither of us would see the light of day."

"Then what are we supposed to do? I can't leave you here like this. I'm driving to Virginia in the morning."

"You're doing *what*?"

Jenna took a deep breath. It was time to tell him what she had found.

"I broke a frame in Mom and Dad's room. Behind the picture of all of us in the lifeboat was a letter and a picture of a small child. Mom was involved in something thirty years ago with some friends. I have no idea what all of it means, but I'm going to Virginia to find out. I contacted one of Mom's friends from college - the woman who wrote the letter."

"Why, Jenna? What's the point? If Mom hid the letter, I'm sure she had a good reason. You should just leave it alone. Besides, with these wackos after us, I don't want you driving anywhere by yourself."

Austin pulled himself to the side of the bed.

"I'm coming with you. I am not going to let anything happen to you. You're all I have left, Sis."

"We don't know anything about these people and why they're threatening us. How would they know I'm going to Virginia? You're overreacting, Austin."

"Yeah, right. Do you want this to happen to you? Well, I don't. So, I'm not leaving you. We go to Virginia together, or you don't go at all."

Austin steadied himself until he got to the bathroom, leaving Jenna speechless.

Austin was right. This made no sense.

But I need to know...

"I'm sorry, Austin," Jenna whispered.

There was no way she was taking him to Virginia.

*****

"We'll leave in the morning," Jenna lied.

"Fine," Austin grumbled, satisfied he had gotten his point across.

"We can leave around eight."

"Whatever."

Austin was in no shape to argue. The four capsules of Advil were kicking in. He just wanted to get back to bed.

Jenna woke up while it was still dark outside. Her clock blasted five-thirty but it seemed so much earlier.

Checking in on Austin, Jenna felt a pang of guilt. He was sprawled on the bed, probably out for at least a couple more hours. By the time he realized she had left without him, she would be well on her way.

Grabbing her small duffle bag, her laptop and her car keys, Jenna closed the kitchen door as quietly as she could. She hated herself momentarily for abandoning him, but she needed to get away without further drama.

As she pulled away from the curb, she passed the Maylors' house, then remembered Teresa wanted to talk to her. It would have to wait until she got back from Virginia. Teresa just probably wanted to reminisce about her parents. Jenna made a mental note to call Teresa and apologize later in the day.

Right now, she was focused on her meeting with Candace Light. Answers about her mother's involvement were waiting for her in Virginia, Jenna just knew it.

She was on her way to finding the truth.

Chapter 5

Mason Hamilton paced his office which was located on the tenth floor of the famed Livingston Museum of Art building. Prime real estate. Prestigious, yet unassuming. He had risen to the top of the Hamilton-Knox Foundation when both of the founding partners had retired several years ago.

A natural move for him.

Primed by his father since the first day he started at H-K, Mason knew this would be his calling. Now, at 65, as he looked out onto the city from his corner office, he was coming full circle. Retirement was a few short months away. A new phase of his life was beginning.

But not soon enough.

Marrying into money, raising an only child, establishing his reputation throughout global museum circles, Mason had proven himself in many ways. Acquiring rare antiquities from his global contacts around the world, turning his Foundation's funding from private donors into large amounts of liquid assets and promoting world showcase exhibits, Mason was at the top of his game.

His success was measured by the highest standards.

Yet he had failed, and never forgave himself.

"That bitch," Mason growled, still harboring resentment towards his former lover, Sylvia Bernard. Even after thirty years, Mason still cursed her memory. She was the one who had deprived him of his precious treasure.

"You cost me, and I hope you're burning in hell."

Mason had never forgotten how his first major exhibit failed. Working tirelessly for months to present the world's first monumental display of Pirate Treasure, he was forced to close the exhibit early due to lack of sales. His planned centerpiece attraction – five gold animal figurines believed to be the lost treasure of the infamous pirate, Blackbeard, had been stolen from him.

His lover had outsmarted him.

A concept which had haunted him ever since.

Mason tossed back a shot of whiskey. Closing his eyes for a brief moment, he could almost see the fear on Sylvia's face the night he had left her.

The night he hid the gold objects in her apartment.

The night she betrayed him.

How could she possibly have known where he had hidden the treasure pieces?

Mason remembered in vivid detail the events leading to his disappointment and loss. He had placed a hit on old Henry Stanick, the man who claimed he owned an authentic piece of pirate history. The treasure pieces were stolen from Stanick's apartment by Mason's men then brought to Mason at his office.

It was too risky to log them into the museum's collection inventory just yet. Mason needed time to concoct a story about finding them in Europe.

The perfect hiding place was in Sylvia's apartment. No one could track his actions here.

But the plan was beset with complications. His incompetent assistants searched the apartment but couldn't find the treasure pieces. Then when Sylvia returned home unexpectedly, they surprised her. Panicking, they murdered her then set her apartment on fire.

Such a waste...of prime real estate, Mason recalled. The apartment in Tribeca had cost him a fortune. Sylvia, on the other hand, was expendable.

Mason refilled his glass. He never felt the first shot. He needed more.

"You died too soon, bitch."

Harboring a grudge for such a long time was insane. But for some unknown reason, Mason couldn't let it go.

Someone had beaten him at his own game.

The treasure pieces had never been found.

At first Mason wondered if his two accomplices could have stolen them, but after hours of torture and their subsequent deaths by dismemberment, Mason was convinced they lacked the intelligence to double-cross him.

There was only one other explanation.

Sylvia. She had hidden the treasure pieces somewhere then returned to her apartment.

Damn her forever.

She had taken so much away from him.

Mason had wanted those treasure pieces for more than one reason.

Prestige. A rare find such as Blackbeard's gold treasure would certainly elevate him to the highest levels in the museum global community. Every curator in the world would be envious.

Money. A private buyer had contacted Mason years ago to entice him to find the rare pieces for a substantial fee. Millions of dollars were at stake which would secure his financial future.

Revenge. The most compelling reason of all. He would only feel a sense of true satisfaction when the treasure pieces were returned to him and he could finally realize retribution for Sylvia's deceit.

Yet he was no closer today than he had been thirty years ago. The treasure was still missing and he had no idea where to search. Sylvia was still taunting him from beyond the grave.

Or had she been resurrected?

Mason stared at the envelope lying on his desk.

Someone was making him nervous as hell.

The envelope had mysteriously appeared on his desk after lunch. None of his staff had seen the person who delivered it.

Who was brazen enough to breach the sanctity of his private office?

No one who wasn't employed by H-K was permitted beyond the front desk, unless it was for a scheduled meeting. Privacy was paramount. Exhibit details were extremely confidential until an announcement was made to the media.

A betrayer in his midst?

Mason ran through the names of his staff in his head. Not one person outwardly appeared brave enough to pull off such a scheme. It had to be someone outside of H-K.

But who?

The night cleaning crew? Doubtful. Most were gone by the time Mason had left for the evening.

The security guards? Unlikely. They were on his secret payroll anyway.

What did it matter? The contents of the envelope had served its intended purpose.

Mason's blood was beginning to boil.

Opening the back clasp, Mason allowed the contents to spill out onto his desk blotter. Three items emerged – a folded piece of white paper and two newspaper clippings.

Mason glanced briefly at the yellowed newsprint. The obituary of Henry Stanick, aged 83, who died in 1980, and an article dated a few days later describing the arson of an apartment building in which one woman had died.

Old news.

But it was the small piece of paper with words scribbled in dark ink which held the greatest trepidation.

ALL LIARS ARE CAUGHT WITH THE TRUTH

Mason dropped the piece of paper then pushed his chair away from his desk.

After all these years, how could anyone know what he had done?

All of the staff at the Hamilton-Knox Foundation had been working there ten years or less. He had made sure none of his former colleagues lasted more than a year after the Henry Stanick fiasco.

Hans Kliric and Dimitri Batrov? No, not his right-hand men. They were loyal dogs. Mason had smuggled Hans out of Russia over ten years ago with a shipment of antiquities for an upcoming exhibit. Dimitri came on board several months ago from one of the Russian mobs in east Harlem. Hans trusted him completely.

Laurence Renault, his former business partner? No, Renault was long dead. A fishing accident off the coast of Fiji had taken Renault at the peak of his illustrious career when he and Mason were delving into the art acquisition business...outside of legal channels. Threatening museum curators to allow their priceless artifacts to be copied and returned to unsuspecting art donors, while Mason and Renault sold the originals on the black market – an ingenious plan until Renault's ways of persuasion became deadly. Not willing to be brought under suspicion, Mason had terminated his relationship with Renault by hiring a hit man to coordinate the boating accident. Another loose end resolved.

Mason was out of answers which drove him crazy. He ran his fingers through his perfectly combed silver hair and stared out the window.

He needed some help to sort this all out.

Within the hour, he assembled his team.

Hans Kliric, Dimitri Batrov, and one other – Jonathan Knox, the junior partner who would succeed him this fall as the head of H-K.

"I'm being threatened, possibly blackmailed," Mason announced when all three men had taken seats.

"By whom?" Jonathan asked as Mason handed him the mysterious note.

"I'm not sure; that's why I need you to investigate."

"I don't understand, Mason. What exactly do you need us to do?" Jonathan asked. This was well beyond his normal executive-level duties.

Hans and Dimitri exchanged glances. They had no problem deciphering Mason's request. They would have to check surveillance footage and find out if there were any recent replacements on the cleaning crew.

Knox was the only one without a specific job task.

Hans almost snickered. He couldn't imagine Knox getting dirt under his fingernails or wrinkling his expensive suit.

Mason's phone rang. Recognizing the number, he knew he had to take the call.

"Wait outside."

After the men had exited, Mason picked up the receiver.

"Talk."

"I have news."

"Obviously, or you wouldn't be bothering me at the office."

Mason's eyes rolled upward in annoyance.

"A letter has been found by the Reeds' daughter, Jenna. She's travelling to Manassas, Virginia tomorrow to meet with a Candace Light. Thought you should know."

"I see. Your call is very timely. I received a package today with a cryptic message. Perhaps there is a connection. Keep me updated."

Mason ushered the men back into his office.

"One of my resources just provided an interesting report."

Mason sat on the edge of his desk with his arms folded. A plan was formulating in his mind. Yes, it would work.

"There is a young woman who I want you to track. Her name is Jenna Reed."

Mason tapped Jonathan on the shoulder.

"She's travelling to Manassas, Virginia to meet with a woman named Candace Light. With the right *encouragement,* Jenna Reed may provide valuable information to the issue at hand."

Jonathan's eyes locked on Mason's face.

"You think this woman is the one blackmailing you?"

Mason shook his head.

"No, but I believe she holds the key to another matter which may be related. Almost thirty years ago, several artifacts...a special *treasure* was stolen from me - five solid gold animal figurines rumored to be the only valuable treasure acquired by Blackbeard. I have been searching for them ever since. Now I have reason to believe they may be resurfacing. I must find them...at *any cost*."

"You think Jenna Reed has the artifacts?"

"Not yet, but my resource believes she has recently received information which could lead to their discovery. I want you to find her...and *persuade* her to tell us where my treasure is hidden. Use whatever methods you feel are...*appropriate*."

"Are you telling me to seduce her, Mason?"

"Jonathan, be your charming self. I'm sure she won't be able to resist. I've seen you in action. The women around here practically fall at your feet. I'm sure you can work your magic on Jenna Reed."

Mason walked back to his whiskey glass after the men had departed. A smile creased his lips.

Closure was coming. He could feel it.

*****

Jonathan had never met Hans Kliric or Dimitri Batrov before this evening in Mason's office. Mason frequently commented about their special *services*, but never in great detail. Now, Jonathan understood the game plan...*clearly*.

If he was unable to persuade Jenna Reed to tell him about Mason's treasure, Hans and Dimitri would be at his disposal to apply additional pressure. Mason was demanding an answer, one way or another.

As he rode in the taxi back to his apartment, Jonathan cursed under his breath. He had no desire to be allied with Hans Kliric or

Dimitri Batrov whatsoever. They were both below his standard of decency.

My *colleagues* for the next few days, Jonathan lamented.

But what could he do?

Mason was his mentor. He taught Jonathan everything he knew about running H-K. Much more than his own father, Elliott Knox had been willing to share.

A financial wizard who wanted nothing to do with the limelight, Elliott Knox preferred to stay in his corner office and read reports. He left the flamboyancy of promoting H-K to Mason, who seemed to be quite adept at coddling the media for his own benefit.

Besides, Mason needed a protégé. His own daughter had no interest in following the footsteps of her father, personally or professionally. They rarely communicated much less bonded. So Mason devoted his time and efforts to Jonathan.

Helping Mason now was the return of that favor.

A favor to one man which would undeniably hurt an innocent woman.

Jonathan wasn't sure he could live with that.

Chapter 6

"To success," Mason toasted himself as he lifted his glass high.

After tossing back the shot, Mason retrieved the envelope he had hastily thrown in the trash can. It would have to be burned. He stuck it in his jacket pocket with plans to toss it into the fireplace when he got home.

God knows he wanted nothing more than to put the murder of Henry Stanick behind him once and for all. He didn't feel the need to share that bit of information with Jonathan, Hans or Dimitri. The less they knew about the origins of the treasure pieces, the better.

Henry Stanick was still haunting him from the grave.

The man who claimed to own a piece of pirate history.

Claiming to be the last known descendant of a young pirate named James Dunn, Stanick felt a certain sense of loyalty to pirate lore. Much to Mason's chagrin, Stanick had insisted upon explaining his ancestry when they first met.

To validate his *treasure*, he told Mason.

So Mason sat at Stanick's kitchen table, counting the minutes until he could make his escape, as Stanick began his story.

Dunn was just a cabin boy of thirteen when Blackbeard and his men commandeered an unsuspecting sailing vessel in the late 1700s. The captured crew, which included Dunn, was offered the opportunity to join Blackbeard's band of pirates. Dunn jumped at the chance to sail with the infamous pirate, and never looked back on his innocent seafaring days. A dangerous mistake on several counts.

During a raid of several small ports in the Caribbean, Blackbeard's men carried off many trinkets from the reigning dignitaries, killing or injuring everyone in sight. The spoils of the pillage were deposited into the ship's hull for safekeeping until they sailed north and could be sold or traded. One night when the pirates went out to celebrate with a night of debauchery, Dunn stayed behind and wandered the ship.

Finding the treasure cove in the hull, Dunn was amazed at what he saw – there were chalices made of silver, fine silk linens, pistols, swords, cutlery, and bags of gold dust, among other trinkets. Tucked inside a small metal box was a set of five solid gold animal figures.

Dunn was fascinated with the little animals most of all. He had never seen such detail in the way the figurines had been molded. He sat down on the wooden planks and laid the animals before him. An elephant, a tiger, a monkey, a giraffe and a lion. He was sure the other pirates wouldn't want these small animals. So Dunn decided to keep them for himself, in addition to a small bag of gold dust.

Since he had been a tailor's apprentice before taking to the sea, Dunn was responsible for mending sails as well as the clothes of the other men. To keep his treasure hidden, he added small pockets into the linings of his boots which he never took off in the presence of anyone.

Dunn slipped off the ship before the pirates returned. He stole a dress from a clothesline and pretended to be an orphaned girl. Soon, he found passage on a ship bound for the northern colonies with a family of one of the sailors to whom he gave the bag of gold dust.

By the time Dunn arrived in Virginia, Blackbeard had been captured and beheaded. He was safe now.

Over time and many bequests, Henry Stanick became the proud owner of the little gold animal figurines.

Now Henry wanted to leave a legacy for the world to see.

Mason quickly became obsessed with the idea of the treasure pieces becoming the main showcase of his new exhibit. It would bring people from all over the world. The Hamilton-Knox Foundation would become famous and most importantly, he would get all the credit.

But for now, Mason needed to convince Stanick of his *honorable* intentions.

Filling Stanick's head with all kinds of accolades, Mason could see the old man was naïve enough to believe whatever he said. Tomorrow, representatives from the museum would stop by with a loan agreement and they would pick up the artifacts.

A handshake and a promise of free exhibit tickets had sealed the deal.

Within two hours, Henry Stanick was dead and the treasure pieces had a new owner.

*****

Alina Catrall, Henry Stanick's niece, was the only person he trusted completely and the only one he told about his pirate treasure.

She researched the gold animal figurines out of curiosity. She found out the small artifacts had once belonged to a local magistrate in one of the ports of the British West Indies. The figurines had been listed as stolen property during raids by Blackbeard's men. Most of the items had been recovered when they were sold up and down the Florida coast, but the gold animal figures had never surfaced.

Alina arrived at Henry's apartment right after work that fateful day in September 1980. She used her key as usual to let herself into his home, calling to him from the front door. Henry always answered right away.

But not today. There was only silence.

Alina called out again. No response.

Where could he have gone?

Stepping into his modest living room, Alina found her uncle lying face down on the floor. She bent down to take his pulse. Alina began to cry. Her sweet uncle had passed away all alone.

As she stood up and wiped away a tear, Alina noticed the oxygen tubing was nowhere near Henry. In fact, the tubing was out of reach of his body. Even if he had fallen, the tubing wouldn't have been knocked off and ended up behind the oxygen tank. It just didn't make sense.

Alina tried to compose herself before calling the police to report his death. As she passed the kitchen table, she saw the newspaper clipping about the upcoming *Pirate* exhibit at the Maritime Museum.

Having an uneasy feeling, Alina quickly ran to the small bedside cabinet next to Henry's bed. Behind a stack of books was a metal box Alina knew was Henry's hiding place for his pirate treasure.

When she opened the lid, her fear was realized. The box was empty.

Alina gave the police officer her report of finding her uncle's body but failed to mention the theft of the gold animal figurines. She had her own suspicions.

The police officer listed the death as 'natural causes.' There was no indication of foul play – no break-in, no missing possessions. Henry Stanick was in his 80s. Case closed.

Alina tried to protest, but the officer said they didn't have the resources to devote to investigating a case of natural death. There was no reason to suspect a crime had been committed unless Alina had another theory.

Alina bit her tongue. She wasn't sharing her theory with anyone, but she knew without a doubt her uncle had been murdered for his treasure pieces. The Dunn legend had claimed another victim.

Death comes to those who dare to hold all five pieces of tainted gold.

*****

Alina arrived at the Hamilton-Knox Foundation right on time for her appointment with Mason Hamilton. She was ushered to the waiting lounge as Mason was still on a conference call.

Alina couldn't help but notice another young woman sitting a few seats over who appeared very agitated, and then got up to approach the front desk.

"You know better than anyone, Sylvia. Mason has his own agenda. Occasionally, he lets us know what it is. If he told you he can't meet with you today, then it's probably true. He does have several appointments and he's running behind."

The receptionist nodded in Alina's direction.

Alina looked up when Mason's door finally opened. As Mason strode out, Alina noted an air of conceit which seemed to embellish his very presence. Alina couldn't help but speculate this man standing before her had something to do with her uncle's death. She shivered as he approached her.

"Miss Catrall, I presume."

Alina felt an icy chill as Mason Hamilton's hand clamped down upon her own. Before she could utter a response, she was interrupted.

"Mason, I need to see you *now*."

The other young woman in the waiting area had jumped to her feet and was standing only a few feet away. Alina immediately let go of Mason's hand and took a step backwards.

"Why, of course. Just let me direct Miss Catrall to my office then we can go over those reports you prepared. I know how anxious you are to get them to the auditors, Sylvia."

Alina couldn't help but notice the glare Mason Hamilton sent in the other woman's direction. He was most certainly annoyed at the rude interruption and wanted to put the woman in her subservient place.

How condescending, Alina thought to herself. She felt sorry for the young woman, who looked so despondent when Mason brushed past her.

"Take a seat, please. I'll be right back."

Alina felt totally uncomfortable as she sat in one of Mason's guest chairs. Mason had forgotten to close his office door. Alina could still hear bits and pieces of his heated conversation. It made her extremely nervous. She hoped she could still remember everything she wanted to say.

After a few minutes of hearing Mason berate the poor woman, Alina couldn't take it anymore. Overhearing a private conversation was one thing, but the threat he was making was too much to bear.

Arriving in the lobby, Alina breathed a sigh of relief mixed with regret. So much for her bravery. She had no evidence Mason Hamilton had stolen her uncle's treasure. And she certainly didn't want to get on his bad side.

As she started to leave, Alina noticed the young woman who had absorbed Mason's wrath. She was sitting in the waiting lounge across from the water fountain.

The woman's eyes were red from crying. Mason had reduced her to a pitiful mess. Alina was willing to bet the young woman couldn't be this upset about some reports. No, this had to be personal.

In the short amount of time Alina had been in Mason's office, she remembered seeing a picture on his desk of Mason and his pregnant wife.

It didn't take Alina long to figure out what was going on.

Mason Hamilton had a mistress.

I wonder, Alina thought. Perhaps she could find out some information another way. It was worth a try to find another angle.

"Hi, I'm Alina. I had requested a meeting with Mr. Hamilton to discuss my uncle who just recently passed away, but…I was too emotional. I had to leave. I'm sorry, I didn't mean to interrupt a meeting you had with Mr. Hamilton."

Alina hated to lie but it was the only chance she had.

"No, I'm the one who should apologize. I was very rude upstairs. Please, forgive me. I'm Sylvia Bernard."

"Nice to meet you. Do you know of any coffee shops around here? I think talking about my uncle has really gotten to me. I could sure use some caffeine right about now."

"Actually, there's a great coffee shop just a couple of doors down. I can show you if you like. I wouldn't mind stopping for a cup myself and I could use the company."

"That would be great. Thanks, Sylvia."

Alina felt guilty using this woman. Ironically, they almost looked alike. Both had long, dark wavy hair and brown eyes. About the same height, same figure. It was almost eerie.

The coffee break turned into lunch.

The more time Alina spent with Sylvia, the more she found they had in common. Most importantly, they had a passion for shoes.

They made plans for a quick breakfast the next morning followed by shopping at Macy's.

"I'll stop down at the bakery when it opens to pick up some croissants."

"Ok, how is seven-thirty?"

"That's fine. If I'm not home yet, my hide-away key is just above my door frame. See you tomorrow, Alina."

Sylvia saw no reason not to trust Alina. She seemed like just another woman who had been intimidated by Mason's manipulative behavior.

Join the club, Sylvia muttered to herself, never realizing she had seen Alina Catrall for the last time.

Chapter 7

She couldn't wait to get off the interstate.

Patience…you're almost there.

Almost was taking forever.

Six and a half hours later, Jenna pulled into the parking lot at the Hampton Inn in Manassas, mentally and physically drained. Austin had called her cell practically every hour. She had no choice but to ignore it.

Jenna didn't have the stamina to get into an argument with Austin right now. She just wanted to push forward. As soon as she checked in and put her suitcase in her room, Jenna headed for the diner where she was meeting Candace Light.

Jenna pushed open the door to the diner and took a deep breath.

"You remind me of your mother."

Candace was standing just inside the front door. She gave Jenna a hug, then stood back to take a better look at her.

"Lois sent me a few pictures of you and your brother. I recognized you the moment you got out of your car."

"My mother is the reason I need to talk to you."

"Let's take a booth in the back."

As soon as they gave their order to the waitress, Candace grabbed Jenna's hand.

"I knew this day would come, Jenna. Your mother and I both knew one day this would all surface again."

"What are you talking about? I don't understand any of this, Candace."

"Lois took every precaution. She kept secrets…from your father, you, and your brother. For your own protection. She loved you very much."

"What secrets? Please tell me. You wrote the letter to my mother which I found at our beach house. Inside was a picture of a small boy you were unable to raise. Why was my mother involved?"

Candace glanced out the window. Each raindrop seemed like a tear falling down from the friends she had lost.

"Did your mother ever tell you about our college days?"

"Yes. Lots of times. Funny stories, sad stories. I still don't see what that has to do with the letter."

"We were all...*bound together*, you might say. Your mother, Mary Fortenni, Gail Tremont, Sylvia Bernard and myself. We promised to look out for each other, even after we graduated. Sylvia stayed in New York, while the rest of us went home. Sylvia got in too deep with a bad relationship, which ultimately resulted in a pregnancy."

"The little boy in the picture?"

"Yes. We named him Billy. Sylvia ran to your mother for help. She was afraid for her life and the baby. The man who fathered him...well...he couldn't be trusted. We all agreed to help. One day when your mother was babysitting, Sylvia told her she needed to run a few errands. She never came back."

"Sylvia abandoned her baby?" Jenna's eyes widened in shock.

"Sylvia had her reasons which I won't go into now. But, suffice it say, the rest of us were suddenly thrown into a situation where we had to act quickly. I brought Billy home to live with me. I really thought I could raise him. He was the most adorable child. But after a few months, I soon realized, being a single parent with a young child and a demanding job was too much to handle. That's when I wrote the letter."

"What happened to the baby?"

"Lois took him to live with Mary Fortenni in Folly Beach. But before they could get settled, Gail called out of the blue. She wanted to formally adopt Billy. We were all shocked of course, but knowing Billy would have a permanent home in Boston, we all agreed."

"I'm sure you were all relieved."

Candace nodded.

"Gail married within a year. She and her new husband formally adopted Billy and changed his name. We never heard from her again. It was so strange."

"Maybe Gail wanted to give the baby a fresh start. But it still doesn't make sense why she cut off communication. Maybe something happened that the rest of you didn't know about."

"Could be. I don't know. We all went on with our lives. I'm sorry, Jenna. I know you were looking for more answers, but I just don't have them."

Jenna sat back in her chair, dumbfounded. What could she say? There was so much more to this mystery, she just knew it. She wondered if Candace knew more than she was willing to share."

"I don't know where to go from here, Candace."

"Go home, Jenna. Forget all about this. It happened so long ago; maybe your mother had her reasons for not telling you."

"Could they be the same reasons you have?"

Jenna surveyed Candace's face. It bore a look of deep concern now.

Candace took a deep breath and leaned closer across the table. Her voice was softer now, almost a whisper.

"If you want more details, talk to Mary Fortenni. She and your mother were very close. Mary will be able to tell you things…I wasn't privy to."

"The woman from South Carolina? Is she still living there?"

"I'm not sure. But I know Mary won't talk to you on the phone either. We were all told…not to use public technology to communicate."

"Told by whom, Candace?"

Looking around the restaurant, Candace felt an eerie sensation.

"Candace?" Jenna repeated.

"Jenna, I think your parents were murdered. The man who Sylvia was running from is pure evil. His name is Mason Hamilton. After Sylvia came to your mother's house and we hid her, we received word Sylvia's apartment had been set on fire and a young woman died. The New York paper indicated it was Sylvia, but we all knew she was alive. Someone set the fire to conceal the murder."

Jenna's hand flew to cover her mouth.

"My God, Candace, what were you all involved in?"

Candace shook her head. She just couldn't give Jenna all the details…*not now.*

"You have to be careful, Jenna. Meeting me here was risky for you. Mason Hamilton won't stop until he gets what he wants. Now, he might be coming after you."

"I don't believe that for a second, Candace. I don't know anyone named Mason Hamilton."

"You won't until it's too late."

"Why are you scaring me like this?"

"Because you need to be scared. You need to watch your back. He will do anything to get his treasure."

Jenna sat stiffly in her chair.

The treasure.

"I've said too much already. I have to go, Jenna."

"Wait, Candace. Why do you think Mason Hamilton killed my parents? They were in a car accident. The road conditions were bad."

Candace looked over her shoulder, unable to shake off the tension which was building inside her.

"Did you ever see the official police report?"

"No."

"Did you have to identify the bodies?"

"No. The police detective told us they were burned beyond recognition."

Candace looked directly into Jenna's eyes.

"Your parents were sacrificed. Someone wanted them dead. I believe it was Mason Hamilton, covering his tracks after he failed at finding his treasure. Now I'm afraid he might be focusing his attentions on you. You need to take care, Jenna."

"Candace, this is crazy. My brother was beaten a couple of days ago. The man who attacked him mentioned something about a treasure."

Candace sunk back slowly into her chair.

"Then he knows. Someone tipped off Mason Hamilton. Sylvia was right all along. She told us to watch our backs. Even after our homes were broken into and nothing was stolen, I knew it was him. Now, he's up to his old tricks again."

"I don't know what to do, Candace."

"Be very diligent, Jenna. Keep a watchful eye. I'm going home to make a few phone calls. I'll try to get you some help."

Jenna couldn't believe what she was hearing. She felt like she had woken up in the middle of one of her mystery novels, but couldn't get out. Her head was spinning.

Candace tore off a piece of the paper placemat. She wrote down a phone number.

"This is Mary Fortenni's cell number. She calls me occasionally to check in. Leave her a message and tell her I told you to call. I'll call you later tonight, Jenna. We'll get together tomorrow morning."

She watched Jenna's car pull away from the parking lot. Candace felt like a huge weight had been lifted but another one had taken its place.

Opening her car door, she felt a chilling sensation she couldn't explain. Her skin grew cold, clammy.

Someone is watching me.

Glancing fearfully around the parking lot, Candace sighed when all she saw was empty parked cars. Her fear was unfounded...*again*. Too many years of worrying, of being frightened, had left her paranoid.

As she turned the key in the ignition, Candace knew why she had felt the iciness creep over her body, but it was too late. Her car's electrical system came to life just in the split second as she took her last breath.

Pieces of metal, broken glass, and body parts skyrocketed into the air, then came crashing down over parked cars, and against the front window of the diner.

Jenna slammed on her brakes a half mile down the road when she heard the loud noise. She spun around to get a better look, but too many people were speeding away from the parking lot.

A cloud of smoke billowed up into the air as she did a u-turn, going back towards the restaurant.

Jenna searched the crowd. Candace was nowhere to be seen. Maybe she had already left.

She dialed Candace's cell. No answer. Maybe Candace was driving and couldn't pick up the phone. The poor woman was so paranoid, Jenna thought to herself. She probably screened every call.

Dragging her tired body up the steps to her room on the second floor, Jenna yawned as she slid the keycard into the slot just above the door handle.

She would check her email then hit the sack.

But the softness of the bed was beckoning her. She climbed up and soaked in the sheer pleasure of the plush softness surrounding her aching body.

It felt so good.

A few seconds of pure relaxation was all she knew.

Rough hands pushed her face forward on the bed, forcing her arms behind her back. Within seconds, rope bound her wrists as she struggled helplessly.

"What the…"

Only a partial gasp escaped her lips before a gag was tied behind her head. Twisting her head, Jenna caught a glimpse of two men, dressed in black, both pinning her to the bed.

Panicking, she desperately tried to roll to either side with the fleeting notion she would have the ability to shake either one off her.

Bad theory.

She was no match for these strong men. Out-numbered and overpowered. Her mind raced with all kinds of thoughts…mostly bad ones.

Was she going to be raped, beaten, or worse…murdered?

Jenna had no time to debate those options. Her body went limp as the drugs took effect.

Her mind was shutting down just as fast.

Can't fight…anymore.

After dumping Jenna's body in the backseat of their car parked just outside the side entrance, both men tore off their black ski masks, revealing their sweaty faces.

"Good work," Hans Kliric remarked as he nodded to his partner, Dimitri Batrov.

"Now we will see what she knows."

*****

Numbness. Darkness.

Jenna's head rolled to one side. She slowly woke up.

Why couldn't she move?

Oh, God, now she remembered.

The hands on her body. Her arms being jerked backward. The sweet-smelling coating on the rag stuffed between her teeth.

Flexing her fingers, Jenna realized her arms were still tied behind her back but now she was seated in a chair.

She was someone's prisoner in a dark room.

"She's awake."

A voice echoed in the room. Someone was standing nearby. Someone with a heavy, European accent. Russian, perhaps?

"Untie her...*now*."

Another man's voice. American. Younger. Authoritative.

Her captor?

A man approached her chair but she couldn't see his face. There was no mistake; she recognized the rough hands and the stench of his cigar residue. He was the same man who assaulted her in her hotel room.

What else had he done to her?

Jenna turned her head away. He was purposely breathing heavy close to her neck, taking time to untie the ropes around her wrists. He repulsed her and made her skin crawl.

"Get your filthy hands off of me!"

Hans Kliric laughed as he licked the back of Jenna's hand before he cut the final rope free. Stepping back, he glared at the man who had just stepped from the shadows and turned on the light which hung above a small table.

Jenna rubbed her arms vigorously. As her eyes flew around the room, she centered on the man who now stood before her. He didn't look threatening at all. Looks could be deceiving.

"Ms. Reed, my apologies for the uncouth manner of my associates."

"Apology *not* accepted. Who the hell are you people?"

Jenna stretched her arms above her head. She was so sore from being confined to the same position for a long time.

The drugs hadn't quite worn off. She was dizzy. The room began to spin around her. She tried to stand then fell back into her seat.

Jonathan steadied her arm as she sat upright.

"Take your hands off of me."

Jonathan stepped back, not expecting such retaliation. He had never strong-armed a woman before and didn't know how to react.

"I don't mean to harm you," he said quietly.

Hans rolled his eyes. Knox had no idea what to do. This was a waste of time.

"Please, stay seated. I'm afraid the effects of the drugs have not yet worn off."

"So you admit you drugged me. Perfect. What the hell do you want? "

"Information."

Jonathan offered Jenna a glass of water, which had been placed on the table. To his complete surprise, she promptly threw it back at him, splattering his suit.

"I'm not willing to share any information," Jenna said with attitude.

Jonathan jumped back. He hadn't expected that move. Brushing the water droplets off his jacket, he held back a laugh. He was going to enjoy getting to know Jenna Reed.

"I hope you change your mind."

"And if I don't? What? Are your boys going to attack me like they did in my hotel room?"

Jonathan hung his head in shame. He had no idea Hans and Dimitri would go to such lengths. He merely had asked them to find Jenna so he could contact her. Instead, they drugged her and kidnapped her.

Jenna folded her arms in defiance.

"Well?"

But as her eyes regained her full vision and she could focus on his face, Jenna softened.

He was absolutely gorgeous. Wavy dark hair, high cheekbones, incredible blue eyes. Just the right amount of sex appeal. Dressed impeccably in a tailored suit, he looked like a model for GQ.

How in the hell was she supposed to deal with that?

Jenna was spellbound.

Jonathan tried to contemplate what was going through Jenna's mind but her tenacity unnerved him. Or was it the low-cut shirt she was wearing? Or could it be her long, dark hair which was tousled and had fallen around her face?

How could he possibly interrogate someone who looked this sexy?

Jenna Reed wasn't at all what he expected. She was beautiful and strong. He couldn't help himself. Jonathan was beginning to smile.

Hans grunted in the back of the room, making Jonathan snap to attention.

If he didn't succeed, then Mason would turn Hans and Dimtri on her. Jonathan dared to think what they might do.

He couldn't let that happen. He had to think of something...*fast*.

"My name is Jonathan Knox. My employer sent me to find you, ask you some questions, then return you to your hotel safe and sound. We mean you no harm."

"Really? I find that hard to believe."

Jenna turned her wrists over to show Jonathan the rope burns on each wrist.

"Try again."

Jenna couldn't help being sarcastic. Fierceness sparked inside her she never knew existed.

Jonathan was appalled to see the remnants of Jenna's abuse. He wished to God he could take back every one of them.

"That was...unfortunate. Please, Ms. Reed, I'm asking for your cooperation."

Jenna fumed. He wasn't going to stop until she played along.

"Ask me."

Jenna locked eyes with Jonathan Knox. She was willing to do anything if it guaranteed her freedom.

"What did you discuss with Candace Light?"

"Wrong question. Next?"

Jonathan shifted his stance. She was good. But he could be better.

"What do you know about the treasure?"

Jenna stiffened. The...*treasure*. It was the topic of too many recent conversations to be a coincidence.

"I don't know what you're talking about."

"We can do this all night, Ms. Reed."

Jenna shook her head.

"Ok. First of all, my conversation with Candace Light was *private* about my mother. Secondly, I don't know anything about a treasure. So, I don't see how I can possibly help you or your employer. Now I want to go back to my hotel."

Jenna rose slowly just as Jonathan stepped forward. They were within inches of each other's faces. She felt a strange intensity growing inside her. She turned to move away as Jonathan touched her arm.

Heat poured into her body at lightning speed.

Her face became warm. Her fingers were tingling.

Her whole body was on fire.

Maybe she needed to throw some water onto herself.

"Jenna."

"Jonathan."

She was now on a first name basis with Jonathan Knox. That couldn't be good.

"Let...me...go."

Jonathan released her arm and took a step backwards. Coolness returned to his body the instant he let go.

What had just happened?

Raising his eyes until they met Jenna's, Jonathan wanted nothing more than to touch her again. To feel what they had both sensed.

But he needed to maintain control. Mason wanted results, not excuses.

"I will meet you tomorrow in the lobby of your hotel at nine o'clock. We will continue our conversation under better surroundings."

"Sorry, I already have breakfast plans."

"With Candace Light, I presume?"

"Yes. Is there a problem with that?"

She wasn't about to let this perfectly-dressed, sexy, arm-twister dictate her plans.

"I'm afraid there is. Ms. Light is dead."

Jenna's expression turned from amazement to horror.

"You bastard!"

"We had nothing to do with that. As soon as you drove away, her car exploded. She was killed instantly."

Jenna felt like she had been sucker-punched. She slowly sank down in the chair.

My God, what had she gotten mixed-up in?

Jenna lunged at Jonathan with clenched fists.

"If you hurt anyone I love, I swear to you..."

Jonathan grabbed the back of Jenna's neck, firmly pulling her head back.

"We had no part in harming Ms. Light. It took us by surprise as well."

Jonathan released his grip but Jenna was still frozen. Her hands were planted against his chest.

Jenna felt Jonathan's heart beating. It scared her yet excited her at the same time. She needed to get far away from him for more than one reason.

"We'll take you back now."

Jonathan motioned to Hans and Dimitri.

"Take Ms. Reed back to her hotel...*safely*."

"I will see you tomorrow morning. Nine o'clock in your hotel lobby...and Jenna, do not think about calling the police. This is another *private* matter we will need to conclude."

*****

Jenna was dropped at the entrance to her hotel as promised. Before going inside, she checked her clothes. She looked halfway presentable. God knows what her hair looked like, but at this point she really didn't care. She was just grateful she was safe...for the moment.

Feeling something in her jeans pocket, she withdrew her hotel keycard. Whatever they had done to her, they took the liberty of sticking her keycard in the front of her jeans.

Jenna shut her eyes briefly and cursed.

It was probably that oaf with the cigar breath. She dared to imagine what other parts of her body he had violated.

Arriving in her room, she made a quick scan of her belongings. Nothing had been stolen except her dignity, and she was damn determined to get that back, too.

But she needed help.

An ally. Someone she hoped she could trust.

Chase Garrett.

Chapter 8

Chase rolled over and opened one eye to look at the clock on the nightstand.

How did morning come so soon?

Most normal people would be up and about by seven-thirty enjoying their second cup of coffee.

He wasn't like most people. He didn't have a normal life-style.

Most people had better sense than to stay awake until two in the morning.

Chase groaned and let his hand fall to the side of the bed. He groped for his cell phone lying on the floor.

She needs to call me.

Jenna.

He couldn't stop thinking about her. Her smile, her wit, her fantastic body...and the kiss they had shared...*nice* memories which had ended way too soon.

Chase's eyes started to close again. He smiled, remembering the way Jenna's eyes sparkled when he had surprised her with a kiss at the restaurant. When he had snuck a piece of her omelet.

He started to laugh.

The phone fell out of his hand as it started to vibrate indicating he had a text message.

What good luck! It was from Jenna.

CALL ME ASAP. I NEED YOUR HELP.

"What the hell?"

Chase punched in Jenna's number and sat upright in bed, waiting anxiously for her to answer.

"Hello?" Jenna said, groggily.

"Hey, it's Chase. Are you ok? You scared the hell out of me with your text."

"Yes...no... sorry...late night. I just wasn't expecting you to call me back so soon. I have a bit of a headache."

"I know what's good for that."

"I'm sure you do."

"Advil."

"Don't make me laugh, Chase. My head hurts too much." Jenna moaned loud enough for Chase to hear.

"I'm sorry. Just wanted to start your day with a little light-hearted humor."

"I could use some."

Jenna hesitated. What was she doing? Involving someone else in this crazy mess? But what choice did she have?

Chase picked up on the silence. She was think-ing...reconsidering, perhaps?

"I'm glad you called, Jenna. But something's wrong, isn't it?"

Jenna chewed on her bottom lip. How could she possibly explain what had happened to her?

"Yes. Something is terribly wrong. I need your help, Chase. This is a whole lot bigger than an old letter and a baby picture."

"I'll come to you. Stay put. What's the name of your hotel?"

Jenna sat on the edge of the bed.

"The Hampton Inn in Manassas. It's right off I-95."

"I'll get directions from the concierge. It might take me a few hours. But I'll get to you as fast as I can."

She didn't realize Chase was so far away. He was over on the coast, and Manassas was west of D.C. He definitely wouldn't arrive before Jonathan Knox made another appearance.

"Jenna?"

"Ok. Please get here as soon as you can. Thank you for do-ing this, Chase. I know when we said good-bye at the beach house..."

"I knew we would see each other again. I don't really be-lieve in good-byes. Get some rest and take care of your headache. I'll see you soon."

Just as Chase hung up, Lloyd Garrett walked through the door from the adjoining room. He was carrying his suitcase.

"Going somewhere, Dad? Why are you up so soon?"

"I'm going wherever you are, Son."

Chase shook his head.

"Sorry, Dad, not this time. Jenna Reed needs me."

"You sure you know what you're doing?"

"I'm sure."

"Be careful, Chase."

"I think I can handle it, Dad."

"That's what you said the last time."

"That was a different story and you know it. Jenna needs me. You know I have to go."

"Watch your back."

"I always do."

*****

This was a living nightmare.

How could she possibly get out of it?

Austin had been right. She should have just forgotten about the letter. Whatever this mystery was, it certainly was not worth their lives.

But something was driving her forward.

She couldn't explain it.

She had no answers, only more pieces of a puzzle which there was little hope of solving. If she drove to South Carolina, would she be putting Mary Fortenni's life in danger also?

She certainly hoped not.

She had no right to take chances with other people's lives.

Yet she had called Chase. He was on his way to her now. Soon he would be involved, too.

She didn't have time to debate her decision.

It was almost eight. One hour until Jonathan Knox came looking for her.

Well, he could look all he wanted and ask her a zillion questions. How many times did she have to say it?

She didn't know anything about a treasure.

Except that her brother had taken a beating for it.

Except that her mother's friend had died for it.

For all she knew, maybe the treasure was the reason her parents had died in the car crash.

God help me.

If Mason Hamilton is the one behind all of this…

A bell went off in Jenna's head.

Could Mason Hamilton be Jonathan's boss?

Jenna couldn't shake the idea from her head as she showered and dressed. Even as she headed down to the breakfast buffet off the lobby, Jenna was bothered with a constant nagging in the back of her mind.

Jenna swirled the cream in her coffee and stared at the other people in the eating area.

Were any of them watching her? Maybe Knox had sent someone to spy on her until he made his grand appearance?

Stop being so paranoid, Jenna tried to convince herself.

She grabbed a couple of banana muffins and walked to the elevator, keeping a keen eye on anyone who looked her way.

Everyone looked suspicious.

This was *insane*.

After last night's nerve-wracking episode, Jenna was so frazzled she almost regretted getting regular coffee. But she had to keep the adrenaline flowing…her life depended on it.

Back in her room, Jenna powered up her laptop. A Google search found an address for a Mary Fortenni on Beechwood Drive in Folly Beach, but the phone number was unlisted.

Of course it was.

Candace had mentioned Mary wouldn't talk on the phone either.

Minutes were ticking away. She needed to come up with a plan to stall Knox until Chase arrived.

But what kind of plan?

She was way out of her league here.

The phone on the dresser rang which startled her.

"Hello?" Jenna asked, timidly.

"Ms. Reed, this is the front desk. Your guest has arrived."

It wasn't even eight-thirty yet.

Knox was early. Purposely to catch her off-guard? If so, why did he have the front desk call up for her?

Arrogant. Did he think for one minute she was just going to come waltzing down when he beckoned her?

"Think again, jackass."

Jenna powered down her laptop, debating what to do.

If she stayed in her room, Knox and his sidekicks would just come after her. And she knew how *pleasant* that was the last time.

But if she ran down to the lobby, Knox would be gloating knowing she was afraid.

What was she going to do?

Confront him loudly in the middle of the lobby. Embarrass him. Make a scene. Perhaps then Jonathan Knox would finally get the message and leave her the hell alone.

It was worth a shot.

Storming from her room, Jenna arrived in the lobby ready to do battle. But Jonathan Knox was nowhere in sight.

"Knox, I'm not in the mood to play your little games," Jenna muttered under her breath as she approached the front desk.

"I'm Jenna Reed in 204. Someone just called me to let me know I have a *guest*."

The clerk nodded then gestured towards a tall, thin, dark-skinned man sitting by the small waterfall, reading a newspaper.

Jenna was notably confused.

"I'm sorry, there has to be some type of mistake."

"No mistake, Ms. Reed. That gentleman specifically asked for you."

Jenna tilted her head. "That man? By the waterfall?"

"Yes," the clerk repeated in an annoying tone.

Jenna approached the waterfall. Could this man be one of Jonathan's envoys? He certainly was dressed the part. A crisp, white linen suit with a dark green tie. Very sophisticated, even if he was on the wrong side of trouble.

"You wanted to see me?"

Jenna kept her distance. She folded her arms and stared as the man neatly folded his newspaper and laid it in his lap. She had no time or patience for any more of Jonathan's games.

"Please sit down, Ms. Reed. I mean you no harm."

"I've heard that before. Try a new line."

The man bowed his head slightly.

"My name is Tumi Carile. I may be of service to you."

"I doubt that. I've seen the type of services you people provide. I'm not interested. You can tell Jonathan Knox he can…"

"I can understand your reluctance to believe me. But I assure you, I am not associated in any way with Jonathan Knox."

Jenna put her hand on her hips. A new player. Great.

"Then who the hell are you?"

Tumi Carile then motioned for Jenna to take a seat across from him.

"Someone who wants to keep you safe. Mr. Knox works for a very undesirable man who will not hesitate to harm you if you do not adhere to his demands. I have been asked to make sure that does not happen."

"Well, you're a day late, Mr. Carile."

"Yes, and you have my apologies. Circumstances out of my control prevented my timely arrival."

"Your arrival for what? You know, I'm so tired of hearing part of the riddle which no one seems willing to explain. Who are you and why are you offering me your protection services? I'm not sure why I even need protection."

"I can appreciate your proprietary sense of inquiry, Ms. Reed. However, suffice it to say, I am on your side and your safety is paramount to me and my associates. Has Mr. Knox questioned you about the treasure?"

The *treasure* again. Jenna was fuming.

"Yes," she responded through gritted teeth.

"As I suspected. You are in danger, Jenna Reed. I will be close by, but for now, I must leave you."

"Well, that's wonderful. You offer to protect me and now you're bailing? Who exactly are you, Tumi Carile?"

Tumi smiled as he tucked the newspaper under his arm.

"I am not permitted to elaborate at this time."

Jenna uttered a short laugh.

"I find that hard to believe."

Tumi nodded curtly.

"I will watch over you. You may need my services one day soon."

"This just keeps getting better and better."

"Do you always talk to yourself?"

Before Jenna could even respond, Jonathan Knox placed a hand on her shoulder.

Instant warmth.

"Good morning."

The sexiness in his voice was undeniably beckoning her to pay attention to his every word.

"Jenna."

She had to fight this. Fisting her hands, Jenna spun around ready to use all the will power she could find.

"I don't know anything about your treasure."

She looked forcibly into his eyes.

Eyes which commanded her obedience. Eyes which made her body lose its rigidness.

"You're very beautiful when you're angry."

Jenna forced herself to look in a different direction.

Jonathan had managed to diffuse her badass stance with just a few words. His charm had cut her down to size in a matter of seconds.

"Leave... me...alone."

One last attempt to demonstrate her fleeting bravado.

"I'd be happy to…if you tell me what I want to hear."

"And if I don't? What's next? Are you going to carry me over your shoulder like the idiots you sent last night to get me?"

Jonathan couldn't hold back his laughter.

"That's not my style."

"Really? Then what is? Are you going to romance me to death? Seduce me with words while you keep asking me the same damn question?"

"If and when I seduce you, Jenna Reed, I guarantee you it won't be with words."

Jenna's breath caught in the back of her throat.

"But for now, we need to conduct ourselves with a certain level of decorum. As you can see, I have come alone. I merely wish to ask you a few questions. Perhaps you know more than you think. Talk to me, Jenna."

Jenna took the seat previously occupied by Tumi Carile. Jonathan sat directly next to her.

The lure of his cologne was intoxicating. She wanted to stand up to catch her breath, but she was paralyzed by the close proximity of his body.

His hand was touching her bare leg now. It felt so good.

Don't stop…

Jenna's eyes were closing, giving in to Jonathan's caresses. She felt her body falling backwards.

"Jenna, my employer is very anxious to find his lost treasure. You may have received a clue to its hidden location from the letter you found or through your conversation with Candace Light. Think, Jenna. My employer will be most appreciative of your cooperation."

Jonathan caught Jenna's back before she lost her balance.

The sudden action snapped Jenna back into reality.

"How appreciative? You mean, he might let me live?"

Jonathan winced. He wasn't very good at this. Jenna wasn't taking his advice.

"I don't want to see anything happen to you, Jenna. You're a beautiful woman. The men who...came with me to Virginia do not...adhere to the same personal values as I do. I'm afraid you will be forced to deal with them if you do not answer my questions."

Jenna looked away. This was no use.

"Alright."

Jenna took a deep breath.

"I have to go to South Carolina. There is another woman who Candace Light told me to contact. I'm leaving today or tomorrow. She may have the answers to where the treasure is hidden."

Jonathan paused for a minute.

"Go to South Carolina, but keep in mind, we will be following you. Any attempt to contact the police or throw us off-course, and there will be dire repercussions. Be very careful with your choices. The only person keeping you safe right now...is me."

Jonathan took advantage of Jenna's dazed look by running his finger down the side of her face. The slight distance of space between their faces was killing him. They were so close now, he couldn't resist any longer.

Jonathan made his move, brushing Jenna's lips with his own.

Without hesitation, Jenna did the one thing she would forever regret.

She grabbed Jonathan's face and kissed him back...very slowly at first, and then with a heated passion she didn't know she possessed.

Pulling back when the blood finally reached her brain and re-lit her senses, she slapped Jonathan Knox as hard as she could, then ran to the elevator.

Chapter 9

Jenna's hands shook uncontrollably. She dropped her key-card in front of her door.

Cursing under her breath, it took her three tries to get the green light on the door slot.

Yanking the door open, and then slamming it shut, she leaned back against it. Sliding all the way to the floor, Jenna wrapped her arms around her knees.

"I can't believe I just did that!"

Sobs and gasps consumed her.

The ground rules had just been set. No police. No sudden moves.

Except for the one she just made.

"Jonathan Knox!"

Jenna pounded the floor in frustration.

The sudden knock made her jump. Pitching forward onto her knees, Jenna began to hyperventilate.

They had come for her. Jonathan and his ruthless men. What were they going to do to her this time? Kill her?

Managing to regain her balance, Jenna fearfully peered into the small privacy hole in the door.

"Oh, thank God!"

Relief set in; she almost fainted. The door couldn't open fast enough.

Jenna fell into Chase's open arms. She was shaking so badly, it took great effort to wrap her arms around his neck and hold on.

"Chase!"

Chase pushed them both inside and closed the door. He leaned against the back of the door for balance. Jenna felt so limp in his arms; she was almost pulling them both to the floor.

"Jenna…"

Jenna's eyes held a deep desperation. She was so vulnerable right now. Her body was tensing again him. Her heart was beating even faster than his own.

She needed him. That was simply enough.

"Tell me what you want…"

Chase's lips grazed her ear.

Jenna inhaled deeply, waiting for his next move…*any* move. What she needed right now from Chase was to feel safe and wanted. He was clutching her protectively, but she needed more. Jenna couldn't take the stillness of the air between them any longer.

"You…I want *you*."

As in retribution for her unthinkable act with Jonathan, Jenna found the strength to clasp Chase's face between her hands, kissing him deeply and forcibly.

Was she doing this to wipe away the memory of Jonathan Knox out of her mouth *and* out of her head? Jenna didn't know…her mind was reeling and her body wasn't catching up fast enough.

Chase responded in the way she was hoping for by pushing her backwards towards the bed. They fell in a synchronized motion, never breaking their kiss. Natural moves took control as they both floated, clearing their minds of anything and everything, but each other.

*****

"I called the front desk and requested your room through tomorrow."

Chase kissed Jenna's shoulder as they lay next to each other both facing the window.

"Thank you," she whispered. Breathing easier now, she never wanted to leave Chase's warm, sheltering arms.

"You want to tell me what's going on?"

Chase gently caressed her arm.

Jenna closed her eyes briefly then rolled over and propped herself up on one elbow. It was time for an explanation. They weren't in Cape May anymore walking innocently on the sand with no cares in the world.

She had left that world behind.

"Last night…after I met with Candace…," Jenna paused. The sound of the car exploding would be forever etched into her mind. "Two men attacked me in my room. They drugged me and

I passed out. The next thing I knew, I was tied to a chair in a dark room. Some kind of warehouse, I think."

Jenna averted Chase's eyes as she continued. "A man named Jonathan Knox interrogated me."

Chase's face registered a startled look, but not complete shock. His arm went protectively around Jenna's waist as he pulled her closer.

"He kept asking me questions about a treasure. I have no idea what he wants me to say. I don't know anything about a treasure. Anyway, I was finally brought back to the hotel."

"Did they hurt you in any way?" Chase's voice began to rise.

Jenna shook her head. "I don't think so. But I don't know, Chase. I was out for...several hours. They didn't take anything from my room. I was so scared but I tried not to let them know that."

"You're very brave," Chase said as he squeezed Jenna's waist.

"Bravery had nothing to do with it. I was shaking on the inside. But for some reason, I knew if I stood up to them, I'd have a chance of getting free. But I'm not *totally* free..."

"What do you mean?"

"Knox came to the hotel lobby this morning. He tried again to get me to tell him about the treasure."

"He threatened you...in a public place?"

Jenna didn't respond right away. Now was not the time to tell Chase the whole story...about the overwhelming sensation she felt when Jonathan's hand touched her...about the kiss... She *never* wanted Chase to learn about that.

"Jenna?"

"He was...very persistent. So, I told him I was leaving for South Carolina to visit another one of my mother's friends. I led him to believe this woman might hold the key to finding the treasure. I lied, Chase. It was the only option I had at the time. Now, I might be putting this woman in danger...just like Candace."

Jenna buried her face in Chase's shoulder.

"Candace?"

Jenna lifted her head. "Candace is dead, Chase. After we met at a diner, we both got in our cars to leave. I drove off first and had made it down a few blocks when there was this awful loud noise. When I circled back, there was so much smoke... Candace's car had exploded...with her inside."

"My God, Jenna! What are you mixed up in?"

"I keep asking myself the same thing. I just don't know!"

Chase's arms tightened.

"When are you leaving for South Carolina?"

"Tomorrow."

"I'm coming with you."

"I was hoping you were going to say that."

"A car bomb...a kidnapping. I'm surprised you haven't lost it by now."

"I was close, believe me. Then you found me."

Jenna rubbed her fingers down Chase's cheek.

"Yes I did, and now I don't want to lose you."

Chase met her halfway for a soft kiss that should have lingered longer, but ended quickly as Jenna's lips trembled.

"I'm the one who is mixed up in all this...insanity. I don't want to put you in danger, too."

"Well I'm not leaving you, so get that through your head."

Jenna's eyes began to mist.

"I'm not kidding, Chase. These men are very dangerous. I don't know what's going to happen next."

"Then we will face it together. I'm staying right here."

"Another protector."

"What do you mean?"

"Before Knox arrived, another man was waiting in the lobby for me. He said his name was Tumi Carile. He knew about Knox, and warned me I was in danger. He told me...I might need his protective services soon. Then he simply vanished. It was the weirdest thing."

Chase looked off in the distance.

Jenna placed her hand on Chase's chest. The warmness from his body was soothing if only for a little while.

"I feel like I'm being torn in half...one part of me wants to find out what my mother was involved in, and the other half...feels like I'm being used for another purpose."

"Then let me help you stay grounded. Close your eyes and get some sleep."

Within minutes of listening to the quiet rhythm of his heart, Jenna fell into a deep sleep, finally succumbing to the letdown of the tension.

Chase stared at the ceiling, still cradling Jenna in his arms.

Too many theories were circling in his mind. He needed to make a phone call. Maybe two.

Sliding out of the bed, Chase grabbed his cell from the side table and slowly closed the bathroom door behind him.

It was time to even the playing field.

"Assistance requested."

"Text me specifics."

"Will do."

Chase opened the door slightly and peered out.

Jenna was still asleep. *Good.*

The less she knew the better.

Shutting the door again, he speed-dialed another number. His friend had some explaining to do...*now.*

*****

Jenna turned on her side and woke up. The warmness which had surrounded her was gone.

"Chase?"

She was freezing. The a/c was on full-blast. She reached for the comforter to cover her naked body. That's when she noticed the bathroom door was shut.

"Chase?" She called again.

Chase hastily emerged, shoving his cell back into his jeans. He pulled Jenna into his arms and rested his head on her forehead.

"I didn't want to wake you. Had to check in with Dad. He's going to re-schedule some dates of the book tour."

Jenna ran her hands up Chase's back, and then pulled back so she could see his face. She had a strange sensation something wasn't quite right.

"Are you ok?" Chase asked.

"Actually, I'm starving. I haven't had much to eat in a long while. Will you take me to lunch?"

"Absolutely."

Chase was almost certain she hadn't heard his conversations behind the closed door. But Jenna seemed a little distant just now.

Maybe he should have lowered his voice.

*****

Jenna's phone vibrated, breaking her train of thought. Another text message from Austin. No rantings this time. No brotherly advice.

This time Austin's message was short and sweet.

Kelly is here.

Jenna had completely forgotten all about Kelly coming down to the shore.

Bad timing. The worst possible time for a visit. Jenna quickly sent a text back to Austin promising to call him soon and begging him to entertain Kelly for a little while.

Within a few seconds, Austin responded. He had no problem being Kelly's tour guide. In fact, he had already taken her to Carney's, one of his favorite pubs, to see a band.

Jenna just hoped Austin's bad habits of sub-par personal hygiene and lack of domestic chore-training would not repel her friend.

Kelly had very high standards in the men she dated. Spending a few days with Austin might send her over the edge pretty damn quick. Jenna could only hope for the best when it came to her brother; the rest was up to him.

*****

Austin chuckled to himself. He had genuine concern for his sister, but she was a big girl. If she felt the need to go traipsing around Virginia to figure out some mystery about their mother, then so be it.

He was cool with entertaining her best friend. Who wouldn't be? Kelly McBride was drop-dead gorgeous. Her long, blond hair and her sparkling blue eyes had stopped him in his tracks more than once since she had arrived.

Austin peeked in the spare bedroom. Kelly was still sound asleep. After driving down from West Chester yesterday afternoon, then staying out until after two, she was obviously exhausted. But it was almost noon now.

Austin couldn't wait any longer. He had some errands to run.

Hearing Austin's car pull out of the stone covered driveway, Kelly opened her eyes. Yawning, she padded into the kitchen searching for some coffee.

A note on the table indicated he was running a few errands. That would work out well.

Austin's absence would serve her purposes today. She had to contact her father's resource.

Obey the master.

Kelly practically choked as she swallowed her coffee. She hated being a part of Mason's little schemes. Over and over again, he dictated her every move. When was it ever going to be enough?

Kelly groaned as she leaned against the kitchen counter. She absolutely detested being at her father's beck and call. Especially when his orders would ultimately hurt her friend.

Kelly grimaced. Every detail she could squeeze out of Jenna...her plans for the weekend, if she was seeing her brother, where they were going...every precise detail had to be reported back to Mason.

Such a major pain-in-the-ass.

None of the lavish gifts, the two apartments or the cars had ever been given without strings attached. Mason Hamilton demanded and always got Kelly's obedience.

She was too afraid to disobey.

Mason was constantly reminding her what happened to people who didn't follow his explicit instructions.

They paid for their mistakes...one way or another.

Fear was her only motivator but it was a strong one.

Kelly's hands shook as she tried to grip the coffee mug without letting it fall to the floor.

"When will you ever let me go?"

Her words echoed in the empty kitchen. Kelly pushed back several tears. She knew the answer before she verbalized it.

Never.

It was a pitiful way to live, but she never knew any other lifestyle.

As she placed the call, Kelly's energy collapsed.

"Corner of Jackson and Carpenter, one hour."

The call ended before Kelly said a word. She grabbed a map of Cape May she had picked up last night outside of Carney's. The intersection where she was to meet Mason's resource was only a short walk away, off the Washington Street Mall.

She arrived at the designated corner a couple of minutes early. She was getting nervous just standing around, and hoped Mason's resource wouldn't be late.

Kelly didn't immediately notice the short, stocky bald-headed man who made his way to her side of the street. He was carrying three large shopping bags from Dellas, one of the landmark stores on the Mall.

Disheveled and obviously flustered, he kept shifting the bags in his hands. When he bumped into Kelly, one of the bags fell to the ground. Bottles of sun-tan lotion and bug spray tumbled out onto the pavement.

"How clumsy of me! Oh, thank you very much!"

Kelly bent down to help pick up the contents of the bag.

As she knelt down to grab the runaway Coppertone, the man leaned closer then shoved a folded piece of paper into her hand.

"Many thanks, Miss!"

Kelly stared in unbelief.

Her father must be desperate if this guy was on the payroll. But he did blend in with the tourist crowd.

No one had given him a second glance.

Chapter 10

Jenna was dreading the long drive to South Carolina.

Afraid to question Chase's motives, she chose the safe route. Clamming up.

She needed allies now, not enemies. Could she trust him? Jenna just couldn't shake the feeling Chase wasn't being totally honest with her.

Jenna stared straight ahead. She was ready to explode. She had never been very good at hiding her feelings.

"Worried?"

Jenna nodded.

"Not sure what I'm walking into. There's been too much deception already."

Chase gripped the wheel.

"I'm sure your mother had good reasons for not telling you everything."

"Maybe, but I still feel…betrayed."

Chase reached over and took Jenna's hand in his own. He could feel her tension. He had to say something. But what? How could he possibly tell her…*everything*?

Jenna laid her head against the window.

She couldn't keep this up. It was eating at her too much not to say anything.

Ask him and get it over with. Stop procrastinating.

Jenna shut her eyes and jerked her head, hoping her conscience would shut up for once.

Chase pulled the car to a stop along the shoulder. He unbuckled his seat belt and put his arm across the headrest of Jenna's seat.

Jenna couldn't face him.

"I'm here."

"Are you?"

"Of course I am."

"Then show me."

Chase drew her face to his lips. Kissing Jenna slowly at first, their kiss became stronger as her body gravitated towards him. She wasn't pulling away now; that was a good sign.

But had he been successful in ridding her mind of any suspicious thoughts?

Chase certainly hoped so.

Jenna was panting by the time he finally let her go. Their kiss had increased to the point of enticing both of them to hold on for dear life. Air supply was the only reason they had pulled apart.

"Chase, please don't keep secrets from me. You'll tear me apart."

"Jenna…"

"If you care about me, then please tell me the truth."

The truth? As much as I want you to know the truth, you're not ready to hear it.

Chase glanced in his rearview mirror. Someone was pulling up behind them. A man in the front seat of the dark sedan was wearing a baseball hat and sunglasses. One of Hamilton's goons? Chase didn't have time to figure it out.

"Hold on, Jenna."

Chase jerked the steering wheel and slammed down the accelerator. Crossing over two lanes, he wove between a cement hauler and a large UPS truck, and then sped up to get back into the right lane. He took the next exit off the interstate. Pulling into a truck stop, Chase finally slowed the car to a stop.

Jenna jumped out and slapped the hood.

"What the hell, Chase? Where did you learn to drive like that?"

Chase ignored her comments. "I thought we were being followed. I wanted to let them know I was paying attention."

"Well you certainly got my attention. Crossing an interstate? Are you crazy? I'd like to get to my destination in one piece!"

Jenna caught her breath, realizing Chase had made the heroic move to protect her.

"I'm sorry."

Jenna started to get back in the car, still noticeably shaken.

As he walked to the driver's side, Chase was caught off-guard and spun around. A gun was jabbed into his ribcage.

"Dr. Garrett, I would strongly suggest you keep the next words out of your mouth to a minimum volume level, or I will make sure your girlfriend bleeds out in the next five minutes."

Chase's attacker was almost twice his size, immobilizing Chase in a matter of seconds.

"And you will die shortly thereafter. Do I make myself perfectly clear?"

Chase nodded begrudgingly. He was outnumbered. Hamilton's men had found them.

He had failed to protect her.

"Let go of me now, you asshole! And tell Jonathan Knox he can go…"

A hard smack across the face prevented Jenna from finishing her sentence. A tight pull of her ponytail followed, assuring her submission.

Jonathan, I'm going to kill you the next time I see you…

Jenna's face was painfully on fire, but she stood rigid.

Her aggressor was tightening his hold. He pushed her firmly against the car door. He had let go of her hair, but the forceful pressure of his body and the gun pressing into her ribs was causing Jenna major discomfort.

She whimpered, unable to keep quiet any longer.

Chase finally broke his silence. "What do you want?"

Without warning, the man pinning Chase against the car eased back, then holstered his weapon.

Over his shoulder, Chase glanced back at Jenna. Her attacker had also backed away.

Jenna stood frozen against the car. Turning slightly, she saw a small card being shoved into Chase's hand. Then both men turned and ran to a black Escalade waiting a few yards away. The car took off, kicking up dust as it raced towards the highway.

Chase jammed the card into his pocket. He couldn't get to Jenna fast enough. Before her legs gave out, Chase pulled Jenna into his arms.

They were both breathing so heavy now, speaking was next to impossible.

Finally, Chase pulled back to look at Jenna's face.

"Please tell me you're ok."

Jenna raised her head, nodding.

"I think so."

Chase immediately noticed the red mark on her face. He admired her fortitude, but it had been a risky move.

"Then let's get the hell out of here."

Once they were on the interstate again, Chase brought Jenna's hand to his lips.

"You were too brave back there."

Jenna rubbed the side of her face.

"Apparently not enough."

"Were they the same men from the warehouse?"

"I don't think so. I would recognize that monster with the wandering hands and cigar breath anywhere. I think he's Russian. He has a thick accent. I don't know who these men are, but I would venture to guess they're after the same thing."

Chase handed the card to Jenna.

"What does it say?"

"Your cooperation is expected."

She tapped the card with her finger.

"How poetic. Guess I haven't been performing up to my true potential."

Jenna tossed the card on the dashboard in disgust. Another threat. How *wonderful.*

Chase took a deep breath. He needed to regain Jenna's confidence. God knows she needed him right now.

"Jenna, I wanted to be the one to protect you. But I realized I needed help. I still do. I called a friend of mine to make sure he looked out for you...when I couldn't. Of course, it would have been nice if he had shown up sooner."

"Who, Chase? Who did you call?"

"Tumi Carile. The man you met in the lobby. I was furious at him. I had asked him to watch over you when you left Cape May, but his team didn't arrive in time. If they had, you wouldn't have been kidnapped."

Jenna's shoulders started to relax. Chase had been trying to protect her, not betray her. She had been such a fool to doubt him.

"I'm sorry...I didn't trust you."

"You had every right. I should have told you from the beginning. I just thought Tumi and his men would be there when I couldn't be...but..."

Jenna gave Chase's hand a squeeze.

"You tried, Chase. You have no idea how much that means to me. Now I know I can trust you."

Chase's eyes flickered as he focused on the road. He couldn't face Jenna right now.

He hadn't completely earned her trust, but he was determined to try.

Chapter 11

Kelly ran to the guestroom on the first floor, locking the door behind her. She took a deep breath and unfolded the note.

God, no. She couldn't do this...

She crumbled the small piece of paper in frustration.

"You bastard."

She had been so naïve.

Go down to the beach. Keep an eye on Jenna and her brother.

It sounded innocent enough.

How stupid she had been to think her father would only want reports of the Reeds' activities.

This was totally different. This order required explicit actions. Not towards Jenna, but her brother, Austin.

In plain terms, Kelly was to seduce Austin Reed. Her father didn't care *to what level* she needed to take her persuasion. He just expected results.

"I'm no better than a prostitute."

Kelly sunk to the edge of the bed. She loathed the very thought of her father. He had no regard for anyone's personal values. He used people for his little games and amusements. It made no difference if people suffered, as long as he got his end result.

Her eyes focused on the mirror above the dresser.

What she saw was the face of betrayal...and pain.

*****

George Maylor did exactly what he had been told to do. He felt like such a fool going into Dellas that morning and buying several bags of junk he really didn't need.

All for the mission. Mason's mission.

George's covert assignments were always dictated by Mason Hamilton. He felt frustrated at times not knowing how he fit into

Mason's grand scheme, but for the most part, George just followed instructions. He was afraid not to.

Results, not failures.

Mason would accept nothing less.

Not that George hadn't been compensated. In fact, Mason had generously rewarded George for his obedience.

Enough to retire in Cape May and buy Molly's Pancake House, just a couple blocks off the Washington Street Mall. Mason had secured George's financial future. Setting up a bank account under the fictitious name of Frank Borgessi in Stone Harbor, George was able to receive Mason's monetary incentives via wire transfer. Mason had also provided George with a fake driver's license and passport. Mason had thought of everything.

A man who could give...*and take away.*

Last December, Mason drove his point home.

To George's own home.

Early last December, George had sent his weekly report to Mason right on schedule detailing the daily activities of Lois and Jim Reed. Same old boring report. They were meeting their children for dinner in Philadelphia.

Just another report on another day.

But oddly enough, Mason never sent an acknowledgment.

George and Teresa were notified the next day when Austin called to give them the devastating news. Lois and Jim Reed had died suddenly in an auto accident.

Teresa was hysterical. George was speechless.

Did this have anything to do with Mason?

George knew Mason had a bonafide mean streak, but to in- stigate the *murder* of two people? No, it couldn't possibly be true. George hurried to his laptop and emailed Mason right way, giving him the news.

This time he received a prompt reply.

Well done.

George sat for hours staring out the window, lost in his thoughts. Teresa finally came into the den wanting him to come to bed at two in the morning, but he just waved her off. He was paying for his own penitence.

George sent an email to Mason telling him he wanted out. The mysterious errands over the years hadn't caused anyone any harm. But now…he couldn't be a part of Mason's murderous plans anymore.

Mason didn't answer right away. George waited for two hours. He fell asleep in front of his laptop. The next morning, George found the most frightening attachment to a message in his inbox. It was a picture of Teresa, sleeping soundly in their bed dressed in the nightgown she had worn the night before. A red "X" was drawn across her forehead.

Teresa had been marked. Unless he did exactly what Mason commanded, Teresa would be his next victim.

George couldn't sacrifice the woman he loved. There was no other choice.

He would do whatever Mason demanded.

George quickly disposed of the Dellas' bags in a trash can next to Collier's Liquors, and then hurried home.

"Hi, Hon."

Teresa looked up from the sink as George hustled in the back door and kissed her on the cheek.

"My cousin Michelle just called."

"The one in Florida, right?"

"She's the only cousin I have, George. Yes, she's in Florida, where she's been for the past twenty years."

"How is Michelle?"

George tried to appear interested, but he was itching to get to his laptop and report to Mason he had made the drop.

"She needs my help. Her mother fell last week, breaking her hip for the second time. Michelle wants me to help her check out some nursing homes. I told her you would be ok with that. Right?"

George let out a sigh of relief with his back turned.

"Of course. Take as long as you need. I'll be fine."

George was half-way into the living room when Teresa called to him over her shoulder.

"Thought so. I'm leaving in the morning."

"Ok, Hon, I'll drive you to the airport."

George's fingers were flying across the keyboard as he did his best to follow Teresa's conversation.

"No need, George. I've already arranged for the shuttle. I know you like to be at the restaurant early."

"Ok, Hon. Whatever you need."

Teresa rolled her eyes. George was probably playing some stupid game on his laptop. She didn't need him to pay attention any more.

In fact, it was better if he didn't.

*****

Austin returned to the beach house, hauling two cans of paint. He struck out at the local Home Depot, trying to match the paint his father had purchased last summer. The front steps were desperately in need of a paint job, but Austin had procrastinated all last summer. Parties or painting? A no-brainer.

But after he found the paint can in the basement yesterday, Austin felt a terrible sense of guilt.

Now his father's simple request had become Austin's own personal mission. The steps would get painted as soon as possible. He owed it to his father to finish the job, or at least start it.

Besides, painting had a certain manly sense to it. He wanted to do anything possible to impress Kelly. He sincerely hoped she would stay awhile longer even if Jenna wasn't around.

He enjoyed Kelly's company. She was fun, smart, and fantastic to look at...she was *perfect*.

Maybe his beach cronies would take notice if he paraded Kelly around town. Making the rounds with a woman who looked like a bathing suit model boosted Austin's morale and his ego.

Austin chuckled to himself. Luck was on his side. At least today, anyway.

Maybe even *tonight*.

Austin let out a low whistle just imagining being intertwined with Kelly in his bed. The thought had him so distracted; he popped the paint lid, splashing paint onto his shirt.

"Terrific."

Austin wiped his hands on the grass and dabbed at his shirt. He hadn't bothered to change yet into his painting clothes. Another one of his plaid shirts had just been ruined.

Recapping the paint can, Austin hustled up the front steps but stopped as soon as he came through the door.

Kelly was lounging on the sofa. She looked so good with her long hair off her shoulders.

"Hi, Austin, I've been waiting for you."

Austin made it as far as the dining room. He spun around
with a glimmer of hope in his eyes. *She was waiting for him?* Oh,
man.

"I spilled paint on my shirt. I'll be right back."

When Austin got to his room, he let out a deep breath. Having carnal thoughts about his sister's best friend was suicide. He
knew better than to let his thoughts take any kind of control.

Kelly was probably bored. His errand had taken longer than
expected. Maybe she wanted to go the beach or out for a late
lunch.

Austin tossed his paint-splattered shirt to the floor. He
stepped back in surprise when Kelly barged into his room.

Austin's eyes locked on Kelly's face.

"Kiss me," Kelly said in a flirtatious tone.

Austin involuntarily shook his head.

Was he dreaming? This couldn't be happening.

Kelly moved forward and kissed Austin fully on the lips.

Austin reacted instinctively. He drew Kelly tighter and returned her kiss with a powerful stance of his own.

Kelly's hands moved in a seductive rhythm down his back.

I'm in deep trouble now.

Austin's lips grounded against Kelly's once again as her
hands drifted lower. She was unrestrained passion as he hoped she
would be.

She wants me.

Austin still couldn't believe what was happening to him.
Kelly McBride had thrown herself at him.

Maybe Kelly was just looking for a little mindless romance
to tide her over until her next conquest. Austin didn't care. All
that mattered was this moment.

He was perfectly ok to be Kelly's temporary lover.

So what if she was using him? He wasn't beneath being
used, as long as he could get Kelly beneath his body. Austin was
losing all sanity embraced in the arms of Kelly McBride.

Passionate kisses weren't enough. Austin could hardly catch
his breath when Kelly's hands roamed where he didn't expect his
sister's best friend would ever be touching him. She was taking
control and he was letting her.

But even Austin had to admit, the pace was too fast. He hesitated for just a brief moment, but the look in Kelly's eyes demanded his active participation, not his reservation.

Kelly withdrew her lips, licked them, and then kissed the side of Austin's neck. His willpower crumpled quickly. His once reluctant hold had changed to a forceful clasping of her body against his own.

As Kelly continued to grind against him, Austin started to push the thin low-cut shirt off her shoulders. But then a major bell went off in his head.

This is your sister's friend – what are you doing?

Austin held Kelly at arm's length.

"Sorry....big misunderstanding."

Austin grabbed a random t-shirt lying on the floor. He put it on in record speed. Austin flew down the steps and out the front door. He couldn't get the paint can opened fast enough.

Focus on the steps, he told himself. *Steps. One at a time.*

"Come back inside."

Kelly sat on the bottom step and touched Austin's shoulder.

"I can't do that."

Austin kept his eyes focused on the wooden stick swirling the paint. He couldn't look at her right now. He had acted so recklessly.

"Can't or won't?"

Austin slowly raised his eyes. Kelly's shirt was unbuttoned now, revealing a lace cami underneath. He swallowed hard as he saw tiny drops of perspiration which had settled just below her neckline.

She's so beautiful.

Austin squeezed his eyes shut, then turned back to the paint can. He laid the paint stick in the grass. His palms were getting too sweaty to hold it any longer.

"Hey, I'm a guy. Don't blame me for trying."

"I was hoping you would *keep trying*."

Austin felt his breath getting ragged. He just couldn't gaze into her eyes. There would be no going back if he did.

Kelly gently tugged on his chin.

It was no use. He couldn't resist. Leaning forward, Austin met Kelly half-way as she opened her mouth.

The paint job would just have to wait...once again.

*****

George Maylor smirked as he watched the little interlude play out at the Reed house. He thought he recognized her. Mason's resource. The blond with the long legs to whom he passed the note. The same woman who was making Austin Reed shake in his shoes.

Austin usually moved in slow motion, but today, he had a certain spring in his step.

George laughed.

Could Austin be that stupid? Why would he think for a minute that gorgeous blond would make a move on him if she didn't have a hidden agenda? Even George had figured that one out.

George wondered what they were doing right now. Having sex on the kitchen table for all he knew. No wonder Austin was oblivious to the fact the girl was using him.

This would make for a juicy report, George thought to himself. He settled back in front of his laptop and sent an email to Mason.

Blond chick has Austin Reed under her spell.

Mason should be pleased. Two reports in one day.

Chapter 12

Jonathan Knox was angry. Just when he thought he was making progress, Mason Hamilton had the audacity to summon him back to New York to make Jonathan account for his actions.

When Jonathan, Hans and Dimitri arrived at the offices of the Hamilton-Knox Foundation, Hans and Dimitri took the back stairs. Their association with Mason was complicated. Jonathan only knew bits and pieces of it.

Just as well.

He had no desire to lay his eyes on either of them again. Not after what they did to Jenna.

Jenna.

Jonathan's eyes closed briefly as he rode the elevator to the tenth floor. He couldn't get Jenna Reed out of his mind. She had mesmerized him from the first time he had seen her. Her resilience, the determination in her eyes, the curves in her body…

He had to put thoughts of Jenna Reed out of his mind.

Good luck with that, Jonathan's conscience bellowed.

Stepping off the elevator and into Mason's hallowed halls, Jonathan tensed.

"You made good time," Mason quipped as Jonathan firmly stood before Mason's huge mahogany desk.

"I thought you trusted me to deal with Jenna Reed."

Mason laughed, and leaned back in his chair.

"Jonathan, you should know by now I trust no man, or woman for that matter. Since you failed to extract the information from Ms. Reed on two separate occasions, I felt the need to send in another more-experienced team to drive my message home."

Jonathan slapped the desk with his hand. He was royally pissed now. Mason had played him.

"I needed more time. She was…coming around to my advances."

"Is that so? One passionate kiss followed by a slap to the face doesn't indicate to me you had control of Jenna Reed. Oh, don't look so surprised. Of course, I had other people in place to watch you. There's too much at stake here."

Jonathan flung himself into a chair. He was just a pawn in Mason's game. Like Jenna.

"You have no right to hurt her, Mason. She is an innocent woman. She doesn't have your treasure. You're wasting your time."

"I never waste a minute of my time. Ms. Reed may not know where the treasure is right now, but I have a strong feeling she will find out shortly. Your inability to persuade Ms. Reed to cooperate was a detriment to my timetable. Your services are no longer required in that capacity."

Jonathan shifted in his seat, extremely annoyed. Jenna was in a lot of danger now. He needed to warn her.

"Come now, Jonathan, you should be thanking me for taking you off such a distasteful assignment. You do not have the stomach for it. On the other hand, you are quite valuable to me on an administrative level. With the upcoming exhibit…"

Jonathan vehemently interrupted.

"You care more about this exhibit than what happens to Jenna Reed. Admit it, Mason, she's just a means to an end. A way for you to finally get what you want."

Mason hid the sneer rising on his lips.

"Ms. Reed has a purpose to serve…on many levels. I have no intention of preventing her trip to South Carolina. She will have her meeting with Mary Fortenni. After which time, my associates will make contact with her. I'm sure they will be very *persuasive* in their attempts to ensure her cooperation."

"Then what, Mason? Are you going to kill her?"

Mason calmly folded his hands.

"I can see Ms. Reed's charm has captured your attention, perhaps even tugged at your heart. You need to learn, Jonathan, to separate business needs from personal ones. This is a business arrangement, nothing more."

"I'm not buying that, Mason. This is a personal vendetta and you know it. Leave Jenna alone. Find your damn treasure another way."

Jonathan felt his temper rising with every snide comment Mason made. He fought the urge to fist his hands.

"As I thought. You harbor feelings for her…in such a short amount of time. How touching. Do not concern yourself with Ms. Reed any longer. She is not worth your efforts. I will deal with her as I see fit."

Jonathan couldn't believe his ears.

"You're fooling yourself, Mason. Jenna is not going to fall for your little games. She is a hell of a lot smarter than that."

"Wait and watch, my boy. You will learn many things. First and foremost, the art of motivation. Money in most cases, fear in others."

Mason paused for effect.

"And I know *exactly* how to motivate Jenna Reed."

*****

Jenna and Chase arrived in Folly Beach, South Carolina, a little past eight p.m. Both had lost their appetites after their traumatic experience at the truck stop. Dinner at a roadside diner a few exits back was a waste of time and effort.

Chase registered at the front desk while Jenna nervously paced the lobby. Being in the car for over half the day was taking its toll. Her legs felt weak due to the lack of circulation.

The lobby was deserted, except for an older couple sitting in the breakfast area enjoying cups of coffee.

Circling back, she caught up with Chase who had just grabbed the keycards off the counter.

"Fourth floor this time."

"The higher the better."

"My thoughts exactly."

Jenna leaned against Chase's arm as the elevator began its ascent. As her fingers closed around his arm, he could feel the tension radiating from her body.

She's going to lose it. I can't let that happen.

Chase kissed the side of Jenna's head.

"I'm here for you."

"I know you are."

Chase just hoped Tumi's team would be here soon. He couldn't protect her by himself.

His emotions were getting in the way, fogging up his clear judgment. How could he possibly keep her safe if he was distracted all the time?

Focus on protection, not your feelings.

Right.

Easier said than done.

Jenna sunk backwards onto the king-sized bed the moment they stepped inside their room. Her eyes were wide open as they stared at the ceiling.

"Maybe a bath would relax you."

"Maybe."

The tension accelerating in every part of her body was agonizing.

Chase looked worn down as well. Jenna glanced in his direction then laid her head down again.

"Hey."

Chase climbed up on the bed and touched the back of her hand.

Jenna closed her eyes and linked their fingers.

"I don't know how long I can keep up."

"As long as you need to. With me."

Jenna managed a slight smile.

"I don't know what I'd do if you weren't here."

Jenna started to cry softly as Chase's arms wrapped around her.

"Well that's something you don't have to worry about. Come on. You need to relax. I'll start the bath for you."

Jenna watched from the doorway. She laughed when Chase dumped the entire small bottle of body wash under the tap. Bubbles were rising quickly as the tub filled.

Inhaling the sweet lavender scent and the steam from the hot water, Jenna eased herself into the tub. It was heaven...if only for a little while.

Exactly what she needed. The bath, the bubbles. Chase.

She reached for Chase's hand and met his gaze.

I'm falling for him, Jenna thought to herself. Against her own mantra of abstaining from any long-term relationships for a while, Jenna could feel herself letting go.

She tugged on Chase's hand until he got the message...*in the tub...now...with me...under the bubbles.*

*****

Jacoby and Thompson had tailed their targets to the parking lot of the Hampton Inn. Now it was the waiting game.

"You know how hot it's going to be sitting in this car all night? It's got to be over ninety. I hate the south – too friggin' hot."

"I'm with you, Mick."

Surveillance jobs sucked at times…especially in the heat.

Even the portable fans weren't providing enough air flow. It would be a long night until the green light was given.

But they had to be ready to move. No question about that.

Mick Thompson was the larger of the two men. At six-foot-three and packing over two-fifty, Mick could intimidate the hell out of most people. Rambo in a suit. Everyone just assumed he was in charge. Mick was the first to clearly deny that assumption. Besides, he didn't want to tick off his partner who held equal ground.

Brett Jacoby made up for his lack of stature and muscle through his sheer mental acuity and uncanny ability to read people. Dealing with the powers-that-be and deciphering their orders, Jacoby was the polished leader of the pair.

Complimenting each other with brains and brawn, it was no wonder they were second-in-command when their senior agent wasn't available.

Jacoby looked at his phone when the text indicator lit up.

"Turette has arrived."

"Bet she's got better accommodations."

"Rank, my friend."

Thompson growled.

Jacoby laughed as he played with his phone.

"Come on, Mick, you know you like stake-outs."

"I like having steak…out…like in a restaurant. Not sitting for hours confined to a car. Turette probably has a flat screen."

"Probably. I can call if you want me to find out."

Thompson muttered an obscenity under his breath.

Jacoby loosened his tie and took off his jacket. He picked up his iPad from the floor of the car.

"Rather be watching the game."

Thompson moaned, breaking the silence. He hated it when Jacoby zoned out, focusing on his electronic toys rather than his partner.

"Here."

Jacoby touched the screen a few times then handed Thompson the tablet. ESPN was playing one of the major league baseball games.

"Satisfied now?"

"You're ok...for a nerd."

"I'll take that as a compliment."

"How long can I watch on this?"

Jacoby just shook his head and leaned back against the headrest. His partner hadn't truly embraced the age of technology.

"You'll be fine through the end of the game."

Thompson seemed genuinely happy for the moment.

Jacoby squeezed the bridge of his nose. He was going to need some coffee to stay awake all night. He had to be sharp and alert if Turette called.

She would expect nothing else.

*****

Jonathan loosened his tie and hailed a cab.

"Where to, Sir?"

"JFK."

"You got it," the cabbie gruffly mumbled as he pulled out into traffic, narrowly missing another two cars which had attempted to skirt around him.

Jonathan shook his head. Everyone jockeying for position in a race where no one ever seemed to win. Sometimes he wished he could just start fresh somewhere else. Anywhere else.

Maybe start a family. If he could find the right girl.

Had he already found her?

Jenna Reed.

Jonathan let the traffic noise filter out his anxieties for a moment as he concentrated on Jenna's face. She held such a fascinating attraction to him.

Who was he kidding?

Jenna Reed had slapped him in public. Their relationship wasn't starting off on the right foot. He needed to change that.

Maybe another opportunity would present itself soon. He'd show her the kind of man he really was. God knows, he wanted to hold her, not hurt her. He had to make amends.

But first he had to find her.

He couldn't let Mason's men get a hold of her.

Jenna Reed needed him whether she knew it or not.

Chapter 13

Midnight.

"Great," Jenna moaned.

Am I ever going to sleep peacefully again?

The bubble bath and the love-making session which followed had relaxed her, but not to the point of deep sleep.

Although Chase's warm arms did feel good. Really good.

But sadly, even his protective embrace wasn't enough. She was just too worried to sleep.

Glancing over her shoulder, she could see Chase's head buried into his pillow. He had fallen asleep with a smile on his face.

But Chase was one of the main reasons Jenna was worried. Frantically worried.

Why was she putting him through all this turmoil? His life had been threatened at gunpoint as well as hers. In an instant, both of them could have easily been killed. But Chase had refused to leave her.

He was just as crazy as she was.

Jenna understood commitment, but they hadn't known each other very long. Still, Chase was adamant. He said he would stay by her side, regardless of the potential danger lurking ahead.

He was such a good man. No one else she had ever dated would have gone the distance like Chase. She really lucked out this time.

I finally met the right one. Now he's lying next to me.

Jenna nestled closer. She would take whatever few moments they had and cherish each one.

Chase stirred. His arm pulled her tighter. Even in his sleep, he was trying to protect her.

Jenna covered his hand with her own. Chase had done this once before...the first time they had spent the night together. It was as if Chase knew she needed to be protected.

But how could he?

She was reading too much into his soothing touches. She just needed to feel the calmness for a little while longer.

Jenna took in a few deep breaths. If it hadn't been for Chase, she probably would have gone over the deep end by now.

She was falling for him. She couldn't help it.

But the annoying little voice in the back of her head was rattling its cage.

Snap out of it.

Jenna squeezed her eyes shut, forcing her conscience to go back to sleep and leave her alone. She was trying to enjoy this perfect moment, lying in her lover's arms. She pulled on Chase's arms until they bound her snugly. Only then did her inner voice fade away.

There was nothing wrong with being hopeful, Jenna told herself. She wanted to find someone to share her life...someone who cared enough to want the same thing. She was twenty-eight, almost twenty-nine in a few months. She wanted stability in her life. And love.

Most of the guys she had dated weren't interested in long-lasting relationships; only the short-lived horizontal ones. Jenna always wanted more. Companionship, excitement, someone she could trust her heart with...each time she came up empty handed.

Her last break-up had disaster written all over it before it began, but Kelly kept encouraging Jenna to give the guy one more try.

After several months of "one more tries", Jenna gave Mark an ultimatum – either he needed to be more committed or she was walking. Mark gave her an answer rather quickly – walking, actually running away, as he left for practice with the track team. They hadn't spoken since.

Which had made for an awkward situation at work.

Mark was the assistant athletic trainer at Myers-Mill, the same school where Jenna taught English. He practically lived on campus. He attended most of the sporting events and practices in case an athlete suffered a sprain or needed to warm up muscles before competing. It was inevitable Jenna and Mark would run into each other.

Avoiding each other's gazes had been easy at first. Jenna simply looked the other way. But it didn't take long for the majority of the faculty to figure out they had broken up. Especially when Mark felt the need to parade around his newest hottie at the end-of-school faculty picnic.

Kelly had tried to make a joke about the whole situation, but Jenna was the one who had suffered in more ways than she confided to her friend. Kelly just didn't seem to get it at times, but then again she wasn't the type to settle down with anyone. She was content to play the field. Commitment was the *last thing* on her mind.

Kelly.

Jenna felt so guilty leaving her friend in the lurch with no definite time she would return to the beach house. She just hoped Kelly would forgive her for leaving her stranded with Austin for a few days.

Hopefully, Austin was behaving himself for once. Jenna cringed just imagining her brother being his usual self – indulging in late night drinking contests with his posse of rowdy beach bums, or leaving his clothes all scattered around the house.

She would never live this one down, Jenna thought to herself. Kelly was probably mad at her right now.

*****

Kelly rolled out of the bed, searching for her clothes.

"Where…?"

She had to stifle a laugh.

Her shirt was on the nightstand covering the clock, her cami was on the floor at the foot of the bed, and her shorts…well, she didn't see them anywhere at first. Finally, she found them lying in the hall alongside of Austin's.

Kelly dressed quickly as she caught her breath. Austin had been such an ardent sex partner. It was refreshing at first, as they grappled across the bed. They were equally matched in stamina and creativity.

But in the afterglow as Kelly laid in Austin's arms, the regret had sunk in. She was using Austin for her father's twisted plan. How could she do that to him?

Austin had completely and unconditionally made love to her, yet Kelly's betrayal began the first time she touched him.

But it certainly hadn't felt like betrayal, not at first.

She and Austin were very compatible in bed. He was very loving, wanting to please her in every way possible.

And she had let him.

But now, Kelly harbored deep, painful remorse. She knew full well what it was like to be used. She had been used all her life by her father. Now, she was doing the same to an innocent guy. Jenna's brother, of all people.

Jenna.

How will Jenna ever forgive me?

Additionally, Kelly wondered if she would be able to forgive herself. No time soon.

Mason was still controlling her every move from his plush office in New York. He was without question, the vilest man. But with Mason's blood flowing through her veins, Kelly doubted if she was any better.

Kelly sat on the edge of the bed. She glanced over her shoulder at the man with whom she had just shared so many intimate moments and smiled.

Austin was the best lover she'd ever had.

She wasn't prepared for that...*at all*.

What she and Austin had experienced was mind-blowing. There was no way she could ask him if he knew anything about her father's treasure. She could hardly catch her breath, let alone form intelligent sentences.

Mason had suggested she get Austin into a vulnerable position, then fire questions at him before he had a chance to figure out what she was doing.

A dumb-ass plan.

She had tossed Mason's suggestion out of her head rather quickly. Her body was moving, not her mind.

Kelly ran her hand up Austin's bare thigh, and then watched him shudder in response. He was still asleep but he was reacting to her touch. Like a lover should.

Kelly frowned, wishing Austin could stay her lover. Their attraction was strong, but not just in the physical sense. She wanted to be with him unlike anyone else she had ever dated.

Austin was different. Not conceited like the majority of men Mason set her up with. If Mason didn't orchestrate Kelly's date card, then she didn't have one. Kelly wasn't permitted to just take up with anyone who didn't pass her father's rigorous standards, whatever the hell they were.

But right now…at this moment, Mason was far away. For just a few more minutes, Kelly could gaze upon Austin's body and enjoy the memories of what they had just shared.

The minutes ticked away.

You are on an assignment, nothing more.

Mason's warning rang loud and clear. She could see her father standing with his hands on his hips, preaching about the ramifications which would arise if she didn't heed his words. If she didn't do her job.

If she didn't fulfill her part of the mission.

Mason and his secretive missions.

Not everyone spent their life harboring a secret agenda. Kelly thought it was so abnormal to be obsessed with obtaining some old artifacts. She had never figured why her father was hell-bent on finding his precious treasure pieces, or why he felt the need to involve her in his little evil plot.

Kelly needed fresh air to clear her head. She quietly closed the door to the guestroom. Grabbing a Diet Pepsi from the fridge, she stepped out on the back deck.

She could get used to living here in the quaint beach town. It had a sense of calmness she never experienced growing up in New York.

New York. Her father. Her assignment.

Mason would be expecting a report right about now.

Kelly went back inside to retrieve her laptop. A late report would most certainly result in a harassing phone call or text.

She had no desire to talk to Mason right now.

It sickened her to think she wasn't strong enough to stand up to Mason, to tell him she was done playing a part in his game. How she wished she had some backbone when it came to her father! She was so tired of being yanked back and forth as if she was a puppet on a string.

But Mason had no qualms about reminding his daughter quite frequently of all the benefits she enjoyed thanks to his generosity, and just how quickly he could take them all away…including her life.

Loyalty and life, disobedience and death.

Repeated over and over ever since she was a child.

She hit the enter button so forcefully, her laptop almost fell to the floor. Her report had been short and to the point, not affording Mason any more lurid details. He could fantasize all he wanted. She was not providing explicit details of her sex life to anyone, especially her father.

Mason's response was instantaneous.

Good. Continue to use your God-given talents as I recommended. Do whatever it takes to get an answer. I will expect another report tomorrow detailing your success.

Kelly cursed in frustration. Mason's comments were so degrading.

Dumping her laptop on the kitchen table, Kelly wandered into the dining room. Several framed pictures of the Reed family adorned the antique buffet chest. Most snapshots had been taken around Cape May. Austin and Jenna as young children, sitting on their grandparents' laps on the front steps. Jim and Lois Reed leaning against the side of the gazebo just behind the Mall. Austin and a few other young guys by the marina. Jenna and her mother sitting on the deck.

Family. A happy, smiling, family.

Kelly sighed. She would have given anything to have that type of family life. She always felt so cheated growing up. She had frivolous, material possessions but not the love and affection she craved. Her parents and grandparents went their separate ways, leaving Kelly to be entertained most of the time by the house staff.

We're busy people, her mother always told Kelly.

Too busy to take a few minutes to read to me? Kelly remembered asking, pleading.

Her mother would then summon one of the housekeeping staff to take Kelly to the playroom and read to her until she fell asleep. Kelly had never forgotten how her mother and her father always found a reason to push her away. Her grandparents on her mother's side were no better.

At first when she was much younger, her grandparents would dote on her and bring her the latest toys and expensive clothes. But as she grew older, they grew more distant, finding excuses to avoid her altogether.

My disjointed family, Kelly thought to herself.

Nothing like the Reeds.

Kelly pushed the sad memories out of her head. What was the use in drudging up the pain? It only made her heart long for something she never had.

Austin leaned against the doorframe watching Kelly pick up frame after frame, looking deeply at the pictures of his family. When she had replaced the last frame, Kelly stood motionless against the back of the dining room table, lost in her thoughts.

She looked so sad. She needed to be held. Austin came up behind Kelly and wrapped his arms around her waist.

Kelly brushed away an errant tear which had made its way down her cheek.

"You have a beautiful family."

Turning, she wrapped her arms around Austin's neck, wishing her life had turned out differently.

"Your family pictures brought back....*memories* of my own childhood."

"Happy or unhappy ones?"

Kelly didn't respond; she just laid her face along Austin's neck.

She wondered how long she could keep up this charade with Austin. The longer she held onto him, the harder it would be to let go.

"I don't want to talk about my family."

"You don't have to." Austin rubbed Kelly's back. The tension in her muscles was so evident; he started to knead her more firmly.

Kelly found herself tightening her grip on the collar of Austin's shirt. She leaned into him trying to soak up every minute she could lose herself in his arms.

"We can make better memories...*together*," Austin offered.

She beckoned Austin to slowly kiss her neck then her shoulders until she could barely stand. It felt so good to be the one being romanced, and she was content with that. The way it *should be.*

Apparently Austin's nap had re-charged him. He was pumped and ready.

"Austin," Kelly said between gasps of air. His kisses were unending. Kelly finally had to push him back.

"We...ah, need to take a break. I'm hungry."

"I can tell."

"Not that kind of hungry. *Food*...Austin. Focus for a moment on something other than...my body."

Austin had to laugh.

"Ok, let's go up to the mall. We can grab a burger at the Mug, or some nachos at the Jackson. It will give me something else to do with my hands."

"That sounds so good. Just let me get...presentable."

Kelly darted into the bathroom while Austin headed for the kitchen to get a glass of water.

Kelly's laptop was open on the kitchen table. Austin couldn't help but notice her inbox had several messages listed from "NYOne" and each brief description was in some type of code. Broken sentences with numbers inserted randomly. Very cryptic.

What in the hell did that mean?

School wasn't in session again until September. Was this some type of summer educational project she was working on with a co-worker? The messages on Kelly's laptop held a certain level of intrigue because of their mysterious codes.

Should he ask her?

No way. Kelly would know he had pried into her personal emails. There was no way he wanted to take a chance of putting any type of distance between him and Kelly McBride.

*****

Jenna made a hasty, fateful decision at four in the morning.

She had to leave Chase behind.

She just couldn't take a chance he would go with her to Mary Fortenni's house. It was one thing to risk her own life, but she cared too much for Chase for him to risk his own.

If something happened, I'd never be able to forgive myself.

Dressing quickly in the dark, Jenna grabbed her car keys and slipped outside the door. The hallway was quiet. Other hotel guests were most likely fast asleep, re-charging for another day at the beach, or the nearby aquarium.

Vacationers. Jenna wished she had time for a vacation. *Anywhere*...away from all the drama she was facing. Another trivial notion she needed to erase from her mind. No time for anything except her escape plan.

Making her way quietly down four flights of stairs, Jenna stepped outside the hotel's side entrance. Except for the small motion light above the door, and the slight illumination from the half-moon, she stepped off the stoop into the darkness.

There was calmness in the air in the wee hours of the morning. Only the local birds and insects were smart enough to be awake before their world became disturbed by machinery and human intervention.

Jenna cautiously made her way towards her car. The hotel was close enough to the beach she could smell the salt in the air. It reminded her of Cape May. How she wished she could turn the clock back and return to her favorite haven.

But instead she was sneaking around in the dark...in a town she didn't know...to prepare for a meeting she had no business initiating.

Craziness and stupidity.

Which one was motivating her more? Jenna wondered as she played super spy in the dark.

No movement in the parking lot. Maybe Jonathan's men had fallen asleep because they didn't expect her up this early. She wasn't supposed to meet Mary Fortenni until nine o'clock, several hours from now. Had she actually succeeded in pulling one over on Jonathan and his accomplices?

Gloating with satisfaction, Jenna carefully removed the car keys from her pocket and approached her Camry. It was still wet from the dew which seemed to have fallen as a light glaze on everything in sight.

Jenna stopped abruptly.

A twig crunched. Had she stepped on something, or was someone right behind her? Goosebumps quickly formed on her arms.

Not now.

She wasn't going down without a fight. Firmly planting her feet to give her full balance, she was ready to meet her attacker head on. She fisted her hands and spun around.

"I'm not going to hurt you."

Jenna exhaled slowly. She wasn't totally surprised. In fact, she was wondering when he was going to show up.

"Really? That's not what happened last time."

Jenna relaxed her stance as she gazed into the tempting eyes of Jonathan Knox.

At first she hadn't recognized him. His tailored suit was gone. No tie and crisp white shirt. He wasn't even clean-shaven. Was Jonathan out slumming, trying to keep up with his cohorts?

Why do I care?

Jenna tried to look away, but she had to choose her battles. She was losing this time.

Jonathan Knox was sexy as hell. She'd be an idiot not to look at him.

But his appearance certainly made her do a double-take. Dressed all in black with his hair pushed back, he looked more like a jewel thief.

Maybe his position had been elevated.

"What the hell do you want?"

Jenna folded her arms as Jonathan put a finger to his mouth, indicating she needed to keep quiet.

Did he know something she didn't? Was someone else close by?

Fearing the unknown, Jenna allowed Jonathan to lead her away from her Camry. They worked their way around a hedge of bushes adjacent to The Barrel Restaurant which shared the hotel's parking lot.

Jonathan nodded towards the back door and then reached back for Jenna's hand. He pulled her inside in one fluid motion.

Once inside, he secured the door but startled Jenna, as he covered her mouth with his hand.

"If you want to get out of here alive, I suggest you keep very quiet and do as I say. I have to tell you what Mason Hamilton is planning. I'm not on board with it...anymore. Do you understand?"

Jenna nodded, but couldn't help inhaling the musky scent of his cologne. It smelled wonderful...rugged.

Had he worn it to wear down her defenses?

God knows it was working.

But she wasn't falling for his sexy cologne, or any other type of seduction. She was going to resist him tonight. At least she was going to try. Maybe a little attitude would help.

"Where are your side-kicks? Ready to jump me the moment I poke my head out the door?"

Ignoring her smartass comment, Jonathan motioned for Jenna to follow him into the back storage room.

"Sit down and shut up. I want to make sure no one else is here."

Jenna threw herself down on one of the over-turned crates. She was downright annoyed. Jonathan had found her before she could even get to her car. Why on earth had she followed him like an obedient little puppy? She didn't have to put up with his little games.

Not this time.

As soon as Jonathan came back, Jenna jumped to her feet.

"I'm not staying here. I need to get on my way. I don't want Chase to find out I've left without him. You're not going to keep me here."

"Chase. Who's he?"

"A friend. Someone who doesn't coerce a woman. Something you obviously know nothing about."

Without realizing it, Jonathan had grabbed Jenna by her forearms, making her face him. He released his grip immediately as she pushed against his chest.

"See what I mean?"

Jonathan held his ground. Jenna needed to listen to him. Her life depended on it.

"Do you have a death wish, Jenna Reed? For God's sake, I'm trying to save your life! Mason Hamilton will not stop until he gets want he wants. For some reason, he thinks you have all the answers when it comes to his treasure. Personally, I think you're just an innocent bystander. But, by all means, barge out the damn door and prove me wrong!"

Jenna couldn't process what Jonathan was saying. Mason Hamilton was the one behind her abduction – he was Jonathan's boss! The man who may have murdered her parents and Candace Light. The same man who was now threatening her. Too much information, too quick. Her head was spinning and her lungs were contracting.

Jenna backed up until she felt the wall for support.

What should she do?

Stay and take her chances Jonathan was telling the truth, or run as fast as she could back to her car hoping no one was waiting in the shadows?

Neither option held promise.

"I meant what I said. I'm not here to hurt you. Only *help* you."

Jonathan took a step closer. He touched Jenna's cheek. For a moment, he actually thought Jenna leaned in towards his hand. Her face was getting flushed. She needed to be held, but he hesitated. He wasn't ready to take a chance she would slap him again.

"I find that extremely hard to believe."

"Let me try to convince you."

Jonathan moved closer, but Jenna held out her hands.

"No, thank you. I don't need to be convinced. I don't need *anything* from you. Your men abducted me, then they threatened me and Chase at gunpoint. What's next, Jonathan? Or do you already have that worked out with bringing me in here? Is it your turn now…to *personally* threaten me?"

"I would *never* hurt you."

"No, that's right. You just send your men to do your dirty work. Do you want to see my bruised ribs where they jabbed the gun into my side?"

Jenna lifted her tank top to show Jonathan the ugly black and purple marks which covered the right side of her rib cage.

"Jenna, I had nothing to do with that! Did Hans and Dimitri…?"

"The men from the warehouse? No, it wasn't them. I just assumed you sent another pair of bad-ass goons to work us over."

Before she had a chance to lower her shirt, Jonathan touched his fingers to her side, but quickly removed them when Jenna drew back.

"Those men hurt me, Jonathan. Chase, too. For God's sake, we thought they were going to kill us! Don't pretend you have no idea what I'm talking about."

"Those men were sent directly by Mason. I was summoned back to New York shortly after you left Virginia."

"Yet here you are."

"I came down here to warn you. Nothing else."

Jenna uttered a small laugh.

"I don't believe that for a second."

He wasn't getting off this easy. Jonathan Knox had a hell of a lot more explaining to do.

They didn't have much time. Jonathan most certainly didn't want to spend it arguing.

"Ok. I came back because I...can't bear to see anything else happen to you."

"Oh, *please*."

Jenna rolled her eyes as quickly as the sarcasm rolled off her lips.

"I can't let Mason win this time. He's playing with your life and everyone you know. He's a sadistic son-of-a–bitch, and he has this all planned out. He won't back down until you give him exactly what he wants."

"How many times do I have to say it? I don't have his treasure!"

Jenna felt her frustration rising to a dangerous level.

"But he thinks you're going to find out. He is hell-bent on getting an answer out of you...one way or another."

"Then I'm just going to have to put up a fight."

"Not without my help."

Jonathan moved closer until he was within inches from Jenna's face. She was doing it again, unknowingly. She was drawing him like a magnet.

He needed to touch her.

Now.

Electric surges pulsated inside her. Every single nerve was poised and ready. When Jonathan lifted her face, Jenna couldn't tear her eyes away.

I'm under his spell.

Her body was reacting in a way she couldn't understand. She could not and would not trust this man. No matter what he said, and *how* he said it, Jonathan Knox was still connected to Mason Hamilton.

He would betray her. Jenna was certain of it.

"Jonathan...what...are...you...doing?"

Forming words was quite an effort now.

Jonathan lowered his head. Jenna found herself sinking into the helpless pit of oblivion. It was frightening...and exhilarating at the same time.

"Jenna..."

When his face was directly above her mouth, Jonathan exhaled, forcing warm air to gently glide across her lips. If he hadn't been holding firmly onto her arms, Jenna would have collapsed that very moment.

"Damn it, Jonathan…"

Jenna's mind spun out of control, sending erratic impulses to her body. She locked her arms firmly around Jonathan's neck and found his mouth.

Tightening his grip, Jonathan pushed Jenna firmly against the wall.

The coolness of the concrete did very little to interrupt the heat rising up her back. Jenna barely felt the wall; she was too focused on Jonathan's body pressing against her from the other side and how good it felt.

Too fast. Too soon.

They were starting to glide down the wall…*together.*

Jonathan knew he had to be the one to break the bond which held them together or he would have no choice but to take her right then and there. Calling on every bit of restraint he could muster, Jonathan pried Jenna's arms from his body.

They were both drenched in sweat. Jonathan's shirt had been ripped open, and Jenna's tank top had been lifted above her chest.

Deep breaths brought much-needed oxygen back to their brains.

She wants me. But not here. Not now.

What was I thinking? He's not the man I want to be with!

A blue jay squawked outside, causing Jonathan to jump. It had been so quiet in the restaurant even an innocent call of nature's watchbird jolted him. His body was still trying to recover from Jenna's sudden and unexpected show of passion.

But he was also wary of any indication Mason's men were lurking outside. In plain terms, Jonathan was a mess. His nerves of steel were letting him down.

"Can't stay here…" Jonathan started to say through ragged breaths.

"Should leave…right now…my car is…just down the road…black Nissan. We need to get there…*now.*"

Once again Jonathan put a finger to his lips. He opened the storage room door slightly, and then peered outside. The door had squeaked, but not enough to send out a flare to anyone lurking in the parking lot.

Quietness hung in the air. It was too quiet. Jonathan leaned further out the door to get a better view through the small binoculars he grabbed from his jacket pocket.

Focusing straight ahead put him at a disadvantage. Jonathan never saw the board swing, or felt the whoosh in the air as it came crashing down. All he felt was one enormous twinge of sharp pain in the back of his head.

Jonathan lay motionless in the doorway.

Now the morning dew wasn't the only glimmering sight to welcome the morning's sunrise.

Chapter 14

Jenna slowed the Nissan to a stop in front of the Fortenni home. It was almost seven a.m. now. She was two hours early.

After escaping from the restaurant, Jenna had driven around Folly Beach to make sure she wasn't followed. At the first light of day, she scoped out back roads which would lead her the fastest way back to the hotel.

Once she had a chance to speak with Mary, she was getting the hell out of there. Enough was enough. The time for secret agendas and death threats was well over.

She needed to get back to Chase. To apologize for running out on him. For making him worry.

Chase was probably furious with her right about now. Not probably. He definitely was. She had the phone messages and texts to prove it.

Jenna leaned over the steering wheel and glanced up at Mary's house. The house at 575 Beechwood Drive looked like any other brick rancher in the quiet neighborhood. An assortment of bushes lined the entranceway in no particular landscape design. Probably planted over the years randomly, Jenna thought.

The drapes were all drawn in the front windows. No indication anyone was at home. Done on purpose?

Maybe Mary had expected trouble to follow Jenna and she was taking extra precautions.

Trouble had been following her. Way too closely.

Jenna leaned back against the headrest, shutting her eyes. She had two hours to wait. Plenty of time to figure out what she was going to say to her mother's friend.

But was she ready to hear the answers?

Jenna could feel her insides tightening. From the moment she found the letter, her life had been thrown into turmoil. She wondered now if her curiosity had pushed her into a downward spiral.

Life had gotten so complicated in a short amount of time. Jenna felt a headache beginning to surface. She wasn't sleeping, she wasn't eating. God knows, she could hardly concentrate.

Stress wasn't the only factor causing her to be on edge.

Jonathan Knox had a lot to do with it.

This whole sexual magnetism business with Jonathan in the storage room made her dizzy, almost to the point of disorientation.

She pounded her fist on the steering wheel.

Had she actually thrown herself at him?

Losing control with a total stranger was so out of character for her. Jenna believed whole-heartedly in passion, but the emotions she felt while wrapped in Jonathan's arms had been a level of wildness she couldn't explain.

God knows she wanted him, and that was the problem.

The wanting.

Jenna's head drooped forward in resignation. She couldn't get past the notion of physically craving him. But not just his body. Jenna wanted everything Jonathan Knox was...inside and out.

How could she possibly want him...when she had Chase?

No sane reason.

But sanity was the farthest concept from her mind when she was pulling Jonathan against her body.

There was no way she could let that happen again. Ever.

Push him out of your head before it's too late.

It was too late already. Jenna suddenly remembered.

She wasn't the one who pushed away.

After Jonathan abruptly pulled their bodies apart, Jenna was sent reeling back into reality. As Jonathan moved towards the back door to scan the parking lot, Jenna slipped out of sight into the kitchen then to the front door.

Surprisingly, Jonathan wasn't following her.

Jenna exited the restaurant, making sure not to slam the heavy glass door on her way out. She needed to find Jonathan's car without a moment to lose. After Jonathan told her about his car, Jenna slipped her hands into his pocket to steal his keys while he stole a kiss.

Just as she stepped outside, Jenna heard a loud noise which sounded like a board cracking.

As much as she wanted to see what was going on, she couldn't risk going back. If someone else had joined Jonathan, she would be captured for sure.

A startling thought went through her mind.

What if Mason's men attacked Jonathan when they couldn't find her?

Mason's men were dangerous, lethal. They could…no, she had to push that thought out of her mind. Jonathan still *worked* for Mason. He wouldn't dare hurt Jonathan. Or would he?

There was nothing she could do. She couldn't fight off Mason's men, and she didn't want to stick around to face another gun barrel.

Keep moving.

Jenna slipped behind a tall hedge which lined the front parking lot of the restaurant. From her hiding place, she could hear footsteps on the pavement. Someone had found the storage room door.

Fear gripped her body. Jenna ran as fast as she could along the hedge, praying she wasn't making too much noise to attract anyone's attention. She didn't look back. Not once.

Finally reaching Jonathan's car, Jenna fumbled with the keys. They dropped on the grass by the car door.

Within seconds, she found the keys, pulled the door open and fired up the ignition. Flooring the accelerator, she had the Nissan hitting sixty before she came to the first intersection.

Jenna slowed to a stop at a traffic light. Sweat beads were running down her face faster than she could wipe them away.

She had gotten away. She was safe. *For now.*

Few cars were on the road. Jenna found herself looking at every driver who passed her way, everyone a potential threat. No one caught her eye or even appeared interested in where she was going.

"I'm going crazy," she said to herself as a tear started down her cheek.

Gripping the wheel, she tried to slow her breathing. No one was chasing her. At least no one she could see.

She pulled into a twenty-four hour Waffle House. Food might help to calm her nerves, if only a bit. If anything she needed coffee to keep her awake.

She took a seat facing the front window, her vantage point to spot anyone who looked suspicious.

Jenna glanced around the restaurant. Just a few tables occupied. Diners were talking to each other or engaged in reading the newspaper.

Jenna picked up a page which had been left on her table. The current events section drew her attention. More *Pirate* events were scheduled along the East Coast. Festivals and ships decorated as replicas of famous schooners complete with costumed interpreters offering tours, and bits of pirate trivia to attract audiences of all ages.

Jenna continued to scan the article as she swallowed a bite of her buttermilk waffle.

What about modern-day pirates, she thought to herself as a nervous laugh tempted her mouth.

Jenna refilled her coffee mug from the carafe on the self-serve counter. Not bothering to look over her shoulder this time, she didn't see the pair of eyes watching her every move.

The woman casually glanced in Jenna's direction then returned her attention to her newspaper when Jenna spun around. Dressed in typical attire for a beach town – khaki shorts, tank top, flip flops and a baseball cap advertising Denny's Bait and Tackle, she blended right in with the Waffle House clientele.

Just a local enjoying her breakfast of coffee and a Boston crème donut. The front page of the paper spread across her table, a cell phone within reach. No obvious signs she didn't belong exactly where she was…except for the pistol concealed in her back waistband and the knife strapped to her inner thigh.

The woman with the short dark hair shot another furtive glance in Jenna's direction. So far, so good. Her target was still unaware.

All of the small pieces of her disguise had been selected carefully. She looked like any other early riser, ready to enjoy a lazy day at the beach after that all-important cup of java and sugar fix. Covert assignments were always the toughest. One small slip could mean disastrous results.

Special Agent-In-Charge Maria Turette sure as hell wasn't going to let that happen.

Sipping her coffee, Maria watched Jenna Reed like a hawk, memorizing every precise detail and movement. Having the ability to zero in on a target had served her well during her tenure at the FBI. Keen observations coupled with the ability to second-guess behaviors always paid off. Even now as she paid close attention to Jenna, she was primed for action if Jenna made a swift exit.

Good thing her partners were taking care of matters at the hotel. One less thing to worry about. Jacoby had everything under control...as usual.

He was also sending her text updates every fifteen minutes.

He and Thompson had pulled Jonathan out of the doorway and into their car. They were now en route to the FBI's safe house. Beside a nasty bruise on his head, Jonathan was ok.

The next phase would be to pick up Chase Garrett.

Maria was anticipating trouble at the Fortenni residence. There was no way she needed Garrett riding in like a cowboy and screwing up a perfectly executed rescue mission, if it played out that way.

Jenna was almost done her breakfast, Maria noted. She would be leaving soon.

Target mobilized, Maria texted to Jacoby then raced to her car.

Stay on her, Jacoby quickly responded.

Yes, Genius, Maria couldn't help but reply right before she pulled out into traffic.

Maria hung back a good distance as Jenna slowed to a stop in front of the Fortenni home. Her car was now just slightly visible behind a large bush in dire need of a good clipping.

Grabbing her binoculars, Maria focused on Jenna's car. Jenna was leaning back, closing her eyes. No doubt exhausted. The poor girl had been on the run from Mason Hamilton for the past several days. Jenna was probably on edge and barely functioning.

Maria knew all too well what Mason Hamilton was capable of...*better than anyone.*

*****

Chase bolted upright when he felt the empty pillow beside him.

She couldn't have...

"Jenna!" Chase yelled, hoping...praying for a response.

A chilling silence made Chase realize he was alone.

"Jenna!"

Chase grabbed his shorts and sneakers from the floor. His t-shirt was neatly folded on the dresser.

She had placed it there after taking it off.

"Why, Jenna? Why would you leave without me?"

Having no patience to wait for the elevator, Chase raced down the four flights of stairs, and then headed straight for the front desk.

"The woman I checked in with yesterday, long, dark brown hair, about this height," he gestured with his hand just below his head level. "She must have left earlier – did you see her?"

The front desk clerk shook his head then turned to ask a couple of other staff members who were also behind the counter.

"No, Sir. But it is quite possible she left the hotel either by a side entrance or before we all came on shift. Did you check the breakfast buffet?"

Chase didn't bother to respond. He knew Jenna wasn't filling up a tray at the buffet.

She had left without him.

It was almost seven-thirty. Due to the exhausting drive the day before and the frightening experience at the truck stop, Chase had slept harder and longer than he had planned. Curling his body against Jenna's last night, he had fallen asleep almost as soon as his head hit the pillow. He never knew she had left the room.

Chase ran his fingers through his hair in desperation. She was driving him insane in more ways than one. He wanted to protect her, but she was running in an opposite direction. Maybe he needed to take a chance and tell her the whole truth. Maybe then she'd listen to his voice of reason and never stray from his side.

Maybe.

Jenna Reed had a mind of her own.

Chase hurried back to their room. He found an address for Mary Fortenni on Jenna's laptop. 575 Beechwood Drive.

He attempted to call Jenna on her cell but it went right to voicemail. Leaving a frantic voice message and text message, he had to move on.

Chase dialed Tumi's number. No answer there either.

So much for the cavalry; Chase had to act *now*.

Chase looked all over for Jenna's car keys, then glanced out the window at the parking lot below. Her Camry was still parked in the spot below their window.

Had she taken the keys so he couldn't follow her? Did she believe for one second he wouldn't try *with or without her car*? How did she get out of here if she didn't drive her car? Had someone taken her again? Too many scenarios were running through his head.

"Front desk," the clerk answered on the first ring.

"Chase Garrett, Room 415. I need a rental as soon as possible. Charge it to my account. Also, please extend our stay for another night."

"Very good, Sir. I will order your rental. We usually receive mid-size sedans, unless you'd like an SUV. I could recommend…"

"The sedan will do. Just get it here…*fast*."

Within twenty minutes, the front desk manager called back. The rental car had arrived. A navy blue Impala was parked to the left of the entrance.

Chase tore down the steps once again. Grabbing the Impala's keys, he nodded in a quick acknowledgment to the front desk manager, then darted out the front door.

Rushing towards the rental, Chase immediately noticed two men getting out of a black SUV.

I don't have time for this, Chase muttered to himself as he reached for the car door.

One of the men reached behind him and slammed the door shut. Chase spun around and stared into the man's chest just as the second man began to speak.

"Special Agent Brett Jacoby, Dr. Garrett. We're with the FBI. We will be taking you to our safe house until the matter is resolved at the Fortenni residence."

The Feds. About time they got here, Chase thought to himself.

"I can't go with you. My *friend*…needs me." Girlfriend, lover, woman on the run…Chase wasn't sure what Jenna was to him at this point.

"We understand your concern, Dr. Garrett, but for her safety and your own, we need you to come with us."

"*She's* the one in danger! Jenna is the one who needs protection. We need to get over there right now!"

"No need to be alarmed, Dr. Garrett. Our senior agent is monitoring the situation. Ms. Reed has arrived at the Fortenni residence and she is safe inside her car. Please come with us now."

Thompson opened the door behind the driver's side as Chase reluctantly got inside.

Once the car was in motion, Jacoby turned around from the front seat to address Chase's mounting concerns.

"Tumi Carile informed us Ms. Reed was in potential danger. We've been monitoring the hotel ever since. Ms. Reed left the hotel very early this morning on foot. She got into a car and drove around for a couple of hours, then arrived at the Fortenni residence."

"But her car is still in the parking lot."

"Ms. Reed used another vehicle to make her escape."

"How in the hell did she do that?"

Jacoby exchanged a glance with Thompson. He had no desire to report on Jenna Reed's extracurricular activities with Jonathan Knox.

"Ms. Reed was aided in her escape. She has been followed by our agent to the Fortenni residence and is still under surveillance."

"I don't care how good your team is! Mason Hamilton and Jonathan Knox have proven they have the manpower to get to Jenna wherever she is. I can assure you, one agent will not be enough."

*****

Jenna ignored Chase's repeated calls…on purpose. She had made a decision to face her destiny alone.

I got myself into this…I'll get myself out.

Battling between a sensible decision and an insane one was riding Jenna's nerves. She jumped as her phone vibrated. Mary Fortenni was texting her.

Ok to come in now. Back door.

Jenna took a deep breath as her hand reached for the car door. She had no idea what she would be facing. This could very well be a trap. Jonathan tried to warn her about Mason Hamilton and his deceptive plan.

Now as she walked briskly to the back door of Mary's house, Jenna felt her legs weakening. Each step closer shot warning tremors up her calves. No one was watching her back. No one was here to help her. Jenna knew her odds of survival were slim at best.

I need to keep going...

The back door swung open and Jenna slipped inside. She was in the kitchen. A coffee pot was half-full, burner still on. A mug was on the small table with a half-eaten muffin. Someone was here...in the house...with her.

"Mary?"

No response. Jenna tensed. Was someone else in the house? Oh, God, she hoped she wasn't walking straight into...

"Mary?" Jenna called again.

"Jenna?" A voice called from another room.

Jenna reached for the kitchen counter. She needed to feel something strong to keep her balance.

Her heart was beating so fast now; she could feel the thumping against her thin shirt. Her mind and ears must be playing a trick on her. Her nerves were raw; she wasn't able to rationalize what was happening. She heard a woman's voice.

It was so *familiar*...a voice she had known *all her life*.

Chapter 15

Kelly changed into a short, white linen skirt and peach tank top. Her skin was flushed due to her multiple love sessions with Austin. She had a glow even better than a suntan.

Twisting her long blond hair upward, she secured it with a clip. She was so warm; it felt good to have her hair off her neck for awhile.

She and Austin were going to drive over to the Lobster House for drinks and dinner, then maybe take a drive out to Sunset Beach, Cape May's perfect spot to watch the sunset.

Looking at her reflection in the mirror, Kelly saw a different person smiling back at her. A *happy* person. Kelly blinked her eyes. She must be mistaken. How could she possibly be happy with the deception she was committing?

Just for a short while, she could pretend. She had grown adept at pretending most of her life. Pretending she had a fabulous family life for the cameras and her father's public image, pretending to be Jenna's best friend.

So what difference did it make now if she pretended she was Austin Reed's new girlfriend, having the time of her life at a romantic Victorian beach town?

Tonight, for once, she wanted a chance to feel what true happiness was like.

She didn't need her father's permission *tonight*. She just needed Austin.

"Hi."

Kelly's face registered her complete surprise as Austin stepped into the kitchen.

Austin had made every possible effort to clean up, shave and actually put on a shirt with a collar. He looked so good. He had gone the extra mile...*for her*.

Kelly nodded in approval, and leaned in to give him a light kiss on the cheek.

"You look...very handsome."

"Why thank you," Austin said, proud she had noticed.

Kelly quickly brushed away a fallen tear. Austin was making her melt inside, and she didn't know how much longer she could push those feelings back.

"You look...*amazing*."

Kelly smiled, masquerading the hurt inside. Before she could figure it out, she pulled Austin's head down so she could easily reach his lips. There was a heated urgency inside her to find her core of happiness until she lost it again.

Kelly searched Austin's eyes. Could he see how much she needed to feel something real?

"I'm sorry," Kelly whispered as she slowly drew her hands down the front of Austin's shirt. "I didn't mean to attack you like that."

Austin's arms were still locked behind her back. Planting light kisses just below her chin and then traveling backwards, he stopped briefly only when he heard a soft moan emit from her lips.

"Never apologize for kissing me," he whispered into her ear.

Kelly smiled.

"As much as I would love to carry you back to bed, we'd better go if we have any notion of eating a meal fully dressed."

"Ok, let's go. No more distractions. I'm hungry," Kelly said as she grabbed her sweater from the kitchen table.

It was a great night for a walk along the marina. Soft breezes were blowing along the dock, as they headed for one of the best seafood restaurants in Cape May.

Thank goodness Austin had called ahead for a reservation. Even at this early hour, the Lobster House had a good crowd waiting for a table.

They were seated by one of the large side windows which provided a picture-perfect view of the dock. It was a peaceful scene. Seagulls gliding back and forth. A few small boats cruising along. A few people walking hand-in-hand.

Kelly sipped her Chardonnay and savored the moment. She could imagine living this life. Having a caring man smiling at her from across the table while they anticipated a decadent meal of local seafood. She could *dream,* anyway.

Which lasted about thirty seconds.

Happiness is just a poor man's way of excusing himself from real responsibility.

Mason and his constant lectures on life. She had heard the dissertation several times, yet Kelly tried to be an eternal optimist. Hope was the only reason she hadn't fallen off the edge yet.

"Another glass of wine, please."

The waiter nodded as he jotted down a note on his tablet then walked away.

Austin reached for Kelly's hand.

"What's wrong? You seem so…far away."

"I'm sorry, Austin. Just daydreaming, I guess."

"Just so I'm the one in your dreams."

Austin squeezed Kelly's hand. A smile spread across her face as he caressed her fingers.

"You are."

More than anything, Kelly wanted to tell Austin the whole story. How her father had threatened her into doing such unthinkable things…maybe with another glass of wine…?

Wishful thinking. She wouldn't stand a chance if her father found out she had confided in Austin. Neither of them would survive if they tried to stand up to Mason Hamilton.

But she had to try.

Questioning Austin was a waste of time. He had no idea what she was talking about. In fact, he thought it was hilarious when Kelly had mentioned little gold animal figurines. His knowledge of antiques was limited to his vintage t-shirts from his teen days and a few boxes of baseball cards. If she still wanted to pursue her search, Austin suggested they check out a few antique shops in town.

Maybe it was the wine getting to her head, but Kelly didn't seem too fazed with her decision. She would tell Mason she was done serving his every need. He would have no choice but to deal with that.

Just as their meals arrived, Kelly's phone vibrated in the pocket of her skirt. She laid the phone in her lap and pulled up the text.

Meeting tomorrow. Time and location to follow.

Mason had a knack for ruining perfect moments.

Kelly swallowed her wine a little too fast, almost choking.

"Are you all right?"

Austin jumped to his feet and knelt beside her.

"Yes," Kelly said as she ran a finger down Austin's face.

A little embarrassed by his darting action, Austin settled back into his seat.

"Just my father," Kelly said as her eyes drifted downward.

"If you have to take the call…"

"No, not right now."

Kelly finished her glass. She hoped to hell it nullified her senses, or at least made her brain a little fuzzy. Maybe then all thoughts of her father couldn't permeate her mind, and she could try once more to enjoy the evening.

Austin could sense Kelly needed a distraction.

"Would it help if I told you how incredibly beautiful you are, how fantastic you look, and how I feel like the luckiest guy in the whole room?"

Kelly's eyes starting misting.

"Yes, that would definitely help. I'm sorry, Austin. My father always seems to find a way to destroy everything. His timing is unbelievable."

"Your father isn't here. So, forget about him for now, and just concentrate on us."

She could try.

Silently, Kelly promised herself she wasn't going to let her father take away the one thing she had yearned for all of her life – a true sense of happiness.

*****

Mason Hamilton fumed when his call to Kelly's cell went straight to voicemail.

"How dare she not pick up my call!"

His patience was growing thin. Kelly was acting impulsively. She was being distracted from her task at hand.

Mason grunted as he cursed her lack of willpower. George would have to provide some prodding. Kelly needed to be taught a lesson.

Reprimanding his disobedient daughter was the least of his problems.

Mason's attention was drawn to his vibrating phone.

Plan is proceeding. Team is in place.

Mason's lips curved into a sneer as he welcomed the good news. Soon he would have the information he needed to find the treasure pieces.

Thanks to The Closer.

A professional assassin known in international circles, The Closer was an enigma. The mere mention of his name brought lesser men to their knees. Even though he frowned upon the cloak-and-dagger tactics The Closer insisted upon, Mason had complete faith in the man who would travel anywhere and do anything for the right price. With no limitations.

Mason shuddered as a nerve rippled his spine. The Closer had no qualms when it came to handling *delicate* matters. In fact, Mason believed The Closer relished the opportunity to instill fear in others through his many creative ways of persuasion and his infamous signature-kill.

Mason had contracted with The Closer on several occasions, and the outcomes were always to his satisfaction. The Closer never disappointed Mason. All plans were executed with precision.

An ally worth his weight in gold. Such a rarity.

Now, if he just had other men on his payroll as equally talented. For general grunt work, Hans and Dimitri would do.

Mason smuggled Hans out of Russia almost ten years ago. Fleeing before the Russian mob had a chance to question him for stealing part of an arms shipment, Hans never looked back.

Hans had been hired temporarily by Mason's crew chief to load a private plane with cargo containing Russian artifacts for a museum exhibit in the States. When Hans overhead Mason's futile attempt to convince the Russian curator it would be the last time he saw several rare pieces, Hans stepped in and proved his mettle. Within an hour, the curator miraculously accepted Mason's proposal, thankful he still had three fingers remaining on his right hand.

Mason immediately saw the value in Hans' unique, yet barbaric talents. Before the plane took off from the airstrip, Hans was smuggled inside as part of the crew. He hoped his family would one day forgive him for abandoning them.

Loyalty had been forged between Mason and Hans that day, as Hans vowed his allegiance. In return, Mason promised Hans freedom in the States, as long as he did *exactly* as Mason commanded.

Hans quickly found life in the States to be agreeable. As long as he kept under the radar of the police, he could come and go as he pleased. Mason provided an apartment and fake ids. Hans soon adapted to his new surroundings, even finding a few bars which catered to other displaced Russians.

Years later, Hans met Dimitri Batrov.

Hearing Dimitri converse in his native tongue, Hans struck up a conversation in one of the bars on the lower east side. Trading stories about some of the old haunts in St. Petersburg, and how Russian women were so much different than Americans, Hans soon had a new comrade.

Hans appealed to Mason. He needed a partner.

Dimitri proved he could hold his own. Roughing up slackers and providing enough intimidation by his sheer size and piercing eyes, Dimitri became very useful. But he told Hans from the start, he would have no part in murder. A promise made long ago to an aging grandmother was a bond he would never break. Hans respected commitment.

So far, murder hadn't been part of their required duties.

Mason had other people who would take care of that.

*****

The Closer requested additional backup when he arrived in South Carolina. Mason quickly complied and ordered Hans and Dimitri back on the road.

A simple task. They were to keep an eye on Jenna Reed. Two over-sized men, one small female. No problem, Hans had told The Closer.

Hans had underestimated Jenna Reed.

And didn't plan on Jonathan Knox being part of the equation.

Hans called The Closer. He had no knowledge of Knox's involvement. He would have to check with Mason.

Hans received a text rather quickly.

Get the girl. Get Knox. Bring them both to me.

Hans showed the message to Dimitri. They had their orders. Time to put them into action.

Dimitri tried the front and back doors of the restaurant. Both were locked from within. Finally able to pry a window open in the coat room just off the main lobby, Hans and Dimitri pulled themselves inside.

Voices were coming from the storage room. Knox and the girl. Then there was silence.

Hans peered around the kitchen door into the storage room to get a better look. Jonathan and Jenna were clinging to each other.

Hans snickered.

"Now we scare them."

"No," Dimitri said as he held Hans back. "Taser. No protests."

"Yes. Did you bring it?"

Dimitri shook his head. "In the car."

"Get it. I will wait here."

When Dimitri left, Hans hid underneath one of the long metal prep counters.

Minutes passed, yet Dimitri had not yet returned. Hans grew impatient. Hearing footsteps, Hans pushed back further under the counter.

Gripping the edge of the counter, Hans peered above. He could see Jonathan moving towards the back door with binoculars in his hand. Had Jonathan seen Dimitri? If Knox called out, he could screw everything up.

Hans couldn't take that risk. He grabbed one of the wooden cutting boards lying on a nearby wire rack and slammed it into the back of Jonathan's head.

Knox was knocked out cold.

Pleased with himself for acting quickly, Hans turned around to check on the whereabouts of Jenna Reed.

She wasn't in sight. That couldn't be good.

Hans ran from room to room, checking all doorways and under counters. Jenna Reed had vanished.

The Closer would not be happy.

Dimitri finally returned with bad news. Jenna Reed was not outside the restaurant.

But the FBI was.

*****

Twilight was beginning now, bringing a mystical glow to the early evening.

Kelly watched other couples embrace as she stood with Austin at Sunset Beach enjoying the ambiance. At the precise moment when the sun had made its final appearance, Austin grabbed her around the waist, squeezing her just a little.

"Kiss me."

Kelly's arms encircled his neck. She needed no further encouragement. Her lips were on Austin's before he could even say another word.

She was *afraid*...afraid to let go. Afraid for the retaliation of her father if she disobeyed. Her momentary defiance at the restaurant was now hitting hard. As much as she wanted to put the past behind her, Kelly knew it was impossible. Mason would never relinquish control of her.

Feeling a tremor rise through Kelly's body, Austin held her closer. He hoped his arms would be the safety net she needed.

"I'm here."

Kelly fell against Austin's chest. His neck was now damp from her tears.

She couldn't take much more. She was crumbling.

Her phone vibrated again. Her father wasn't giving up.

Austin surprised Kelly by grabbing the phone out of her hands. "I have no problem tossing this damn thing into the ocean. Just give me the word."

If she continued to ignore her father's phone calls and texts, another form of retribution would follow which would be much worse.

"I'll call him back later."

"Turn the phone off, Kelly," Austin pleaded.

"I can't, Austin."

"Yes, you can. For one night, *tonight*, please forget about your father. Give *me* all your attention. I promise you, you won't be sorry."

Kelly wished Austin could make that promise come true. She turned the phone off and put it back into her skirt pocket.

"Thank you."

Austin cupped Kelly's face between his hands. He barely touched her lips, and then moved lower to plant light kisses on her shoulder.

Kelly felt light-headed. She was free, if only for a short time. She wanted to make time stand still!

"Take me back...*now*," Kelly murmured before Austin's lips came crashing down on her own.

Their kiss was interrupted by three small children who ran around them tossing bread crumbs in the air for the seagulls. Yet another reminder of living a simple, peaceful life at the beach.

A life he wanted to share with Kelly McBride.

But as they walked back to the car, harsh reality set in.

Who was he kidding?

Kelly was smart, sexy, and used to the finer things in life.

How could he possibly be enough for her?

Austin's hand lingered on the door handle as he took one last look at the family with the small children chasing the seagulls.

How can I make that happen?

In an instant, Austin felt a miraculous change come over him. He had something to strive for, and he was determined to take his best shot. Even if he failed, and Kelly left him, at least he could say he tried. He was willing to do just about anything to win Kelly's heart.

Kelly was his sole motivation now.

Tonight he would show her just how far he was willing to go. Tonight, he wasn't just giving her his body.

Austin was giving Kelly his heart.

Chapter 16

Jenna was following the voice calling to her.

It couldn't be....

Turning the corner into the living room, a woman stood facing the front bay window. A hauntingly *familiar* silhouette.

Jenna stopped in her tracks, afraid to take even one more step.

Tingling sensations reached out to her from across the room. The woman at the window was slowly turning.

This couldn't be happening...

The woman at the window knew her visitor had arrived. She cocked her head to make sure, then simply nodded.

It was time.

Flexing her fingers anxiously, the woman breathed deeply. All these years she had been so afraid to reveal herself...and the truth which she had promised to keep hidden for so long.

Turn around now, she told herself. *Put your own fears aside.* For the sake of the young woman who had just entered her house. For the memory of her friend.

Mouthing a silent prayer, calmness seemed to engulf her.

This was the right thing to do...

She pivoted.

The soft glow of dimmed sunlight seemed to form an ethereal backdrop. Jenna gasped in total surprise, falling backwards onto the sofa.

Standing before her...was her mother's best friend, Teresa Maylor. Jenna was too stunned to even respond. Teresa ran to her side.

"I'm so glad you're all right!" Teresa exclaimed. "I know you want answers. I promise you, I will tell you everything. My real name is Mary Teresa Fortenni. I changed my last name to Maylor for George, even though we never officially married."

Jenna's mouth hung open. She was hearing Teresa's explanation but it wasn't sinking in. Another deception she had lived with all her life.

Her mother, now Teresa?

"I thought it would be best to keep my former identity a secret. Your mother agreed. We had so much to deal with just out
of college. So many decisions to make which would impact our
families down the road."

Jenna felt a tremor go through her body. A secret shared between trusting friends, but not with Lois' own daughter.

"Your mother prepared for this day, Jenna, from the time
you were born. She always knew you would learn the truth. She
entrusted me with a letter I've kept hidden for you. Lois wanted to
explain the actions she took so many years ago for what we all
believed in...for what we were willing *to sacrifice for...*"

Jenna felt her face getting hot. All she could feel was anger...frustration.

"Past actions...sacrifices...*for what?*"

"Jenna, I know this is hard to hear."

"Teresa, I feel like I never knew my mother at all."

Teresa squeezed Jenna's hand.

"Lois never wanted anyone to get hurt because of what she
did. She loved you all very much. Please don't blame her for not
sharing this with you. Lois thought the longer she kept you out of
all this mess, the safer you would be. Unfortunately, her theory
was flawed. Now you are right in the middle."

Jenna shook her head, trying to comprehend.

"In the middle of what, Teresa? I have no idea what any of
this means!"

Teresa held back. She had to tread lightly. Jenna needed to
keep her wits about her and not fall apart. But she also had a right
to know the danger she was facing.

"Jenna, listen to me. Mason Hamilton is behind all this.
There's no other logical explanation. I'm convinced he ordered
your parents' deaths. Lois confided in me she thought she was
being watched for several weeks. Then a few days before the
accident, she told me a man came to their house demanding to
know where the treasure was buried."

Jenna shook hearing the word *treasure.*

"Lois told me she slammed the door in his face and threatened to call the police. He never returned. She was so scared.
This man could have been the one who made her swerve off the
road. I am so sorry, Jenna. I know you and Austin believed at the

time it was an accident, but I'm telling you…your parents were *murdered.*"

Jenna covered her face with her hands. Both Candace and Teresa had the same suspicions. It had to be true.

Leaning against the back of the sofa, Jenna waited for Teresa to continue.

"This all goes back thirty years, Jenna. Thirty *long* years of keeping a secret. Candace probably started to tell you what happened with Sylvia Bernard. Sylvia had to run for her life after she overheard Hamilton bragging about the murder of an old man. He killed someone to get his hands on the treasure pieces! Hamilton planned to hide the objects in Sylvia's apartment until he could sneak them into the museum foundation's inventory. Apparently, he planned to take credit for finding them. He needed the old man out of the way so no one would question him."

Teresa noted Jenna was listening…intently.

Good, she thought. *You need to hear every word. Your life may depend on it.*

"Next Hamilton said he was done with her! Sylvia took that to mean he was going to kill her as well. She was at her wit's end! She had no family. She just found out she was pregnant. She didn't want Hamilton to find out about the baby. He was…a murderer with no conscience at all. She had been so foolish to get too close to him. We all kept telling her she was getting in too deep, but she wouldn't listen."

Teresa looked away, remembering the late night discussions about the extreme risk her friend was taking.

"Sylvia found where Hamilton hid the treasure pieces. She took them to hold over his head if he ever tried to hurt her or her child. Sylvia fled to your mother's house and begged us all to help her. What could we do? She needed our help."

"What's so important about this treasure? Why not just give it to Hamilton and be done with it? It's caused so many problems. For God's sake, Teresa, people are *dead*. Isn't it about time we just hand it over to Hamilton? Maybe he'll finally leave us alone."

"I wish it was that simple, Jenna. I really do. But it's not. We can't let Hamilton win. Everything we've done, all the lives which have been lost, will be for nothing if he gets his hands on the treasure pieces. Mason Hamilton won't stop until he kills us all."

Jenna gripped the edge of the sofa. Teresa's words were cutting too deep.

"Sylvia and Lois felt as long as the treasure was hidden, we could keep everyone safe. As long as Mason Hamilton never found out where it was buried, he wouldn't harm us or our families."

"So much for that line of thought."

Her mother's actions had now become her burdens.

"It was the only solution we could think of at the time. We were all drawn into this situation together. We did as Sylvia asked. Your mother let her use your Aunt Marge's summer beach house in Stone Harbor. We took turns going down to the shore, taking care of Sylvia. Gail was the only one who wasn't able to come down often. She lived in Boston and the drive was too long for just a two-day weekend. But Gail helped financially, sending monthly checks which were very generous."

"Sylvia just abandoned her baby?"

"It wasn't like that, Jenna. Sylvia had no choice. Her baby was in danger the longer she was around. Sylvia feared Mason would finally figure out she wasn't the one who died when her apartment in New York caught on fire. But I don't know if he ever did."

"Someone else died in her apartment?"

Teresa nodded. "Sylvia believes it was a woman named Alina Catrall. They were supposed to meet for breakfast the morning after Sylvia escaped to your mother's house. She tried to call Alina for several days but she never got an answer."

Jenna was confused. "Why wasn't the body identified?"

"Remember this was thirty years ago, Jenna. DNA analysis wasn't perfected. The burned body found in the apartment matched Sylvia's general height and proportions. There was no other indication it was someone other than Sylvia. Whoever killed this woman took her purse so she couldn't be easily identified."

"Where did Sylvia go, Teresa?"

Teresa hesitated. She wasn't ready to get into that explanation. She switched the subject hoping Jenna was just too overwhelmed to pay close attention.

"We ended up calling the baby *Billy*. We kept thinking...*hoping*...Sylvia would come back. We waited for weeks. Finally, Candace said she would take him to live with her in

---

Virginia. Her mother had recently died and her father had gone back to live in New England. Candace needed someone to fill the void in her life."

"But Candace couldn't keep him. That is what she was writing to my mother about in the letter I found at the beach house."

"I'm afraid your discovery of that letter somehow got back to Mason Hamilton. He must have assumed the contents of the letter contained information about the treasure."

Jenna sat rigid.

"How, Teresa? How did Hamilton find out about the letter?"

"I'm still working on that, but I have some theories. Once I know for sure, I'll let you know."

"I still don't know why Hamilton thinks I know anything about his treasure. Candace's letter only talks about the baby."

"Your mother hid the artifacts at Sylvia's request, but she never told the rest of us where they were buried. She and Sylvia thought it would be best for our own protection. But Hamilton figured out we were Sylvia's friends. One by one, our homes were raided, but nothing was ever stolen. He never contacted any of us directly. He was probably afraid to tarnish his public reputation."

"You never found out what the treasure pieces were? My mother never told you? I find that hard to believe, Teresa. You and my mother were best friends. Best friends trust each other completely."

Teresa was tempted to say more but knew it would be best if Jenna heard it from someone else.

"You need to read your mother's letter."

Teresa took a book down from the bookshelf which lined one wall of her living room. She opened the back cover and pulled out an envelope which she handed it to Jenna.

"You need to read this alone. I'll be in the kitchen."

Jenna ran her fingers gingerly over her name written in her mother's handwriting. It was the last personal message her mother had left for her. She was almost afraid to open it.

Finally, she mustered enough courage and carefully opened the envelope.

Dearest Jenna,

I know if you're reading this, then I have already left you. From the first moment you were born, I felt an obliga-

tion to explain. *How I chose this path, the consequences of the decisions I made, and what I would be asking you to do.*

Please know this, you were such a blessing to me. A bright spot in my life which will always shine no matter what lies ahead. I ask you to forgive me for not sharing this with you before now. You must not blame Teresa for keeping this secret from you. She has done exactly as I asked, providing you with this letter at the best time in her judgment. She has been a true friend for many years. Do not hesitate to trust her.

The actions I took several years ago at the request of a friend have haunted me for many years. I knew the day would come when Mason Hamilton's obsession would surface again. He is the most evil man imaginable. I pray you will never have to gaze into his eyes because they are hollow, except for the madness which consumes him.

Sylvia asked me to hide five small objects which she overhead Mason Hamilton describe as his treasure. Sylvia believed he murdered a man to acquire them because they are extremely rare and valuable. I did as she asked, fearing for her life and her unborn child.

I let her use Aunt Marge's beach house as it was secluded in Stone Harbor. After the baby was born, Sylvia took off unexpectedly. The four of us - Teresa, Candace Light, Gail Tremont and I, tried to find a solution of raising a baby on our own. Gail finally adopted him.

Jenna, you need to find the package containing the treasure pieces and re-bury it. Mason Hamilton is NEVER to get his hands on it! But you need to be diligent. You must stay strong and defiant. Sacrifices have been made, and now I'm asking you to make another.

You must do whatever it takes to keep the treasure hidden. Be very careful with the people you trust. Mason has legal and political ties which are far-reaching. Only use the treasure as leverage if it is a matter of life and death.

I have buried them in the beach house. You will know where to find them. The catch-all. Take out the bottom drawer and reach back as far as you can. You will find a small box. Inside you will find five small animal figurines – an elephant, a tiger, a monkey, a giraffe and a lion.

Remember the game we used to play when you were younger? I have left a few clues for you – there is a small note tucked inside the box. If you think hard enough, you will remember these places. Bury them while it is dark outside.

I wouldn't ask you to do this if I didn't feel completely confident you could achieve success. I pray you will never need to touch the treasure pieces again once you hide them.

Some treasures are better left buried.

Carry my love with you, Jenna. It will keep you strong.

I will always love you,

Mom

By the time Jenna reached the end of the letter, her hands were shaking. She could hear her mother's voice resounding in her head, each word articulated, drilling into her memory. This wasn't just a final letter from a mother to a daughter. This was her mother's last wishes with precise instructions.

You can do this.

Lois' familiar words of encouragement, which Jenna had heard so many times before, were loud and clear. Her mother was counting on her. She couldn't let her down.

Teresa returned from the kitchen carrying a tray with tea cups and a small plate.

"Do you understand what needs to be done?"

Jenna slowly nodded.

Teresa laid her other hand on top of Jenna's.

"You have to understand. I've been preparing for this day for quite some time. Candace was ready also. She knew the risks. She agreed to meet with you anyway. We *all* knew the risks. But now, I'm more afraid for you. Something is going down."

Jenna immediately tensed.

"What do you mean?"

Teresa's eyes darted towards the front window.

"There are people surrounding the house. When I was in the kitchen, I saw a man crouching in my shed. We don't have much time. We have to act quickly."

Teresa took a pocket lighter from her pants' pocket. She lit the corner of the letter, letting it drop to the plate.

"Teresa, what are you doing!"

Teresa pushed Jenna's hand away when she tried to reach for the burning letter.

"No one else can find this letter."

Jenna sat back, resigned. Teresa was right.

As painful as it was to watch, both women intently stared as the memorial flame to Lois Green grew brighter, then finally died out.

A daunting silence covered Jenna and Teresa for a few brief seconds with only their nervous breaths billowing between them.

Jenna's cell vibrated, drawing her attention. She cradled the cell in her palm but already knew who was calling.

Chase.

Her rock in all this madness. Jenna momentarily lost her train of thought.

She wanted to hear Chase's voice more than anything right now. But she just couldn't pick up the phone.

Not yet.

Jenna looked warily at Teresa then sat up straight. She knew she had to finish what her mother had started.

This *task*...Jenna regrettably realized...had cost her mother her life.

*****

Chase felt helpless and frustrated staying in the safe house when Jenna was the one in danger.

He needed to get to her. She needed *him*.

Chase slapped the wall; the pain rising up his arm began to keep time with his anger level.

"Jenna, why did you leave me?"

The agents in the front room were too engrossed in searching their laptops to pay any attention to Chase's outburst.

They were unofficial bodyguards, that's all.

Not that he needed one. Special Agent Turette just didn't want him in the way.

But he couldn't just stand around and do *nothing*.

I have to get to her.

Chase paced the floor of the FBI safe house, which looked like any other upscale residential home in the small town of Daniel Island, just off the coast of Charleston. Except for the electronic fencing and the strategically-placed surveillance cameras, it looked like a normal split level single-family residence. Tan siding with dark green shutters, two car garage, and azalea bushes lining the front walkway.

In fact, *most* of the homes on this part of the island looked this way. It was one of the FBI's gated communities along the East Coast. *Probably safer than the Pentagon,* Agent Jacoby had quipped as they pulled into the driveway.

Chase had been too annoyed at the time to appreciate the agent's dry sense of humor. But it was probably true. At least it felt that way. It felt like a prison.

"Can you at least check with your team to see if Jenna has left the house yet?"

Chase stood his ground. He wasn't leaving until one of the agents made the call. He was determined to get an answer, one way or another.

Agent Derek Bromley frowned as he looked up from his laptop. He had been told by Jacoby not to ignore Garrett *completely.*

Bromley spun around in his chair.

"Sir, I'm waiting on a report from Agent Jacoby right now. You'll have to wait this out like the rest of us. If you'd like something to eat, please help yourself to anything in the kitchen."

"I don't want anything to eat, damn it. I want answers. Get Jacoby on the line. *Now.*"

Agent Bromley tossed his pencil down. He desperately wanted to avoid a lengthy discussion about FBI protocol to a *civilian.*

But something in Garrett's authoritative tone made his hair stand on edge. Bromley glanced over at his partner Agent John Matthews, who was seated across the table. Neither had time for personal drama, but Agent Jacoby had told both of them to take special care of Chase Garrett.

An order was an order, and Bromley wasn't about to question his superior. But he still wondered why Garrett was getting special treatment.

Whatever, Bromley thought. He still wasn't going to let Garrett boss him around. He'd have to put Garrett in his place. Besides, Special Agent Turette was expecting a report soon from the surveillance equipment installed around the Fortenni residence.

"We'll call Jacoby now. I'll let you know when he gets back to us."

"Thank you."

Bromley breathed a sigh of relief when Chase headed for the kitchen. Another stall technique. Apparently, it had worked this time, but Bromley wondered just how long it would take for Garrett to come storming back.

Chase stared at the kitchen cabinets with empty eyes.

He wasn't hungry, but his insides were caving.

Jenna.

Leaning against the counter, he tried to push away disturbing images of Jenna being hurt again. After their frightening episode at gunpoint, Chase was certain Jenna was facing yet another threatening situation and he couldn't do anything about it. Not yet anyway.

Chase shrugged as he pulled out his cell phone. He had to keep trying.

Jenna, please pick up the phone.

He just needed to hear her sweet voice. To know she was safe.

The number was ringing...again...and again. Soon it would go to voicemail.

"Chase?"

Chase fumbled the phone when Jenna answered.

"Jenna, thank God, you're all right!"

Chase heard nothing but silence. The line had gone dead. Jenna's phone had been shut off or...destroyed.

Chase tore into the living room, shoving his phone in front of Agent Bromley's face.

"Jenna was on the phone...then the line cut off. Something is definitely wrong – we need to get word to your agent. We need to get Jenna out of there...*now*!"

Bromley speed-dialed Jacoby. He wasn't going to act on another round of Garrett's rantings without approval. His pay grade wasn't high enough for that.

"Sir, Agent Bromley here. Garrett says Ms. Reed answered her cell then the line went dead. Is she still inside the house?"

"Affirmative. We'll check it out. Haven't seen anyone else enter. Garrett's getting hard to handle?"

"You could say that, Sir."

"Bring Garrett here, but you're in charge of him. Keep him out of sight. If Turette sees him, we'll have hell to pay. You got it, Bromley?"

"Yes, Sir."

Bromley powered down his laptop then turned to his partner.

"Get the car ready, John…field trip."

"Not without me," Chase interceded.

"You're coming with us, Garrett. Here are the ground rules. You stay in the car. You do exactly as I say. You're on a short leash. You got it?"

Chase nodded. Hell, yeah, he got it.

Bromley opened the car door as Chase climbed inside. He was surprised to find someone else already flanking the backseat.

"I don't think we've met. By the way, I'm Jonathan Knox."

Chapter 17

Agents Jacoby and Thompson arrived at the Fortenni residence to give Turette back-up. They pulled into the driveway of
the house next door all the way to the backyard. Both agents
unsnapped their holsters.

Jacoby scanned the backyard with his infrared binoculars.
He picked up movement in the shed.

Jacoby's fingers swiped a message to Turette.

Check shed. Perp with gun.

Jacoby slowly opened the car door then withdrew his gun.
He nodded to Thompson who was also ready to spring into action.
All they needed was Turette's command.

Jacoby's phone vibrated.

Stand down. Going in.

"Damn it, Maria. Why don't you let us handle this?"

"You going to tell her that?" Thompson asked.

Jacoby shook his head. They both knew better. Turette
knew what she was doing.

FBI Special-Agent-In-Charge Maria Turette was running on
pure adrenaline. She had been up almost twenty-four hours preparing for the mission. She was losing steam fast, even after
several cups of coffee.

But there was no other choice. She had to stay alert.

She had to keep Jenna Reed alive.

Maria pulled the pistol from the back of her waistband and
checked the clip.

Creeping along the hedges connecting the houses, she
stopped mid-way to update Jacoby.

"Circling around to the shed. You two cover the front door
and the patio door in the back. We'll cover all the exits."

"Roger that."

Here we go, Jacoby thought, shoving his phone in his pocket. Both men took their positions as instructed.

Jacoby was glad he had the foresight to contact the neighbors yesterday in the immediate vicinity. Families in a two-block

radius were required to vacate their homes. This gave the FBI some well-needed leverage as they anticipated a showdown with the most notorious of Mason Hamilton's known associates, The Closer.

Maria wasn't taking anything for granted. Approaching the back of the Fortenni house with her weapon drawn, she hoped to use her taser instead. She wanted Mason's man *alive*. No one had to die today. She was after answers, not a body count. But first she had to see who she was up against.

Maria stopped in her tracks behind the shed which took up a sizable portion of the backyard. The shed had two small windows on the side panels and a double-wide door in the front. The back wall was solid with no windows which provided Maria's concealment.

The back wall rumbled against her. Someone was moving inside. Slowly, she curved around the left side. Lifting her head slightly, she was able to peer inside the window.

The man was facing the other way. She couldn't make a positive ID just yet.

He appeared to be getting anxious.

So was she.

Perspiration dripped in a steady stream collecting at the top of her waistband. Maria exchanged her gun for her taser. She was willing to take the chance she could immobilize him before he pulled the trigger.

Maria edged her way under the side window. Even if he peered out the window, he wouldn't be able to immediately see her. She would be in position by then.

The door to the shed was partially open. Perhaps the man was anticipating an attack. *He must be as keen as I am*, she thought, but with one disadvantage.

Size.

Maria was petite and could move a hell of a lot faster than the large man inside the shed. Her reflexes were on point as she crouched down behind the shed door.

No problem, Maria said to herself. At least she wasn't coming up against The Closer. Maybe just one of his hired hands or Mason's.

Although it had been several years since Maria first encountered The Closer on a mission in Alaska, she memorized every detail recorded about him, and his weapon of choice. The FBI's Facial Recognition Database had no definitive matches, but after her quick glance into the shed Maria knew without a doubt, the man hiding inside the shed was *not* The Closer.

Besides the man inside was wielding a gun, not a *knife*.

Almost all of the kills attributed to The Closer involved the same type of hunting knife. The Closer's trademark *slice-and-dice*, as Jacoby liked to call it.

Maria breathed a little easier. She could handle a minion with a gun.

Maria backed up and checked the window again. She watched cautiously as the man rolled up his shirt sleeves, revealing a tattoo of two intertwining snakes on his left arm. The mark of the Russian Alliance, known to be based in New York City.

Still unable to see his face, Maria focused on the man's profile. His left ear was pierced with a large emerald stud. A two-inch scar was evident just south of his left sideburn.

Maria knew *exactly* who was hiding in the shed.

Picking up an empty plastic flower pot lying on the ground, Maria banged it slightly against the door.

The man stepped out, cursing in Russian. He pointed his weapon, ready to launch an attack.

Maria grabbed the edge of the door and slammed it forward, knocking the gun out of his hand. Before he could respond, Maria yanked his arm downward, and threw her body against him. The man fell backwards, unable to regain his footing just as Maria aimed her taser at his ribcage.

Maria locked eyes with him.

Jerking uncontrollably for a few seconds, the man fell sideways then laid still.

Ripping open a flap on her vest, Maria withdrew duck tape and plastic binding. She secured the man's hands, feet and mouth in quick motions.

"One down," she said into her phone.

"Good job. I would expect nothing less."

Maria laughed at Jacoby's comment then got back to work pulling the man's body inside the shed.

*****

Bromley pulled the black Suburban directly behind Maria's car. Keeping the vehicle out of sight was one thing, but he couldn't see what was going on at the Fortenni house. A big disadvantage.

He turned around to address Chase and Jonathan.

"Sit tight. No one is to get out of this car unless I give the word, understand?"

Chase couldn't believe he was stuck in the backseat with Knox of all people. Jenna's kidnapper. Mason Hamilton's errand boy.

Every muscle in Chase's body was flexing, getting ready to lunge. He could feel his fingers closing into tight fists.

More than anything, he wanted to pound Knox to the ground. One smart-ass remark from Knox was all it would take.

Stay in control. For Jenna.

Chase stared straight ahead. He couldn't let Jonathan Knox get to him. But he couldn't help but wonder why Knox was rubbing elbows with the FBI.

Was Knox turning rogue, turning the tables on Mason Hamilton?

Doubtful. Even Knox didn't seem that stupid.

It was more plausible to believe Knox was trying to infiltrate the other side. Whatever Knox's motives were, Chase didn't trust him.

But apparently Jenna did, which irritated Chase.

Jenna had been taken against her will, drugged, and bound by Knox's accomplices. She could positively identify Knox. But yet she flatly refused to file any charges.

There had to be a reason.

*****

Jonathan sized up Chase very quickly.

Tense. Frustrated. Jealous.

Rightly so.

Garrett now had competition.

Jonathan also felt possessive about Jenna, especially after their brief but dynamic interlude in the storage room. Part of her undeniable charm was her fierce, yet vulnerable way of dealing with the crisis moments in her life.

Driven. Passionate. Explosive.

Jenna Reed scared him senseless.

He couldn't breathe much less think when she was close to him. All semblance of reasoning was cast away.

If they had just met under different circumstances, he would have no problem wooing her away from Garrett.

Jonathan hated himself for what he had done.

Why did he let Mason talk him into playing such a role?

Mason's obsession had propelled Jonathan in a direction he wished he'd never gone. Except for meeting Jenna. The only bright spot in this whole mess.

Mason's creative methods of dealing with people were too manipulative and dangerous. Jonathan wanted no part of it.

Had he known Mason Hamilton was capable of such atrocities, Jonathan would have distanced himself years ago.

Now he wished he'd never met Mason Hamilton.

When his father, Elliott Knox, had passed away, Mason stepped up and took Jonathan under his wing. A surrogate father-figure. A teacher. A friend.

Or had Mason been grooming Jonathan for another role?

Jonathan looked away in disgust. Now he was in the FBI's custody. What was next?

Jonathan couldn't figure out why the FBI agents had taken him back to their safe house. After finding him unconscious just outside the restaurant, he was driven to their covert station instead of a hospital.

Were they expecting him to testify against Mason? That had to be it. Yet no one had even mentioned Mason's name.

The agents tended to his head injury, gave him some Advil and told him to lie down in one of the bedrooms.

Without explanation, Jonathan had been summoned by Agent Matthews. He was stuck in the backseat of the SUV, and joined shortly thereafter by Chase Garrett.

Jenna's *friend.*

Just how *friendly* was Garrett? *Apparently not much,* Jonathan speculated. Jenna wouldn't have lost control in his arms if she was tethered to Garrett.

Maybe she's attracted to both of us?

A possibility, but one Jonathan hoped to conquer if given another chance.

Right now he had to focus on something else. Getting away from the FBI.

Jonathan couldn't take a chance the agents would finally get around to questioning him about Mason or his own role in Jenna's kidnapping. He needed to find a way to escape.

Jonathan snapped to attention when Agent Matthews opened his car door.

"Just got a text from Jacoby. He wants me to run recon along the common area behind the neighbors' houses. Turette is expecting more trouble. She's already caught one perp. Doesn't want to take any chances. I'll let you know what I find."

"Ok," Bromley answered, disappointed he had to stay behind and babysit.

Jonathan watched carefully as Agent Matthews moved out of sight. One agent down. It was time to make his move.

When Bromley turned his head to say something to Garrett, Jonathan took his chance.

He jumped from the car, taking off in the opposite direction. Fleeing down a side street, he never looked back although he heard Bromley calling his name.

"Knox! Get the hell back here!"

Bromley got out of the car, but hesitated, trying to decide whether to pursue Knox on foot or stay with Garrett.

Bromley's indecision made him a viable target. As he turned back towards the car, a shot rang out. A bullet pierced his left shoulder causing him to pitch forward.

Bromley had failed to put on his Kevlar vest back at the safe house. His only assignment was to be the driver. He felt no need to wear the heavy vest sitting in a car for a couple of hours. An extremely bad decision.

Fearing additional gunshots, Chase crouched as low as possible in the backseat. Waiting for a few seconds, he peered over the front seat to grab Bromley's cell phone from the center console.

Bromley moaned just outside the car door.

Chase tossed the cell aside then jumped from the car. He dragged Bromley into the back seat. Finding the cell on the floor, Chase pulled up the call log and dialed Jacoby.

"It's Garrett. Bromley's down. Shot rang out when Knox left the car. Get over here quick! Not sure I can stop the bleeding!"

Chase applied pressure to Bromley's wound with both hands. Blood seeped through his fingers and dripped onto the floor.

His actions weren't enough. Bromley's eyes started to close.

"No, you don't. Bromley, you stay with me! Do you hear me? I am *not* giving up and neither are you!"

Bromley coughed as his eyes strained to stay open.

"Bromley, look at me *right now*. I am not going to let you go. Help is on the way."

Chase heard footsteps coming from behind the car. Within seconds, he was pulled backwards.

"Back away, Garrett."

Jacoby and Chase stepped aside to allow the paramedics to climb in the car.

"Good job."

Jacoby tossed Chase a towel from the back of the SUV.

"Ambulance with no siren?"

"Didn't want to set off any flares. We still think we have a good chance of catching whoever is nearby."

"You caught one?"

"Yes. We think he might be one of Hamilton's men. Turette is expecting more to come crawling out of the woodwork."

"Is Jenna still safe?"

"The Fortenni house is covered. Ms. Reed is safe as long as she stays inside."

"Hope you're right about that."

"So do I."

Jacoby grimaced as he watched the ambulance pull away from the curb.

Too many empty houses.

The sniper could be hiding anywhere.

*****

The sound of gunfire outside the house made Jenna and Teresa dive to the living room floor.

"Jenna, get down and stay away from the window!"

Teresa pushed Jenna ahead of her.

Cowering against the side wall, Jenna felt her teeth rattling. She positioned herself to dart into the dining room which was darker and had a higher window.

Strangely, Teresa didn't seem as scared. Jenna wondered if living in fear had hardened Teresa in some way, or maybe she had just developed a stronger sense of bravery.

One shot ringing loud and clear was enough to make Jenna's nerves crumble.

"I just saw a man run across the yard," Teresa whispered as she crept over to where Jenna was crouched. "Stay here. I'm going to the kitchen to get a couple of knives."

"Don't do it, Teresa! I didn't lock the back door. Someone could barge right in!"

"Well I can't sit here and do nothing. The front door and the windows are locked, so at least we will have some notice before they break in."

Jenna watched Teresa sprint to the kitchen. Reaching into her pocket, she closed her fingers around her cell.

Thank God she didn't put it back in her purse!

Jenna's hands were shaking so badly, the cell fell to the floor. She scrambled to pick it up then speed-dialed Chase.

Jenna almost cried when Chase answered.

"Jenna!"

"Chase, you have to help us! We're trapped inside the house! We just heard a shot! I'm so scared!"

"Stay put, Jenna! Don't come outside!"

Chase's voice was drowned out by a deafening sound.

Jenna lifted herself so she could peer out the window. She couldn't believe her eyes. A helicopter was landing on the front lawn.

"They're coming...Chase!"

Jenna scrambled to her feet as Teresa pulled her into the kitchen.

Motioning for Jenna to get behind her, Teresa stood strong as she saw the kitchen door being yanked open.

"Back inside," Maria Turette said forcefully. She ripped open the outside flap on her Kevlar vest to reveal her FBI badge.

"Now!" Maria pushed both hands forward then shut the back door.

Teresa and Jenna retreated to the back of the kitchen, catching their breath.

Maria dialed Thompson, knowing Jacoby had left his position to check on Bromley.

"I'm in the house. Scan perimeter and report. Sniper located?"

"Negative. Additional teams have arrived. We'll spread out and search."

"Keep me updated."

"Will do."

Maria turned back to face Jenna and Teresa.

"FBI Special-Agent in-Charge Maria Turette. Are the two of you ok?"

Jenna and Teresa nodded, but gasped almost in unison as Maria withdrew her gun.

"Need to search the house. Stay put." Maria started to leave, but Teresa stopped her.

"No one else is here. I'm sure of it. Just Jenna and me."

Maria shook her head. "Humor me. I'll be right back."

Darting downstairs, Maria made a quick check of the basement then proceeded upstairs. In a few minutes, she returned to the kitchen.

"All clear," Maria called into her phone, this time directing the call to Jacoby. "Update on Bromley?"

"En route to Charleston General."

Maria dropped her head. "Let me know when you have details. Bring Garrett to the house. Did you find Knox?"

"MIA. We'll keep looking."

Jenna jerked her head, surprised to hear the agent mention Jonathan's name.

"Is Jonathan ok?"

Maria cast a startled look in Jenna's direction. After all, wasn't she supposed to be with Garrett? A love triangle, perhaps?

"We're not sure. He escaped when one of my agents was shot. He took off on foot and no one has been able to locate him yet. How do you know...?"

Maria's question was interrupted by Chase bursting in the back door.

He pulled Jenna into his arms and held on tightly.

Jenna's arms dropped to her sides. She had a dazed look on her face.

"Jenna?"

Chase rubbed his chin on her forehead.

"I don't know what I would have done if I had lost you."

Before Jenna could respond, Agents Jacoby and Thompson barreled in through the back door.

"Still no sign of Knox," said Jacoby.

"I don't think he'll surface."

Conflicting theories were overshadowing Maria's reasoning. Something wasn't adding up. Instead of a sniper aiming for the house, one of her agents was targeted? Someone had created a diversion. Knox's escape was most likely part of a well-calculated plan.

Jacoby turned towards Chase and patted him on the back. "Nice work. You probably saved Bromley's life."

"Yes, thank you," Maria said as she shook Chase's hand. "I'm personally grateful to you for taking care of my agent."

"I'm just glad the paramedics got to him in time. Hey, when can we get out of here?"

"Right now. We'll take you back to your hotel in a few minutes. Get packed and check out. You'll spend the night in our safe house. One of my agents will bring your car there. In the morning, we'll see about getting you home. Where is home by the way?"

"Cape May, New Jersey, for the summer. My brother and my friend are waiting for me there. Do you think it's safe for us to go back? I don't want to bring any trouble there."

"We'll know more tomorrow after we check with some of our sources in the area. I'm not going to sugar-coat this for you, Ms. Reed. We have reason to believe a contract killer was dispatched here on the orders of Mason Hamilton," said Maria.

Jenna tensed as she gripped Chase's hand.

Jacoby took a step towards the door. "The car is in the driveway, black SUV. We'll cover you and Garrett. When I open the back door, I want you to run alongside of me." He glanced back at Maria, "I'll check in when we get to the safe house."

"Thank you. Good work, guys."

Maria and Teresa watched the car pull out of the driveway then took seats at the kitchen table.

"Did you tell her everything?" Maria asked as she unlatched her vest. She tossed it on one of the empty chairs.

"Not everything. I thought I would leave the important parts for you."

Teresa got up from the table. She took two beers out of the fridge. Clanking her bottle against Maria's, she smiled.

"Too early for a beer?"

"Not early enough, old friend."

Chapter 18

Mason Hamilton signed a promotional release and tossed his pen aside. He abhorred the paperwork associated with his position, but nonetheless it was a necessary component to his job.

Placement details, timing of press releases, organizing the extravagant opening gala were just a few of the tasks he gladly delegated. He simply supplied the authority to make the wheels turn.

Dumping the stack of paperwork on his senior administrator's desk, Mason whirled around and headed back to his office. He stopped momentarily to cast a glance over his shoulder.

His staff was scurrying around at a quick pace.

Minions.

No matter what inane request Mason generated, his subordinates heeded his wishes, almost groveling at his feet.

It was almost pathetic.

For what, Mason wondered. Money? His staff made decent salaries. Pride in their jobs? Maybe for some when the exhibits opened. No, it was something else.

Mason held back a snicker as he watched his nervous employees trying to focus on their job tasks with his eyes bearing down on them.

Fear, the best motivator of all.

Leaning in the doorway of his corner office, Mason felt cocky as hell. He had his staff right where he wanted them. They were afraid *not* to do a good job.

Mason rubbed his hands vigorously as he anticipated the next round of profitability reports. Checking his pc for the current projections, his grin grew even wider.

Pre-order ticket sales were booming. The exhibit's advertising ran the gamut of printed materials, radio, television and the internet. The exhibit was even on Facebook this year.

Mason couldn't be happier.

Actually, he could.

Finding his treasure pieces would make him ecstatic.

"Jenna Reed," Mason said between gritted teeth. "I know you have what I want. I can *feel* it. I am so close."

There was little satisfaction in coming close.

There was only agony knowing success was yet to come.

Mason gripped the arms of his chair as a wave of heated tension washed over him. He was tired of waiting. Thirty years was more than enough.

Patience, The Closer had told him in his last report.

Patience and strategy will bring the desired result.

"Patience, my ass," Mason grumbled.

The Closer didn't seem to fully appreciate Mason's timetable. But what could he do? The Closer was the best, and he could get the job done better than anyone.

Even if he felt the need to change Mason's plans from time to time.

The modified plan in South Carolina had worked. The FBI had been fooled to believe Jenna Reed's life was in danger when the real purpose of the diversion was to get Jonathan Knox out of the FBI's clutches.

Mason was concerned Jonathan would only incriminate himself if the FBI started grilling him or worse yet, cast another dark shadow over Mason himself. Mason had no trouble throwing doubt on federal allegations, but Jonathan wasn't quite as finessed.

Besides, there was really no need to track Jenna Reed any longer. She would be coming to New York soon enough on her own accord. The Closer could deal with her there.

Right now, Mason had to focus on another matter.

Meet with Kelly. Tell her I expect her cooperation. I will not tolerate her inability to do her job. She should know the consequences by now.

Mason hit the send button which forwarded his email to George Maylor. The next phase of his plan would begin soon.

Everything had to be in place and *everyone* had to be onboard.

*****

Kelly left a note for Austin before she left for the Promenade. Another meeting with George was taking up precious moments she'd rather be spending with Austin at home.

Home, Kelly mused as she jogged up Congress Street. *Home* had such a nice ring to it. *Home with Austin.* All these days and nights they spent together curled up on the old sofa, walking along the beach hand-in-hand, cooking pancakes together...made her feel so good, and so sad.

How she wished she could tell her father what she really thought of him and his stupid treasure hunt. Mason was becoming too neurotic, and Kelly wondered how many more people he would hurt before his little game was over.

Her cheeks were getting hot as she picked up her pace. Remembering her last meeting with Mason was making her extremely agitated.

"I need you. You are part of the plan," Mason had drilled into Kelly before she left for Cape May.

"Right," Kelly said as she pounded the pavement harder.

Much to Kelly's chagrin, Mason's cruel plan was progressing. Although she still didn't know all the details, Kelly received a text to meet George Maylor on the Promenade this morning.

Nothing could make her feel worse.

She was forced to leave the comfort of Austin's bed to meet her father's envoy.

Once again, Mason was ruining her happiness.

But Mason would be the first to tell her he didn't care about her happiness or anyone else's, for that matter. He was only concerned with *obedience*.

It was a horrible way to live. Kelly wondered how she had possibly survived this long without falling over the cliff.

Kelly slowed her pace to avoid being run over by an older couple riding a tandem bike. As she neared the end of the Promenade, she spotted George seated on a bench watching the ocean.

Blending in just like one of the tourists.

Except he was one of the bad guys.

Kelly wondered if Mason was holding any type of threat over George's head as well, or if he had been merely sent to Cape May to make sure she did her part. One thing was for sure, Mason's methods of motivation were extreme, one way or another.

And that was the only reason she was heeding his threats.

Kelly slowed to a stop taking a few deep breaths. There was no way she wanted to sit on the same bench with George. She bent down to tie her shoe.

George leaned closer.

"Your father is not happy with you."

"I'm not happy with him, so we're even."

George laughed. Either Kelly was being downright defiant, or she was too scared to think straight.

"I could care less what you think of your father. You got a job to do and so do I. He's expecting you to do what he says. He's got no patience for people who don't follow his orders. Oh, and he wanted me to tell you, you should know what the consequences will be."

Kelly couldn't even look at George. She barely heard what he said. She was too focused on Austin. Her betrayal was going to devastate him.

"Tomorrow night. We're having *company*. Make yourself presentable."

George snickered as he got up to leave.

Kelly turned and ran in the opposite direction.

She couldn't even justify George's degradation with a single word.

*****

Hans Kliric kept his eyes on the road and his mouth shut.

The Closer insisted they take a car to New Jersey instead of the helicopter to keep a low profile. The FBI would be searching all major airports, train stations and bus terminals along the East Coast. A car and back roads were the way to go.

Hans had no desire to engage in a conversation.

Mason had put The Closer in charge and told Hans he was to obey every word the man said.

Hans didn't like it when the rules changed.

But he would never question Mason's authority. He saw firsthand what happened to people who did.

Finally, The Closer broke the silence.

"We'll stop in Virginia overnight. I need supplies. I don't like to depend on anyone even though Mason tells me his New Jersey resource is reliable."

"You think of everything."

"I have to; reliance on others can be quite detrimental."

Hans cracked his knuckles. He wondered if The Closer's comments were directed at him or at Dimitri, who had chosen to hide in the shed instead of following The Closer's instructions to take out the female agent.

Dimitri's untimely mistake had cost him his freedom.

Hans cursed in Russian. He could think of no words in English to describe how much he disliked The Closer.

"Keep your comments to yourself," The Closer stated in a harsh tone, "Or I'll have to show you how I got my reputation."

Hans jerked his head in astonishment. Just his luck.

The Closer understood Russian.

*****

Kelly ran an extra mile trying to shake thoughts of her father and George Maylor out of her head. But it hadn't worked.

Pent up anger was consuming her.

She needed a cool drink and a shower, in that order. Grabbing a water bottle from the fridge, she noticed her laptop was open on the table. Her inbox was glaring at her.

She hoped Austin hadn't seen her messages.

How could she possibly explain herself?

Kicking off her sneakers, she threw them in the guest bedroom in frustration.

She certainly hoped the shower would calm her nerves.

The bathroom on the lower level had an antique claw-foot tub which had been updated with modern fixtures. Stepping inside, Kelly immediately felt relief as the pulsating water soothed the muscles of her back.

"Ahh…"

As the steam rose, her body began to ease out the rigidness. She closed her eyes and breathed deeply. Oblivious to anything but the sound of the soothing waterfall, Kelly didn't hear the door open.

The shower curtain parted slightly.

"Beautiful."

Kelly smiled before she turned around. She had grown accustomed to Austin's voice, always appreciating his compliments.

"Like what you see?"

"Absolutely."

Within seconds, Austin stripped down and joined her.

"There's not much room in here."

Austin pulled Kelly's arms up to his neck.

"We don't need much room."

The old tub creaked as their bodies swayed in a gentle motion. As the water cascaded down their bodies, Kelly felt completely at peace. She was lost in Austin's arms, where she wanted to be more than anything.

*****

George sauntered into Swain's Hardware, pulling out his list. Mason had been very specific regarding the items George needed to purchase in preparation for The Closer's arrival. He grabbed a cart and made his way down the first aisle.

"Hey, George," Malcolm called, giving a wave.

Malcolm had been at Swain's for as long as George had lived in Cape May. The tall, thin man with the wiry hair always made George uneasy. Malcolm had eyes like a hawk. He always made a point to hover. It was so annoying; George could barely stand it.

"Malcolm."

"Need help, George?"

Shifty eyes watching his every move. George wished he had driven the extra few miles up Route 9 to the Home Depot. At least he wouldn't be hounded.

"No, I can find everything myself. Thanks, Malcolm."

"No trouble at all, George."

George hurried off with his cart. He didn't have time for this...*not today*. George hoped Malcolm would just go back to the registers and leave him the hell alone.

"Buying some things for your restaurant, George?" Malcolm asked as he followed George down the paint aisle.

Was Malcolm following him on purpose?

"Just some things I need for the house."

Malcolm tapped his finger on the tarps in George's cart.

"A paint job? You know we have a few college guys here who could help you with that. They're always looking for some odd jobs. Extra money for school."

"No, thanks. I can handle it."

George quickly steered around the corner. As he picked up a bundle of rope, George glanced over his shoulder and let out a deep breath. Malcolm had disappeared.

Finally.

As George turned around to face the cart again, Malcolm was standing in front of him. George jumped backwards.

"Didn't mean to startle you, George. We have a sale today on bird seed. You need any for your bird feeders?"

How could Malcolm possibly know he had bird feeders in his backyard?

George panicked. Maybe Malcolm was one of Mason's spies. What other explanation could there be?

George pulled out his handkerchief and wiped the sweat running down his sideburn.

"No...thank you. I don't want to keep you from other customers, Malcolm. I can find my way around the store. It's not like I haven't been here before."

"No problem at all, George. We're a little slow anyway. I'm here to help you in any way I can."

What was that supposed to mean?

George focused on his list and tried to steady his hands. Just a couple more items to go.

Tossing a box of large black trash bags and a roll of duck tape into his cart, George quickly headed for the register.

Casey Reynolds, the daughter of George's neighbor two doors down, was working the register. On summer break from Penn State, she had been working at Swain's for the past two summers. She waved at George to come to her register.

"Hi, Mr. Maylor."

Seeing a friendly face, George breathed a sigh of relief. He started to unload his cart.

Just as George put the last item on the belt, Malcolm stepped up and gently pushed Casey aside.

"Take your break now, Casey."

"Figures," George muttered as the young cashier left her post.

George swore Malcolm was taking special note of everything he seemed to be buying. Nosy pain-in-the-ass.

"Fifty-five ninety-three, George."

Fumbling with his wallet, George withdrew three twenties and practically rammed them into Malcolm's hand.

He just wanted to get home. Away from Malcolm's watchful eyes.

"Take care, George," Malcolm called as George practically ran to his car, the bags jostling in his hands.

Malcolm couldn't suppress his laughter any longer. George certainly had been flustered. No wonder. It wasn't every day meek and mild-mannered George Maylor got to play ball with the big boys.

As soon as George's car sped out of the parking lot, Malcolm's cell phone was in his hand. It was time to call in.

"Maylor just left. You're good to go."

*****

It was late by the time The Closer and Hans arrived in Virginia, finding a nondescript motel just off the interstate. The Closer paid for separate rooms, assuring him the privacy he needed to make a couple of phone calls.

"I miss you," he said in a low, hushed tone.

"Then get yourself back to Texas."

"As soon as I can, I promise. Then I'm all yours."

"Hmmm..."

"Still there?"

"Yes, just thinking about the possibilities."

A smile formed on The Closer's lips. Her sultry voice and innuendos always did a number on him.

"Keep your mind *and* your body focused. We will need to get re-acquainted at a fast pace."

"Looking forward to it," she said before blowing a kiss through the phone.

The Closer tossed the phone on the bed with regret. He had pacified his woman in Texas, once again with necessary lies.

Now for the second call. Another woman. Different priorities.

"I've been waiting to hear your voice."

The Closer let his eyes fall. He knew his betrayal would haunt him forever.

"I need you to do a job for me."

"As always, you know I can't resist."

The Closer paced the floor, hoping to end the conversation soon. But he knew it was almost inevitable. The teasing. The phone sex foreplay.

Mallory Kincaid wouldn't settle for anything less.

"I'll be in touch in a few days."

"We need to meet, so I can *feel* your touch."

"Mallory...," The Closer groaned.

His heart was promised to another, but his body was always the price Mallory demanded.

"Oh, quit the drama. I know what you need and it isn't always *mission-related*."

"You know where my priorities lie."

"Obviously, they lie with me or you wouldn't be calling."

Mallory Kincaid was too close of an ally to turn down. She knew his secrets better than anyone.

He had to keep her satisfied, one way or another.

Chapter 19

George dialed Teresa's number before he went to bed. He needed to hear her voice, which reminded him of the *only* reason he obeyed Mason Hamilton's every command.

She was worth every sacrifice he had to make.

"Hi, Hon, how are you doing?"

"Fine, just fine, George. How was your day?"

Teresa balanced her cell against her ear as she continued to pack her suitcase. It was time to go home. She had played her part. She needed to get back to Cape May as quickly as possible so George wouldn't be suspicious.

"I'm coming home in a couple of days. I was trying to get a flight out tomorrow, but they're all booked, so you can expect me the following day."

"That's great. Can't wait to see you. Need to get some sleep now. You know I rise early to get to the restaurant. Love you."

"Love you too, George. I'll call you when I get to the airport. If you're not too busy, maybe you can pick me up. Talk to you tomorrow."

Teresa hung up quickly. She was afraid if she kept George on the phone any longer, he would start asking her about her dear old aunt who didn't exist, or her cousin who didn't live in Florida.

Besides, it was time to check in with Maria.

"I'm just about done here."

"Ok, I'll let Jacoby know and he'll dispatch a team. We have to gut the house. We can't have any evidence linking you to your alias in Cape May."

"Such a comforting thought...*gutting* the house."

"Ok...sometimes I don't choose the right words. Too many years of chasing the bad guys. Guess I've lost some of my softer touches. Would you prefer...?"

Teresa laughed.

"No, Maria, don't change on account of me. Stay the way you are. Are you back in D.C.?"

"Just got home a few minutes ago. We hit a lot of traffic around the airport."

"Guess you had some time to apologize to your husband."

"He told me he wouldn't accept an apology until we got home and up the stairs."

"Then I better let you go. I'll call you when I get back to Cape May."

Teresa grabbed her bags and headed out the back door. Taking one last look at the house where she had perpetuated her alias for over thirty years, she whistled.

Time had passed too quickly.

She wondered if there was any chance to catch up.

*****

Austin was gently snoring in her ear. Kelly couldn't imagine ever falling asleep again without his arms wrapped around her. She didn't want to imagine it. The thought of waking up alone without him was too painful.

She had fallen in love with Austin Reed.

Love. Was she fooling herself? With Mason Hamilton as her father, was she even capable of loving anyone?

Kelly wanted to believe she could. She just needed the right man. And he was holding her right now.

Kelly shuddered against Austin's arm, hoping she wouldn't wake him.

In less than twenty-four hours, he would be taken away from her. They would never have a chance together. If Austin ever found out what she had done, he'd never want to lay his eyes on her again.

Kelly ran downstairs to get dressed, and wiped the tears from her eyes. Today was the day she would betray her lover. She hated herself for it.

When Kelly arrived at the arcade along Beach Avenue, George was already there. She spotted him immediately. He couldn't be missed in his loud Hawaiian shirt.

Kelly could hardly bear the thought of actually working closely with George tonight. He made her skin crawl.

"Not sure why your father wanted us to meet again. Guess he still has doubts about your *capabilities* for tonight's activities.

He thinks you need a reminder. He's very *concerned*," George said as Kelly slid onto the stool next to him.

"My father wouldn't know *concerned* if it came up and bit him in the ass."

"You got attitude, that's good. Should help you stay focused. Anyway, the team will be arriving after dark. You should get ready just after dinner. I'll be over around seven or so. I'll come in through the basement. Don't worry; I'll bring the items we need. All you need to do is entertain Austin in the living room and give him some of his *special* beer."

George peered around to see if anyone was within earshot. No one was in their immediate vicinity, except for two teenage boys playing skee-ball in the back.

"Is that all?"

"Got somewhere to be? Can't stand to be out of the sack for too long? Yeah, that's right. I figured out how you're distracting Austin. I know you're not playing cards over there."

Kelly felt so ashamed. She hurried out of the arcade as fast as she could.

She had no desire to spend even one more second in George Maylor's company.

*****

Austin rolled over and felt Kelly's empty pillow.

"Another run?"

He yawned which turned into a big smile.

He was happy. Happier than he had been in a long time. Kelly was definitely the reason.

Grinning profusely, Austin padded down the steps to the kitchen in search of some coffee.

Kelly's laptop was partially open and email was up. Austin couldn't help but notice her in-box.

Who the hell was this character named "NYOne"? The same person had sent her dozens of messages since she arrived in Cape May.

Her father?

Kelly said he lived in New York. Had to be.

What a major pain-in-the-ass. Kelly never had a moment's peace. No wonder she couldn't stand him.

Her father was driving her crazy. Calls, texts, emails. *What was his problem anyway?*

Austin shut Kelly's laptop and carried it to the guestroom. Her father had pestered her enough.

She needed to relax. No distractions.

Whatever her father's petty needs were, they would just have to wait. Austin planned to occupy all of Kelly's time today. For once, she would belong *only to him.*

Hearing Kelly's footsteps on the stairs, Austin held the door open for her. "Did you have a good run?"

Kelly didn't answer. She reached up to touch Austin's face. He hadn't shaved yet, and she felt the early morning stubble on his chin.

So incredibly sexy. She couldn't resist rubbing her hand across his cheek.

Kelly pulled Austin's lips to her own. She kissed him ever so lightly, knowing from prior experience, it drove him crazy.

Austin responded by pushing Kelly down on the table.

"Don't you dare."

"Then tell me to stop," Austin teased as he playfully bit her ear.

"I…can't."

Kelly was enjoying every moment, every bit of affection Austin wanted to give her.

Her phone buzzed inside the pocket of her shorts. All Kelly could do was shake her head while Austin fumed in frustration. He backed away and pulled Kelly upright.

"Your father?"

"Yes."

Austin felt his temperament rising. He hated the man already and he hadn't even met him.

In a sudden move, Austin grabbed Kelly's phone and stormed out of the kitchen. He threw the phone next to her laptop on the bed in the guestroom.

Kelly was hunched over the kitchen table, crying when Austin returned.

"Why can't he leave you alone?"

"I don't know, Austin."

"Whatever it is, you don't have to take it anymore. I'm here and I want you to stay with me. Do you understand, Kelly? I want *you* to be with *me*. You don't need your father...*anymore*."

Austin bent down to scoop Kelly into his arms.

She let her tears flow. Tears stored up so long inside her, she had been afraid to let them come out.

Until now.

Chapter 20

Jenna balked at Jacoby's suggestion when they were taking a break at a rest stop in North Carolina. Driving straight to Cape May from Folly Beach? Even without traffic, the journey alone would take over twelve hours.

"Are you out of your mind?"

Jenna shook her head in between sips of her Diet Pepsi.

"If we don't stop overnight, you may have a mad woman on your hands. I can't stand to be in this car much longer."

Jacoby frowned, but relented not wanting to deal with a frustrated, hysterical female.

"I'll call Turette. We'll stop somewhere in Virginia."

Jacoby nodded to Thompson and they both started to walk back to the cars.

"Thank you," Jenna called over her shoulder. She squeezed Chase's hand to hold him back. She wanted a few moments alone with him.

"I'm sorry. I guess I'm still on edge. A lot has happened the past few days. It's hard to deal with all of it."

Chase rubbed Jenna's shoulder. "I think you're holding up pretty good. Don't be so hard on yourself."

"I'm glad you're here," Jenna said as she nestled closer.

"I'm glad you want me here."

Jenna pulled back to look into Chase's eyes. What was she seeing? Commitment, passion...*love*?

Everything she wanted.

And was afraid to lose.

*****

Maria Turette knew her job, and she did it well. Recruited by the CIA in her junior year of college, she took an undercover assignment as soon as it was offered to her. She learned quickly there were consequences to every action done wrong, and she tried her best not to repeat any.

But in the beginning of her illustrious career which spanned over three decades now, she had certainly made quite a few.

Some which would haunt her forever.

Maria never turned down any assignment, no matter how dangerous or mundane. She was revered within the rank and file. Even her superiors took notice. Maria Turette wouldn't back down. *Not ever.*

Against insurmountable odds in Alaska, she led a team against a hostage situation. Taking out two snipers, she maneuvered her way inside the rigged building, retrieving the young family taken against their will. Within minutes, Maria and her agents pulled the family to safety before the building exploded.

Her first encounter with The Closer.

She would never forget it.

He had escaped, but not before Maria had come so close to shooting him. Her decision to retrieve the family first allowed The Closer to slip through her clutches dressed as a paramedic.

Later when surveillance scans were being reviewed, Maria spotted him, realizing her team had let a known assassin walk right through a crime scene.

Maria and her superiors had mixed feelings about the outcome of the mission. It certainly had been successful on a personal level. All four hostages had been rescued, unharmed. But The Closer had gotten away. A win and a loss for the FBI.

Seemed to be a recurring theme. The Closer. Mason Hamilton. Always a few steps ahead of the law.

There had to be a reason.

Maria wracked her brain. None of the answers she came up with made any sense. Except one which made her sick to her stomach.

A traitor in her unit.

She refused to believe it.

The theory kept proving itself over and over. Someone on the inside was feeding Mason Hamilton and The Closer enough details about her unit so they could circumvent Maria's missions.

But who?

Not one of her agents had a questionable background that she knew about. They had all passed screenings, excelled at Quantico, and took risks right alongside of her.

In successes…and failures.

Maria recalled the numerous times she attempted to bring down Mason Hamilton and it gave her a headache.

Countless accusations and three arrests. All shot down. The most time Mason spent behind bars was two hours, only because his lawyer had been stuck in traffic.

The District Attorney's office wouldn't even talk to Maria's unit anymore. Filing charges seemed to be a complete waste of time on everyone's part.

Mason would waltz into the court house and right back out again. But not before he bent the ear of the press. Mason made sure he got his air time...spouting off how it was a case of mistaken identity, or the FBI was running out of suspects, or...

God, Maria groaned.

She felt so alone in her pursuit.

Mason Hamilton was the one case she had never closed. It was the one she wished to God she had never opened so many years ago.

Maria closed her eyes, wondering where the years had gone. It seemed like yesterday she was graduating from college and looking forward to a lucrative career. The CIA *wanted* her! She had been so thrilled to be selected by such a prestigious organization.

How naïve and stupid she had been.

Too young and inexperienced to figure out she was being used, over and over. Too driven to excel, at any cost.

Shot twice, beaten unconscious, left for dead, not to mention sacrificing her personal happiness along the way. Had it been worth it? Maria wasn't so sure now.

Yes, she had earned a reputation for being at the top of her game. A time or two she had been thrust into the spotlight, catching the eyes of the powers-that-be at the FBI. During a joint task-force assignment, the FBI made her an offer she couldn't refuse.

She traded one badge for another. But yet here she was, still chasing her tail. Same target, different agency.

Too many years of fighting uphill battles was starting to wear on her.

She was getting tired. At 51, she had seen too much violence, too many lives severed or damaged by the horrific acts of madmen. She had caught quite a few.

All except one.

And she was willing to do just about anything to make that happen.

*****

A soft knock came to George Maylor's back door. Anxiety swelled inside him, but also a level of confidence. He had successfully done his part in the plan. Mason would be pleased. Now, The Closer's team could do the rest.

George opened the door and joined The Closer and Hans outside. He said nothing, merely pointing to the basement entrance of the Reeds' house and led the way.

Once inside, George turned on a battery-powered lantern he had placed just inside the door.

As the room lit up from the lantern's muted glow, The Closer and Hans finally saw the *package* they had been commissioned to bring to New York.

On the floor was a rolled up rug from one of the upstairs bedrooms.

Inside was Austin Reed, unconscious, bound and gagged.

"Check outside. Make sure no one is around," The Closer indicated to George.

Hans kicked one of Austin's shoes but there was no response. He shook his head.

"Good. Let's move."

The Closer and Hans hauled the rug into the van as George gripped the edge of the van door to keep it open.

They're going to kill him; I just know it.

George was noticeably shaking now as the van door wobbled.

Hans gave George a disgusted look, conveying his disdain for George's cowardice. He couldn't understand how Mason could choose such resources without an ounce of bravery. Hans spat on the ground as The Closer shut the van doors.

"Get in the van," The Closer ordered Hans in a low tone. "I'll be right back."

Time to tie up loose ends, The Closer chuckled to himself. Wasn't that one of Mason's favorite phrases?

"Where is the girl?" The Closer asked George as they returned to George's house.

"Probably still crying her eyes out. She could hardly do what she was supposed to, but I made her come around. I had to slap her a couple times," George said, trying to brag. Maybe a little show of backbone would impress Mason's number one hit man.

"A man who takes charge. I like that, George."

"I did everything Mason wanted. Once Reed passed out, I carried him down to the basement. Actually, I just kind of rolled him down the steps. I'm sure he didn't feel anything. He was out cold after she drugged him."

"Did you take the picture?"

"Yes. It's in an envelope on the kitchen table. I wrote the note on the back exactly like Mason said."

"Good. I'll be back in a few minutes. Stay here."

"Where are you going?" George asked, nervously.

"Hunting," The Closer replied as he unsheathed his knife. Keeping it close to his leg, he walked back to the Reeds' house.

George could hardly breathe. He knew The Closer was undoubtedly searching for Kelly…and what he would probably do to her if he found her.

A few minutes later, The Closer returned.

"Did…you find her?" George stuttered.

"No. She must have taken off. I don't have time to deal with Kelly McBride right now. Mason can track his daughter himself. Other tasks demand my attention. Where are the supplies I requested?"

"Right here." George led The Closer into the dining room. He had lined up all of the items neatly in a row. Large plastic trash bags, rope, towels, disinfecting wipes, and paint tarps.

"Is everything to your liking?" George asked, painfully aware his hands were shaking. He shoved them in his pants pockets so The Closer would not notice.

The Closer said nothing. Instead, he began to lay the trash bags on the floor, overlaying them so no parts of the floor were bare. He motioned to George to help him until the entire box was empty.

George was puzzled, but didn't dare question The Closer's methods.

"That will do," The Closer said, tossing the empty box aside. "We need to move the table. Push it to the wall."

George leaned against the table and pushed until it banged against the wall. Teresa wouldn't be happy. He had nicked the paint just below the windowsill. George made a mental note to touch it up before she got home.

Assuming the windows were all closed due to the a/c blasting, The Closer nodded. There was no need to alarm the neighbors.

"Close the blinds."

George obediently ran around to shut the blinds in the living room, dining room and kitchen. He finally returned as The Closer finished sending a text.

Probably to Mason, George thought. Even a professional hit man had to check in with the Great Man himself. George hid a smile, realizing Mason trusted him enough to be an assistant to The Closer, of all people.

"Do you need me for anything else?" George asked, with a renewed sense of pride. His nervousness was gone now.

The Closer beckoned George to join him in the middle of the room on top of the trash bags. The Closer's lips curved into a twisted smile.

George was bewildered. *How could he possibly...?*

"Your services are no longer required."

The Closer grabbed George from behind and thrust the knife into his side. The upward tilt and jerking motion was all that was necessary.

George had followed his last command on behalf of Mason Hamilton.

The Closer withdrew his knife, and then wiped it on a towel. Turning on his heels, The Closer never looked back.

What was the point?

This was just another business arrangement. Nothing more.

Once inside the van, The Closer made another call.

"Clean-up requested."

Malcolm responded immediately.

"Confirmed."

His crew would arrive at daybreak to take care of what The Closer left behind.

*****

Kelly held her breath. She couldn't believe she had been spared.

Just a few minutes ago, she heard footsteps approaching the bedroom across from Austin's where she was hiding.

Whoever was in the house was looking for her. To hurt her. Or kill her.

After George had slapped her several times, Kelly ran upstairs. She was hysterical after seeing Austin collapse on the sofa. He had taken the beer she offered him without question.

Trusting her completely. Not realizing what she had done.

What she had been forced to do.

George repeated Mason's warning. He would tolerate no failures. If she didn't do her part and drug Austin, Mason would send someone to kill her. Plain and simple.

Hiding was the only answer. Thankfully, she knew of just the place.

One day when Austin was giving her a tour of the house he showed her a small compartment behind the closet in his parents' room. He and Jenna had discovered the "little room" when they were children playing hide-and-seek.

Barely big enough to contain her adult body, Kelly had crouched inside and closed the small door behind her. She could taste the salt from her tears. She closed her eyes and prayed.

She lifted her head and listened.

The footsteps were going down the stairs. Whoever had come inside was now gone.

Too afraid to move, she remained still.

Within a few minutes, she heard the tires crunching on the stones. The van was leaving.

They were taking Austin away…from her.

Crying softly, she finally let her head drop to her knees. It was hot inside the small room and Kelly finally succumbed to her exhaustion.

Morning came sooner than she expected. Light snuck under the door to wake her.

She was grateful to be alive.

By telling Kelly about the little room, Austin had saved her life. Now she was determined to save his.

Kelly climbed out of the room, her back and legs aching from being in a cramped position for several hours. She glanced out the bedroom window which looked down onto the driveway.

She heard voices and was puzzled. A white truck with "Peterson's Painting Service" etched on the side was now parked in the driveway.

George was having his house painted?

How could he possibly go back to his normal way of life after what he did to Austin?

How could she?

Kelly's hand trembled as she slowly opened the door to Austin's room. She didn't want to go back to any life that didn't include Austin. She wanted *him*.

Kelly curled herself around Austin's pillow. More than anything she wanted to rewind time until she was surrounded by Austin's warm body and his sheltering arms. But the tighter she held Austin's pillow, the colder it became.

The longer she lay in the bed alone, the more depressed she felt. Finally, Kelly pulled herself up. Wishing wasn't going to bring Austin back.

Walking into the kitchen, Kelly immediately noticed the large tan envelope addressed to Jenna. George must have left it because it hadn't been there earlier.

The back flap was not closed. Pulling out the contents, Kelly nearly choked from the bile rising up in her throat.

It was a picture of Austin tied up and unconscious.

Kelly turned the picture over and saw the written message: *Call when you get to New York.* Underneath the words, a phone number was listed.

She knew that number. *Quite well.*

Jenna was being lured to New York to hand over the treasure, and Austin was the bait.

Chapter 21

Jonathan rode the elevator with his head hung low.

What could he say to account for his actions?

I can't get Jenna out of my mind.

Mason would never understand.

Jonathan stopped short just outside Mason's door. Mason was on the phone, but as usual he was spouting off loudly. Jonathan had no trouble hearing part of the conversation.

"Well done. Your payment has been wired. Yes, I'm sure you checked the house thoroughly. Kelly will find her way home eventually. Sometimes I just have to yank on the chain a little harder."

Mason laughed.

"Yes, I'm sure. I need you to stay in the city to guard my *package*. I will speak with you tomorrow."

Mason hung up the phone then opened his door.

"Jonathan, please come in. How was your flight? I understand it was longer than expected."

"Cut the crap, Mason. You and I both know you don't give a damn about my travel arrangements."

"Such crass terms. Perhaps Hans and Dimitri corrupted you. Be assured, I do care about your travel plans, especially when they go *against* my direct orders."

Stab number one, Jonathan thought, averting Mason's glare.

"What do you want from me, Mason? To run H-K when you step down? I'm prepared to do that. But don't send me on a fool's errand and then reprimand me when I don't play according to your rule book. It's a waste of my time."

Mason clapped Jonathan on the back.

"Nothing I require of you is a waste of time. I merely thought we could approach Jenna Reed from a different angle, but it didn't play out that way. I arranged for your return to the city because this exhibit goes live in less than two months. You needed to come back where you belong."

"With you."

"Precisely."

Jonathan began to fume.

"Your little escapade has been forgiven. We must now focus on the exhibit. Other matters involving Jenna Reed need to be tabled for now. Do you understand?"

Jonathan looked away.

"Well?"

"I heard you the first time."

Mason knew he had touched a chord of discontent.

"We will meet with Media Production tomorrow to preview the layouts for distribution. That will be all."

Jonathan was dismissed with a wave of Mason's hand.

Mason leaned back in his chair, lacing his fingers behind his head.

Jonathan needed to be put in his place.

Just like all the other players in the game.

*****

Chase pulled alongside the curb at the Reeds' beach house. He had been told to wait while Jacoby and Thompson searched the house.

A few minutes later, Jacoby came bounding down the steps and leaned in Chase's side window.

"All clear. You're free to go inside. Here's my card...call us if you need anything. We'll be nearby keeping an eye on the house. A team from the Atlantic City field office will be here tomorrow."

Jenna didn't even wait for the agents to get in their car. She raced up the side steps.

"You know, this is precisely the place where you dumped me the first time. It's like déjà vu, don't you think?"

Jenna stopped on the landing. Chase's stinging remark cut her deeply.

"You're right," Jenna said, not knowing quite how to respond.

Chase hustled up the steps to join her.

"I am *not* leaving you unless you tell me to go."

"I'm sorry," Jenna said, feeling a drain of energy. She opened the kitchen door and her eyes fell on the envelope.

Reaching inside, she withdrew the photo.

"Oh, God, Chase!"

Jenna stared in horror as the picture fell from her hand.

"Is this your brother?"

Jenna's blank stare confirmed his guess.

"Hamilton wants to trade Austin for…the *treasure*."

"What haven't you told me, Jenna?"

Jenna laid her head against Chase's forehead.

"You should leave…right now. Get on the first plane to Boston. Let me go to New York…*alone*."

"Not going to happen. What kind of man do you think I am?"

"Hopefully the kind who's smart enough to know when it's time to quit and go home."

"Well I guess I'm an idiot then, because I have no intention of…."

The house phone rang, startling them both.

Jenna grabbed the receiver, assuming she knew who was calling.

"Hello?"

"Good afternoon, Ms. Reed."

*****

Teresa was annoyed. George wasn't picking up the house phone, his cell, and no one at Molly's had seen him all day.

"Where are you, George?" Teresa muttered to herself as she headed to the shuttle desk at the Atlantic City airport.

At three p.m., she finally arrived home. The house seemed strangely different for some reason, Teresa thought as she deposited her suitcase by the stairwell.

Heaviness hung in the air. Something she just couldn't put her finger on.

Teresa headed into the kitchen. Something was definitely different. The dishes were actually in the dish rack and the garbage had been taken out.

Maybe George had missed her so much he was trying to impress her. Probably not.

Maybe Jenna had stopped by and tidied up. That was a much better theory.

She hadn't noticed it the first time since she had been anxious for a cup of coffee. But now, as Teresa brought her mug through the dining room, her eyes focused on the floor.

"Oh, George," Teresa complained as she ran her fingers over the deep indentation. "What in the hell were you doing?"

Last August, they spent thousands for a floor specialist to re-do the hardwoods, wanting the old distressed look which had recently become popular again.

Teresa was now seeing stars.

"George!"

No answer.

*****

"Ms. Reed, I trust you arrived safely in Cape May," Mason Hamilton said sarcastically into the phone.

Jenna fought the urge to scream or provide a smartass remark. She needed to focus on getting Austin back in one piece.

"I got your calling card."

"You know what I want then. I'm sure you don't want to see your brother pay for the sins of your family."

"He better be alive when I get there."

"Of course, Ms. Reed, you have my word. Bring me my treasure and I will reunite you with your brother. Come alone. Call me when you get to New York."

Jenna slammed the phone down so forcibly it fell out of its cradle.

"The son-of-a-bitch was taunting me. *Call me when you get to New York* – that's the same friggin' message on the back of the picture."

Chase turned the picture over. Sure enough, Hamilton had repeated his threat.

"I was right about the trade."

"And you're going to just hand it over to him?"

"Not without a fight."

"Then I'm fighting with you."

"You're not going to leave no matter what I say, are you?"

"Not a chance. Do you want to tell me how I can help or should I just continue to get in your way?"

"You're pretty awesome when you get riled up."

Chase pulled Jenna towards him.

"So are you."

"Ok then. Follow me, *Dr. Watson*."

Jenna led Chase down to the basement. She knelt in front of an old metal cabinet at the foot of the stairs.

"Please tell me you're saying a prayer."

"Not exactly."

Jenna pulled the bottom drawer of the cabinet towards her until it stopped on its track.

"What are you doing?"

"When I was meeting with Teresa, she gave me a letter from my mom. She's the one who buried the treasure."

Chase's jaw dropped.

"It's here? In this cabinet?"

"That's what we going to find out."

Jenna yanked on the drawer harder until it came off its track. Pushing it aside, she laid down on her stomach and stretched her arms until they couldn't go any farther.

Her fingers groped in the darkness. Finally she felt it. The box.

Jenna's heart was pounding with anticipation. Tugging on the corners, it came free. It had been wedged behind the back of the track where it couldn't be easily seen when the drawer was opened.

Jenna slid out from underneath the cabinet. Sitting on the floor with the box in her lap, she didn't notice her face and t-shirt were covered with dirt. She was too mesmerized.

"I can't believe this."

She was almost afraid to open the lid.

Was this worth killing for?

Chase watched intently. Jenna slowly opened the metal box. Inside was an old handkerchief tied in a knot. Jenna untied the knot to reveal five individually-wrapped bundles.

The first one she uncovered was a small gold elephant.

Chase clasped his hand over top of Jenna's.

The curse might be true. He wasn't taking any chances.

"Don't do it."

"Chase, what is wrong with you?"

Chase quickly wrapped up the elephant in the handkerchief and returned it to the metal box.

Chase pulled Jenna to join him on the step.

"Do you have any idea what this is?"

"Hamilton's treasure. Blood money as far as I'm concerned. The reason my parents and Candace Light are now dead."

"That's probably true. But these gold animal figurines could very well be the lost treasure pieces of Blackbeard."

"Blackbeard? The pirate? I don't believe that for a second. It's just some treasure Hamilton wants for God knows what reason."

"Think about it. Why would Hamilton kill for these small objects? They must be worth a fortune. What's more valuable than lost pirate treasure that goes back centuries?"

"I still don't see what..."

"Not just any pirate treasure. Blackbeard's *lost* treasure. It was stolen from Blackbeard. There is a legend that says the treasure is cursed."

"It does have a curse as far as I'm concerned, and it doesn't go back as far as Blackbeard. It's cost innocent people their lives."

Chase pushed the box away with his foot.

"I'm not willing to risk it. The legend states anyone who holds the five gold animals together in their hand will die a mysterious death. It's been documented, Jenna. The people who have inherited these objects have all died in strange ways. Do you want to dismiss this as just a myth?"

Jenna sat back and wiped some dust off of her forehead. Chase was serious and maybe it was time she was, too.

"Tell me more about this legend."

"James Dunn was a cabin boy in Blackbeard's days. He was captured when his ship was overtaken by Blackbeard and his men. Dunn smuggled the gold pieces off the ship and made his way to Virginia. Each one of Dunn's descendants died strangely. Accidents, unexplained deaths, graves disturbed."

"And you believe in the legend, don't you?"

"I'm afraid not to. I think you should, too."

Jenna and Chase stared at the box for a few minutes in silence.

"Death comes to those who dare to hold all five pieces of tainted gold."

"What is that?"

"That's the pirate curse. Please, Jenna, do not unwrap the gold animals and hold them in your hand at one time. Promise me you will *never* do that."

"I promise."

Chase relaxed his shoulders.

"What are we going to do now?"

"The only thing we can do…go to New York. I have to get my brother back."

Chase wiped a smudge off Jenna's cheek. "Together?"

Jenna nodded. "Together."

Chase picked up the box then extended his hand to Jenna, pulling her to her feet. They were surprised by a knock on the back door.

Teresa burst inside.

"George is missing… I have a bad feeling."

Chase tapped his fingers on the box.

"I told you it's cursed."

Both women just stared back at him with fear in their eyes.

Chapter 22

Kelly had barely pulled around the corner when she saw Jenna's car in the driveway.

"Not good," Kelly said to herself. She couldn't let Jenna see her. How could she even begin to explain what had happened?

Gripping the wheel tightly, she could feel the sweat beading up on her palms.

She needed to leave...*now*. Why was she still driving around Cape May?

Because leaving Cape May meant leaving everything good that had happened to her the past few weeks. Laughter. Romance. *Austin*.

All the happy moments she had shared with Austin were clinging to her, begging her to stay. But they meant nothing if Austin wasn't with her.

Kelly slapped the steering wheel in total frustration, almost running a red light. She slammed on the brakes at the last minute, cursing out loud. She needed to calm down or she was going to get herself killed.

She desperately wanted to make things right. She had to find a way to save Austin's life.

But she couldn't do it alone. She needed help.

Someone who could get Mason's attention. Who could be an ally if approached the right way? One name came to her mind.

Jonathan Knox.

Young, impressionable, but with a good head on his shoulders. Mason was always singing Jonathan's praises.

It was worth a try.

Kelly pulled into a gas station off the New Jersey turnpike. She placed a call as she waited for the attendant to pump her gas.

"Hamilton-Knox Foundation."

Hearing the high-pitched female voice, Kelly cringed. Mason's administrative assistant, Suzanne Carter, was at the helm, filtering calls as usual.

"Jonathan Knox, please."

Kelly covered part of the phone receiver, hoping Suzanne didn't recognize her muffled voice.

"Mr. Knox is in a meeting. He should be free in about an hour. Would you like to leave a message?"

Kelly exhaled slowly. So far so good.

"I'll call back."

Kelly ended the call before Suzanne could reply. The less she spoke to the current object of Mason's affection, the better. It was no secret around the office. Kelly knew exactly what her father and Suzanne were doing after hours in the privacy of his office, and it had nothing to do with Media Production.

Tall, blond with a slender body. Designer clothes. A small rose tattoo on her right ankle. Almost a carbon-copy of her own mother, without the tattoo and half her mother's age, Suzanne Carter had attracted Mason's roving eyes several months ago. Surprisingly, he was still captivated, which had to be a new record. Usually, after Mason broke in the new girls, he moved on to the next conquest.

Whatever, Kelly thought to herself. She had no desire to waste any more time thinking about her father's indiscretions. Mason never apologized for his behavior anyway.

Kelly jumped when the gas attendant knocked on her car door. He handed her back her credit card.

"Ma'am, your card was declined. Can you give me another one to run?"

The young, lanky attendant with major facial acne seemed extremely uncomfortable approaching the subject.

Kelly cursed under her breath. She rapidly pulled out the correct amount of cash from her wallet and stuffed it into the attendant's hand. Firing up the engine, she sped away as fast as she could.

She knew exactly what was happening. Mason was tightening the screws until she was forced to come crawling back to him, begging for forgiveness and another chance.

But this time he had gone too far.

He was cutting her off financially. Her credit cards, probably her bank accounts. Mason knew no limits when it came to humiliation.

Thank goodness she had been smart enough to take a few thousand in cash out of the bank before she left for Cape May. Most of the money was still left.

She could survive for about a week in the city, but then she would be tapped out. If Mason had frozen her financial sources, she was on her own.

She was also afraid to go to her apartments in New York or West Chester. Mason's men were most likely waiting inside at both locations. She had little money and no familiar place to go.

She prayed she was making the right decision.

To contact Jonathan Knox. He was her only chance.

*****

The meeting with Media Production concluded right on time.

Jonathan flung his portfolio down on his desk and loosened his tie. All he wanted was to get the hell out of the office today. He had no motivation. His mind was on other things...other people...*Jenna Reed.*

He continued to daydream for a few extra minutes until his phone rang. He didn't recognize the caller ID.

"Hello?"

"Jonathan? Are you there? Please, say something! I need your help. This is Kelly!"

"Kelly?"

Mason's daughter? Why would she be calling me?

"What's wrong, Kelly? Do you need me to find your father for you?" Jonathan offered. "I think he went back to his office after the meeting."

"No, no, Jonathan...listen to me...something...*terrible* has happened. I need to talk to you, but you can't tell my father. Can you please meet me somewhere? I'll be in the city within an hour."

At first Jonathan didn't understand why Mason's daughter would be calling *him*. But it didn't take long for Jonathan to get onboard. Kelly was clearly upset. He had no doubt Mason was the reason.

"Can you get to Harrigan's on 47th and Lex?"

"Yes...I'll get there as soon as possible."

"Ok, Kelly. I'll see you then."

Jonathan could tell from Kelly's voice how upset she was. He couldn't imagine what Kelly had to tell him but whatever it was, he probably wouldn't be surprised.

Mason Hamilton was capable of too many bad things.

*****

Mason watched Austin's body react as The Closer slapped him hard across the face to wake him up. Blood spurted as his lip cracked, dripping down the front of his shirt.

Mason winced. He never acquired the tolerance for watching torture, necessary as it was. It seemed too barbaric, but nonetheless, he understood the benefits.

Austin jolted awake, feeling the stinging sensation.

Where the hell was he? He glanced around the room. A basement, a warehouse? He doubted he was still in Cape May. He couldn't smell the salt in the air.

Austin tried to move, unsuccessfully. His arms were tied behind a chair and his legs were bound to the chair legs.

"Where's Kelly?"

"Ah, Mr. Reed, so good of you to join us."

Mason stared at the man who had prompted Kelly's disobedience. It was a pity, really. She could have done so much better.

"I want you to tell me right now what you have done with Kelly!"

Austin's outburst earned him yet another round of head poundings, courtesy of The Closer. One eye was now swollen shut. His cheeks and nose were bloody.

Austin tried to take a few deep breaths to stave off the pain. But it was no use. His body convulsed, as he braced for the next blow.

"Kelly is not worth worrying about, I can assure you. However, if you insist, I am more than willing to tell you all about...my *daughter*."

Austin spit out a mouthful of blood and saliva.

"You just couldn't leave her alone, could you? She hardly had a moment's peace because of your excessive hounding. It's a good thing I'm tied up, or I'd be the one throwing the punches."

"Ah, Mr. Reed, do not bother yourself with idle threats. You are here for one reason. Leverage. Your life for my treasure pieces. Your sister and I have an understanding."

"Jenna will never give in to your demands."

"Mr. Reed, you underestimate your sister's devotion. Right this very moment she is planning on coming to New York as soon as she retrieves the treasure pieces. How very...*touching*."

Mason paced the floor as The Closer stood ready to inflict more pain.

"Now, as to the matter of my daughter. I assume you enjoyed her in your bed?"

Austin didn't flinch.

"As I thought. Did it ever occur to you *why* Kelly was allowing you to romance her? Certainly it must have crossed your mind why a woman of her caliber would be bothered with a laggard such as yourself? The only reason my daughter showed up on your doorstep was because she was following my orders."

It couldn't be...not Kelly. Not after what they had shared.

Austin refused to believe it. Hamilton was baiting him and using Kelly as an excuse. He had to play along for now.

Mason was pleased with the reaction he was getting. Austin Reed looked positively shocked.

"I sent Kelly to Cape May to get the location of the treasure from your sister. Imagine my surprise when Jenna decided to travel unexpectedly to Virginia. A change of plan was required. You were the next target. Kelly was to use her mind *and body* to entice you to reveal any knowledge about the treasure. Such a wasted endeavor. When I ordered her to return to New York, she chose to disobey me."

Austin shut his eyes.

Kelly had chosen him over her sadistic father. At risk to her own life.

She's in love with me.

"...a miscalculated, dangerous decision on her part. However, she partially redeemed herself when she aided my team in your abduction, even though one of my associates had to...*force* her hand."

Austin took in a deep breath. *What had they done to her?*

"Where is she?" Austin said between clenched teeth.

"On her way back to New York, I assume. I'm sure she will try to appeal to my sense of decency to plead for your release. Another waste of time. I assure you, Mr. Reed, you have seen the last of my daughter."

"She loves me, Hamilton. She chose me over you."

Austin forced himself not to cry out. The Closer had swung a heavy board against his leg. The pain shot through his body before he could even react.

"A mistake Kelly will regret sooner or later."

Mason stepped out of the way as The Closer moved forward. He had traded the board for a metal pipe.

"I am through discussing my wayward daughter with you. Kelly will see the error of her ways and return to me shortly."

"I wouldn't count on it."

"Don't test me, Mr. Reed. I may not be so benevolent the next time you see me. It would be a shame if you didn't get to say good-bye to your sister."

*****

Kelly waited in a back booth at Harrigans. Drumming her fingers on the table, she scoped out the bar. Not one person was casting a glance her way in the popular Irish pub.

Most of the patrons appeared to be socializing professionals out for an extended lunch hour, or sales reps trying to impress out-of-town clients.

What was taking Jonathan so long? Was he going to stand her up? Or worse, tell her father where he could find her.

Kelly nervously checked her watch. Jonathan was twenty minutes late. Soon she would have to leave.

Kelly's eyes fell to the table. She was stuck with nowhere to go.

"Been waiting long?"

Jonathan slid into the booth across from her with a beer in one hand.

Kelly let out a sigh of relief. "I was afraid you weren't coming."

"Just being careful. I wanted to make sure I wasn't being followed, so I got out of the cab a couple of blocks away. I'm learning to have a basic distrust of most people these days...especially your father."

"I'm sorry, Jonathan. I didn't want to involve you, but..." Kelly's voice trailed off.

"This has something to do with Mason, doesn't it? When is it ever going to end? I'll never forgive him for what he did to Jenna."

"*Jenna Reed*?"

Jonathan was afraid to admit what he had done.

"Is Jenna ok? What did my father do to her?"

Kelly wrung her hands together in anguish.

"Mason thinks Jenna has found the treasure. He's not going to stop until he gets it. Mason sent me to seduce her, to make her tell me about the treasure, but I...never got that far. He got impatient with me, and sent another team."

Kelly's eyes fell.

"Jenna was drugged, kidnapped and threatened at gunpoint. The FBI stepped in, so hopefully she's under their protection now."

"Where is she, Jonathan?"

"I don't know. I tried to warn her, but someone ambushed me. I woke up in the FBI's safe house. I was afraid they'd start grilling me, so I escaped when I was in their car. One of Mason's men picked me up. Instead of going after Jenna, they were told to get me away from the FBI."

Kelly reached over and laid her hand on Jonathan's arm.

"You can't blame yourself, Jonathan. My father has everyone wrapped around his little finger."

"Well, that's not where I want to be. *Ever again.* How can I help you?"

Kelly understood Jonathan's shame better than anyone.

"I need to find Austin, Jenna's brother. He's being used to lure Jenna to New York. He was kidnapped last night from their beach house. I was there, Jonathan. I know what they did."

"Then you're in danger, too."

"I'm sure my father is quite annoyed with me. He sent me to ...persuade Austin to tell me about the treasure. But...the more time I spent with Austin, the more I wanted to be with him."

"Mason didn't count on that, did he?"

"I'm in love with Austin. But I hate myself for betraying him. Mason has an accomplice...George, the Reeds' own neighbor...who told me Mason would kill me if I didn't go through with his plans."

Kelly's voice cracked as she continued.

"So I gave Austin a beer laced with a sedative and..."

Tears were starting to fall down her cheeks.

"He slapped me...hard. I was so afraid. I didn't know what else he would do. I ran upstairs and hid until the next morning. When I woke up, Austin was gone."

"Two pawns in Mason's game. We need to make things right."

Kelly wiped a tear away. "I don't know what to do, Jonathan. My bank accounts are frozen and I'm too scared to go to my apartment."

"I'd take you to my place, but I don't trust your father either. I know someplace else...where no one will find you."

Jonathan jotted down an address on the back of his business card.

"This is my grandmother's house. She lives about thirty minutes south of the city. I'll call her to let her know you're coming."

"I don't want anyone else to get hurt by my father. He's done enough damage."

"My grandmother is a tough old bird. Besides, Mason doesn't even know I have a grandmother. You can trust her. She'll take good care of you."

"Thank you. This means a lot to me."

"Looks like we're in this together. We'll figure it out. We owe it to Jenna and Austin."

Jonathan flagged the waiter to bring menus. He was too engrossed with talking to Kelly to notice two men moving closer to the bar stools opposite their booth.

Except for the guns hidden by their suit jackets, the men fit in perfectly with the afternoon crowd, ordering two pints at the bar. Even when they swiveled in their chairs occasionally and glanced at the table behind them, Jonathan and Kelly were oblivious to their watchful eyes and ears.

After their lunch was finished, Jonathan laid a fifty on the table then escorted Kelly to the front door.

"Call me when you get there."

"Ok," Kelly said as they parted ways.

The two men assigned to follow Jonathan Knox sprung from their stools. They needed to follow Knox at a quick pace or they would lose him in the pedestrian traffic outside the restaurant.

"Back up...*now*."

Out of nowhere, two extremely large dark-skinned men blocked the doorway. With stern looks on their faces, they strongly encouraged the two spies to retreat to the rear of the restaurant, then through the back door until they were in the alley.

Another man stepped from the shadows and nodded. In a thick accent, he spoke to the two captives, who had been forced to their knees.

"You will not follow Jonathan Knox or Kelly McBride. You will not speak of this meeting to anyone. You will not...see tomorrow if you do. Do you understand my words?"

Both men nodded in silence.

Without warning, their heads were twisted and squeezed with enough pressure forcing them to fall forward and pass out.

Tumi Carile snapped his fingers. The bodies of the two men were rolled behind the trash receptacle.

"Enough for tonight. Is your team in place?"

Phillip, Tumi's right-hand man, nodded.

"Good. There is more work to do."

Chapter 23

Haunting darkness filtered into the bedroom as if to tap Jenna on the shoulder. Her eyes flew open as she read the time on the clock. Four a.m.

Get up...now.

Every minute counted. Her brother's fate was in her hands. She had one chance to get this right.

Jenna quickly dressed. She smiled at Chase, who was sprawled out on the bed. The ceiling fan and cross-breezes from the open windows had lulled them to sleep at an early hour. Tedious driving along the interstate coupled with the stress of the drama in South Carolina had drained them both.

But now Jenna felt recharged. She was ready to go.

Chase placed the box with the treasure pieces in Austin's room, next to hers. Chase didn't feel comfortable having the *cursed* objects in the same room where they would be sleeping.

The damn legend. Maybe it was true after all.

Her parents, Candace Light? Who would be next?

Jenna shuddered to think. If she didn't get to New York soon, she knew what the answer would be...Austin.

Jenna wrapped the little gold elephant figurine in the old handkerchief and returned it to the box. She stuffed the remaining four objects into the pockets of her shorts. Tiptoeing down the old wooden stairs, she hoped Chase was too far gone to hear the squeaks her feet made on the last couple of steps.

Jenna grabbed a pair of scissors and a box of sandwich baggies from the kitchen, and then headed for the dresser in the guest room. Austin would never miss one of his worn-out Van Halen shirts he kept downstairs for a quick change. There were at least ten or more in the drawer and most had holes in them.

With a few quick snips, Jenna cut four small pieces of cloth. After wrapping up the gold animals, she placed them in separate plastic bags. Grabbing an old backpack which hung on the back of the basement door, she deposited the baggies inside.

Jenna paused as her hand touched the doorknob. *Not again.*

Quickly, she scribbled a note for Chase.

Coffee run – be back soon. Don't worry.

Minutes were ticking away. It was now four-thirty on the kitchen clock.

Sunrise would be coming in about an hour. She had just enough time to bury the artifacts in the dark before daybreak threatened to reveal her secret hiding places.

Jenna withdrew the small piece of paper with the clues her mother had left her. She had almost missed it when she first opened the box.

She hadn't shared this bit of information with Chase. At the time it seemed like the right thing to do - keeping one element of this mystery to herself. Just in case.

Just in case...for what?

Oh, hell, she didn't have time to debate the issue right now. It was time to go.

Darting between Victorian homes and businesses, she made her way around town. Only a few people were up at this hour, most likely employees starting the early shifts at restaurants. Otherwise, the town was deserted.

Five a.m.

Jenna caught her breath. She was almost done. She had successfully found the hiding places her mother had referenced in her encoded note. Two more to go. Jenna pushed on, crouching behind a short hedge.

She jumped back, stifling a scream when a long-haired gray cat jumped off a porch to chase a squirrel. Catching her breath, she continued on her way down Howard Street.

Peering around the corner in between two small shops, she closed her eyes briefly.

What in the hell am I doing?

Jenna paused for a few precious seconds. There was no use trying to rationalize the insanity which had overtaken her life.

Re-burying treasure?

This had to be some kind of strange dream.

But it wasn't.

A simple child's game Jenna played with her mother had now become a very strategic method of staying one step ahead of Mason Hamilton. Her mother's clues about various landmarks in Cape May had proven to be a modern day treasure map.

Five-thirty. She was done.

Jenna made her way to the Washington Street Mall. A last stop for coffee. *Her alibi.*

Café Buongiorno opened early for energetic morning risers. *Thank God*, Jenna thought to herself. Another twenty minutes and this place would be hopping.

The house was quiet as she crept upstairs. Slowly pushing the door open to her bedroom, Jenna fully expected to find Chase still fast asleep.

The bed was made. Chase was nowhere in sight. Jenna sat down on the bed after placing the cups on the nightstand. The note she had left on the kitchen table was now on her pillow.

Great, Jenna said to herself as an unsettling chill washed over her.

Jenna took the lid off her coffee and drank it down mindlessly. She noticed how the sunlight was starting to brighten up the room yet it wasn't doing a good enough job on her spirit. Chase was gone.

Without thinking, Jenna opened the second cup of coffee and took a sip.

"Either you're extra thirsty this morning, or it's caffeine you're craving. Two large cups, Jenna? You're going to be wired."

Chase appeared in the doorway.

Jenna jumped in surprise, spilling part of the coffee down her tank top. Startled by Chase's sudden appearance, she didn't notice her shirt was drenched.

Coffee ran down her neck and arm. Placing the cup on the nightstand, she grabbed Chase around the neck as he came closer.

"I thought you left me," she said, pressing her face into the curve of his neck.

"No. That's your little trick. But I've figured you out by now."

"Really?"

"Really. This is the first time you left me a note, so I figured it was a safe bet you'd be coming back."

Chase tugged on Jenna's shirt. His eyes drifted downward following the trail of coffee droplets.

"I think the wet-shirt look is incredibly sexy…or maybe it's the coffee running down your body."

Chase kissed Jenna's neck and licked his lips.

"Oh, it's definitely the coffee."

"I could spill my coffee every morning."

"I'd like that."

Chase pushed Jenna back on the bed, leaning down for another kiss.

Jenna slid out from underneath Chase's arms.

"We need to get on the road...so, don't get any ideas. I'll just be a minute. Let me change and..."

Chase caught Jenna's arm.

"Don't change...*ever*."

Jenna gave Chase a friendly push backwards. She sprinted towards the closet so he would take the hint.

Chase followed at a quick pace, trapping Jenna between his body and the closet door.

"Chase, please..."

Jenna's protests were muffled by the sound of their bodies crashing to the floor. Chase was taking her to a new level of adrenaline-pumping fervor.

Making love to Chase hadn't been part of Jenna's plan this morning. But the caffeine was definitely kicking in...and so was her heart.

*****

Maria looked up when Jacoby poked his head into her office.

"Line two. Teresa."

Maria nodded as Jacoby shut the door on his way out.

"What's wrong, my friend?"

Maria knew Teresa would never call her at the office unless something had happened.

"It's George," Teresa blurted into the phone, knowing full well every phone call to the FBI was recorded and traced.

"I need to talk to you."

"Let's get together for drinks...can I call you back?"

A coded conversation they had both used many times.

"Ok, I'll give you a ring later."

Maria darted from her office.

"Errand. Back in twenty minutes."

Code to Jacoby she was taking the call outside.

Maria speed-dialed Teresa on her way to the fountain plaza. She had worked for the CIA and FBI for too many years. All conversations even behind closed doors could be overheard. She wasn't taking any chances.

Maria waited until the third ring then ended the call. A signal to Teresa it was safe to call back.

"Seems like we can never avoid the cloak-and-dagger, can we?"

"Not this time, I'm afraid. George has disappeared. Maybe for good this time. I found traces of dried blood in the house. Probably a contract kill. Neat and tidy."

"I guess they didn't figure on a trained agent to find tiny specks of evidence. Did you send it to the lab?"

"Courier picked it up this morning. I called my contact. She's going to try and rush it. Should hear back later today."

"I'm sorry, Teresa. I know you had grown fond of George over the years. I'm willing to bet Mason had no further use for him and wanted to clean the slate."

"You're probably right," Teresa said, sadly.

"Hold on a minute." Maria hit the button to bring Jacoby on the line. "What's up?"

"Targets on the move. Thought you'd like to know. Dispatch team?"

"Yes," Maria said flatly.

Maria shook her head. She knew exactly where Jenna and Chase were headed.

"Field trip. Tell Thompson to pack his bag."

Maria got Teresa back on the line.

"I need your help. Can you get to the safe house in New York at Reddington? Jenna and Chase are headed straight for trouble. Did you see them leave a few minutes ago?"

"Yes, that was the other reason I was calling. They seemed to be in a hurry. Chase was driving but Jenna was looking at a map. I'll leave within the hour. I have to clean up a bit. If I'm wrong and George does surface, I don't want him finding out he wasn't the only one harboring a secret identity."

*****

"I am so tired of being in this car!" Jenna exclaimed as she threw the map on the dashboard. They had just pulled onto the Jersey turnpike bound for New York. "I'm sorry...venting again."

"Vent all you want. I'm not going anywhere."

"You have the patience of a saint to put up with me."

Chase laughed at Jenna's last remark. "No one has ever called me a *saint*. And please don't start now, especially after what we just did on the floor. You know, we could have made it back to the bed. I was in no rush."

Jenna raised an eyebrow. "Bullshit."

"Why, Jenna Reed, you hurt me with your lewd accusations."

Jenna shook her head, as her lips curved into a smile.

"Call it whatever you want. You were the one pushing me against the door."

"I didn't hear any complaints."

"I didn't have time."

Jenna grabbed Chase's hand and held it in her own. Stroking his fingers, she felt a brief calmness rush over her. Their sexual banter had always taken the edge off of the drama which seemed to be constantly unfolding.

"This is your fault."

"My fault?" Chase looked bewildered.

"Yes, Chase Garrett. I made a commitment to myself to swear off men for the summer."

Chase couldn't help but smile.

"You're kidding me, right?"

"Then you came along and...well, let's just say my resistance level was shot to hell. I was all set to spend my summer lying on the beach... *by myself*...in my string bikini."

"A sight I still hope to see." Chase said, wetting his lips.

"Don't change the subject. I wasn't planning on falling for anyone so soon."

"Well, you certainly had no problem falling to the floor."

Jenna was the one laughing now.

"I know...and you love me when I'm bad."

Too late. She had just said the "L" word...out loud. Jenna's face registered a look of panic, unsure of Chase's next move.

But what he did next totally shocked her.

Chase took the next exit off the interstate then stopped along the road.

Good job, Reed, the little voice inside her head echoed. *Chalk another one up to stupidity.*

Chase walked around to Jenna's side, threw the door open, and pulled Jenna into his arms.

"I didn't plan to fall in love with you, Jenna Reed, but I can't help myself."

"You know, your timing is..." Jenna couldn't find the right words...*any words.* She was tongue-tied.

Chase wanted to search Jenna's eyes, but she had closed them too quickly. Why? He wondered.

Jenna desperately wanted to tell Chase she felt the same, but the words wouldn't come.

She did the only thing she could.

Jenna got back in the car and stared straight ahead.

"Drive, Chase. Please...drive...*now.*"

Chapter 24

"Damn helicopter!" Maria shouted as the pilot landed the bird in the backyard of the FBI's safe house just outside of New York City. As the wind from the blades smacked her in the face, Maria's mood further deteriorated.

New York was the last place she wanted to be. But here she was; it was unavoidable.

Jacoby and Thompson were driving up. Recognizing Maria's urgency to meet Teresa as soon as possible, Jacoby had arranged for the chopper.

Maria felt certain this time her team had a bona fide chance to take down Mason Hamilton; catching him with his hands so dirty they would never come clean. She had waited for this opportunity for many years. Now, it was about to be handed to her...*with the help of Jenna Reed.*

Jenna's terrifying phone call left Maria with a sick feeling in her stomach. Mason was branching out. He wasn't just rubbing elbows with contract killers; he was now adding abduction to his repertoire. His obsession was driving him to a new level of menacing acts.

One stupid mistake and she would have Mason right where she wanted him. Behind bars or dead. Preferably dead.

Maria nodded to an agent on security detail as she held up her badge. Finding an empty bedroom, she dropped her duffle on the bed. Maria's hand lingered on the carrying strap as she remembered her conversation with Damian right before she left.

"He's got you on a short leash. He's toying with you, Maria. Can't you see that?"

"Damian, for God's sake, what do you want me to do?"

"You know the answer." Damian gathered Maria into his arms. "The answer I've been giving you for years. Give up."

"And you know why I can't."

Maria sighed as she recalled the agony she felt leaving Damian's embrace to finish packing. She hated arguing with her husband. It wasn't fair to either of them. Mason Hamilton was still wreaking havoc even when he wasn't around to see it.

"I'm coming with you."

Damian threw his own duffle on the bed.

"I was hoping you were going to say that."

Damian kissed the back of Maria's head before he turned to leave. "But I have to finish up on a couple reports from my 'Dimitri Batrov' days. I'll get up there as soon as I can."

"Don't take too long...I might miss you."

"I'm counting on that," Damian said right before he closed the bedroom door. Instead of leaving the room, he surprised Maria by wrapping his arms around her waist and kissing her on the back of the neck.

"Now show me how much you're going to miss me," he said before Maria had a chance to respond.

Maria recalled how both duffle bags flew across the room with a wave of Damian's hand clearing their lofty bed.

"I do miss you, Damian," Maria murmured as she sat on the edge of the bed and rummaged through her bag.

"And I need you here...with me."

*****

"Bout time you got here."

Jacoby flung his suit jacket across the back of a chair then rolled up his shirt sleeves. Stretching from the long drive, he let out a long yawn.

"Some of us with shorter titles have to drive everywhere."

"Moaning and groaning won't get you any sympathy. Grab a couple beers from the fridge. I need your expertise. I can't get the SMART board to key up. We need to go over these blueprints. I want to make sure I have all my bases covered."

"And my day was looking so promising," Jacoby teased as he headed for the kitchen.

"Give me your gun," Mick Thompson said as he held out his hand.

"Aren't we in a wonderful mood? Looking forward to the long meeting, Mick?"

"You know I can't stand sitting still for too long. I'd rather be doing something useful. I'm going to clean my weapon.

Thought I would do yours, too, but if you're going to be a smartass..."

Jacoby laughed then handed his gun over.

"Make sure it's in tip top condition," he said before walking back into the meeting room.

"Don't push me, *Genius*."

Jacoby stopped to glare back at Thompson. Only Maria was allowed to call him that nickname. He'd have to set Thompson straight the first chance he got.

But he didn't have time for that now. Maria needed help.

Maria rubbed her eyes as Jacoby approached her carrying two beers. He handed one to her.

"Take a break."

"Did you come all this way to mother me?"

"Someone has to. Where's Damian?"

"Still in D.C. Paperwork, what else? He's wrapping up his 'Batrov' assignment. So, of course, the brass wants a full report. He's not happy."

Jacoby took a swig. "Because he had to stay and write up reports or because he'd rather be here with you?"

"Both."

"Guess we'll see him tomorrow then?"

"That's the plan. I may need his sniper skills. I'm not putting anything past Mason this time. He's luring Jenna Reed into his web, and he's probably got her brother somewhere inside the museum. I'm trying to plan for every possible scenario."

Maria squeezed the bridge of her nose as she tightly closed her eyes. Eye strain was wearing her down.

"Let me take over," Jacoby offered. "You've been at this too long. Why aren't you wearing your glasses?"

Maria sat back and scowled. She lifted a piece of paper covering them.

"Some of the younger agents might see them as a sign of weakness. I can't have that. I need them to respect me."

Jacoby picked up the glasses and placed them on Maria's face.

"Well I can attest to the fact that you're a tough broad, if you need me to...and secondly, if anyone doesn't give you respect, I'll sic Thompson on them."

Jacoby pulled Maria to her feet and pushed her towards the staircase. Maria started to protest but knew it would be a wasted effort. Jacoby was only trying to help and deep down she appreciated it.

"Go get some rest. I'll bring the SMART board to life."

"One hour. If I'm not back in one hour, you come and get me. We don't have a lot of time to waste. Minutes are ticking away and I've got to come up with some solutions."

"Not by yourself, you don't. We're working on this together. I'll have some answers for you when you come back."

Maria stopped halfway up the steps.

"I want another unit on them. I just hope Jenna and Chase aren't stupid enough to tangle with Hamilton by themselves."

"Already done."

"Thanks. You're the best," Maria called before heading up the steps.

Thank goodness she had good people to rely on. Whoever came up with the theory someone in her unit was a traitor needed to get their head screwed on tighter.

*****

Mason Hamilton kissed his wife Ellen gingerly on the cheek on his way out the door.

"Have a nice day, my love."

"You too, Mason."

A daily routine perfected through years of practice.

As his driver pulled away from the front door, Mason gazed upon the Italian stone fountain positioned in the middle of his circular driveway. The partially-nude sculpture of an angelic boy holding two doves always captured his attention.

Mason never grew tired of looking at it. The cherub held the doves by one hand and motioned to the sky with the other. It was obvious to Mason what the statue represented - a man's ability to keep or release anything he *controlled*. Dominance.

Mason puffed out his chest. He knew exactly how to dominate. He had been doing it for years with his wife.

Once he set the appropriate boundaries, Ellen never once gave him reason to doubt her loyalties.

Always the dutiful wife for the cameras, Ellen participated in Mason's public events, accompanying him to press conferences and museum exhibits. She hosted lavish parties for his high-end donor constituents and political allies. She made herself available to his every wish and command.

Such an obedient wife.

Not that Ellen had much choice in the matter.

From the start, she had been manipulated. First by her parents, who had insisted she marry into an affluent family. The Chandlers pushed their daughter into an alliance with young entrepreneur Mason Hamilton through the encouragement of their friend and confidante Mason Hamilton, *Senior*. They wanted a prominent son-in-law. What better man than the one who would head the Hamilton-Knox Foundation, their primary recipient of massive donations?

It was a win-win situation, so the Chandlers thought. Even when Ellen became pregnant soon after their marriage, her parents tolerated Mason's growing egotistical mannerisms, knowing they had a grandchild on the way. An extension of the illustrious family tree.

Mason soon took over the role of controller as their marriage got underway. Laying out his stipulations, he set Ellen on a straight path. If she behaved in accordance with his rules, then she would have every material pleasure she wanted. If she strayed, there would be repercussions. Dangerous *and* lethal.

Surprisingly, Ellen never complained, which was the one thing Mason never figured out. Perhaps Ellen had made up her mind she would use her husband as much as he was using her. She did take advantage of what Mason's reputation in various international circles provided for her – access to practically any location around the world in luxurious comfort.

Even after all these years, Ellen was still a mystery to him.

Ellen peered through the lace panels which covered her bay window. She stood back far enough so Mason wouldn't notice her curiosity.

Any other day, she could care less when he left after he kissed her good-bye. His gesture was nothing more than a perfunctory show for the house staff's benefit. It was never meant as a sign of affection.

But today was a whole different story. Ellen was getting ready to pull out her trump card. The day of reckoning was finally here. Mason was about to get what he deserved.

"The lies we live," Ellen said, not caring if any of the house staff was within earshot. What did it matter? She wasn't planning to be living here much longer.

With any luck, today would be the last day she'd have to endure being married to such an evil man.

Ellen grabbed her gold Michael Kors purse and headed for the garage. She had no need for her driver today; she had to get to her destination *alone*.

Her four-inch heels clicked out a cadence on the metal floor of the underground garage. Ellen paused to view the vast collection of cars at her disposal. Some vintage, but mostly modern indulgent play toys of her husband's.

A black Lamborghini, a red Porsche and a silver Aston Martin greeted her down the first row as she ran her fingers along each one. Tempting her like a stimulated lover.

Too extreme. Too showy. Too *Mason*.

She moved to the second row and selected a more conservative car. One which would blend unassumingly into traffic.

Sliding into the leather seat of the Toyota Highlander, she turned the key in the ignition. The engine roared to life, echoing loudly in the garage.

As she pulled out the side driveway, Ellen waved to one of the landscaping staff who was trimming cherry laurels. None of the Latino gardeners ever spoke English to her. But they always understood. Ellen was certain of that.

Tomas nodded politely as Ellen's car passed through the front gate. As soon as her car disappeared, he took out his cell.

"She just left," he said, his Spanish accent fading into perfect English.

"Tracking device activated?"

"Of course, Sir."

"Good. Now, we'll see exactly where my wife is headed."

*****

Teresa Maylor burst through the back door of the safe house, bringing lunch for everyone. She was balancing several large boxes of pizza.

"Safe travels?" Maria asked, handing a few boxes to Thompson, who had just cleared the kitchen table of gun parts and lubricant.

"No problems. Smooth ride until I got closer to the city. Sitting in traffic is *not* my idea of fun. I suppose you're thrilled to be back here as well. Am I right?"

Maria made a face.

"Beyond words."

"Oh, I don't know about that. You had a few *choice words* you were sharing with the class a few moments ago," said Jacoby.

"Thank you so much for picking up on that."

Maria sunk her teeth into a piece of sausage and mushroom pizza then elbowed Jacoby who reached for a pepperoni slice.

"I was just briefing the guys. You want to sit in?"

Two mushrooms hit the floor and were scooped up faster than Teresa could even bend down.

"Nice to see you still have quick reflexes," her friend teased.

"I have my moments."

"That's what I hear."

"From my husband?"

"No, I haven't been talking with your gorgeous man! I was speaking with Thompson when we were cleaning up at my house in Folly Beach. When the rest of you *left*...I might add. Thompson told me you can really kick ass when the need arises. Good to know."

"I try to keep in shape. I don't always want to use my gun."

"Uh-huh..." Teresa muttered as she folded her pizza slice in half. "I'll stick with my nine millimeter, thank you very much."

"Classic."

"Are you referring to me or my weapon of choice?"

"Both and I'll leave it at that. Come on."

She motioned Teresa into the meeting room.

"So, what's the plan? Are you positive we can pull this off and get Jenna and Austin out safely? Or do we have Plan B if we can save only one?"

"Not an option," Maria said confidently. "Everyone is coming out alive."

"What do you need me to do? You know I am capable of *many* things." Teresa cracked a smile.

"There is *one job* I need you to do…because of your *special* talents."

"Can't wait to hear what that entails."

Jacoby cleared his throat and pointed towards the window. A car had pulled into the driveway behind the other SUVs.

Teresa parted the curtains and took another glance.

"You're expecting someone else?"

"You'll see," Maria said, moving towards the back door.

She held the door open as the sunglass-clad woman sauntered in.

Teresa gave Maria a questionable glance as she sized up the visitor. Dressed in designer clothes and sunglasses which probably cost more than her entire wardrobe, the woman seemed quite out of place. *This should be good*, Teresa thought to herself.

"Hi," the woman said as she made her grand entrance.

Both Jacoby and Teresa stared at each other. They couldn't wait to hear Maria's explanation.

Maria rolled her eyes. "Oh, give me a break. We don't have all day for this. Teresa, Jacoby, this is Ellen Chandler Hamilton. She's been helping us undercover for about a year now."

"Did you say *Hamilton*?" Jacoby stuttered as his eyes widened.

"Yes," Ellen said, as she carelessly tossed her sequined jacket across the kitchen counter. She picked up a slice of veggie pizza with her perfectly manicured hand, took a small bite, then wiped her mouth daintily with a napkin.

Uncapping a bottle of beer, she took a sip.

"My husband is Mason Hamilton, and I want to nail that jackass to the wall. Tell me what you need me to do."

Chapter 25

Jenna grimaced as she glanced out the hotel window. Wind and rain. Darkened skies. Matched her mood, actually.

"Figures," she moaned.

The rain hadn't let up for the past hour. She would look like a drowned rat if she went out in this mess. But there was no getting around it. She needed help.

She made a phone call earlier when Chase had gone out for some burgers. Jenna secretly made arrangements for a meeting in one hour at the Starbucks just down the block.

She had to leave now while Chase was in the shower. He would never let her leave alone...especially when she told him who she was meeting.

Sneaking out on Chase...*again.*

Jenna felt a deep sense of guilt as she slowly shut the door to their hotel room. It couldn't be avoided. She would just have to make it up to him later.

"I'm sorry," Jenna whispered as she laid two fingers against the door.

Heading out with only a small umbrella, Jenna knew instantly she hadn't come prepared to deal with pounding rain and high winds. When they left Cape May, it had been sunny and warm. Two opposite ends of the spectrum.

An omen...perhaps?

As expected, Jenna was practically drenched when she arrived at the Starbucks. The umbrella had kept the top of her head dry, but the wind had slammed the rain onto the rest of her body.

She quickly ordered a mocha latte then headed for a back table trying not to drip on anyone. No one looked her way. No one cared she was there. Just another soaked customer trying to dry out from the storm.

Jenna gripped the paper cup with clammy hands. She was actually shivering. With the air conditioner blasting down from a ceiling vent, she couldn't get warm.

A problem which only lasted a few minutes.

Her body temperature began to rise. Starting in small spurts, Jenna felt every nerve in her body stand to attention, then gradually contract in an orchestrated motion.

She didn't need to look up; she knew who just arrived.

"Hello, Jenna."

Jenna purposely kept her eyes lowered. She knew full well if she dared to look into those electrifying blue eyes right now, her coffee cup would be air-bound. Jenna wrapped both hands tighter around the small cup, hoping it wouldn't cave in due to the added pressure.

God knows she was ready to cave in herself.

"Jonathan."

Jonathan slid into a chair right next to Jenna. He grabbed her knee under the table and squeezed it, sending familiar, intimate impulses through both of them.

It felt so good to touch her again.

Jenna wasn't cold now. A steady wave of warmth had encased her from head to toe.

Maybe she should have ordered an iced coffee instead.

"Jonathan, stop it!"

Jenna pushed his hand away, oblivious to the fact several customers had looked their way at her sudden outburst.

"Jenna, I'm not doing anything. We're doing this…*together*."

"Well I don't want to do anything…*together*…with you. Back off, Jonathan. Stop touching me."

Jenna could tell where this meeting was going. Not in the right direction, that was for sure. She had to get back on point, or she feared they never would.

"Focus, Jonathan, *please*. Do this for me. I need your help."

Jonathan pushed his chair a few inches away.

"What do you need me to do?"

"Hamilton has my brother. I want him back."

Jenna slid the picture of Austin across the table.

Jonathan swore under his breath. No wonder Kelly had been so worried.

"I found the treasure. I'm going to trade it for my brother's life."

"That's a mistake and you know it."

Jenna nodded. "I don't have a choice. But Hamilton is not getting the treasure pieces all at once. I need some leverage."

"Be careful, Jenna. This is all just a game to him, and he's determined to win."

"So am I. I have too much at stake."

"You're playing with fire if you tangle with him."

"Then I just have to figure out a way not to get burned."

Without thinking, Jenna stared into Jonathan's face.

She felt the air leave her body. How in the hell was she supposed to concentrate? Jonathan's chiseled face, clearly unshaven, made him look like a model for Calvin Klein. He was so incredibly handsome and sensual; Jenna couldn't tear her eyes away.

"Jenna?"

His voice was alluring. She was losing ground. Jenna knew it, but she couldn't save herself. It was becoming unbearable to be this close to him and not...*touch him.*

"Jonathan...please..."

Jonathan didn't realize at first he had leaned closer.

She's drawing me to her. I can't resist.

Jonathan sat straight in his chair and cleared his throat.

"I need to apologize to you first."

"For what?" Jenna gasped. "For your part in my kidnapping, for seducing me in the storage room, or...*right now?*"

Jonathan looked away. She was keeping score. He was losing.

"I had no idea Hans and Dimitri would take you against your will. Mason must have set that up. I told them to find you and call me when they did. As for my behavior in the storage room and right now...well...we have *chemistry*, Jenna, whether you're ready to accept that or not. We are naturally moving in the same direction."

"Then we need to change course. You're driving me crazy and I can't think straight."

Silence crossed the small space between them and hung in the air for a few seconds.

"I never wanted to hurt you, Jenna. You have to believe me. I want to help you. What can I do?"

"Tell me something I can use to my advantage when I meet with Hamilton."

Jonathan shook his head. "It doesn't matter what I tell you. Mason will always have the upper hand. He always finds a way to bring people under his thumb. Kelly told me Austin was taken to lure you here. Can't you see what's happening? You step inside that museum and you might not come out."

Jenna was surprised to hear her friend's name. "Kelly *McBride*?"

Jonathan hesitated, but knew he had to tell her the truth. It was the only way to gain back a small degree of respectability.

"Kelly McBride is actually Kelly Hamilton. She's Mason Hamilton's *daughter*."

Jenna fell back against the chair. The reality of Jonathan's words were crushing her.

"No way."

Her friend with whom she had confided, trusted completely, and was like a sister to her...this *same* person was the daughter of the evil mastermind himself? This had to be a mistake...a twisted, horrible mistake.

"I don't believe you. That's a cheap trick, Jonathan."

"Pictures don't lie."

Jonathan pulled a picture out of his shirt pocket. Mason, his wife and his daughter had posed for the latest edition of the Hamilton-Knox Foundation's annual report.

Smiling for the camera. A perfect family *image*.

Jenna crumbled the picture and tossed it aside.

Pain welled up inside her. Used again, this time by her best friend. Jenna fell against Jonathan's shoulder, unable to control her sobbing.

"Mason set this up, Jenna. Kelly didn't have a choice. He threatened her life."

Jenna squeezed her eyes shut, trying to force the anguish to go away.

"There's something else you need to know. Mason ordered Kelly to...*gain* Austin's confidence."

Jonathan's eyes fell. There was no easy way to tell her.

"She threw herself at my brother? Unbelievable."

"Kelly didn't want to do it, Jenna. Mason gave her an ultimatum. She's been used all her life by Mason. She's not the same person you want to hate right now."

"I don't want to hate her, Jonathan. Kelly is my best friend. If Hamilton is capable of kidnapping and murder, I'm sure he has no qualms about using his own daughter for his deceitful purposes. Nothing is beneath him. A snake can't get any lower than the ground. But I feel like I'm coming unglued. My head is pounding right now."

Jonathan couldn't help himself. He knew Jenna needed to be comforted. He pulled her closer and kissed her lightly on the forehead.

"Kelly cares a lot for your brother, and she feels so guilty about what happened to him. She went against Mason's orders and stayed with Austin. Now Mason is punishing her. He put a hold on her bank accounts and she's afraid to go to her apartments. She asked me for help, so I sent her to stay with my grandmother."

Jenna shuddered as she stared blankly at the table. Her life and everyone in it was falling apart. How could she possibly put the pieces back together?

Too many challenges were hitting her at once. Jenna zoned out as her mind went into overload.

What should I do? I can't focus when she's this close.

Jonathan wracked his brain. Jenna was distracting him, in a good way, but nonetheless, he couldn't come up with any answers with her body so close. He needed to put some space between them although he was finding it too hard to let go.

She feels too good in my arms.

Jonathan gradually removed his arm from Jenna's back. He forced himself to stand, but Jenna pulled him back down.

"Don't leave me until we have figured this out. Or I swear to you, Jonathan, I'm going to walk right up to Mason's office and take my chances without you."

Jonathan's eyes grew bigger.

"You are the most fearless and captivating woman I have ever met! But I want it noted I tried to talk you out of your idiotic plan."

"Duly noted. Now, tell me what I need to know to deal with Mason Hamilton."

Jonathan didn't get a chance to respond.

"That won't be necessary."

Maria and Teresa took the two chairs across the table.

"I'm going to tell you exactly how this is going to play out. You, Ms. Reed, will *not* be facing Hamilton alone....and you, Mr. Knox, will *not* be going into the office tomorrow. The FBI will be coordinating a rescue mission, and I will not have it compromised by a couple of amateurs."

Jonathan and Jenna exchanged a hopeful, but worried glance.

"Intel indicates your brother is most likely being held somewhere within the museum or nearby. Getting him back safely will be our top priority. I give you my word on that, but at the same time, we need to have Mason play into our hands. He has escaped us too many times. So please, let my team handle this."

Teresa gazed in Jenna's direction.

"I saw you leave the house very early this morning. What were you doing?"

"I buried four of the gold pieces around Cape May based on the note my mother left. I brought one with me – the elephant."

"What note? We burned the letter."

"My mother left a small note in the box with the artifacts. Clues to places where I could safely hide them. For now, I need to keep these places a secret...for everyone's safety."

"Sounds familiar," Teresa quipped. "That's exactly what Lois said when she buried the treasure the first time."

Maria understood...more than she was willing to share at the moment. Secrets kept for the safety of others. It was her job to keep everyone safe, and bring Mason to justice. But in order to do that, she had to explain herself.

The time had come. It was long overdue.

"Ok, this is what we're going to do tomorrow night. We need time to get everything in place. I know you're worried about your brother, Jenna, but believe me, Mason knows how to play his hand also. He has to have a carrot to dangle in front of you."

"I hope you're right."

"Finding the treasure pieces has become his personal quest. It always has been. Trust me on this one; I know what I'm talking about."

Teresa sucked in a sharp breath. She knew what was coming next.

Maria folded her arms and leaned on the table.

"You need to know how I fit into all this…and not just from the FBI's perspective. This is *personal*. I have a score to settle with Mason Hamilton."

Maria was holding everyone's attention now.

"When I was recruited by the CIA in my junior year of college, my first in-depth undercover assignment was to infiltrate the Hamilton-Knox Foundation. I was to spy on Mason Hamilton. He and his father were suspected of illegally obtaining rare art objects through a variety of channels, forging reproductions to be given back to the owners. My team was collecting evidence and we were getting so close. We just needed to get…*closer*. I fell in way too deep."

Jenna was too stunned to even react.

"Mason rose quickly through the ranks, thanks to his father. He soon found *creative* ways to work around the law. We tried our best to nail him more times than I could count, but we kept coming up short. The evidence was tampered with, or witnesses weren't cooperative, the list goes on and on. I can't even begin to tell you how frustrating it was to come up empty-handed time and time again."

Maria took a deep breath. This was taking longer than expected but they needed to hear everything.

"My superior told me there was only one option left to produce the results they wanted. I had to…get *close* to Mason Hamilton. He had a reputation for getting to know most of his female co-workers, some better than others. At first, I was appalled at the idea, but I was told it was just temporary. If I felt uncomfortable at any time, I could signal to my handler and I would be pulled from the mission. So, being young, naïve and eager to please the senior officers, I agreed to let Mason flirt with me."

Maria struggled to continue.

"Mason didn't stop with a few advances. He…became very intense. We became lovers, and for some insane reason, I couldn't let go. I foolishly believed the more I convinced Mason I wanted him, he would confide in me, giving my team the information we needed for a conviction. Mason set me up with a furnished apartment so he could visit me whenever he wanted, unnoticed. He was cheating on his wife. It was more than I could handle. I contacted my handler. I wanted out. But I was told…"

Maria paused, feeling the shame all over again.

"I was told to continue the mission for just a little while longer. The evidence was mounting. Just a few more weeks and the District Attorney's office would be filing criminal charges. I would be credited with a successful mission and a promotion would be in my immediate future. What could I say? So reluctantly, I played along. It was the worst decision I ever made."

Maria sighed as Teresa nudged her for support.

"One night, Mason came to my apartment and I overheard him talking to someone on the phone. I had gone back to the bedroom to lie down. Mason was so loud and boisterous. He started bragging about murdering an old man for five pieces of gold which he planned to hide in my apartment. I was in total shock. Then I heard him say, when he was done with me, I would be taken care of the same way. I panicked. When Mason left, I found where he had hidden the package. I grabbed it and drove to my friend's house in New Jersey. Jenna, your mother and a few other friends...saved my life. They hid me where Mason couldn't find me."

Jenna's hands flew to cover her mouth.

"My God...you're...Sylvia Bernard."

Maria nodded. "Yes, that was my alias years ago. If it hadn't been for your mother, I don't know what I would have done. I owe her my life...and the life of my child."

"Your son?" Jenna's voice was breaking up.

"My son," Maria repeated.

Then Maria took another deep breath and turned towards Jonathan, giving him the most shocking news of all.

"Jonathan, I am...*your mother*."

Chapter 26

Ellen Chandler Hamilton actually felt free for the *first* time in her married life. Siding with the FBI had been the best decision she ever made. The shackles would soon be breaking. Mason would be out of her life once and for all.

Mason behind bars. Ellen laughed out loud. The mighty man brought to his knees. And she had contributed to his fall. She couldn't wait to see the look of surprise on Mason's face when he found out she betrayed him. It would be priceless.

Leaving the FBI safe house around dusk, she started to drive home. Only a few miles down the road, her cell rang. Ellen cringed. Mason was calling her.

Ellen rolled her eyes. What in the hell did he want...*now*?

"Hello?"

"Ellen, my love, where are you?"

"Heading home. I ran a few errands."

"Perfect. I'd like you to take a detour. I just finalized a deal on a new boat. We're celebrating by having dinner aboard. The marina, slip 29. I'll expect you within the hour."

Ellen practically choked. The thought of spending another moment in Mason's company was making her sick to her stomach.

Keep your cover, Maria had coached her before she left the safe house. *A little while longer.*

"Of course, Mason. I'll see you shortly."

"Wonderful. I'll be waiting, my love."

Ellen hurriedly hit the end call button. *Love.* Mason couldn't possibly understand the concept. He was incapable of it.

Ellen made a U-turn at the next intersection, cursing in disgust. Mason didn't need another boat; he already owned five. Just another indulgence to flaunt in front of the people he wanted to impress. Well it wasn't working on her. Not this time. Not ever again.

Ellen arrived at the marina forty minutes later. Walking to slip 29, she wished she had grabbed her jacket from the car. A strong wind had picked up. How fitting. She was actually experiencing a chill when the temperatures in New York had been hovering in the upper nineties for most of the summer.

She could get through this. Only an hour or two.

Ellen pasted a smile on her face. Docked in front of her was a beautiful forty-five foot cabin cruiser with custom decking and polished mahogany wood trim. Without a doubt, the boat was quite magnificent. Except for the fact her deceitful husband was glaring down at her. Was he smiling or smirking? Ellen couldn't tell. She didn't give a damn either way.

Mason offered his hand to Ellen as she climbed aboard.

"Your thoughts, my love?"

"It's wonderful, Mason. You chose well, as usual."

Placate him. Act normal.

"Are we sailing or having dinner now?"

"Sailing. May I pour you a glass?" Mason asked as he lifted the champagne bottle out of the ice bucket.

Several, Ellen thought to herself as she nodded. God knows she would need more than one glass to dull her senses until the evening was over.

Mason waved his hand and the engine was started. Ellen couldn't tell who was piloting the boat. The man behind the wheel had his back to her. He was wearing a baseball cap and sunglasses. How odd, Ellen mused. The skies were still gray from the storm.

Ellen leaned against the railing as the wind pushed her hair away from her shoulders.

"I rarely see you with your hair down. You look ravishing this evening."

Put up with anything he says. Just for tonight.

"Thank you, Mason. I'm flattered you noticed."

"Would you like to freshen up before we have dinner?"

"Yes, I believe I will."

Ellen descended to the lower deck, as she heard Mason pop a cork. She paused for a moment. Why was the fool opening another bottle? They barely touched the first one.

Ellen splashed cold water on her face. *Do whatever it takes...you'll get through the evening.*

"Hurry, my love," Mason called as the foam from the champagne ran down the side of the bottle onto the deck.

Ellen dabbed a wet towel around her face. A lame excuse of a headache would curtail Mason's maiden voyage. Drinks, dinner and then a migraine. She could do this. She could outsmart her husband one more time. Maria would be proud of her.

Someone was moving behind her.

Ellen gasped, hoping to hell it wasn't Mason who would try to force himself on her. In the few times during their marriage when Mason insisted on having sex with her, he was either drunk, or furious something hadn't gone according to his plans. No pleasure, only a controlling act. Nothing more.

Remnants of spicy cologne hung in the air. The man standing behind her definitely wasn't Mason.

Ellen eyes darted to the mirror above the sink. The man with the baseball hat and sunglasses was standing in the doorway.

What the hell did he want?

Ellen reached for the hand railing to propel herself to the upper deck. Her foot had barely touched the first step when she was yanked backwards. A thin metal cord quickly found its way around her neck, competing for space with her strand of cultured pearls.

"What...help...me," Ellen tried to say but the words barely escaped her mouth.

She couldn't breathe...or scream. Ellen desperately groped for the cord as it cut into her hands. As her throat compressed, air flow decreased at a rapid pace. Her hands were becoming too bloodied to hold on much longer.

Ellen twisted from side to side, trying to shake her attacker's balance. It was no use. Her energy was subsiding. Her vision was blurring. Short, jagged breaths became her only means of survival. As her consciousness floated, Ellen's tragic attempts to prolong her life ended quickly.

In the fateful moment before she suffocated, Ellen's last view was watching her husband sneer at her from the upper deck as he raised his glass.

"To you, my love," Mason said with sheer contempt. He turned and faced the back of the boat, hearing Ellen's body fall at the bottom of the stairs. No need to watch any longer. It was done.

The deceitful bitch was dead.

As thoughts raced in his mind about Ellen's treachery, Mason commiserated with a shot of whiskey. He had tossed the champagne bottle over the side of the boat. He needed hard liquor now. Plenty of it.

The tracking device in Ellen's car and the electronic bug placed in her cell phone had confirmed Mason's suspicions. Ellen had been working with Special Agent Maria Turette. Spying on him.

Mason growled. Once again, Turette was trying to catch him at his own game. He would definitely have to retaliate, but not now. There was still another phase to this evening's little adventure.

Satisfied his job had been completed ahead of schedule, The Closer gave the signal for Hans to rev the engines.

Hans steered the boat further out into the Hudson. A half hour later, he signaled to another nondescript boat cruising nearby. The smaller vessel coasted until it was alongside of Mason's yacht.

The Closer smiled. She looked perfect.

A woman with long, blond wavy hair was stepping on deck as she took The Closer's hand. It was uncanny. The resemblance was remarkable. Same hairstyle, same clothes, same body shape...actually, a more sculpted body-shape. She could easily pass for Ellen Chandler Hamilton in her better days.

Mason was truly amazed.

The woman smiled and tilted her head, looking first at The Closer then at Mason.

"Mason," The Closer began. "Allow me to introduce...*your wife*."

*****

Chase was in a foul mood by the time Tumi Carile finally arrived. He was two hours late.

"Come in," Chase said in a gruff tone, holding the door open.

"My apologies. Traffic prevented my timely arrival. However, I do have news for you."

"Where is she, Tumi?"

Chase was ready to explode. Jenna's little escapades were draining him of the small iota of sanity he still possessed. They were in New York City now, not a safe little beach town. She was being reckless going out on her own.

"Jenna Reed is quite safe, my friend. My team has her under surveillance. She is at the Starbucks just down the street."

"For the past *two hours*? What in the hell was so important she couldn't wait for me?"

Tumi hesitated in responding.

Chase clenched his fists. He knew the answer before Tumi had a chance to speak.

"Jonathan Knox."

Chase wanted to pound something, anything...in the worst way. Jenna was siding with the enemy to make a deal. She wasn't thinking clearly.

Chase grabbed his jacket.

Tumi stopped him, blocking the door.

"You must stay here. I anticipate her return very soon."

"If she met with Knox, then she's agreed to something. He can't be trusted. Why can't she see that? He could hurt her again. I can't just stay here when..."

Tumi shook his head.

"She is in no danger. My men are very close. We will not allow any harm to come to Jenna. Besides, Jonathan Knox has already departed. Jenna was still meeting with Maria Turette and Teresa Maylor a few minutes ago. She has allied herself with people who can help her. She is a very smart, capable young woman. You must not chastise her for taking whatever steps she feels necessary to secure her brother's release."

"Tumi, she needs to trust *me*! I'm the one who needs to protect her. You know that."

"And you shall."

Chase tossed his jacket back on the bed. He just couldn't understand why Jenna didn't trust him enough. Or why she felt the need to meet with Knox. But he didn't have to wonder for too long. The door swung open as Chase lifted his head.

"What's going on?"

Jenna was startled to see Tumi in the room, but she was grateful at the same time. Maybe he was here to help get Austin back. Right now, she'd take all the help in the world.

Tumi slightly bowed to Jenna as he stood in the doorway.

"I will be close by…if you need me."

"But…"

Tumi closed the door on his way out.

Jenna braced herself for the onslaught of Chase's accusations. But instead of anger, she only saw anguish. It struck her deeply.

"No note this time."

"No…I'm sorry." Jenna felt her stomach tighten.

"You were right, Jenna." Chase threw his suitcase on the bed. Tossing his jacket and some toiletries inside, he tried to gain a focus, painful as it was.

"About what?"

"I shouldn't have come with you. You obviously don't need *me*. You have the FBI, Tumi's secret police, Jonathan Knox… everyone else at your disposal. You think you need them all to get Austin back. I can understand that. But what I don't get is why you pushed *me* away."

"Because I didn't want to take a chance with your life."

"But you'll take a chance with your own…and make me stand in the shadows…*and watch*. I can't do that."

Chase headed for the door but his hand never reached the doorknob. He was frozen in place as Jenna leaned against the door.

"Stay with me," she pleaded. "I'm sorry for hurting you…again. This is crazy, Chase. But I can't imagine spending a day…without you."

Chase dropped his suitcase at the door. Leaving Jenna was not an option. He knew that from the start. He had acted recklessly. Something they both seemed to be doing.

He needed to focus again on what was important. Chase pulled Jenna into his arms.

She was wet from the rain. Her hair and clothes were soaked. He needed to warm her.

Jenna clung to Chase's body, feeling the dampness start to recede.

"I will make it up to you."

"You will."

"Right now?"

"Right now."

Jenna closed her eyes. Chase's arms were tightening around her and he was kissing her face.

"I need you," she whispered.

"Yes, you do. Don't ever forget it."

She had come so close to losing him tonight. She couldn't bear the thought of that right now. Chase had stayed to give her a second chance…a chance she probably didn't deserve.

*****

Jonathan drove straight to his grandmother's house in Woodmere, southeast of New York City. After his meeting with Jenna and the revelation thrust upon him, he needed answers he hoped his grandmother would provide.

He was still reeling from the startling news laid at his feet just a few hours earlier. His *real* mother. Maria Turette. An agent with the FBI.

Unbelievable.

Well…*not entirely.* Jonathan always suspected he was adopted. Little nuances he always wondered about. He didn't share any physical traits with his parents, Gail and Elliott Knox. Not one feature was the same. Jonathan had wavy dark hair. Gail and Elliott were both fair-skinned and blond. His blood type was different than both of them. Jonathan's doctor had told him this was a very rare occurrence but still possible.

Had the doctor lied to him, on purpose?

Jonathan wondered how many other lies had been told to cover up the true identity of his birth mother…and father.

Jonathan jerked the wheel to avoid a car coming up on his left side. The driver repeatedly honked his horn. Jonathan snapped to attention. He gripped the wheel tighter even though his hands were beginning to shake.

Realizing Mason's blood was running through his own veins had been too much of a shock.

His stomach was churning. His head was hurting.

Not much further now. He could make it. A couple more exits.

Think about the positive facts. You have a mother…and a sister.

Maria and Kelly. He would always be grateful for his parents who raised him, but now he had a chance to experience another level of family. Two people he cared about were now gone, but two others were about to take their place.

Jonathan pulled into his grandmother's driveway and immediately knew his presence was being announced. The front curtains were quickly parted by four brown noses. His grandmother's Labrador retrievers were barking happily at his arrival.

Why his grandmother felt the need to keep four large dogs, he never knew. But he was glad in a sense. No one snuck up on Mabel Tremont without the canine cavalry bolting from their beds.

"Jonathan, get in here! The dogs can't wait to see you!" Mabel yelled from the front door.

As soon as he got to the stoop, Mabel pulled him into a bear hug. The labs fought for his attention. After a few slobbery kisses, the dogs finally backed away so Jonathan could step inside the small brick rancher.

Jonathan was ready to crash, and the old canvas sofa with Mabel's crocheted blanket was beckoning him. In three strides, he sunk into the comforting embrace of the worn piece of furniture while Mabel corralled the dogs in the back bedroom.

"Hi," Kelly said as she took a seat in one of the recliners next to the fireplace.

"Hi, yourself. You look a hell of a lot better. You doing ok?"

Kelly nodded as she laid her head against the back of the chair.

"Mabel's been great. I can see why you love her so much. She's a very gracious woman. She made me feel right at home."

"I'm glad to hear that."

Jonathan threw his jacket over the back of the sofa. Kicking off his shoes, he stretched out and finally closed his eyes.

Kelly covered Jonathan with the multi-colored blanket.

"Get some sleep. We can talk tomorrow."

Jonathan nodded without saying a word. He was too wiped out to carry on any type of conversation right now. Thank goodness Kelly wasn't pushing him for any answers.

Kelly met Mabel half-way down the hallway.

"Jonathan's exhausted. We better wait till tomorrow to ask what happened."

Mabel nodded then gave Kelly a hug. "Don't worry. Jonathan will tell us when he's ready. I think we all need some rest right now."

Kelly headed for the guest bedroom. As much as she wanted to take Mabel's advice, all kinds of thoughts were running through her mind.

Austin. Jenna. Now Jonathan.

And her own heart-pounding news.

*****

"Excellent."

Mason was proud of himself.

The note he had written on the back of the photograph would undoubtedly generate a surprise reaction. Perhaps even fear. He certainly hoped so.

He wanted to make sure Agent Maria Turette knew he was taking the game up a notch.

"Ready for the next round, Agent Turette?"

Mason chuckled.

"I am," he said as he confidently sealed the envelope.

Chapter 27

Hans Kliric wasn't happy. He was downright annoyed.

It was stifling hot inside the basement storage room of the museum. A small fan was blowing tepid air across his stern face. Sweat was pouring down his chin faster than he could wipe it away.

His patience was dwindling as the minutes ticked by.

Hans spit on the floor. A waste of time to watch a body which could not move. Austin Reed's arms and legs were tied tightly with heavy, thick rope. Even if he could pull himself up, he wouldn't be able to walk. Especially after the multiple beatings provided by The Closer.

Yet Mason had been very clear in his instructions. Austin Reed was to be watched...*not touched.*

Hans cursed in Russian as he walked to the far end of the room. Lighting one of his cigars, he inhaled the sweet aroma between his nostrils. Nodding, he recalled the last time another member of the Reed family was bound with ropes. A smile creased his lips.

Jenna Reed.

Ahh...

The memory of Jenna Reed struggling against the cords which bound her to the chair at the warehouse...or when she was lying face down on the bed in her hotel room...brought a warm sensation to Hans' body.

Her skin was so soft. He wanted to touch that skin again...

Hans closed his eyes as he fantasized about stroking his calloused fingers all over Jenna's body. Perhaps he would have a chance once again. Hans laughed boisterously as he recalled Jenna's temperament. Maybe she wasn't used to a little forcefulness.

Glancing towards his captive, he wondered if Reed was awake enough to hear him. What did it matter? He would be dead soon.

Hans grunted as he flicked his cigar butt across the floor. Enough of this guard duty. He needed some air.

Hans ripped off a piece of duck tape and slapped it on Austin's mouth to keep him quiet. Shutting the lights off in the storage room, Hans left Mason's little prey in the dark.

Hans walked up the delivery ramp and out to the street. He debated his options. Within a couple of blocks, there were several bars, some seedy and some even respectable, lots of shops and restaurants. If he ventured down a few more streets, he was sure to find some type of female companionship.

A multitude of possibilities. He fully intended to indulge.

Two blocks down and around the corner, Hans sauntered into McMurphy's. He was lucky to find an empty bar stool towards the back. A bar definitely popular with the locals. Practically every seat was taken. Waitresses were finding it quite difficult to navigate in the crowded room, balancing trays of drinks and finger foods. Laughter and toasts were competing for attention-getters. McMurphy's was the place to be.

Hans slapped the bar to get the bartender's attention. In less than a minute, he was served his first two shots of whiskey. Tossing the glasses back, he initially felt searing pain trickle down his throat. Then a relaxed feeling emerged as the liquor dazed his senses.

Hans motioned for the bartender to fill his two glasses with another round. Obediently, the youthful-looking, red-headed bartender didn't blink an eye. Sean McCallister had been tending bar at McMurphy's for the past year. He was in his last year of college. Bartending was good money. Working only a few nights a week, he brought in more with tips than his roommates did working almost thirty hours at fast-food joints.

"Drink up, you fool," Sean said between his gritted teeth. The more drinks he poured, the higher his take-home pay would be. He didn't care if half the patrons drank themselves into oblivion as long as they dropped bills on the bar.

Only on occasion did Sean have to get physical with a drunk. Most of the time, he just kept busy filling glasses at the bar, and watching people. His favorite pastime.

Like this big Russian dude, for example. Badass, no doubt.

Sean was sure his newest customer could hold his liquor. He had downed two straight shots of whiskey like it was water, barely flinching. Now he was on round two. Oh, yeah, definitely badass.

"Another round?" Sean asked the burly man as he picked up the whiskey bottle, ready for round three. Keep 'em coming, he thought to himself. Tonight's take-home would be well worth the crap he had to put up with if his customers started to get mean.

Hans jerked his head and stuck out two fingers.

"You got it," Sean said as he filled the shot glasses then moved hastily to the next poor slob who was demanding another beer. But although he was moving down the bar, Sean was keeping his eyes on the man with the Russian accent. That's what the people in the back were paying him for.

Hans tilted on his barstool. The room seemed to be moving. The laughter was getting louder. Conversations were buzzing around him. It felt pretty good. He could sit here all night.

A redhead two stools down was smiling at him. She was nursing a drink and had one hand on her hip. She was a looker! At least he thought she was. His vision was starting to blur. But he wanted to find out.

Sure enough, as he moved closer, the redhead was smiling at him *again*. Time to get friendly. He started to reach for her. She beat him to it.

Hans was caught off guard when she tugged on his shirt collar, pulling him closer. She smelled of rum and coconut. The scent of her body mixed with the alcohol he had just consumed was making him dizzy. He was too far gone. The woman in the tight, low-cut dress with the tantalizing red hair had slipped her hand inside his back pocket. She was squeezing his ass. The night was getting better.

Sean looked up from wiping the bar and just shook his head. What a sucker, he thought.

You have no idea what's about to go down.

The redhead nodded to Sean as she continued to distract her conquest with her roving hands. She pulled back slowly, speaking to Hans in a low, provocative tone.

"Let's go in the back," she whispered as her tongue glided across Hans' ear.

Hans didn't care if he wasn't picking up every single word she said. Her gestures were definitely in the universal language.

Taking Hans by the hand, the redhead moved seductively towards the back storage room just off the side of the bar.

Hans shuffled down the small hallway allowing her to lead the way. He would let her do anything she wanted right now.

Hans was thrust against a metal rack filled with boxes containing an assortment of bottled beers.

Rough. His kind of woman.

Hans' grin widened as he anxiously awaited her next move. She was batting her eyes at him now and licking her lips. Her hands were groping under his jacket. He had waited long enough.

Grabbing her rear with both hands, he started to make a move of his own.

Mistake. *BIG* mistake.

In three quick seconds, Hans was on the floor with his arms pinned against his back. A strip of packaging tape was thrust across his mouth while his arms were secured with plastic binding. He was yanked to his feet by two men who had come out of nowhere. His wallet had been stripped from his pants. His gun had been taken from its holster.

Several pairs of hands had attacked him in a precise, orchestrated fashion.

Feds.

Hans fought against his restraints. He could hardly move and he couldn't speak. *Not good.*

The woman was rifling through his wallet now.

"Hans Kliric. Mason Hamilton's side-kick. My lucky night," she said sarcastically.

Hans tried to respond as he struggled against the tight grip of his assailants. He could feel the barrel of a gun jammed into his back.

"Consider this a warning, Hans Kliric. Don't mess with Jenna Reed."

Hans cocked his head at the mention of Jenna Reed's name. But what about *her brother*? He would say nothing. He would not betray his boss, Mason Hamilton, under any circumstances.

The redhead tugged on Hans' chin until her face was within inches from his own.

"Anything happens to Jenna Reed, and I will find you again. I won't be so forgiving next time."

Hans stood steadfast, not moving a muscle. He needed to stay strong. These were just threats.

"Good. I can see that we understand each other. Just remember, if any harm comes to Jenna Reed, all kinds of hell will crush you."

The redhead started to move away but then turned to face Hans again. Without warning, she brought up her knee swiftly between his legs.

Hans doubled-over in pain.

"That's for grabbing my ass."

She jerked her head and Hans was pushed towards the back door.

"Now get this piece of trash out of my sight."

Taking in a deep breath, the redhead smiled. Her performance was over.

Annoyed with the way her tight clothes were feeling at the moment, she tugged on her short dress to move it down a bit. Fluffing her red wig, she downed the beer left by one of her associates, then nonchalantly sauntered back into the bar.

*****

Mason watched the ripples cascade across his pool. A relaxed feeling swept over him.

For just a few seconds.

"Mason."

Mason jumped at the intrusion then gripped his chair. It was so irritating how The Closer could sneak up on him whenever the hell he felt like it.

"I...didn't expect you." Mason said nervously as he motioned for The Closer to take a seat.

"You should know by now, I like to come unannounced."

Mason made no comment.

"I trust you are getting acquainted with...*your wife*?"

"Yes, she is playing her part quite well."

The Closer nodded. He had no doubts; Mallory was the best. She took on any role with such vigor, he wondered how she could separate fantasy from reality, but she always did. A trained professional...in *every* regard.

"Very good."

The Closer scanned the poolside area for any other staff who might overhear their conversation. They were alone.

"Tomorrow evening this matter will conclude...in your office?"

Mason sipped his martini, wishing to hell The Closer would leave as soon as possible.

"I'm expecting Jenna Reed to arrive at eight. She left a message. Although, I'm sure she's being counseled to avoid me altogether by her friends at the FBI."

"They'll be watching her every move."

"You do have people in place to handle the FBI's interference?"

"I have resources at my disposal, always. I will make sure your meeting with Ms. Reed is undisturbed. I can restrain her, if you wish."

Mason waved his hands. "That won't be necessary. Hans will be with me. I will have Jenna Reed's undivided attention."

The Closer laughed.

"Kliric? He's an idiot. My men tracked him to a bar earlier this evening when he was supposed to be watching your prisoner. He is obviously incapable of following simple commands."

Mason ground his teeth. It was unsettling when The Closer felt the need to zero in on Hans' incompetency.

"Very well. Maybe you should be there. Just for back-up. I still think Hans..."

Mason turned around. He was talking to himself. The Closer had disappeared as mysteriously as he had appeared. Mason felt a chill go up his neck.

The Closer moved like a ghost.

*****

Maria tossed and turned, then pounded her pillow in frustration. She wasn't in her own bed. Hotel beds, no matter how nice they were, always made Maria fully aware she wasn't at home. She flung herself to the left, this time knocking into her husband Damian. She lovingly patted him in a silent apology, letting her hand linger on the small of his back.

How she wished she could just close her eyes, curl against his warm, muscle-toned back and forget the cares of the world. A nice thought, but that's all it was. *For now.*

Maria made a mental note to schedule a few days off when they got back home to D.C. She needed some down time.

The room wasn't so dark now. Dawn was approaching. She needed to get moving.

The rest of her team had bunked at the FBI safe house. Jacoby was probably barking orders right now, rousing the other agents from their beds.

Maria smiled, thinking of Jacoby being in charge. He was a natural leader and someone she could rely on in her absence. But Jacoby always gave her back the reins. He would never disrespect her by competing for the unit. They were a team, first and foremost.

But today, she wished Jacoby was the one wearing the *Special-Agent-in-Charge* badge.

Maria groaned. The weight on her shoulders was pushing her down making it harder to get up. She had a solid plan for the mission but there was no marginal room for error. Her team needed to be in sync.

The FBI would begin its convergence on the museum, putting their undercover agents in place around the perimeter. All exits would be secured with tactical teams placed strategically inside. Jenna would enter the museum fully protected.

With luck on their side, Mason Hamilton would be in FBI custody by this time tomorrow morning. Austin Reed would be returned safely to his sister. Jenna Reed could get on with her life.

Maria could get the hell out of Dodge, or New York, actually.

If her plan worked out. 'If' was such a big word. A major pain-in-the-ass word.

There were still too many unpredictable variables. What if Mason anticipated her attack? He wasn't stupid by any stretch. If anything, he was the most sadistic, calculating person she knew. What if he wasn't holding Austin Reed in the museum, or worse…if he had killed him already? What if Jenna caved at the last moment, or was caught by Mason's men?

No matter what, Maria couldn't let the 'ifs' bring her confidence level down. She had faced immeasurable odds before. She had a job to do, and she would tackle it the best way she knew. Without fear. Without reserve.

Get in and get it done.

The ceiling fan hummed above her. Maria could see the outline of the blades spinning slowly in a gentle rhythm. She rested her arm on her forehead and closed her eyes, forcing her body to relax for a few more minutes.

Slim chance of that happening.

Sensing her agitation, Damian laid his arm across Maria's stomach and pulled her closer. He brushed his lips against her shoulder.

"You're not sleeping, Sweetheart," he murmured as he opened one eye.

"Can't. Too much to think about."

"I know."

"Yes…you do."

Maria snuggled against Damian as he lifted his head to face her. Grateful for his comfort now and all the years they had been together; she dreaded having to leave the warm coziness of his arms. They had endured so much over the years, fearing for each other's safety when one or both of them were on dangerous assignments. But somehow, fate always managed to bring them back together.

Where had time gone?

She had met Damian shortly after being assigned to a surveillance team tracking a drug cartel out of Atlanta. Security feeds were being routed to the CIA's main office in Langley. Maria and Damian spent countless hours deciphering taped footage in order to spot identifying markers which could lead to arrests of known felons.

Long, tedious hours of peering at the same terminal intensified their mutual attraction. Their faces were within inches of each other. It wasn't too long before a short distance was even too painful to maintain.

When the mission ended, the field operatives and the technical staff wanted to celebrate. Maria and Damian never made it to the group party. They had holed up in a cozy bed and breakfast overlooking the St. James River, never coming up for air for almost a week. The first of many passionate marathons they had shared over the past thirty years.

At first, Maria never thought she stood a chance with Damian Pierce. He managed to catch the eye of every available female in the surveillance division.

Maria wasn't the type to flaunt herself like so many of the other young CIA operatives. But she could still look his way occasionally...frequently...and *fantasize*.

Young, self-assured, but without an ounce of conceit, Damian Pierce exuded sexuality whenever he strode into a room. His golden-bronzed skin, his muscles taut from extreme workouts, and his scintillating green eyes mesmerized Maria from the first time she had seen him.

Maria studied the security tapes for hours at a time. If her eyes were glued to the terminal, they weren't darting in Damian's direction. She was too afraid to look at him. How could she possibly explain herself? It would be humiliating to say the least.

Her superiors took notice of her dedication to the job. They were impressed she was taking her assignment seriously, but Maria was concentrating on her job only because she had no other choice. She knew gazing into the tempting eyes of Damian Pierce would have damaging effects on her.

Maria replayed the tapes over and over because she was so distracted. When Damian leaned over her shoulder, Maria could hardly breathe...or speak...or think.

In a few incoherent words, she said yes to his offer of drinks after work.

A date with Damian Pierce?

Maybe she misunderstood. He was probably just being considerate since they were always the last two people left in the office. It wasn't really a *date* in the traditional sense.

Then why was she so nervous? God knows she didn't want to embarrass herself in front of a co-worker. It would be all over the office the next day. But Damian was so handsome. So what if she called it a date in her mind. He didn't have to know.

It turned out to be the date from hell.

Maria didn't hold her liquor well. They both found out the hard way.

The first whiskey sour went down very smooth. They began to laugh and kid each other as the music blared in the background. Maria was starting to feel good, relaxed.

But when the second round of drinks arrived, Maria took one sip, then bolted to the ladies room. She couldn't get there fast enough. She finally returned to the table looking so pale, Damian was afraid she was going to pass out. He promptly told her he was taking her home.

Their enjoyable evening had turned into a personal rescue mission. After helping Maria out of the car, Damian scooped her into his arms, carrying her up three flights of stairs to her apartment.

Maria would never forget his kindness, the way he never judged her or made fun of her inability to indulge in a couple drinks. Instead, Damian helped her into the shower with comforting words, staying just outside the door to make sure she was ok. Wrapping Maria in a towel, he helped her to the bed, then sat beside her until she fell asleep.

In the morning, Maria woke with a major headache, cursing herself and wondering who would tease her first when she arrived at the office. Dragging herself out of bed, she padded to the kitchen. She almost dropped the coffee decanter.

Damian was smiling at her from the sofa. He had spent the night to make sure she was fine.

Maria did the only thing she could think of at the time. She pushed Damian out of her apartment so he wouldn't see her shame.

Would he give her a second chance?

She didn't have to wonder for too long. When she arrived at work, there was a bouquet of yellow roses on her desk. At first she didn't want to read the card, but she was glad she did.

"Best first date I ever had."

Maria was ready to laugh and cry.

Damian snuck up behind her and kissed the side of her neck. Maria was gone. There was no going back. She knew Damian Pierce was the only man she would want for the rest of her life.

After several months, forced separations were making their lives too complicated. Different offices, different states, different levels of clearance. Pulled apart by their jobs, Maria and Damian soon felt the strain on their relationship. It was becoming unbearable.

Something had to change.

Regrettably, Maria made a hasty decision. She told Damian they were over. She had to focus on her assignment in New York. The mission was heating up. She would be going deep undercover for several months.

Damian was devastated. Maria had a hold on him. She was young, driven, and the sexiest woman he ever met. He was so amazed at her ability to try anything and keep at it with such determination. She never gave up...on anything. He just couldn't understand why she was giving up...on *him*.

Unable to deal with her absence at the CIA, he resigned. Within two months, Damian was recruited by the FBI. He needed a fresh start. But what he needed most was Maria. No matter where he went, he couldn't escape the memory of what they had together. He was losing his mind. He wanted her desperately.

Maria couldn't take it any longer. Even though her highly confidential assignment was taking up most of her time, she missed Damian more than anything.

Taking a chance he would still want her, Maria called him. Within hours, Damian arrived in New York. They met outside the city, away from anyone who could jeopardize her cover. Every other weekend, Damian drove up from D.C. to be with her.

And every time he left, he took another part of Maria with him. She kept promising Damian her assignment wouldn't last much longer and then they could be together.

But something went terribly wrong. Damian always called right before he was leaving to make sure Maria could still rendezvous with him. Maria wasn't answering her phone at home or her cover job at the Hamilton-Knox Foundation. When Damian arrived at hotel and requested their usual room, the manager told him Maria had not yet arrived.

Damian waited all night, still trying to reach her. He had been told never to go to her apartment in the city or her cover would be blown. After several more unanswered calls, he returned to D.C.

He contacted her handler but was told he didn't have enough clearance to warrant a status report on her assignment. Maria had simply vanished.

For the next several months, Damian didn't know if Maria was dead or alive. Exhausting all of his resources at the CIA and

FBI, he was just about ready to give up when Maria came bounding through his door.

Damian didn't care. He didn't want explanations. He knew Maria would tell him everything eventually. She was back...and that was all that mattered.

Within a couple of weeks, Maria was assigned to a joint task force comprised of CIA, FBI and various local law enforcement agents on an undercover assignment in Boston. During this mission, Maria was directly recruited by the FBI at Damian's suggestion.

After she completed her part of the investigation, Maria flew back to Langley and promptly resigned. She wasn't going to make the same mistake twice. She would never let her job interfere with her relationship with Damian ever again.

Aware of her relationship with Special Agent Damian Pierce, her superiors cautioned her, even suggesting she terminate the relationship if she wanted to succeed. The FBI was getting ready to implement a policy stating agents were not encouraged to date, or marry. The policy would take effect in sixty days. There was only one way to get around it.

Damian and Maria were married two days later. But the FBI made no promises. Assignments could take them in different directions, but for the most part, they would be able to stay locally in D.C. It was the best arrangement they could hope for as they once again tried to balance their commitment to each other and their careers.

Those early years seemed so far away now, Maria thought as she lay in bed. *And I'm still chasing my tail.*

Damian rubbed Maria's cheek. "I'm here for you," he said in his raspy, sexy voice which always drove Maria a little crazy even after all these years.

As Maria leaned over to kiss him, Damian grabbed her by the neck and rolled on top of her.

"I have to jump in the shower and get over to the safe house in about..." Maria's eyes darted over to the alarm clock. "...forty-five minutes. You're good, but..."

Damian didn't let her finish. He was too busy occupying her mouth. Finally, he let them both come up for air.

"Oh, we both know how good...and *quick*...we can be. So, stop wasting time. You have work to do today."

Maria felt herself giving in. Damian still tempted her with the same fierceness she experienced the first time his lips had found hers.

As much as she wanted to stay in bed with Damian, Maria reluctantly pushed him on his back. She ran her fingers over the bruise that was just starting to fade just above his hip.

"I'm still sorry about that," Maria confessed as she bent down to kiss him lightly, keeping one hand firmly planted against his chest.

Realizing it was her own husband in his covert role as Dimitri Batrov in the shed at the Fortenni house, Maria had to make her assault look as real as possible. She had rammed her taser gun against Damian's side with a little too much force so he could pretend he received an electrical jolt.

"Still hurt?" Maria asked, trying to look apologetic.

"Not too much. Stop changing the subject. I want you."

Damian allowed Maria to momentarily hover over him, as he ran his fingers through her hair. He kissed her gently this time on her chin, as she regrettably shook her head.

"No time," she sighed, once again contemplating just how much her job...and her obsession with catching Mason Hamilton had consumed her life.

"Make time....*for us*."

One more kiss perfectly placed and she....Damian smiled as he heard Maria moan softly.

Worked every time.

Maria let herself go, as she always did when Damian tugged on her heart strings. Like so many times neither one of them could go into a dangerous situation before they showed each other why they were still together after so many years. It had always been more than love and frenzied embraces.

It was knowing they *belonged* to one another.

Chapter 28

Jenna was restless. As her fingers grabbed clumps of the sheet, she stared into the darkness. Her mind was too preoccupied. Dangerous thoughts of facing Mason Hamilton, rescuing Austin and staying alive were keeping her awake.

Stay focused. Keep confident.

Agent Turette and Teresa both told her there was nothing to worry about. FBI agents would be swarming the museum. She would be fully protected. Just follow directions. Piece of cake.

Right.

She needed to get Mason's attention and stall for the FBI.

It sounded easy enough.

Then why was she scared beyond words?

Chase stirred, distracting her. Jenna breathed steadily. She had almost lost him. Chase couldn't understand why she called Jonathon Knox to help her. Jenna wondered the same thing.

Desperation. *Was that the only reason?*

Jenna forced doubts out of her mind.

She closed her fingers around his hand. A safe haven. All she had to do was reach out and Chase would be there for her.

"Hi," she whispered, after kissing his eyelid. A subtle attempt to make amends.

Chase opened one eye and smiled. Jenna looked so good in the morning after spending the night in his arms. How could he possibly stay mad at her?

"Are you always going to wake me with a kiss?"

"I just might, you never know."

"I'm willing to take that gamble."

Chase's arms closed the small gap between them. "You feel good," he whispered into the hollow of her neck.

"Chase…

Jenna tried to disentangle their arms, but Chase had no intention of letting her.

"We don't have time."

"Yes, we do. The FBI can wait."

"I need to take a shower, grab some breakfast..."

"Excuses, excuses."

Chase locked his arms. He wasn't giving up. He needed to show her just how much he cared.

"Chase, please. I just can't...*focus* right now."

"You don't need to focus. Just let go."

Chase rolled Jenna onto her back despite her feeble attempts to push him away.

"Are you really going to tell me not to make love to you?"

Jenna couldn't hide her smile. And despite her minor protests, she was happy he was standing his ground.

"Well?" Chase asked knowing full well the way Jenna's body was responding she had already made up her mind.

"Don't stop," Jenna said between short breaths. She never wanted to push Chase away again.

She needed everything he was...everything he could give her. Promises. Hope. Love.

She needed to feel it all...before she walked into the fire.

*****

Jonathan awoke with stiffness in his neck. Falling asleep on the sofa last night had resulted in a strained neck muscle.

He struggled to sit up then caught a whiff of unmistakable aromas coming from the kitchen. A smile spread across his face.

Breakfast...his grandmother's way.

French toast, Canadian bacon, scrambled eggs with onions and peppers. The good stuff only his grandmother knew how to make all at once. It was a home-cooked buffet. He was dying to get started on it.

Darting for the kitchen, Jonathan stopped short at the doorway. To his surprise, it wasn't his grandmother cooking at the stove.

Kelly flipped the French toast on the two-burner griddle.

Jonathan stared in amazement.

"Something wrong?" Kelly asked.

"I...just expected my grandmother to be at the stove."

"Mabel went to the store. She was out of creamer. Sit down and I'll get you some coffee."

Kelly turned the Canadian bacon, then placed a cup of steaming hot coffee on the table.

"You look like hell."

Jonathan laughed after taking a sip. "Thanks...you look *good*, too."

Kelly looked down and saw powdery white specks on the over-sized t-shirt she was wearing. "I'm trying a new *adventure*...cooking."

"Well it smells great. Learning secret recipes?"

"Sort of...Mabel made most of the food. I'm just putting on the finishing touches. I hope you don't mind I borrowed your shirt. My clothes are in the wash."

"Take whatever you like. I'm only here on weekends."

Kelly took the golden brown slices off the griddle. Sprinkling them with powdered sugar and cinnamon, she plopped a plate down in front of Jonathan.

"This looks amazing. Thanks."

Kelly wiped her hands on her jeans then took a seat.

"What's going on, Jonathan? Please tell me you have news about Austin."

"Not yet, but we're working on it."

"We?"

Jonathan put his fork down and took Kelly's hand.

"I have a lot to tell you, but first I have to ask my grandmother a few things. Can you give us a minute when she gets back?"

"No problem. I'll take a shower and get out of your way."

Jonathan's comments sparked Kelly's curiosity but she didn't want to pry. She was in Jonathan's debt for letting her stay with Mabel. She would just have to be patient even though it was killing her not to hear news about Austin.

The back screen door swung wide open. Mabel Tremont marched in, carrying not one, but two grocery bags. Jonathan immediately got up and took the bags out of her arms.

"It's about time you got up. Kelly and I were beginning to wonder if we should fix lunch instead of breakfast."

"It's only eight o'clock."

"Well, when you get up at four-thirty like I do to tend to the dogs, eight o'clock seems like half the morning is over."

"I love you too, Grandmom. Breakfast is great by the way. I see you're training an apprentice." Jonathan hurried back to his chair and stuffed his mouth full of French toast.

"Best one I ever had. Not that you were too interested in cooking...only eating."

Kelly rose, as if on cue. "I'm going to take a shower."

Mabel watched Kelly leave, then poured herself a cup of coffee. "Why did you ask Kelly to leave?"

"Perceptive as ever. Actually, I asked Kelly to give us a few minutes. I need to ask you something."

Jonathan gulped down his coffee, hoping the caffeine would give him the jolt he needed.

"Was I adopted?" Short and to the point was sometimes the only way.

Mabel gripped her coffee mug to keep it from falling.

"Yes," she said matter-of-factly. Honesty was always best even though it was shocking to hear. "Gail adopted you when you were only a few months old."

Jonathan's eyes closed slowly. Maria had told him the truth. She was his real mother.

"Gail and your mother became very good friends. After you were born...well, let's just say, your real mother found it hard to keep you. Gail brought you back to Boston to live with me. That is, until she married Elliott, then the three of you became a family."

"Thank you...for telling me, Grandmom. I needed to know."

"Gail didn't want to tell you. She thought she was protecting you, but I really thought you had a right to know."

"I know now; that's all that matters. I always thought I wasn't their son by birth. But I didn't let it bother me. My parents loved me. You loved me. I had a great life growing up. No complaints."

Mabel pulled Jonathan into her arms. "Then you shouldn't have any worries now. I will *always* be your grandmom."

"I want you to know something else, Grandmom. My birth mother has introduced herself to me."

Mabel clasped her chest. *It couldn't be.*

"Are you sure, Jonathan? Gail thought...well, she told me your real mother went away and was never heard from again."

Mabel tried to remember. Too many years were fogging up her memory.

"I'm sure, Grandmom. She's quite *alive*."

"Why did she wait this long to come back? I don't understand." Mabel got up to pour another cup of coffee. She needed more than one this morning.

"I'm not sure. Hopefully, one day she'll tell me. All I know is she wanted to make sure I was safe."

Mabel drank the rest of her coffee straight down. She wondered if Jonathan knew the rest...the absolute worst part of the story.

"Did she happen to tell you...who your real father is?"

Jonathan nodded slowly. "Mason Hamilton."

Mabel cringed.

"Your boss."

"Yeah, that does complicate everything. I have no desire to share that bit of news unless I have no other choice."

"Be careful, Jonathan. Mason Hamilton can't be trusted. You take care of yourself."

"I will. One day Mason is going to get exactly what he deserves. I'm bound and determined to see that day come, believe me."

Jonathan felt a rage building inside him.

"Don't do anything foolish. I'll worry too much about you."

Mabel got up to rinse out her coffee mug.

"I'm going to check on Kelly."

When Jonathan left the kitchen, Mabel let her shoulders sag. "God help you, Jonathan," she said as she tossed pieces of French toast to her faithful four-legged friends.

Kelly stepped out of the bathroom, barely having time to tie her robe before she jumped back. Jonathan was sitting on the bed in the guest room.

"What are you doing in here?"

"Waiting for you."

Startled, Kelly pulled her robe tighter. She quickly grabbed her bra and panties from the corner of the bed.

"I need to talk to you."

"You couldn't wait until I was dressed?"

"Sorry about that. I have a lot to tell you. Grandmom just confirmed my suspicions. I was adopted."

Kelly sat next to Jonathan. Hearing such news was probably a shock, although in her case, it would certainly be a blessing.

"Which brings me to the next round of earth-shattering news…You're my… *sister*."

Kelly's mouth flew open. *Then that would mean…*

"Mason Hamilton is my father, too," Jonathan said with a tone of sadness.

"How do you know this?"

Kelly felt remorse wash over her. Jonathan now had the same cross to bear.

"I met my mother…my birth mother…last night."

Kelly was speechless.

"My mother and Mason had an affair thirty years ago, when your mother and Mason were first married. I was born first and then a few months later you came along."

"This is incredible."

"Everyone thought my mother supposedly died in an apartment fire but it was someone else. She's alive and kicking….kicking ass, as a matter of fact. My mother is an FBI agent."

Kelly stared in amazement.

"Her team is going to rescue Austin, and hopefully find enough incriminating evidence to bring Mason down once and for all." Jonathan paused.

"What are you not telling me?"

"Part of the plan requires Jenna to walk into Mason's office and stall him until the FBI gets there. Jenna found the treasure pieces, Kelly. They were buried in Cape May…at her family's beach house all these years."

"Jenna is taking too much of a risk."

"That's what worries me, too."

Jonathan glanced at his watch. "I need to get going. I'm helping the FBI decipher the museum's blueprints."

Kelly grabbed Jonathan's arm. "Promise me you won't do anything to put yourself in danger."

"I'll be as safe as I can, Kelly. Please don't worry. Stay here with Grandmom. I'll call you as soon as I know anything."

"Be careful. I don't want to lose you. Besides being my brother, you're going to have another role to play soon."

Now Kelly had Jonathan's undivided attention.

"Uncle," she said as her voice wavered.

Kelly's face held mixed emotions. She was happy to finally be able to share her good news, but hesitant because her future was so uncertain.

"Does Austin know?"

Kelly bit her lower lip. "Not yet."

Jonathan put his arm around Kelly and she laid her head on his shoulder.

"We'll find him, Kelly. I promise you. I'll do whatever I can to find Austin."

"Thank you, Jonathan."

Kelly nodded, but felt helpless all the same. When Jonathan left, she fell backwards on the bed, resting her hand on her stomach.

"Stay safe for me, Austin," she prayed. "For both of us."

Chapter 29

"I don't mind helping, you know I don't," Teresa Maylor announced as she leaned against the table in the kitchen of the FBI safe house.

"But, damn it, don't make me wear tight clothes again and dress up like a hooker! I don't have the shape I used to. Those days of tight miniskirts draped over my ass need to be over!"

"Oh, I don't know, you filled out the costume just fine. I heard you even got a few whistles from some of the patrons."

Maria stifled a laugh, trying to look serious.

"Uh…huh. You have no idea how close I came to decking a couple smartasses saddled up at the bar."

"I'm sure you gave them a dignified response."

Teresa smirked. "I wouldn't exactly say it was dignified, even for an undercover agent. Let's just say, I got my point across. No one messed with me after that."

Maria doubled-over. "You still have your touch."

"Oh, yeah, I still have the touch. In fact, Kliric is probably still seeing stars from where my knee *touched* him."

Maria had to steady herself against the counter. Her face was turning red from hearty laughter.

"Next time you wear the disguise. I'll be the one sitting behind the desk, thinking up our next move."

"Is that all you think I do?"

Teresa gave Maria another snarled look then folded her arms. It wasn't long before she was laughing, too.

"Where is everyone?" Teresa asked, changing the subject.

Maria finally gained her composure. "Everyone should be arriving soon. But I'm worried about Ellen. I couldn't reach her last night."

"Probably too busy getting her manicure perfected. I'm sorry, Maria, but that rich bitch really irritated me yesterday. Did you see the way she expected us to clear off her trash? She couldn't even get off her ass to drop the paper plate into the trashcan!"

"She comes from another world, Teresa. She's probably never used a paper plate before."

"Oh, don't get me started."

"I know better than that."

Teresa set down her mug and cooled her tone. She could see Maria was genuinely worried.

"Maybe Hamilton was within earshot. She's probably on her way."

"Let's hope you're right."

"New subject. How do you think your son is taking the news?"

Maria shook her head and kept her eye on the window.

"Not sure. Devastated, shocked, relieved...I'm not sure how I would react. Finding out you're adopted can be traumatic enough. Then to top it off with finding your birth mother...who is about to arrest the man who was your business mentor...only to find out he's really your father and...finally to learn you have a sister. I'm sure Jonathan's head is spinning."

"I would say so."

"What was I supposed to do, Teresa? I'd be worried sick about him getting involved, and he would probably wonder why I was acting so strange." Maria shrugged her shoulders.

"Stranger than usual?" Her friend teased.

"Keep it up and I will make you go undercover again. I hear tube tops are making a comeback."

"In your dreams," Teresa said as she reached for the coffee decanter.

"Trading undercover stories again?" Jacoby asked as he strode into the kitchen and grabbed a mug off the counter. Looking inside, he grimaced and decided it needed a good rinse.

"Not enough hours in the day for our stories," Teresa chimed.

"Too bad. I was hoping to hear something I can use for blackmail."

"Girlfriend code. We do not divulge our innermost secrets. You're out of luck."

Maria shoved Jacoby out of the way. He was blocking her access to the donut box.

Thompson poked his head around the corner.

"Everyone's here except Hamilton's wife. You want to get started?"

"Yes, let's move."

Maria headed for the meeting room after gobbling down her Boston crème. The worried look returned to her face. Something must have happened. Maybe Ellen felt compromised and had to stay home. But no calls or even a text? Maybe she was worrying for nothing.

In less than twelve hours her tactical teams were set to converge on the museum, and she had to play mind games once again with Mason Hamilton. This would require precise planning, coordination, and a hell of a lot of luck.

"This is what we're going to do," she said as she glanced around the room. Her team had assembled and was focused. Now it was time to outsmart the mastermind.

*****

Mason paced his office. He was getting too old for this game with Maria Turette and her cohorts at the FBI. Yet he enjoyed the entertainment.

Mason stared out his windows at the pedestrians several floors below him. It wouldn't be long until he said good-bye to the city life, taking up residency in the Hamptons with an occasional trip to his secret villa in Venice. Without the family baggage. A smile emerged. A vindictive smile.

Mason took a break from daydreaming about his retirement to skim through the pages of his scheduling book. Conference calls, staff meetings, rubbing elbows with donors, and the endless stream of paperwork. Mundane tasks which should be delegated. But where was Jonathan?

It was almost ten o'clock. Did Jonathan think being an executive entitled him to sleep in late on a work day? Jonathan needed to be reminded of his office responsibilities, and his corporate image.

Later. Jonathan's disregard for his business duties were the least of Mason's concerns.

Something else required his utmost attention.

His treasure was coming home.

Mason could hardly contain his excitement.

Thirty years of searching would be ending tonight.

The Lost Treasure of Blackbeard...placed in his hands.

Other artifacts had surfaced dating back to Blackbeard's time, mostly items taken from the Queen Anne's Revenge located off the coast of North Carolina. Parts of the ship and some small trinkets had been retrieved, but no significant treasure pieces.

Not until tonight.

Within hours, Mason would be holding the only known gold treasure acquired by the infamous pirate. What a remarkable find! Mason could just hear the accolades now. He would be the envy of every museum curator in the world!

When Jenna Reed placed the gold animal figurines in his hands, Mason knew he would feel pure ecstasy.

Then, of course...he would have to kill her.

*****

Jenna squirmed in her chair. She wasn't bored, but she was baffled by all the FBI jargon.

"Vantage points need to be tri-angulated. NYPD needs to be on-board. I need their point person's name. Thompson, get on the horn with Central. We may need to pull another team."

Jacoby was taking notes as Maria barked commands.

"We've got a tech van coming. We can set up across the street."

"Good to know." Maria scanned the blueprints and maps covering the large table in front of her.

Turning sideways, she checked the SMART board. Data was compiling faster than the human brain could comprehend. It gave her a headache just watching the percentage computations going up and down. Success and failure rates were constantly re-adjusting when new data was entered to the sophisticated data system. Only Jacoby could understand it.

"A sniper will be in place. Should give him direct sight into Hamilton's office. Success rate 86.93 percent. Knox, do you know the type of glass installed in the offices? It will make a difference for shot calcs."

Jonathan jerked his head. He had been overly distracted worrying about Jenna's involvement to pay close attention to anything being said.

"Not sure. It's not bullet-proof, if that's what you're asking. I have no idea about thickness of the glass, though. Isn't that listed somewhere in the architectural documents?"

"Nothing's listed. Can someone please check with the insurance company or the security firm?"

"On it," Jacoby said, sensing Maria's frustration. He punched a number on his cell, then walked towards the back of the room.

"Thompson, you got your team sites down? I don't want any surprises at any exit," Maria said as she looked up briefly from the blueprints.

"Ready. Waiting on green light to move out."

Maria looked over at Jenna and nodded. "Jenna, you will proceed through the main entrance at approximately eight-fifteen. Hamilton is expecting you at eight, but we'll add in a few minutes to your scheduled arrival. Let him sweat it out."

Jenna snapped to attention and felt her body going rigid. Maria's announcement was going to catch Chase off-guard. Fearing his reaction, she hadn't told him ahead of time.

Jenna didn't have to turn in Chase's direction. She could sense his anger. It was vibrating off his skin. Chase was gripping the seat of his chair.

"Don't underestimate Hamilton. He knows full well Jenna won't be coming alone. We need to anticipate a reaction. I have no doubt he's got someone on board," Maria cautioned.

"The Closer?" Jacoby asked, as a hush fell over the room.

"Could be. We have to take that into consideration."

Maria looked around the room. Several faces were drawn tight. The mere mention of the notorious assassin always put her team on edge.

"Who is The Closer?" Jenna asked, finally breaking the brief silence.

Some of the agents exchanged worried looks. Maria shook her head, conveying to her team to go silent.

"Basically, he's an extremely well-paid hit man with a signature kill style...his weapon of choice is a rare hunting knife which he uses with precision. He has quite a reputation in international circles, although occasionally he does make an appearance in the States. Intel indicates he may be rubbing elbows with Hamilton. Unfortunately, we haven't been able to determine his true identity.

He surfaces then goes under the radar for months. He's very elusive."

Jenna sank back against her chair. *God help me.*

Chase jumped to his feet, practically propelling himself across the room. Two agents grabbed him before he could get close to Maria at the head of the table. Chase shook them off, and then straightened up.

"You mean to tell me you're going to let Jenna walk right in the front door without any type of escort? With the possibility an assassin is lurking somewhere inside! Are you all crazy?"

Maria maintained her composure. "Dr. Garrett, I appreciate your concern…"

Chase cut her off. "No, I don't think you do. Jenna is risking her life for your mission! None of you get that!"

"I get that, believe me," Maria emphasized as she exchanged a glance with Jonathan. "Please sit down. We're working every angle to make sure Jenna is fully protected."

Chase walked back to his seat. He didn't like these odds. He didn't need the SMART board to tell him what the risks were.

Jenna tugged on Chase's arm. "Please, Chase…for me, please sit down."

Chase reluctantly took his seat and pushed Jenna's hand away. He couldn't even talk to her right now. She was as blind as the rest of the people in the room.

"Let's take a break," Maria said after sizing up the tension. "Ten minutes."

The room started to break up. The agents headed straight for the coffee pots, and a few went outside for smokes.

Maria pulled Teresa aside, watching Chase storm out.

"Get him the hell out of here. He's making Jenna nervous. I can't have her distracted today."

"He's worried, Maria. You're putting the woman he cares about in a very risky situation."

"Teresa, don't you think I know?"

"He needs to blow off some steam. I'll talk to him." Teresa started to leave, then pulled Maria's arm motioning her friend to follow.

"What?"

"You know what…get your ass out of this room…*now.*"

Maria finally relented, following Teresa to the kitchen. "I was just trying…"

"I know what you were *trying*. You need to stay out of it. I'm telling you right now that love triangle is going to be trouble."

Maria waved off her friend.

"I'm not sure about that. Chase Garrett is headstrong. Jenna may get tired of that."

"Headstrong or not, he's in love with her. So don't interfere."

"Alright. I get the picture. Let's get more coffee." Maria moved towards the coffee pots.

"Maybe you should switch to decaf."

"Not today."

Filling her mug to the brim, Maria stepped outside to get some fresh air.

*****

Jenna sat frozen in her chair. She was stunned by Chase's temper and the way he rebuffed her in front of everyone. She should have told him…about going into the museum *alone*. One little detail. Actually, a major detail. The omission was now looking like a lie. Irreparable damage was done. Jenna dropped her head into her hands.

Jonathan knelt down in front of Jenna and gently pried her hands away from her face.

"You're in good hands."

"Yours or the FBI's?"

Jonathan smiled. She had seen right through his little comforting gesture.

"Touché, Ms. Reed."

"I just want to save Austin. Why can't Chase see that?"

"I'm sure he does. Garrett doesn't want you to be put in danger. He's afraid for you."

"Oh…so now you're defending Chase?"

"Not defending…just understanding."

Jonathan rubbed her hands. The electricity was building. Slowly at first but it was definitely rising. The friction between their hands was causing a heated sensation to run up his arms.

Was Jenna feeling it too?

"Jonathan…"

Jonathan was here and Chase wasn't. She couldn't push him away when he was the only one who stayed behind. But Jenna still felt guilty all the same.

"Jenna, listen to me…"

Jenna felt the magnetic pull again. She was so tired of resisting. Another slight tug and she would be gone. No matter how hard she tried to avoid it…Jonathan was irresistible. When he locked eyes with her, Jenna felt herself drowning, forgetting everything that was happening.

"I don't want to…"

Jenna tried to utter words, but her brain was slowing down. When Jonathan squeezed her hands again she couldn't see anything but him.

"Let me…"

Jonathan moved closer. He was inches from her face. Leaning in, he knew Jenna would let him kiss her…she was looking at him now, completely vulnerable. Her breath was coming in short gasps as he neared her lips.

Jonathan heard footsteps coming from the next room. Dropping her hands, he rocked back on his heels and cursed silently.

Their moment had been lost.

Jonathan quickly returned to his seat. Break time was over. Back to business. The FBI was as regimented as possible.

Damn them for being so efficient.

"Mr. Knox, could you take a look at this floor plan? We need to confirm the layout of the offices so we can strategically position our teams," Jacoby said.

"Of course."

"Can you think of anyone besides the security guards who would possibly be in the offices after eight o'clock besides Mason Hamilton?"

"Mason will probably have Kliric there. Not sure of anyone else since Batrov was captured."

Maria looked away, trying to hide a smile. Her agents knew about Damian's undercover role, but she wasn't ready to divulge that information to civilians.

"We've taken that into consideration. Thank you."

Chase was fuming. His arms were folded in disgust. Why was Jenna looking over at Knox now? Was she so impressed with his willingness to help the mission? Or was it something else?

Chase could hardly contain his anger. As soon as Maria announced the lunch break, he bolted from the room. He needed as much fresh air as he could get...to push the jealous rage out of his head.

*****

As the room emptied, Jenna and Jonathan found themselves alone again. Jenna started to rise out of her chair, but Jonathan pulled her back down.

"Look at me," he said. His voice tone was deeper, forceful.

Jenna shook her head. Not this time. She couldn't. Her eyelids shut instinctively.

"Jenna...don't fight me." Jonathan's fingers traced Jenna's jawbone stopping at her neck.

Every touch was branding her, forcing her obedience, but Jenna remained still, willing herself to stay strong. It was agonizing. When she felt Jonathan's breath hover above her lips, her eyes began to flicker. Her willpower was fading. She was surrendering.

Jenna opened her eyes expecting Jonathan's lips to come crashing down on her own. Instead, to her surprise she was alone. Suddenly she could breathe again. At least she thought so.

Not really.

Jenna choked trying to get enough air inside her lungs. Gripping the table, she tried to stand. It was nearly impossible...her legs felt weak. She fell back into her chair.

"My God, Jenna, are you alright?"

Teresa raced over and put a hand on Jenna's back.

"You look like you're going to pass out. Here, drink some water."

Teresa shoved the water bottle into Jenna's hand.

"Did you eat breakfast?"

"Didn't have time," Jenna said, clutching her chest.

Teresa ran out of the meeting room. Returning a few minutes later with a plateful of food, she placed it on Jenna's lap.

Jenna took a small bite out of the turkey sandwich. Even though her stomach was growling, she hardly had an appetite for anything.

You need to eat to gain strength.

Chase's reassuring words were echoing in her head. He was always worried she wasn't eating enough. Chase. Worrying. Caring. Not by her side.

Oh, God, what had she done?

Jenna shut her eyes as they began to mist. She had pushed Chase away. The best man she had ever met.

Teresa noticed Jenna wipe a tear away from her cheek.

"You want to talk about it?"

"Not really."

"Try."

Jenna reached for her sandwich then let it fall to her plate. "Chase and I....well, let's just say, I didn't tell him *everything* last night. He's freaking out right now because I failed to mention the part about me going in *alone*."

"I wasn't talking about Chase."

Jenna leaned back in her chair.

"The blood has completely drained from your face. Does Jonathan have that effect on you?"

Jenna could barely answer. She couldn't even begin to explain the effect Jonathan Knox had on her. Words only touched the surface.

"Teresa, you have no idea."

"Try me."

Jenna took a deep breath. She couldn't break down. Not now. Not here.

"It's not just the attraction to Jonathan, is it? I'm sure the mission must seem extremely overwhelming to you. If you don't think you can do this, I'm sure Maria can find someone else...another female agent. Hamilton has never met you; we could use a stand-in."

Jenna shook her head. "He would know, Teresa. I'm certain of it. No, I have to be the one to do this. It's the only way...I'm just....hell, I don't know what I'm feeling right now. There are so many things racing around in my head, I think I'm going crazy. Maybe I just need some fresh air."

Jenna stood up. Her legs were working now. She took a couple of steps towards the kitchen before Teresa gently grabbed her arm.

"Keep your chin up."

"And my heart open?"

Jenna forced a smile, remembering Teresa's encouraging words whenever she was dealing with a crisis moment.

Maria joined Teresa in the meeting room as Jenna left for the back door.

"Is Jenna getting cold feet?"

"Not about the mission. She's resolved to play her part. But she's got other things on her mind. Namely Chase and Jonathan competing for her attention. We need her focused tonight. They both need to be out of the picture."

"Agreed. We'll keep Chase and Jonathan here."

"And we'll sneak Jenna out."

"Exactly. When we're ready to move, Jenna will roll with the team. You're the master of disguises – I'll leave this one up to you."

"Thought you might." Teresa smiled as she picked apart her brownie.

"If you keep eating those things, the spandex is going to get tighter."

Teresa swallowed her last biteful of brownie then threw her napkin at Maria.

"Keep it up and I'll tell Jacoby about the time we had to go undercover at the convent, and you had your gun strapped to your bare thigh."

"Point taken."

"Did I hear the word *thigh?*" Jacoby asked as he rounded the corner.

"Don't ask," Maria and Teresa said in unison.

Chapter 30

Mason wiped the sweat from his brow with his paisley silk handkerchief. *Why was he worrying?* The plan was still on schedule. But time was ticking away ever so slowly.

He absolutely hated to wait.

Tapping his pencil on the top of his desk blotter, Mason's mind played a variety of scenarios. Against the same driven adversary.

Turette.

Mason cursed under his breath. Agent Maria Turette had now drawn Jenna Reed into her fold. Jenna's arrival would be well-guarded. The Closer had his work cut out for him. Turette was relentless. She would try every trick in the book.

Turette needed to be taught a lesson this time, Mason convinced himself. Involving a civilian in her latest game of tag. Pathetic, really. The FBI was resorting to using civilians as bait. Obviously, they were running out of fresh ideas.

The pencil broke, and Mason tossed it into his trashcan. Patience was not boding well with him. His eyes came to rest on the pink message slip Suzanne had handed him earlier.

A message from an anonymous caller. The meeting would be delayed.

"Arrogant son-of-a-bitch," Mason growled. The Closer was dictating orders. Mason didn't like it one bit. "The man doesn't understand my priorities, my risks..."

A knock interrupted Mason's ranting.

"Your appointment is here, Sir. He refused to give me his name. He said you were expecting him."

"Yes, Suzanne. Show him to my office."

Mason stood up from behind his desk. His right hand began to twitch nervously, and he stuck it in his jacket pocket. There was no need to advertise his anxiety.

"Mason."

The Closer strode into Mason's office dressed in a navy pinstripe suit. His hair was styled and he was clean-shaven.

Mason did a double-take. He had never seen The Closer dressed in such professional attire. He looked like a Wall Street lawyer or an impressive marketing executive. Another alias?

Mason nodded in approval. A man worthy of his own fine tastes but with cold-blooded undertones. So be it.

"Are you prepared for this evening?"

"Of course. My team has been briefed. They can handle whatever the FBI throws their way. As for Jenna Reed and her brother, you want to kill them tonight, but not here, correct?"

"That is my intention. I do not want dead bodies in my office or anywhere near my exhibits. Make sure everyone is aware of those stipulations."

"Understood. Just another thought...what if she doesn't bring the artifacts with her? Tonight's meeting could just be a ploy by the FBI to draw you out."

"An interesting theory...but not past the realm of possibilities. I don't put anything past Agent Turette. But I don't think she'd risk Jenna Reed's life without upping the ante. I have a strong feeling Jenna has found the treasure. Now, whether she has brought all five pieces with her, I can't be sure. Hans will search her when she arrives."

The Closer grunted in disgust. "Kliric. He can't follow simple directions. Why you keep him on the payroll is beyond me."

"Loyalty. Hans will always do as I command without question. I do not care if he left the museum last night for a few hours. You, my friend, have no cause for alarm."

"First of all, never attempt to confuse our business relationship as a friendship. Secondly, Kliric does not impress me."

"The man has his faults, but I trust him."

"Trust is an overrated concept...resulting in fallibility. Keep Kliric out of my way."

"Excuse me for a moment. I'll be right back."

Mason headed for Suzanne's desk, glad to have a momentary breather from The Closer's derogatory remarks.

"Suzanne, I'll be leaving shortly to finish packing."

"Yes, Sir."

Suzanne bit her tongue, wanting to say more but hesitated because there were co-workers within earshot. Mason had promised her he would soon be dumping his globe-trotting wife. *But when, exactly?* Suzanne was getting antsy; she couldn't wait to have Mason all to herself.

"You have my contact information. You can always reach me on my cell or through the hotel, if necessary."

Suzanne flipped through her folder of Mason's travel records. She panicked. "Sir, I don't seem to have a confirmation from the airline."

"Not to worry. I've made private arrangements."

Mason was smiling when he returned to his office.

"Just establishing my alibi."

"And the office staff?"

"At our meeting this morning, I told them to leave no later than five o'clock. A last minute private reception would be taking place in the Main Exhibit Hall."

"Very good. My team will be dressed as caterers and guests. Weapons will be hidden very discreetly."

"Ingenious."

"My team will lock down the building. We'll transport Reed and her brother in a van I'll have positioned at the delivery entrance off the basement level. Once we're out of the city and you give the word, we'll kill them. My cleaning crew is standing by to dispose of the bodies. In the meantime, your exit will be facilitated."

"Excellent. You have thought of everything."

"I always do," The Closer answered smugly.

His plan was flawless.

*****

Maria Turette studied her team as they suited up for the raid. Additional agents from Central and two units from the NYPD would join them on-site. Probably more agents than she really needed, but Maria wasn't taking anything for granted.

Mason wasn't getting away this time. Too much was at stake.

"Team Leaders, I want stats every fifteen. No one makes a move unless the green light is given, understood? Move out. Good luck, everyone."

Maria pointed two fingers at Chase and Jonathan, then cocked her head towards the next room. As soon as they were behind the closed door, she let them have it.

"You two are compromising the mission by upsetting Jenna."

Chase was immediately defensive.

"I care about what happens to her! You have no right to use her as a guinea pig. You want to bring down Mason Hamilton, I get that. You want to rescue Austin Reed, I'm with you a hundred percent. But what I don't get is the risk you're willing to take with Jenna's safety. She hasn't been trained to deal with assassins or rescue maneuvers. For God's sake, what the hell are you doing sending her in there all alone?"

Jonathan was in agreement, but tactfully approached the subject from a different angle.

"How closely will Jenna be guarded when she gets inside the building?"

"We have a plan in place. It will work. Jenna's every move will be monitored. But I can't have the two of you interfering. You're grounded."

"Grounded? What the hell does that mean?" Chase yelled.

Maria glanced at Chase and Jonathan with stern eyes.

"It means…you and Jonathan will be stationed here until the mission is complete…for your own safety and the sake of my team. I can't have their efforts wasted keeping an eye on you while we need to remain focused on the task at hand."

"There is no way I'm staying here when Jenna's life is in danger. She needs me."

"I'm with Garrett. You can't hold us against our will."

"I'm afraid I can. Do you want me to quote federal law to you? As the Agent-in-Charge, if I feel you are interfering in the commission of a federally-sanctioned mission, then yes, it is within my power to remand you to the FBI safe house. Besides, Jenna is well on her way by now."

Chase and Jonathan exchanged worried looks.

"What do you mean, she's on her way?" Jonathan asked.

"It means they snuck her out dressed like the tactical teams. Am I right, Agent Turette?"

Maria turned on her heels. Garrett was highly perceptive.

"Yes. It was the only way we could get her out undetected. Now, I have to get on the road myself. I will send a car for you once we have secured the building."

Chase peered out the front window watching Maria's SUV leave the driveway. He was so angry to be left in the dust. To add to his aggravation, his cell mate was Knox.

"She had no right to do this," Chase said as he pushed the curtain back, almost ripping it from the rod.

"I'm with you on that. They used me for inside information, and then tossed me aside. I can't stand this...doing *nothing*." Jonathan flung himself into a chair.

Chase scanned the room and looked outside again. Two young FBI agents were standing by the last remaining car in the driveway, puffing away. He had to formulate a plan...*fast*.

Chase pointed towards the window. "Our babysitters probably drew the short straws due to their inexperience. They don't look much older than college students."

Jonathan joined Chase at the window.

"What are you thinking, Garrett? A little diversion, perhaps?"

"That's the only way we're going to get out of here."

"What did you have in mind?"

"Something *messy*."

"Whatever it takes. Once we're out of here, I can get us into the museum. There's an underground passageway which connects to the building behind it."

Jonathan walked over to the blueprints still lying on the table. He pointed to the tunnel area which was not clearly marked.

"I neglected to mention this today in front of everyone. I thought I might need a bargaining chip. We can get inside undetected. It leads to a room on the basement level just outside the stairwell."

"Ok. Let's focus on getting the car. Once we're on the road, we can work out the other logistics. Stay here while I search for the keys."

Maria is going to be mad as hell, Jonathan thought to himself.

Chase ran back dangling the car keys.

"That was too easy," Jonathan stated.

"They were on the kitchen counter. There's only one car left in the driveway and it's a Chevy."

"What's our next move?"

"How are your plumbing skills?"

Within a few minutes, the toilet in the powder room was overflowing. Water was seeping out into the hallway, saturating the rug.

Chase ran to the front door, trying to look serious.

"Hey, we have a little problem with the downstairs toilet. It's backed up. Water is getting all over the place. You guys know anything about plumbing?"

Agent Luke Jensen dropped his cigarette and crushed it with his foot. It was only his third month on the job. He wanted to catch bad guys, not handle toilet problems. He hadn't signed up for something this lame. First babysitting, now this. He was going to request a transfer first chance he got.

"Pain-in-the ass job," he mumbled as he hurried inside.

His partner, Agent Jordan Galindez, a lanky young man just out of the Academy, took his sweet time following several steps behind.

"You insisted on coming. You practically begged Jacoby. We could have stayed in D.C working surveillance from the comfort of our office. Now, you're griping about this chump assignment and the john backs up."

"Shut the hell up and get in here," Jensen called over his shoulder.

Both agents had frustrated looks on their faces when they met Jonathan in the hallway.

"It's not pretty," he said, pointing to the bathroom.

Chase was bailing water into the sink. Both agents tried to step out of the way, but soon their shoes and pant legs were soaked.

"Great..," Agent Jensen complained loudly.

"Disgusting is all I'm going to say," Agent Galindez echoed.

"I'll look for a mop," Jonathan offered, running past the agents.

"Get a bigger bucket!" Chase called after him.

Jonathan snuck out the back door, sprinted to the car and fired up the engine. Plowing out of the driveway, he sped off before any of the others could figure out what he was doing.

Instead of circling back to pick up Garrett, Jonathan crushed the accelerator. Change of plans.

Jonathan grinned. "Too bad, Garrett. Guess you underestimated me."

*****

Maria peered through her binoculars. Museum workers were starting to exit the building. Within the hour she could get her team inside.

Her hopes were quickly dashed. Two catering vans pulled up to the side entrance.

"You have got to be kidding me!" Maria screamed, forgetting her team was wearing earpieces. She came close to bursting a few eardrums.

"No events were scheduled for tonight. I want to know what's going on. Get someone on this...*now!*"

Jacoby quickly dialed Jensen at the safe house. No answer.

"Jensen, pick up the phone! Get back to me right now! We have a problem with the museum's schedule."

His phone buzzed within seconds.

"What? Get Central to dispense a plumber."

Maria gave Jacoby a puzzled look.

Jacoby mouthed "plumbing issue."

Maria rolled her eyes. She didn't need this today.

"Ok. We'll handle it. Keep Garrett there. I don't care if you have to tie him to the friggin' bed. Just do it, Jensen."

"What now?"

"Knox is MIA. Apparently, there was a plumbing problem in the bathroom just off the kitchen. Water was gushing from the toilet."

Maria wrinkled up her nose. "Staged?"

"Sounds like it. When Jensen and Galindez were helping Garrett bail out the water, Knox took off in the car. What do you want to do about it? I can call in a pickup."

"No, don't bother. He's on his way here. I'll reprimand Jonathan when he arrives. Tell Thompson to keep an eye out."

Damn you, Jonathan. I don't have time for this.

Jacoby called his contact at Central. "Get me the museum's schedule and forward it to my cell. Thank you."

A few minutes later, he showed Maria the screen.

"I don't get it. No events are listed."

"Better check it out. Could be trouble in disguise."

Maria nodded. "Do it discreetly. I don't want to scare any civilians. We'll have enough drama later on."

Jacoby took Maria's binoculars. He zeroed in on the catering vans. Large covered trays and chafing dishes were being carried into the museum. Looked legitimate. But something wasn't quite right; he had a bad feeling.

Maria contemplated her next move. Whatever event was going on would definitely impact the FBI's plan of action. She couldn't send a tactical team in until the lower level was evacuated. It would send off too many bells and whistles.

"Get someone to check with the catering staff...*now!*"

Jacoby keyed-up Thompson.

"Mick, get an undercover agent over to the catering van. Find out what's going on. Nothing's on the radar."

Maria tensed. In just a few hours, Jenna was supposed to walk in the front door. The building needed to be secured; she had given Jenna her word.

"Ok, thanks." Jacoby pocketed his cell.

"Private donor reception. Caterer just got the call this morning. About twenty people. Main hall. Starts at seven. Caterer expects to be out by nine at the latest. Apparently, these last minute receptions are scheduled all the time with little notice."

"Perfect timing," Maria chimed, sarcastically.

What choice did she have? She'd have to work around this reception to be as covert as possible and not tip-off Mason.

If he didn't know already. Maria wondered.

"I need some air."

Maria stepped out of the van. Popping the tab on a Diet Pepsi, she took a long drink. It was going to be a long night.

Pulling off her earpiece, she speed-dialed her husband.

"Hi, babe."

Stationed on the roof of the M&T Bank building across the street, Damian looked through the sight of his sniper rifle. He had a perfect view of his wife, but she couldn't see him.

"I want you to know how sexy you look in that 'Linens of the Week' uniform."

Maria smiled and bobbed her head.

"I could keep it for role-playing at home."

"I'm game if you are."

Damian laughed.

"I miss you."

Maria looked up in Damian's direction.

"I'm right here."

"But not close enough."

"You've done this before, Maria. You know what to do. Stay focused. Actually, I'm focusing on you right now. I'm getting a close-up of your cleavage. And a drop of sweat is running…"

"Damian, don't do this…*not now*." Maria blushed, as her hand flew to her chest.

"Oh, we have time for a little foreplay. Hamilton's not going anywhere."

"Damian, you're distracting me."

"Ok, Sweetheart. I'll behave…but I meant what I said about the uniform."

"I'm hanging up now. You've managed to turn my frown into a smile. Go do your job."

"You do yours. I love you. I'll report in later."

Maria felt a brief sense of comfort wash over her. Damian always knew what to say and when to say it. When the day was done, and her mission had succeeded…or failed, Damian was her rock and always would be.

Chapter 31

Jonathan weaved through traffic, glancing every few seconds in the rearview mirror. No one was tailing him...*yet*. Perspiration dripped off his face and down his neck.

He repeatedly beeped his horn allowing him prime access. The black SUV was ominous, giving the impression it was carrying law enforcement or a political official.

He was making good time; rush hour traffic hadn't hit its peak yet. Commuters would just be starting to head home.

Arriving at his parking garage four blocks away from the museum, Jonathan circled around to his spot. He had an elite corner space on the first parking level.

Jonathan raced to the State Farm office building just behind the museum. He darted down the steps and swiped his museum ID just outside the storage facility on the basement level. He quickly made his way to the back of the room. Large canvas paintings blocked the tunnel access door.

"For God's sake, Nigel," Jonathan complained as he tugged on an over-sized wooden frame.

The current curator, Nigel Remington, always insisted the door be covered with large, heavy artwork in case of theft. He believed thieves would only take small artifacts and not discover the access tunnel if they were forced to move heavier canvas paintings.

Jonathan could appreciate that theory now.

His shoulder burned as he struggled to push the huge frames out of the way. Finally, Jonathan cleared the door just enough to wedge his body inside the tunnel.

Total darkness enveloped him. Lighting throughout the tunnel was sporadic. Small motion-detector lights were Jonathan's only source of guidance.

Moving too fast, he stumbled over a tunnel connector.

Regaining his balance, Jonathan picked up speed again. He soon figured out the connectors were positioned right below the lights. It didn't take him long to arrive at the door which led to the museum's lower level.

Now he needed to get to the stairwell and up ten flights of stairs. He hoped to hell he had enough stamina.

As he started to move across the room, Jonathan sensed another presence. Cautiously stopping in his tracks, he knelt down and wrapped his hand around a storage crate. He peered around it slowly.

"Over here," a scratchy voice called from the darkness.

Jonathan hesitated. The voice didn't sound threatening. Relaxing his grip on the crate, he stood up then took a couple steps closer.

"Who's there?"

"Over here...please help me."

Jonathan could barely hear the muffled voice.

"Tell me who you are, or I'm not coming any closer."

Silence.

Jonathan retreated a couple of steps.

"Reed."

Did the man say his name was *Reed*? My God, could it be Jenna's brother?

"Help me...," the voice begged.

Jonathan rushed forward. His face registered total shock.

Bruised and bloodied, a man was against the wall in a contorted position. Jonathan knelt down to loosen the ropes binding the man's hands and feet.

"Are you Jenna's brother?"

Austin nodded then hung his head. Pain was shooting up his chest and neck with every movement. "You know my sister?"

"I'm Jonathan Knox. Your sister and I...met recently. We need to get out of here, Austin. Hamilton's men could come back any minute."

Jonathan grabbed Austin around the waist and pulled him to his feet.

"God, this hurts," Austin said as they moved towards the tunnel door.

They were moving as quickly as possible, but it seemed like slow motion. Austin's one leg was barely moving.

Jonathan recoiled, thinking about the kinds of torture Mason's men must have inflicted on Austin. But at least he had survived. *Thank God.* Jenna would be so happy.

For a brief moment, Jonathan imagined Jenna running to him...thanking him for saving her brother...kissing him...

Austin's body started to slip out of Jonathan's grasp.

"Hold on, Austin. Not much further."

The tunnel door was in sight. Dragging Austin the final few steps, Jonathan reached for the doorknob. Once inside, he let Austin fall slowly to the floor.

"We made it."

"Thank you," Austin said through labored breaths right before he passed out.

Jonathan called Maria.

"Where the hell are you?" Maria demanded. "Do you have any idea the trouble you're in especially after stealing one of my cars?"

"Maybe I'll get a reprieve. I just found Austin Reed."

Maria was astounded. "How?"

"There's an access tunnel which connects the museum to the lower level of the State Farm Building right behind it. Can you get someone over here fast? Austin is in really bad shape."

"Good work, Jonathan. I'm proud of you. We'll get a paramedic to you right away. Now about the car you stole..."

"Can't talk right now. Gotta get back to Austin."

Jonathan hung up abruptly. His first priority was getting back into the museum to save Jenna.

Mason would be expecting some type of ambush, but not from someone who knew the office floor plan better than anyone.

Jonathan realized he was Jenna's only chance.

*****

"Thompson, get an ambulance and a team over to the State Farm building behind the museum. Basement level. Jonathan will meet you there. He rescued Austin Reed. Go now!"

Jacoby passed Maria a bottle of water.

"You don't look so good. You need some air."

"Just a few minutes." Maria jumped out of the van again, then leaned against it.

She had trained for this type of take-down. She knew how to remain calm during times of crisis. Her tactical training, though, hadn't taught her motherly instincts.

She dialed Jonathan's number, promising herself she would not get upset.

"Jonathan, please tell me you're ok."

"I'm fine. A little wiped out from dragging Austin through the tunnel, but I'm ok. I'm sorry I hung up on you before. Guess I have some explaining to do. How much do you know?"

"Enough. We'll talk about it later. Help is on the way."

"Hope they get here soon. Austin just passed out. He was roughed up quite a bit. Don't give Jenna all the details."

"We'll choose our words carefully. We need Jenna to remain as calm as possible."

"Are you kidding? She's probably freaking out right now. I still don't think..."

Maria cut Jonathan off. "Jenna wants this over as much as I do, maybe even more. She's willing to do her part."

"She's not thinking clearly. If she knows her brother is ok, then she doesn't have to go in at all. Pull her out. She doesn't have to take this risk."

"It's too late for that. We're on schedule and we're going to execute the mission."

"This is a total mistake."

Jonathan ended the call. Maria wasn't listening. She was too focused on catching Mason and not thinking about the ramifications of her decisions. He couldn't waste any more time.

He had to find Jenna and get her out of whatever danger Maria had put her in.

*****

Jenna rode in the SUV with the FBI agents. She was suited up just like the rest of them...except she was the only one not carrying a gun. She felt extremely intimidated.

Jenna sat wedged between two massive men. Their eyes were focused ahead as they cradled their rifles on their laps. Trained agents willing to risk their lives for the mission...and for her. They weren't having second doubts, Jenna thought to herself.

But I certainly am. Big time.

The nagging little voice in the back of her head had magnified, causing a headache to emerge.

Sneaking out without saying good-bye? Good job, Reed. They're both hurting now.

Jenna shut her eyes, trying to keep images of Chase and Jonathan out of her head. What if she didn't come out of this alive? Chase...and Jonathan would be devastated.

And what about Austin? He tried to warn her. But she didn't listen to him.

What a fool she had been.

The SUV ran over a manhole in the road jolting Jenna back to her senses. She banged against the elbow of one of the agents flanking her.

"Sorry," the agent said gruffly as he shifted in his seat.

"No problem," Jenna responded in a meek tone. She wanted to stay brave and confident, but there was no way around it. She wasn't cut out to go shoulder-to-shoulder with the FBI.

You can do this. You have to do this.

The plan was set in motion.

All she wanted was a restful summer vacation in Cape May, her favorite place in the world. Spending quality time at the shore, not rescuing her brother from a murderous mad man.

Crazy-ass drama...and she had the starring role.

Her hands trembled. Jenna tucked them under her knees.

Focused. Confident.

Maria's words echoed in her head.

Distracted. Intimidated.

That just about summed it up.

Jenna bent her head and brushed away a wayward tear.

All the agents were facing forward. Either they were extremely regimented or they were ignoring her. Just as well.

Jenna's attention was drawn to an ambulance parked ahead on the same side of the street. A stretcher was being loaded. Jenna swore she saw blood covering the person's arms and legs.

A terrifying thought pierced her mind.

Oh, God, what if the person was one of Maria's team?

Agent Jason Monroe, a huge man with the largest hands Jenna had ever seen, was standing by the car door, blocking Jenna's view. He nodded to his fellow team members after receiving a message through his earpiece.

"Yes, Ma'am," the agent said. He turned to look at Jenna.

"Time for you to change. Agent Miles will escort you to the rear entrance of the restaurant next to the State Farm building. A green Audi will be parked in the back. You will be dropped off at the main entrance of the museum. Agent Turette has already briefed you. Any questions?"

Jenna could barely speak. Maria had gone over the plan with her several times but now as she stepped from the SUV, the reality of what she was being expected to do hit her hard.

Agent Monroe gave her a slight push towards Agent Sam Miles, the young undercover agent with the surfer-boy look. His shoulder-length brown hair and Ray-Bans made him look more like a California lifeguard than an FBI agent.

"Ladies' Room is the first door on your right."

Agent Miles stood guard at the door with his gun drawn.

Jenna made her way down the darkened hallway. Closing the door behind her, she fell against the nearest tiled wall. Her hands were shaking so badly she could barely unfasten the Velcro tabs on the FBI vest.

"How am I going to get through this?" She asked herself.

Changing into her own clothes was a monumental struggle. Her body had perspired so much; her tank top and shorts were sticking to her like a second skin.

Jenna pulled her hair into a ponytail and secured it with a rubber band. Glancing in the mirror, she was startled.

Puffy eyes, pale complexion, shallow cheeks.

A total wreck.

Jenna splashed water on her face.

"Reed, get a grip."

Jenna stuffed the FBI gear into a duffle bag Agent Miles had handed her. It was time to go.

Jenna reached for the door then paused. A rush of anxiety made her double over.

"I can't do this."

Agent Miles pulled the door open.

"Listen to me. You're going to walk right in that door and stand up to that son-of-a-bitch. We have your back. Every step is one step closer to saving your brother. You can do this. Ok?"

Jenna appreciated Agent Miles' words of encouragement. Before she had a chance to respond, he snapped her earpiece into place and pulled her out the back door.

The green Audi was idling in the alleyway. Jenna climbed in the backseat, as Agent Miles joined the driver in the front.

"Don't buckle up," he cautioned. "You might need to jump from the car if there's trouble."

Within seconds, the car sped off and turned onto a side street. The plan was to circle the museum a few times before stopping in front.

Jenna leaned her head against the window. All she could do at this point was pray. For Austin's safe return...for forgiveness from Chase and Jonathan for not telling them good-bye and...for herself to have enough courage not to let anyone down.

The Audi swerved to avoid hitting a car which had cut into the same lane. Grabbing the door handle, Jenna held on tightly to keep from sliding across the seat.

"Sorry about that," Agent Miles said as he tilted his head in Jenna's direction.

"I'm ok," Jenna said as she sat back upright.

For now.

*****

Maria's binoculars were trained on Jenna.

"She's heading up the steps."

Maria chewed on her bottom lip. She was worried as hell. Her team had not yet gained access to the main level. Jenna was on her own. Unprotected.

Why hadn't she told Jenna about Austin's rescue?

Jacoby sensed Maria's apprehension and tugged on her arm. "She'll be fine."

"I just hope to hell she doesn't get creative."

Maria had just broken her promise of protection. She could have pulled Jenna from the mission from the start, sending in a decoy agent.

But she didn't do it.

She could have told Agent Monroe to change plans and return Jenna to the tech van.

But she didn't do that either.

The anticipation of capturing Mason with his hands dirty was too great of a temptation.

Maria hated herself at the moment. She was trading a young girl's life for the chance to nail Mason Hamilton once and for all. It wasn't an even exchange. Instead, it was bringing Maria down to Mason's level.

Each time she heard Jenna's labored breaths through her earpiece, Maria felt like her stomach was being punched.

All she could do was hope and pray Jenna had enough courage for the both of them.

*****

Jenna neared the front security desk, clenching her hands at her sides. One of the security guards pointed to the elevators.

"Tenth floor. Mr. Hamilton is expecting you."

Jenna briskly walked past the guard station. Both of the men seated at the large console were wearing gun belts. They could shoot her in the back at any moment...but they hadn't.

Keep going. Head straight for the elevator.

She punched the elevator button and apprehensively waited for the doors to open.

Distant voices and muted music were coming from another room farther down the hall. For a brief instant, Jenna felt the urge to veer off in that direction. Then she caught herself as the elevator doors opened.

Do not deviate from the plan.

Maria had been very specific.

"Ok," Jenna commented out loud, as if to confirm the voice in her head.

As soon as the elevator door closed, Jenna turned towards the wall as she had been instructed. According to the elevator specs, only a video feed was being monitored. No audio had been installed.

She would be able to speak freely as long as she faced the back wall.

"In the elevator now. Heading up to the tenth floor. Your team is in place, right?"

"Yes," Maria said, hesitantly. She had no other choice. She had to lie.

"Good, because I'm really nervous."

"Just do what I asked you to do. Take your time. Nice and easy, do you hear me, Jenna?"

Through her earpiece Maria heard the elevator bell and the auto attendant announcing the tenth floor. It was now or never. She was out of options.

Get the team in place. To hell with the reception. Maria scribbled on a piece of paper and handed it to Jacoby.

Jacoby buzzed Thompson.

"Mick, green light. Evacuate...*now!*"

"Affirmative. Green light." Thompson motioned to his team leaders. The party was over. He would have the building cleared in the next few minutes.

"Jenna!" Maria shouted.

No response.

"Jenna! You wait for my team!"

Maria's decision to act was a few seconds too late.

When the elevator opened on the tenth floor, Jenna did exactly as she had been told. She immediately took off her earpiece. Jenna tucked the small device inside a tissue box behind the counter at the receptionist's desk. Maria didn't want to take a chance Mason or his men would retaliate if they found the wire.

"Jenna!" Maria tried again.

A deafening silence was the only response.

I've put her in too much danger.

Maria's body sagged against the van. Dropping her head in resignation, Maria suddenly realized Jenna was following her exact orders.

Jenna was now on her own...walking dangerously towards the man who could easily order her death with a snap of his finger.

Chapter 32

Mason walked the length of his antique Persian rug and then back again. Hans and The Closer stood silently in the shadows watching him.

"Where the hell is she?" Mason growled as he checked his watch. "She's late."

"Patience," The Closer uttered.

"Not one of my virtues."

"I can see that."

Mason reached for his whiskey decanter on his bookshelf. The Closer's hand came down hard on Mason's wrist.

"You don't need a drink. You need to stay sharp."

"Easy for you to say. Whiskey always calms my nerves. The FBI is after me; they don't even know you're here."

"I wouldn't be so sure about that. The FBI keeps tabs on me."

"Don't flatter yourself. They're after me tonight, not you. Agent Turette is probably chomping at the bit right now."

The Closer laughed at Mason's comment. He didn't fear anyone, especially a *female* FBI agent. Mason needed to gain the right perspective.

"She's no match for me and you know it. Stop fidgeting."

Mason just glared back at The Closer. The man thought he was invincible. One day, Mason thought to himself, The Closer's arrogance would circle around and be his downfall.

Mason knew from experience how driven Agent Turette was, and he wasn't about to discount her thoroughness. The Closer better be damn sure he knew what he was doing.

"I will check the offices again," Hans offered as he started to move towards the office door.

The Closer held up a hand before Mason could utter a word.

"Stay put."

Hans turned his head. He was tired of taking orders from The Closer. Mason was his boss. Mason treated him with respect. Most of the time.

Mason walked towards the window. It was too dark outside to make any positive assessments. He couldn't see any cop cars or black vans parked below, but it didn't stop his suspicions.

"The FBI is anxious to see me fall."

"We won't give them that satisfaction. No one knows you're in the building. You left earlier by the front door and we sneaked you back in through the delivery entrance. Your exit has been arranged. Stop worrying. Leave the details up to me. That's what you're paying me for."

Mason nodded as he stopped in front of The Closer.

"You're right, of course. I shouldn't have any doubts. You always do a good job."

He patted The Closer on the shoulder, then immediately regretted his gesture.

The Closer's eyes flared. He grabbed Mason's wrist forcibly and promptly flung it aside.

"Don't ever touch me again."

Mason suppressed the urge to cry out in pain. He fell against his desk.

"I'm...sorry. A misunderstanding on my part."

"Sit down," The Closer said with an air of authority.

Mason quickly took a seat in one of his guest chairs, wishing he had downed a couple of drinks before The Closer had arrived. He couldn't wait till he was on the plane to Venice. Then everything would be better. Much better.

The Closer's cell vibrated with a text message.

"She's on her way up now. The front doors and the side entrance have been locked. My team is in place. I'll be next door if you need me."

The Closer entered the massive conference room. A long polished glass table and wide leather chairs took up most of the space. Too corporate for his personal tastes.

Suiting up to walk in the front door of Mason's office this afternoon had been a stretch. He loathed the constricting feel of a suit. His preference was always a black shirt and black jeans, although Mallory was always telling him he needed a more extensive wardrobe.

Mallory.

His accomplice...partner. Right now a few other words came to mind.

She was constantly driving him crazy with her incessant demands. Money. Clothes. Sex. But she was the best...at *everything*.

If Mallory could convince the world Ellen Chandler Hamilton was still alive for a few more weeks, then she was definitely worth the price he had to pay, financially and physically.

He sent her a text to tell her to be ready. The private plane he had arranged to carry Mallory and Mason to Venice would be departing within a couple of hours. She needed to be at the hangar right on time. No delays.

Her response was immediate.

Of course, darling.

The Closer rolled his eyes. He would deal with Mallory later. Right now, he had a job to do. Mason's extraction would require precise coordination.

Mason needed to conclude his session with Jenna Reed in about twenty minutes.

No more time for stupid games.

*****

Hans shifted his feet in anticipation. He was counting the minutes until he could put his hands on Jenna Reed again. All over her. He would enjoy every minute as he searched her body.

"I am ready." Hans nodded to Mason then stepped back into the shadows.

Putting a finger to his lips, Mason motioned for Hans to keep quiet. The elevator had just chimed. Within a few seconds, Jenna and his treasure would be coming though his door.

Mason wiped his perspiring hands on his trousers. He straightened his tie and pushed out his chest. His confidence had returned. He was in control once again.

"Good evening, Ms. Reed," Mason said as his door slowly opened.

"Won't you sit down?"

*****

Jonathan approached the agent stationed outside the entrance to the storage room.

"I need to make sure the artwork and tapestries are secure. The museum curator will have my head if there's been any kind of damage. Can I get back in the storage room for a few minutes?"

Agent Ian Donnelly, who sported a strict military-style haircut and stance, was on security detail after the paramedics had taken Austin Reed to the ambulance. Standing over six feet with a muscular upper body, he was intimidating to most people, especially when armed with a high-powered rifle.

"Go ahead."

Agent Donnelly turned back to his post. No one was getting past him tonight.

Jonathan made his way back to the tunnel door. Glancing over his shoulder, he made sure the agent was still facing in the opposite direction before he slipped inside the tunnel.

Triggering one of the motion-detector lights, he checked his watch. Eight-thirty. He needed to hurry. Jenna was probably inside Mason's office. She was supposed to stall for as long as possible to make sure the FBI teams were in place.

Jonathan crossed the basement storage room cautiously. Before heading out into the hallway, he noticed a van parked on the ramp, blocking the loading area. It was dark-colored without any markings. Not a museum van.

Jonathan looked closer. Two men were in the front holding guns.

He had to warn Maria.

Van. Loading entrance. Two men. Guns.

Jonathan bent down and crept towards the stairwell at the end of the hallway. When he opened the door, Jonathan heard muffled voices coming from the kitchen right above him. It sounded like a party.

What was going on? Nothing was scheduled for tonight.

Something wasn't right. He just knew it.

GET OUT OF THERE NOW. Maria's text was in all caps.

Jonathan shook his head as he typed a reply, one he knew would raise Maria's blood pressure.

Not without Jenna.

*****

Maria almost dropped her cell when the text appeared.

Instead of replying, she speed-dialed his number.

"Talk to me right now!"

"Can't," Jonathan whispered. "I'm in the stairwell. Call you back."

Maria shoved her cell into Jacoby's hand.

"I'm ready to wring his neck!"

After reading Jonathan's latest text, Jacoby stifled a laugh.

"He's trying to help."

"Don't take his side. He's going to get himself killed. And he's going to give me a heart attack in the process!"

"What do you want me to do?"

"Get through to him. Maybe he'll listen to you. He's not responding to me. He needs to let me handle this. Oh, and find out how he managed to get back inside."

"Obviously...he's Houdini."

Jacoby's attempt at humor was wasted on Maria.

Maria's cell buzzed again.

"Through the tunnel entrance. We need to get a team in the same way."

"Do it."

Jonathan found a vantage point...*on his own.* Maybe there was some of her resourcefulness and tenacity in him after all. But why did Jonathan withhold such vital information about the tunnel until now?

It didn't take long for Maria to come up with an answer.

To be Jenna's hero.

Maria grabbed Jacoby's arm. Her face was taut.

"Get a team to find Jonathan. Get him out of there. *Right now.*"

Jacoby got his partner on the line. "Mick, get a team into the tunnel from the State Farm storage room. Find Knox...*now.* What? Are you sure?"

Jacoby relayed Thompson's update.

"All of the outside entrances are locked. Someone has activated the security system. This was planned...and we fell for it."

"As soon as Thompson and his team are through the tunnel, I want those damn doors open again."

"Maybe there's a faster way. We can bypass the master lock system if we can get the override code."

Jacoby tapped one of the agents stationed at a laptop inside the van. "Get the museum's security company on the phone, Cowboy. We need that override code now."

"On it," Agent Trent Carroll replied. An integral part of Maria's unit for five years, Carroll was Jacoby's go-to person when it came to analyzing security systems. He could bypass technology glitches better than anyone in the D.C. office. At twenty-six, Carroll was the sought-after computer geek who looked more like a model for Stetson cologne. With his rugged looks, sandy-brown hair and a Texas drawl, he had earned the dubious nickname, Cowboy.

"What do we have?" Maria asked as she leaned over Carroll's shoulder to check the screen.

Carroll had pulled up a schematic of every lock in the museum from the architectural blueprints. Jacoby had guessed right. All locking mechanisms were part of a systematic shut-down system, controlled by a pre-set computer code. Without the exact numerical sequence, the steel doors were practically impregnable.

"Nothing yet. On hold with annoying music. Not even country."

"Stay on the line and get a manager."

"Yes, Ma'am," Agent Carroll replied.

Maria stepped from the van, looking first at the museum, then at the building where Damian was positioned. Before she could call his number, Damian beat her to it.

"Calling for an update, Sweetheart, or did you just need to hear my sexy voice?"

Maria smiled. "Both. What do you have for me?"

"Two men in Hamilton's office. Looks like a third man in the room next door and..." Damian hesitated.

"And?"

"Female just entered."

Maria felt a tension headache crossing her brow.

Jacoby joined Maria outside the van. "Jonathan was right about the men in the van. We took them out and replaced them with two of our own."

Maria didn't ask for further details. At this point, she really didn't want to know. Just as long as her team was in control.

"Mick's team just entered the stairwell. Surprise attack in the kitchen. The caterers and guests were all armed. Two men down. No report yet on casualties."

"What about Jonathan?" Maria asked nervously.

"He's ok. Mick told him to vacate the building and get over to our van."

"That's not good enough. Tell Mick to make sure Jonathan gets out of the building. I don't care if they have to cuff him and drag him. I want him out...*now*."

*****

Jonathan got in the maintenance elevator and pulled off the "DO NOT USE" sign. Just another ploy to trick the FBI.

Whoever was spearheading this plan for Mason was good, but not good enough. Punching the button for the ninth floor, Jonathan smiled as the elevator started its ascent.

"Coming to get you, Mason."

He was the eyes and ears for the FBI now, whether Maria liked it or not.

Chapter 33

Jenna took a deep breath before wrapping her hand around the edge of Mason Hamilton's door. Pushing it open, she heard her name being called. Taking just two steps, she finally laid eyes on the man who ordered the deaths of her parents and Candace Light...and abducted her brother.

Mason Hamilton. The epitome of evil.

He wasn't at all what Jenna had imagined. Dressed impeccably in a tailored suit, Mason Hamilton appeared to be an established businessman at first glance.

A murderer and kidnapper in reality.

The man who was responsible for the unending drama which had consumed her life for several weeks now. Mason Hamilton stood before her now, his teeth gleaming as his mouth curved into a sneer.

The Devil personified.

Before Jenna could even utter a word, she was grabbed from behind. She recognized the man from the warehouse in Virginia. The disgusting one with the bad cigar breath. He was binding her once again to a chair rendering her helpless.

Calloused hands began to grope her body. Jenna pulled back, straining against the ropes. He wasn't just searching her; he was taking perverse pleasure in touching her skin.

Help me get through this.

She wanted to cry out so badly. To tell him to get his despicable hands off of her. To scream for help before he violated her even more.

Jenna clenched her teeth instead.

Stall for as long as possible.

Jenna's skin burned as the hideous man pressed and prodded. She tried not to flinch when he tucked his fingers underneath the edges of her shorts. But as he worked his way up her belly, reaching under her shirt to fondle her breasts, she finally gasped...unable to resist his torment any longer.

Hans grinned as Jenna's body tensed under his hands.

"You like that?" He asked as he watched her head turn away. "I can see that you do."

He was getting the reaction he was hoping for, and the stimulation his body was craving even if it was only temporary. Hans was pleased with himself.

As his hands moved to the back waistband of her shorts, Hans paused when his fingers found the top of her lacy black thong. He was amused. Hans pushed his hands lower.

Hearing Jenna make a choking sound, he pulled back just in time to see her eyes widen.

Good. He wanted her to be afraid. Fear made it so much better.

If Mason would just leave him alone with her, he could do so much more…

Almost to his disappointment, Hans found a small object in Jenna's back pocket. He hoped to prolong her body search for as long as possible, but now it was inevitable, he had to end his little sadistic game of touch-and-seek.

Hans reluctantly handed Mason the small bundle encased in an old cloth.

Mason carefully unwrapped the handkerchief. He stood motionless, cradling the gold elephant. He stared in awe and was too dumbstruck to pay close attention to what Hans was doing.

Hans knelt in front of Jenna. Blowing hot air on her neck, his hands moved ever so slowly up her thighs, pushing her legs apart.

"Get away from me, you nasty pervert!"

Hans stood up slowly, drawing Jenna's attention to his own body's reaction. A wicked smile emerged on his thin lips as his hands flexed at his sides. He howled at her outburst.

Hans' distorted fantasy came to an end as Mason grabbed him by the shoulder.

"Step back, Hans."

Jenna was seething, with the urge to kill. If she could loosen the ropes, she knew she had the courage to fight off both men. The adrenaline was rising in her body.

But she needed to stall for as long as possible, the way Maria had coached her.

But for how long? Where was the FBI team?

Mason was tired of waiting. If Jenna Reed could produce one of the artifacts, she knew exactly where the others were hidden. It would only be a matter of time until she gave up the location.

"Ms. Reed, thank you for your contribution."

"Bondage seems to be your favorite way of controlling people, doesn't it, Hamilton? Should I get out my whip?"

As if on cue, Hans grabbed Jenna's ponytail, jerking her head backwards. Her throat was exposed and he imagined licking his tongue...oh, it was so tempting. If Mason would just turn around...

Jenna jerked as a sudden wave of pain shot through her head and neck. She breathed through her nose to steady herself.

Staying alive to bring Mason Hamilton down was the one thing she wanted more than anything at this moment.

Mason finally waved his hand and Hans let go.

"Bastard."

"A wake-up call, Ms. Reed. My associate doesn't take too kindly when you address me in such vulgar terms. We are trying hard to remain civilized."

"Civilized? Is that what you call the invasive body search? I don't think your associate can comprehend the word *civilized*. He seems like a savage ass."

Hans shot Jenna a stern look. He started to approach her, but Mason reached out and threw a hand across Hans' chest.

"Come now, Ms. Reed. Don't insult Hans. He really is useful in his own way which I don't believe you wish to experience any further."

Hans nodded in acknowledgement and folded his arms.

"Ms. Reed, I need information you are going to provide one way or another. If, however, you persist in dragging me on another wild goose chase, there will be consequences to pay."

"Oh, I can't wait to hear what that entails."

She could do this. She could empower herself to keep Hamilton ranting for as long as possible.

"Your brother, Ms. Reed."

"Where is he?"

"Close by. I'm sure you will agree your brother should not suffer immeasurable pain for the sins of his sister. Nonetheless, I am perfectly willing to sacrifice his well-being for your refusal to cooperate. First and foremost, Ms. Reed, I am a businessman. I am very well accustomed to making deals. So, just to make sure we are clear on the matter, when I ask a question and you do not provide the answer I want to hear, my men will take liberties to hurt you...or your brother at my discretion. Do we understand each other?"

Jenna tilted her head.

"Very good. Then let us begin."

Mason leaned against his desk.

"Hopefully, with a little encouragement, you will be more cooperative than *your mother*."

Jenna's eyes flared. Was Hamilton going to confess he murdered her parents? Now, she wished she was still wearing the wire.

"Panic, Ms. Reed. Your mother panicked, causing the untimely death of herself and your father. If she had just been more willing to hand over my treasure, you and I would not be here right now. For you see, Ms. Reed, every action has a reaction, and every play has a counterplay."

"You murdered my parents, Hamilton. Your obsession with the treasure pieces is your own rationalization. I don't care what you say."

Mason contemptuously laughed. Another feisty adversary. Now he had two.

"I must say, Ms. Reed, you have made this little adventure very interesting over the past few weeks. I'm almost sad to see it come to an end, but here we are. I must move on. I'm leaving for Venice soon, and I do need to wrap this up. Now tell me, where are the other four pieces of the treasure?"

As Mason leaned in closer to Jenna's face, he could almost feel the rage radiating from her skin. Her chest was rising fast and her breathing was labored. Yet Jenna remained steadfast.

Mason was puzzled. Jenna Reed wasn't at all what he expected.

"I don't know what you're talking about. I only found the gold elephant."

Jenna fought the compulsion to spit into his face.

"Indeed? Well, perhaps we need to jog your memory."

Mason backed away as Hans circled Jenna's chair. Catching her at an unexpected angle, Hans slapped Jenna hard across the face. Her bottom lip cracked open. Blood spurted, running down her chin in a steady stream of droplets.

The second slap dazed her as it knocked her head sideways. Jenna shook her head to regain her focus but pain was coming now in sharp, biting jolts.

Jenna spit out a mouthful of blood.

Mason moved closer to survey the damage Hans had done.

"Ms. Reed, I loathe resorting to such...brutal tactics. I just want answers. I know you can provide them. Why not just tell me what I want to know and avoid all this...*unpleasantness*?"

Jenna's cheeks were swelling as saliva oozed out of the corner of her mouth. She could hardly see out of one eye and felt certain tears were falling uncontrollably from the other one.

Mason looked away. No matter how many times he personally witnessed the results of a beating, it still repulsed him, especially when it disfigured a beautiful woman.

"Go to hell, Hamilton."

"I assure you, Ms. Reed, Hell wouldn't even want me. But I am your host at the moment, and I can make all of this stop with a wave of my hand. Just tell me where you have hidden the treasure pieces. They are worth nothing to you."

"You're wrong about that."

"Honestly, I do not see the point of your personal vendetta. Your parents are gone, your brother will suffer the same fate...there is no need..."

"You have no idea what you have done."

Despite the heightened level of pain, Jenna's resolve was building. Each strike was weakening her body but her fortitude was getting stronger.

For the sake of her parents, her brother, and everyone else Mason Hamilton had hurt and destroyed along his evil pathway, Jenna vowed she would fight him until her last breath. She didn't need Maria's encouragement any longer. She had found some of her own.

Mason stepped away and gave a nod to Hans.

Hans pulled the knife from his waistband and moved closer to Jenna's chair, grinning profusely.

Jenna sucked in a sharp breath. She wanted to remain defiant, but couldn't push one frightening thought from her mind.

The FBI might not get here in time.

Jenna tried to hold her head straight, staring right into Mason's eyes. If this was her last stand, then she was going to burn her image into Mason's brain.

Mason held up his hand. Hans locked his stance.

Lifting Jenna's chin, Mason peered deeply into her eyes.

"Ms. Reed, let me approach this from a different angle. My associate, Jonathan Knox, has taken quite an interest in you. Although I've cautioned him to avoid such trivial matters and pursue someone equitable to his stature, he would be quite upset with me if I deprived him the pleasure of your company. Tell me where the treasure pieces are, and I will call Jonathan to come to your rescue."

"I'm not interested...in Jonathan Knox." Jenna wrestled in her seat. The ropes were cutting into her skin, and Hamilton had struck an unexpected nerve.

"I beg to differ on that matter. My associates tell me you and Jonathan have grown...*quite close.* Do you need me to refresh your memory with vivid details, Ms. Reed? If you like, I can be very *descriptive.*"

Jenna twisted her head to one side. Someone had been watching in the restaurant's storage room. Whoever it was had seen plenty.

"Now then, let us continue. The location, Ms. Reed?"

Jenna took a couple of deep breaths to gain clarity. She was starting to feel dizzy. A concussion, maybe? She had been hit pretty hard.

"You'll never find them."

"Wrong answer, Ms. Reed."

Jenna sat frozen in shock as Hans skillfully sliced through the top section of her tank top, exposing her lacy bra underneath. She opened her mouth to scream, but no sound emitted through her bloodied lips.

What in God's name was he going to do to her?

Licking his finger, Hans ran it along the edge of the blade. Hans laid the flat edge just below Jenna's neck. He could feel her trembling.

Hans jerked his head but kept his blade steady. He wanted her to be afraid.

Slowly, Hans began to draw crisscrossing lines at the top of Jenna's chest. Thin slits drew just a trickle of blood at first. But the closer he got to the top of her breasts, the deeper the knife travelled in its threatening pathway. Several streams of blood pooled together before running down between her breasts.

The more Jenna gasped, the wider Hans grinned. She would cry out soon. He wanted to hear her beg. Her pleas would stimulate him. A scream would even be better...any sound to know the pain he was bringing.

But all he heard was broken breaths. It wasn't enough.

Hans' frustration grew to an intolerable level. Maybe he needed to push the knife deeper. He should have started at her neck. Hans repositioned his knife along Jenna's neckline. Her body was withering but her eyes remained focused.

Hans did not understand. Why wasn't she giving up like all the other women he had tortured?

Mason grabbed Hans by the shoulder to make him stop. Perhaps Jenna would reconsider. He hoped so. He couldn't watch much longer. Too much blood. His stomach was in knots.

Jenna tried so hard not to whimper as her body convulsed, but she couldn't hold back any longer. She didn't want to die slowly. If they were going to kill her, she wanted it to end, right now.

"Get it over with," she said, realizing her next breath would most likely be her last.

Hans glanced back at Mason as his knife hovered.

"The location...*now*."

Jenna blinked her eyes to push away the glaze which was forcing their closure.

"Never..."

"Continue," Mason commanded as Hans turned back towards Jenna.

Hans pressed the blade deeper as he carved a line right above her heart. Her chest was so splattered with blood; he could hardly find an open space to wield another carving. Soon, he would have to start on her face.

Jenna dared not to let her eyes fall. She knew the knife's tip was disfiguring her in steady, deliberate motions taking her agony to a horrendous, unimaginable level. Tears were flowing down her cheeks as her chest was being sliced wide open.

She tried to breathe through the sharp, searing pain, but she was losing ground. Did they want her to beg for mercy...or for death?

Soon she would have no choice. She wouldn't be able to beg at all if the knife cut into her vocal cords.

"Ms. Reed, Hans finds you very tempting and would like nothing better than to have a few quality minutes with you...alone. Personally, I find his methods of persuasion too distasteful to mention or watch. I will not be able to control him much longer, so I will ask you one final time. Where are my treasure pieces?"

Jenna struggled to look at Mason as she shook her head. Her vision was blurred now and her body was numb. As much as she wanted to hold on, she had reached her breaking point.

Keep strong. Your brother is depending on you.

Austin. Jenna found a small degree of stamina as she thought of her brother. She had one more stall technique she could try.

"I...will tell you...what you want to know," Jenna said between quick gasps of breath. "Need some water...please?"

Mason debated what to do. He hadn't been prepared for this.

"Hans, find some water. Hurry."

Hans stormed out of Mason's office. Another waste of time. She would die anyway.

"Very well, Ms. Reed, we will accommodate your request. Then, we will conclude this matter. Time is of the essence, I'm afraid. Your brother's life hangs in the balance. One call from me and my men will kill him without hesitation. He seemed as uncooperative as you. It must run in the family."

Hamilton's words were drifting in and out now. Jenna could barely comprehend anything he was saying.

Jenna's eyelids fluttered. She was losing blood and the ability to keep her body from collapsing.

"Hans!" Mason yelled from his doorway.

Mason peered out into the hallway. Hans was nowhere in sight. The idiot was probably searching every cubicle which would take several minutes. Mason couldn't wait that long.

He had to take action now.

Chapter 34

Jonathan cautiously made his way up the stairwell to the tenth floor, where he was certain Jenna was being held by Mason and his merciless lackeys.

He opened the door slowly and peered out. Just a few feet away, he could see Kliric checking cubicles. *What was the idiot looking for now?*

Kliric passed the receptionist's desk and went down the row behind the massive marble wall displaying the Hamilton-Knox logo.

Jonathan ran to the receptionist's desk and ducked beneath it. He listened intently to determine Kliric's exact location.

Kliric was now three rows behind him making all kinds of noises as he searched the empty work areas.

"Stupid jerk," Jonathan muttered under his breath. The office staff would certainly be pissed tomorrow when they arrived to find someone had been ruffling through their belongings and office supplies.

Jonathan could hear Kliric grunting in frustration. Whatever he was searching for, Kliric obviously didn't have the brains to find it. No surprise, Jonathan thought. Hans Kliric was clearly out of his element.

It was time to make a move while Kliric was distracted by his unsuccessful search.

As Hans started to check another desk unit, Jonathan sprang around the corner, slamming an electric stapler against the side of Hans' head. Hans fell forward against the desk, scattering file folders everywhere. As he began to fall to his knees, Jonathan whipped out a can of pepper spray and doused him in the face.

Hans ranted loudly in Russian as his hands flew to his eyes. The sting from the pepper spray was blinding and painful. He swung his arms in different directions trying desperately to connect with his attacker.

Jonathan backed away. A couple swift kicks to the backs of Hans' knees made him collide with the cubicle wall. As Hans sunk to the floor, Jonathan slammed a metal trashcan on top of his head.

Hans' body twitched for a moment then went still.

Jonathan nudged Hans' boot to make sure he was out. No reaction.

Jonathan wasted no time in grabbing the knife and gun from Han's waistband. He backed against the cubicle wall then stepped out into the corridor.

Armed with the weapons he confiscated, Jonathan made his way through the maze of cubicles closer to Mason's office. Jonathan stuck the gun in his waistband, but closed his hand tightly around the handle of the knife. He noticed a red, sticky substance on his fingers.

Blood.

Jonathan almost dropped the knife, thinking the worst.

It could be Jenna's blood.

Fear turned to anger.

I swear to God, I'll kill you Mason, if you've hurt her.

Crouching around the perimeter of cubicles across from his own office, Jonathan neared the conference room. Taking a step closer, he positioned himself just outside door. He could hear a voice. A man was talking. But the voice didn't belong to Mason.

Was this the same man who had organized the staged reception to throw off the FBI...who had positioned men in a van to prevent the FBI's entry into the museum...who was the ringleader in setting up Austin's kidnapping?

Someone hired to do Mason's dirty work. Someone who obviously knew the operating protocols of the FBI and could work around them.

Jonathan retreated around a corner of cubicles. He sent a quick text to Maria to give her the update on Kliric, half expecting another negative response.

Jonathan was totally surprised.

Good job. Team on the way. Stay away from Mason.

Jonathan shoved his cell back into his pocket, ignoring the vibration when Maria's call followed. He made it this far by his own intuition. He certainly wasn't going to back down now.

Jonathan hid in the cubicle directly across from Mason's office. Minutes ticked away. No FBI team. No elevator.

The hell with this, Jonathan cursed under his breath. Looking around the cubicle wall, he could see Mason's door was partially open.

As he stepped closer, he could hear Mason's loud voice. Mason was angry for sure.

*****

The Closer swore under his breath. Only one of his team had checked in. It was possible his other men were making sure the building was secure. No cause for alarm. Not yet.

It was time to take control in Mason's office. Enough fooling around. As The Closer reached for the door knob, his phone vibrated with an incoming call.

Mallory.

"I can't talk right now," The Closer said in a quiet tone, lowering his voice more than usual.

"I miss you," she said in an alluring voice.

The Closer exhaled heavily. He had no time to play Mallory's little games.

"Were you breathing heavy at the sound of my voice?"

"Not exactly. Mallory, I don't have time for this. I need to keep moving. Stick to the plan. We'll be together soon."

"But not soon enough. Are you coming to Venice?"

"Mallory, please. You know I can't be seen anywhere near Mason. The whole purpose of going to Venice is to show you off to the media so we can establish his alibi. You need to be on Mason's arm."

"He repulses me. I can't bear to have his arm on me or any other part of his body."

"A few more days, that's all. Then you can come down with a stomach virus or whatever you want to get out of the public eye."

"Promise?"

The Closer felt the urge to bang his head against the wall, literally. Mallory was so skillful at playing him.

"Yes. Now hang up so I can do my job."

"I'm doing this for you...you know that. Everything I do...is all *for you*."

The Closer felt his heart sinking. He couldn't hurt her right now with the truth. He needed Mallory to continue the charade as Ellen Chandler Hamilton.

"I know, Mallory. You are the best."

"At everything?"

"Yes...at everything." The Closer rolled his eyes. *Was she ever going to get off the phone? How many times did she need to be reassured?*

"I'll wait for your call. Good luck, darling."

The Closer rammed the phone back into his pocket. He checked his watch again. It was time to make a move.

He couldn't wait any longer for his men to respond. There had to be a complication.

The FBI most likely had gained access to the building. The van option was no longer available. He would initiate Plan B.

"Status?"

"Landing now. Ready."

"Good." The Closer breathed a little easier. The extraction was still on schedule.

As he made his way toward the stairwell, The Closer had a premonition someone was hiding in the cubicle area just ahead, but he didn't take time to conduct a search.

Whoever it was, if anyone was even there to begin with, was definitely not FBI. The FBI would never send just one person. They were all about the team approach when it came to take-down situations.

But who else would be brave enough to venture into Mason's private torture chamber? The Closer mulled on that question as he took the stairs two at a time. Pushing the door open on the roof level, he waved to his pilot.

It was time to go.

*****

Jenna's head rolled to one side. The room spun around her until she fell into the vortex where only darkness reigned.

"Wake up!" Mason yelled at Jenna's unresponsive body. She couldn't pass out now.

Mason was beyond reasoning. His temper flared. He lost control taking his frustration out on Jenna's face and shoulders, almost knocking her to the floor.

Mason took a step back and stared at his bloody hands. How utterly disgusting, he thought to himself. He had no idea how Hans and The Closer could administer such vile measures of human punishment.

He inspected his suit to make sure there was no evidence of Jenna's blood. None that he could see right away, but he couldn't take any chances. As soon as he was on the plane, he would change immediately. The suit would have to be burned when they landed in Venice.

Rushing into his private bathroom, Mason scrubbed his hands meticulously until they were bright red from the hot water. He hated the thought of carrying the remnants of Jenna's resilience on his body.

For a brief moment, Mason pondered the idea of killing Jenna now and getting the whole ordeal over with. It wouldn't take much; she was already out. Just a quick snap of her neck and...

What was he thinking?

If he killed her now, he would never find out where she was hiding the other four treasure pieces.

"You will give me those treasure pieces if it's the last thing you do."

Sanity had returned to him. Taking a deep breath, Mason regained his composure.

Yes, he would let Jenna Reed live...*for now*. Mason's lips curved into a sneer. He would concoct another scheme to retrieve the remaining pieces of the treasure.

Time was of the essence now. His departure was more of a demanding priority.

Mason rapped on the door of the conference room. Expecting an instant response from The Closer, Mason was puzzled as to the delay. Finally, he pulled the door open and stared into the empty room.

Mason walked out into the hallway. He randomly checked several of the cubicles. The Closer was nowhere to be seen. Hans had never returned. Fear gripped him.

I can't be caught here.

Rounding a corner, Mason stopped short. He was shocked to see a gun pointing directly at him ...held by his soon-to-be successor, Jonathan Knox.

"Jonathan, thank God."

Mason leaned on a nearby cubicle wall for support.

"I thought...never mind what I thought. You need to get me out of here. There is a car waiting to take me to the airport. Ellen and I are flying to Venice. I'm afraid if I don't leave now, I'll miss my plane. Let's get going." Mason started to push past Jonathan toward the stairs.

"Not this time, Mason."

Jonathan kept the pistol aimed. He motioned for Mason to back up past the supply closet and down the first row of cubicles.

"This time, you're..."

Jonathan's body pitched forward onto the floor.

Mason jumped back in surprise. He didn't recognize the man who struck Jonathan down. But he didn't care. Right now all that mattered was his escape.

The man standing before Mason was dressed all in black. Dark sunglasses concealed his eyes and a dark baseball cap hid his hair. He did not say a word but jerked his head toward the main-tenance elevator, pointing upward.

The mysterious man shoved Mason inside the elevator, touching the button for the top floor, and then turned away as the doors closed.

Kliric had been rescued a few minutes ago, and now with Mason on his way to the roof, his job was done. Stopping at the supply closet, he removed his hat, leaving on his gloves. He deposited the hat into a huge bag of shredded documents. No one would realize the bag held anything but scraps of paper headed for the shredding company. Evidence destroyed without anyone's knowledge.

"Perfect."

Securing his FBI Kevlar vest and tucking his sunglasses into the front flap pocket, he then closed the supply closet door. He headed for the stairwell. It was time to rejoin Turette's team.

Chapter 35

The maintenance elevator stopped at the roof level. Mason warily stepped outside. Gusts of wind from the helicopter's blades were making it hard to see. The Closer hung out the side, beckoning Mason on board. As soon as Mason was buckled in, The Closer gave the thumbs-up signal to the pilot.

The local news helicopter flew away into the night with no fanfare. A familiar sight in New York shouldn't raise anyone's suspicions. Not tonight. There was too much commotion on the ground.

Gunfire inside the museum. NYPD and the FBI running in circles. Pedestrians panicking. Chaos all around.

The Closer smiled. Another diversion perfectly planned and executed. He was good, very good.

*****

Jonathan shook his head and tried to focus. His vision slowly regained sharpness as he pulled his head off the floor. Reaching back, he felt dampness at the back of his head. His fingers were red. Blood.

"Not good," Jonathan mumbled.

He grabbed the closest cubicle wall and pulled himself upright. Surprisingly enough, the knife and gun were still on the ground where he had fallen.

Knocked out but not disarmed? Jonathan didn't understand. Whoever attacked him wasn't interested in taking his weapons.

He looked around. Mason was gone. He got it now. Someone had nailed him so Mason could escape. Once again. Mason and his little disappearing acts. Whoever Mason relied upon to get him out of sticky situations knew what he was doing...*extremely* well.

A disturbing chill ran up Jonathan's spine.

Jenna!

Jonathan approached Mason's door. No sound. Maybe she was still inside. He barreled against the door, falling forward as the door swung open.

Jonathan went down to his knees. His eyes flew upward and he was rendered speechless.

Jenna was tied to a chair and she had been...

Jonathan couldn't even begin to comprehend what had happened to her. He placed two fingers along Jenna's neck, finding a weak pulse.

"Oh, thank God," Jonathan said as he regained his speech. His hands flew to his phone and he speed-dialed Maria.

"Jonathan! Please tell me you're ok! Where are you?"

"Mason's office. Jenna...she's hurt...really bad. Get up here...*fast!*"

Tossing his phone aside, Jonathan wrapped his arms protectively around Jenna's limp body.

"Jenna, can you hear me?"

Pressing his face against Jenna's forehead, Jonathan felt his heart breaking at the sight of her.

"Jenna, I'm here. You're going to be ok."

Jenna stirred, hearing Jonathan's voice. She wanted to cry out to him but she had no strength. Her eyes flickered open only for a brief second.

Jonathan untied the ropes and caught her as she slid off the chair. Jenna's body was dead weight falling against his shoulder. He carefully laid her on the floor.

"Jenna, I won't leave you. Help is on the way."

Jenna moved her head slightly as Jonathan brushed a strand of hair from her face.

"Jonathan...," Jenna murmured just above the level of a whisper. Feeling the comfort of Jonathan's arms, she let go. She didn't have to hang on any longer.

"Oh, God, Jenna! Don't leave me, please!" Jonathan shouted just as Maria's team barged through the door.

"Jonathan, get back."

Maria pulled Jonathan to the side, making room for the medical team.

"What can you tell me?" The first paramedic asked as he took a pulse reading. His partner quickly unwrapped a bag of oxygen tubing.

"Found her unconscious just a few minutes ago. She tried to say a few words, but she passed out."

Maria put her arm around Jonathan's shoulders as his voice wavered. It was the first time she had held her son in such a long time. But it was just the degree of comfort both of them needed

"Pulse is weak; I'm barely getting a reading. Get that tank going."

The two paramedics worked in tandem to fit an oxygen mask over Jenna's face, then covered her chest with a sheet.

"Dispatch, this is Harbeson from 407. We're at the Livingston Art Museum, tenth floor. We have a female, late twenties, multiple lacerations to the upper body. Unconscious. Request destination for transport."

Jenna was quickly lifted onto the stretcher and then wheeled to the elevator. Jonathan and Maria followed close behind in silence.

Jonathan held Jenna's hand as they rode down in the elevator. He couldn't believe anyone could hurt her in such a gruesome way.

"I'm going to kill Mason for this," Jonathan said as he glanced up at Maria.

"Not if I get him first," she responded then squeezed Jonathan's arm.

Jonathan and Maria raced alongside the stretcher as it headed for the ambulance. In their haste, they didn't notice who had fallen in behind them. As Jonathan started to climb in the back of the ambulance, he was quickly shoved aside.

"How could you let this happen?" Chase yelled. "Jenna trusted you to keep her safe. We both did. Now just look at her! Damn you for screwing up! For putting your mission ahead of everything and everyone else. Tell me right now, was your mission worth her sacrifice?"

Chase jumped inside the ambulance before Maria or Jonathan could utter a response. They both knew Chase was right.

Maria felt despair wash over her body. When was it ever going to end? Mason had successfully escaped once again. How could he possibly have left the building with her team storming every exit?

Jenna would be the only one who could point a finger at Mason. But her testimony would be shaky at best due to the trauma she had endured. One of Mason's high-end attorneys would have no trouble throwing doubt on the questionable validity of Jenna as a witness.

Unless the Crime Scene techs discovered trace evidence tying Mason to Jenna's assault, criminal charges would go unfounded once again. Mason would just get his picture in the paper alleging another false accusation.

More press coverage. Exactly what Mason wanted. He thrived on it.

But it wasn't just the defeat of losing again to Mason Hamilton which brought Maria to her knees. She made a promise to keep Jenna safe and she didn't honor it.

Maria's hand closed around her clip-on badge. She almost felt the urge to throw it to the ground.

"I didn't do my job today."

"You can't predict his every move," Jonathan said, trying to understand some of Maria's frustration.

"Well I should be able to by now. I've certainly had plenty of opportunities."

Jonathan grabbed Maria's hand and squeezed it. He was dog-tired also, his energy completely gone, but somehow he knew they both needed some encouragement.

"You did accomplish what you set out to do. You got both of them out."

"With your help," Maria quickly added. A moment for mother-son bonding was all she had time for.

"I've got to go," Maria said as she released her hand.

Jonathan nodded as he stared off into space.

"I know you took a lot of risks tonight…even against my advice. But I want you to know, Jonathan, I am very proud of you."

Maria patted Jonathan on the shoulder then walked away. It was time to fall back into command and manage the recovery of the mission.

"Jacoby?"

"Right here." Jacoby stepped up to stand alongside of Maria, where he would always be.

"Get Thompson to round up the team leaders and give me finals. I want updates on all causalities. Also get NYPD to make sure traffic is flowing again and to check on any pedestrians who may have gotten injured. We need Crime Scene techs here as soon as possible."

"You got it."

"Thank you," Maria called as Jacoby took off to search for Thompson.

Maria turned her sights on the M&T Bank building where her husband had been holed up for several hours. She just shook her head, conveying to Damian how discouraged she felt. Her phone buzzed in response.

"Would it help if I told you I love you right now?"

"Yes, it would."

"I love you, Sweetheart."

Maria's head turned in the direction of the one voice which could sustain her through any mountain of despondency. Managing a half smile, she spun around to gaze into Damian's comforting eyes. He had left his post to join her.

So much for protocol.

Maria fell into Damian's arms and held on tightly. She didn't care if her gesture was deemed a sign of weakness. It felt too good to be held right now.

"It wasn't a total loss."

"You may be the only one to see that, Damian."

Damian pulled back and rubbed Maria's arms.

"You executed the plan to the best of the FBI's ability. The reception ambush was unexpected and your team dealt with it. There were casualties, and they are significant losses, but there were also achievements. You saved the lives of two people, who Mason could have easily killed. If your team hadn't taken the steps to storm the building and Jonathan hadn't been lucky enough to find Austin, you would have two more deaths to report."

"But he got away...again."

"And I know how he did it."

Maria stared back at her husband.

"News copter. Landed just as I was pulling out of position. I tried to call you but my earpiece malfunctioned. I guess you were too focused on getting inside to hear my cell."

Maria glanced down at her phone. Sure enough. She had missed Damian's call.

"Did you see anyone else?"

"A pilot and one other man."

"What was the other man wearing?" Maria knew the answer before Damian uttered it.

"All black."

"Then he's back. I just knew The Closer would have a hand in all this. He's quite adept at diversions. I have no doubt he coordinated the Folly Beach fiasco as well."

"We'll get him. Go do your job."

Maria headed back to the van and yanked open the door.

"Let's lock this down," she said to her team.

Hopefully within a few hours, everyone could go home. She would close the scene, but regrettably, not the final chapter on Mason Hamilton.

*****

Mason settled into a plush leather seat on the private jet. Leaning against the headrest, he felt his body beginning to relax. Soon he would be landing in Venice, and Agent Turette wouldn't be able to touch him.

"How do you feel now, Agent Turette?" Mason gloated.

Mallory looked up from her magazine. She shook her head without commenting.

Just a few days more... her lover had promised. She would hold him to that. Mallory went back to Cosmopolitan. She planned to read it cover to cover so she wouldn't have to engage in another pointless conversation with Mason.

"You are the first," Mason said as he pulled the small gold elephant from his pocket. Mason wasn't so much interested in the artifact for its intrinsic rare value; he merely was in awe of the fact it had survived. Yet its owners had not.

The Dunn legend filtered through his mind.

Death comes to those who dare to hold all five pieces of tainted gold.

Mason laughed. What nonsense! He didn't believe in such childish tales. A curse? He doubted it was true. If the descendants of James Dunn had died mysterious deaths, that was their problem.

What did it matter? He wasn't planning on holding onto the treasure pieces forever. After he showcased them for the world to see, Mason planned to sell them to the highest bidder. An anonymous buyer had already made an offer. Two-hundred-fifty million if Mason could procure all five pieces.

Two-hundred-fifty million dollars for five little pieces of gold.

Not a curse by a far stretch. A fortune, indeed!

With that kind of money he could hide from the FBI and Agent Turette...*forever.*

Oh, Agent Turette, will you miss me?

Mason sat upright with a new devilish plot swirling in his brain. He smirked. There was a new game waiting to be played.

Mason took out his cell and speed-dialed the first number on his call list.

As he always did, Mason shuddered when the formidable voice answered.

"Target?"

"Maria Turette."

Now, the *real* challenge would begin.

Chapter 36

Jenna awoke to streaming white lights and a throbbing ache on the right side of her face. When she tried to move her head, sharp twinges of pain made her snap to attention.

"Oh, God."

She glanced under her flimsy hospital gown. She was wrapped in bandages from her neck to her stomach. Terrifying memories rushed to her brain. Tears streamed down her face. She could almost feel the tip of the knife touching her skin.

"No!"

Jenna bolted upright. Her eyes darted frantically around the room, finally centering on Chase. He was asleep in a chair by the window. Jenna fell back against her pillow and let out a deep breath.

Hearing Jenna's scream, Chase woke up and practically fell out of the chair. He couldn't get to her bedside fast enough.

"Jenna, don't try to move. You'll pull out the IV."

Rubbing Jenna's forehead, he tried his best to calm her.

"Chase, I hurt...*all over.*"

Jenna bit her lip as another wave of blinding pain tore through her. She squeezed Chase's hand until the tremor subsided.

"I'll get someone in here as soon as possible."

Chase pushed the call button several times.

"Your pain meds are probably wearing off. I'll get the nurse." Chase headed for the door.

"No, don't leave me. Chase...please, come back!"

Chase spun around, almost afraid to look into Jenna's eyes. More than anything, he wanted to take her pain away. It was too hard watching her suffer.

"I'm not going anywhere. I'll stay right here with you."

Jenna nodded then closed her eyes. Not all of the pain she was feeling was from her superficial wounds.

She was aching from the inside out.

As much as she couldn't bear the thought of Chase not being with her, Jenna knew she needed time alone to figure things out. There were too many unknown variables now.

When would Mason make another attempt on her life? Would he try once again to hurt the people she cared about... including Chase?

Staying by her side would only put Chase in danger. If they were to have a chance together, she needed to know he was safe. There was only one way to ensure that...*she had to push him away.*

Nurse Anne Bailey ran into the room responding to the repetitive alert call signals.

"Sir, one press of the button gets our attention. It's not necessary to keep pushing the button several times."

"I'm sorry...but she woke up in a lot of pain."

"She's due for another dosage." The nurse connected another bag to the IV drip. The result was almost instantaneous.

Chase breathed a sigh of relief as he watched Jenna's body begin to relax. He nodded in appreciation to the nurse.

"Thank you....she's been through a lot. I guess I'm just being overprotective."

"You have every right to be. I read her file. I'd say she's quite a survivor."

"Yes, she is."

Jenna's eyes were glazing over.

"Chase....I... want..."

"We can talk later, Jenna. Get some rest."

"But...Chase..."

"Not now. Close your eyes. I'll be right here when you wake up."

Jenna fell back into the safeness of the darkness where there was no fear of hurting Chase's feelings or her own.

Nurse Bailey picked up Jenna's chart. "She'll be out for the next few hours. If you want to grab something to eat or take a walk, we'll watch over her for you."

"Thanks. I won't be gone long."

Nurse Bailey checked the stats on the monitors recording Jenna's heart rate and pulse, and added the readings to the file.

The nurse shook her head in amazement. It was evident from the extensiveness of chest and facial wounds, Jenna had suffered extensive degrees of torture. But she had survived.

"Keep up the fight, Jenna Reed," Nurse Bailey said as she tucked in the sheet around Jenna's waist. "We're all pulling for you."

*****

Kelly watched Austin's chest rise up and down in a peaceful tempo. Even in a dream-state, Austin managed to hold onto her hand. Somehow he knew she was by his side, and he *wanted* her right there.

As much as Kelly wanted to keep her hand linked with Austin's, she had to finally let go. Her back was aching from sitting in the same position in the metal guest chair. She needed to stretch her legs and get some fresh air.

Kissing Austin's hand then laying it on his stomach, Kelly rose from her chair. She paused to look at his bruised face which made her feel another piercing stab.

How can I ever get past the fact I caused him so much pain?

Every mark on Austin's body was a stinging reminder of her part in his abduction and the suffering he had endured.

Kelly leaned against the wall outside of Austin's room and rubbed her tired eyes. She was exhausted. But she couldn't be anywhere else.

She was in love with him, and she would stay until he pushed her away.

Austin's body was in bad shape now, but it would heal. It was his heart Kelly was more concerned about. She had broken that as well through her betrayal.

Jenna was three floors above. The two people Kelly cared most about had been hurt on the malicious orders of her father.

Kelly's stomach churned at the mere thought of Mason and what he had done. As she approached the water fountain at the end of the hallway, Kelly became nauseated. Her legs felt weak, but somehow she made it to the nearest bathroom. After throwing up twice, she was finally able to catch her breath.

Wiping her face with a damp towel seemed to help. But it wasn't just the disgust she felt being the daughter of such a loathsome man; she was suffering from morning sickness.

She needed something to calm her stomach. Maybe a ginger ale from the cafeteria would do the trick.

Taking a seat at a table in the deserted corner of the eating area, Kelly laid her head down on her folded arms. All she wanted to do at the moment was fade into the background where her shame wasn't as noticeable.

"This spot taken?"

Kelly lifted her eyes, recognizing the voice.

"Hi, Chase. How's Jenna doing?"

"Still in a lot of pain. She keeps waking up and screaming when the meds wear off. I can't stand it. I feel totally helpless."

"I know what you mean."

Kelly got to her feet. She just wanted to be alone to wallow in her own despair.

"Hey, don't leave. I could use the company. Is it true? Is Mason Hamilton really your father and...Jonathan's?"

Kelly gripped the back of her chair steadying herself. She nodded and lowered her head.

"Then how did you turn out to be so good?"

Kelly was surprised at Chase's comment.

"Chase, you have no idea how wrong you are. The things my father made me do..." Kelly's voice drifted off. Tears were starting to cloud her eyes.

"Hey, listen, I didn't mean to upset you. You don't need to explain. Just seeing what Hamilton did to Jenna was enough for me. I can't imagine what he did to you all these years. Sit down, Kelly," Chase said as he patted the seat beside him. "I need the company. I'm sure you do, too."

Kelly felt another fit of nausea ready to erupt as her stomach contracted.

"Gotta go, Chase. Not feeling well."

Kelly flew from the cafeteria to the ladies room around the corner. Within a few minutes, she emerged, pale and sluggish. She hadn't expected Chase to be waiting for her.

Chase caught Kelly as she leaned towards the wall.

"You're really wiped out."

"I should go back to Austin's room now."

"I don't think that's a good idea. You need to see a doctor right now. You might have caught something in here. You know hospitals carry the most germs." Chase laughed, trying to lighten Kelly's mood.

Kelly shook her head as she pushed forward towards the elevator.

"Austin could catch whatever you have."

Kelly managed a slight smile.

"I don't think so, Chase. Although, Austin is part of the reason I'm not feeling well."

Chase shot Kelly a puzzled look.

"I'm pregnant."

"Does Austin know?"

Kelly shook her head. "I don't know how he'll react."

"Well, I'm happy for you. I'm sure Austin will be, too. Congratulations, Kelly."

"Thank you, Chase."

Chase steered Kelly towards Austin's room as they walked past the nurse's station.

"Thanks for walking me back, Chase."

"My pleasure. I'll keep your news a secret for now. You can tell Austin and Jenna when you're ready. Take care of yourself."

Kelly was totally surprised to find Austin propped up in bed. Hesitantly, she kept one hand on the door to dart out quickly if he rejected her.

The decision was made for her in two seconds.

Austin reached out his hand. "Come over here," he said with a weak voice.

Kelly gently put her arms around his neck and kissed him several times, trying to avoid the bruises on his face.

"Tell me you love me. That's all I need to hear right now. Please, Kelly, just tell me…"

Austin's eyes were starting to close.

"I love you, Austin," Kelly whispered then laid her head on his shoulder. Austin fell asleep, this time with a smile on his face.

*****

"Hi," Chase said as he neared Jenna's bed.

"You have to go," Jenna blurted out.

"What do you mean...*go*?"

Chase was totally confused.

Maybe the drugs were impairing her ability to think straight?

"Leave me...*now*. For your own safety. You'll get hurt because of me. I can't handle that...if something happened to you, I..."

Chase wasn't prepared for this conversation.

"Jenna, we've been over this before. I can take care of myself. Besides...I love you. I can't just leave you."

Jenna shook her head in frustration. "Can't you see, Chase? Staying with me puts you in danger. It hurts me too much to think I'm the reason you could get hurt. Give me...*give us*...some space...some time."

Jenna braced herself for Chase's arguments but surprisingly there were none.

"I'll give you whatever you want, Jenna. Space. Time. My heart. But I won't be far away."

Jenna broke down and cried against the pillow. Maybe she had made a mistake. She needed Chase. Why did she think pushing him away was the only answer?

But it was the answer she received.

When Jenna finally opened her eyes, Chase was gone.

Chapter 37

Jonathan watched the flat screen in the hospital lounge with a look of disgust. Mason's face was plastered on the screen. The news reporter was going on and on about the Hamiltons vacationing in Venice right before the launch of the upcoming *Lost Pirate Treasure* exhibit.

"Who the hell cares?"

Jonathan changed the channel. Mason Hamilton didn't deserve any air time. In fact, Jonathan thought to himself as he headed in the direction of Jenna's room, Mason Hamilton didn't even deserve...*any air to breathe.*

As he rounded the corner to Jenna's unit, he ran smack into Maria as she exited Jenna's room.

"Sorry. Is Jenna awake?"

"She is at the moment. Are you always this anxious to see her?" Maria asked, as she took a step backwards to regain her balance.

"I wanted to stop by before I rode over with Kelly to her apartment. She wants to pick up a few things. Thanks for sending Thompson and Jensen over. I'll feel better knowing Kelly and I have some back-up just in case Mason's men are lurking."

"I'm sure they'll scatter when they see Thompson."

"You're right about that. But I appreciate the gesture. I'm sure Kelly does, too."

"I think you're going to be a very good brother."

Maria smiled. *And a good son,* she thought to herself.

"Yeah, I'm pretty excited about that. And some other news about Jenna."

Maria raised her eyebrows. "What are you talking about?"

"The nurses told me Jenna gave Garrett the boot. I think it's my turn now."

"Be careful, Jonathan. Jenna may not be thinking clearly if she's dealing with a break-up."

"I can handle what Jenna throws my way. Don't worry about me. I'll talk to you later."

Jonathan pushed Jenna's door open after Maria left.

"Want some company?"

"Ok." Jenna pushed herself up to a sitting position.

Her gown fell off her right shoulder, exposing her skin to Jonathan's wandering eyes. He kissed her lightly just above the neckline of the gown then reached for her hand.

Jenna was dumb-struck, caught off-guard by Jonathan's sudden move. She didn't know how to respond...in words.

"Are you going for the off-shoulder look? Because I find it very, very...*sexy*."

Jenna tried to pull the gown back into place without luck. She had no desire to feed Jonathan's sexual fantasies, but he had certainly awakened hers.

Her entire body was resonating with a combination of hot and cold twinges. She was tingling from anxiety and excitement.

"You seem like you're doing a lot better...*now*."

Jenna looked at him hesitantly. "I am, but I'm still really sore."

"I wish I could take your pain away."

Chase had said almost the exact same thing.

Chase. Who she had pushed away. The worst decision she ever made.

"Jenna?"

"I'm sorry. I just got lost in my thoughts for a moment."

"Just so your thoughts were of me."

"Why would you think they would be?"

Maria was right; Jenna was obviously still reeling from whatever happened between her and Garrett.

"I have my suspicions. Besides, I want you."

Jonathan leaned in closer. He was hovering above her face now. The temptation was bearing down on both of them.

"I know you do, and that's the problem."

Jonathan backed away just a little.

"Why would that be a problem?"

"Because..."

"I don't want to hear any explanations."

Jonathan bore down on Jenna's lips with a powerful kiss that rocked her entire body. As his arms pulled her closer, Jonathan almost lifted Jenna out of bed.

The sensation was dynamic. A magnetic pull so strong and exhilarating neither Jonathan nor Jenna could find the energy to pull away. But finally Jonathan found an ounce of willpower coupled with his concern of holding Jenna too firmly he would hurt her.

"I don't think there's any problem with me wanting you. Or you wanting me."

Jenna tried to compose herself, but it wasn't easy with Jonathan grinning at her.

"I lost myself for a moment...*that's all.* Obviously, it's a reaction from the drugs. I'm not thinking clearly. There is *nothing* between us."

Jonathan couldn't do anything but laugh.

"Deny it all you want. Your lips were telling me a different story. But for now, I'll play along. I suppose you think I'm trying to come between you and Garrett."

"That's exactly what you've done and what you'll continue to do! As long as you keep interfering in my life, Chase and I are going to have problems."

"A friendly competition, that's all."

"There is no competition. I don't want you; I never did. You're the one who can't get that through your head."

"Perhaps you need another reminder." He started to reach for Jenna's face but she pushed his hand away.

Jonathan caught her hand in mid-air. He kissed her palm.

The heat returned to Jenna's body within seconds.

"Didn't want you forget me anytime soon."

Glancing over his shoulder before he left the room, Jonathan saw the bewildered look on Jenna's face.

Good, he thought to himself.

I'm not giving up now...or ever. Our attraction is too strong.

*****

Kelly stopped short in front of her apartment door. Although Jonathan and two FBI agents were right behind her, her hand paused as she reached for the doorknob.

"Let me help you," Jonathan offered, sensing her apprehension.

"Thank you. I guess I'm just a little nervous."

"Can you guys take a walk-through before we go in?"

"Of course, Sir," Agent Thompson said, leading the way with Agent Jensen right behind him. In less than a minute, they returned to the hallway.

"All clear. We'll wait for you here."

Jonathan pulled Kelly inside. "Do you need me to help you?"

Kelly placed a hand on his arm for support.

"Jonathan, I'm scared to even be here. It doesn't feel like home anymore. I guess it never did. Mason bought and paid for practically everything in my apartment. I just want to grab a few things then get straight out of here."

"I understand. Get what you need then we'll leave."

As Kelly headed for her bedroom, Jonathan looked around the lavishly-furnished apartment. Expensive leather furniture. Fifty-inch flat screen. Crystal everywhere. A fully-stocked bar.

All for show. *Mason's show.*

He couldn't imagine Kelly wanting to spend any time here.

Kelly filled a small suitcase with a few clothes and shoes. She grabbed a framed picture of herself and Jenna taken when they went on a retreat together with the freshmen class. It was the only personal memento she had. Glancing around the room with the four poster bed, she felt nothing.

She wanted to put the past behind her, and start fresh with Austin and their baby. She just prayed Austin would remember the good things about their relationship when he wasn't so drug-induced. He had fallen asleep too soon before she had a chance to tell him she was pregnant.

Kelly had no regrets when she joined Jonathan in the living room. She was letting go of this part of her life...*forever*.

"All set?"

"I just remembered something. I'll be right back."

Kelly returned to her bedroom closet and pulled up a small piece of rug in the corner. She grabbed an envelope containing her stash of emergency money, shoved it into her pocketbook, and then ran from the room.

"Ready."

Before they made it to the door, Kelly wondered what Jonathan really thought of her now. She had prostituted herself for her

324 S.A. Van

father's benefit, and befriended the woman Jonathan cared about only to betray her in the end. How could he ever forgive her?

"I'm sorry, Jonathan," Kelly started to say. "I don't even know where to begin."

Jonathan turned around and placed her suitcase on the floor. He grabbed Kelly's shoulders and searched her eyes. They held such sadness; Jonathan could barely focus.

"Stop blaming yourself for things you had no control over. Just try to think of better days ahead. Ok?"

Jonathan gave Kelly a hug.

"I am so glad you're my sister. I always wanted a sibling. Didn't realize I'd have to wait almost thirty years, but you are definitely worth the wait. Let's get out of here. We'll drop your stuff at my grandmother's house then I'll take you back to Austin."

*****

Kelly gingerly walked into Austin's room and her eyes immediately locked on him.

Austin was awake and grinning so widely Kelly was at a loss for words.

Austin held out his arms. "You're too far away."

Kelly melted inside at such a loving gesture. She ran to Austin and fell against his shoulder as his arm encircled her waist.

"Tell me about your news," Austin said before he kissed Kelly's forehead. "One of the nurses let me in on a little secret."

"A secret?"

Austin rubbed his hand on Kelly's stomach. He watched as her eyes sparkled with anticipation. Then he cradled her face in his hands.

"Our baby. I love the sound of that! If you told me yesterday, I'm sorry I don't remember. I was really out of it. The nurse came by this morning and congratulated me. At first I thought she was just happy I ate all of my breakfast."

Kelly laughed softly. She felt such a sense of relief.

"I didn't get a chance to tell you yesterday; you were so tired. I guess I wasn't too discreet making mad dashes for the ladies room. Morning sickness. It's making me a little weak."

"Sit down then."

Kelly shook her head.

"I'm ok for now. Just hold me, Austin. I'm just so glad you want me."

Kelly couldn't hold back any longer. Tears ran down her cheeks before she could utter another word.

"Of course I want you. Why would you have any doubts?"

"Because of what my father and his men made me do. Then I realized I was pregnant and I...."

"Before your father ordered his boys to rough me up, he told me you disobeyed him to stay with me. That's all I needed to hear. As far as I'm concerned, you don't belong to him anymore. You belong...*to me*."

Kelly sighed heavily as he stroked her back. It felt so good to be in his arms once again. Nothing else mattered. She had everything now.

"Look at me, Kelly."

Austin lifted Kelly's face so he could look into her eyes.

Her cheeks were so wet from her tears; Austin's heart ached for the pain she was finally letting go.

"I need you to forgive me, Austin."

"Kelly, I know."

"No, Austin, I need to tell you. I was the one who drugged you before you were taken to New York. I didn't want to do it. George forced me."

"George...*Maylor*?"

Kelly nodded. "He works for Mason. He was spying on you and your family for years."

"Did George hurt you?"

"He hit me. I was hysterical when you passed out. I ran away from him and hid upstairs in the little room you showed me. Someone searched the house looking for me. If you hadn't shown me the little room, I...don't know what they would have done. You saved my life, Austin."

Kelly felt her body collapsing, but Austin held her face steady.

"I don't blame you for anything. You were forced to do things against your will. How can I possibly hold that against you? I love you, Kelly. That's all I want to focus on right now."

"You really *love me*? You're not just saying that because of the baby?"

"I want to show you how much I really love you, but the nurses might run in. I'm sure it would set my heart monitor up a few notches." Austin laughed. "I fell in love with you the first moment I laid eyes on you. You're beautiful, kind, and incredibly sexy. You're everything I want. But I do have a question for you."

"What is it?"

Austin kissed the palm of her hand then placed it against his face.

"Will you marry me, Kelly McBride?"

*****

Maria rubbed her aching neck. It had been several long days following the raid on the museum. Now it was time to clean up the paper trail. Multiple reports justifying the actions of three FBI field offices in addition to the NYPD were taking an enormous amount of time to complete.

Where were the SMART boards when she needed them? In the age of technology, Maria still wondered why so many paper reports had to be processed. It was mind-boggling and brain-draining, but she couldn't get out of it.

Administrative punishment.

Her superiors obviously felt the need to teach her a lesson. One she should have learned years ago. Three decades of playing cat-and-mouse with such an elusive mastermind had cost the FBI countless hours of manpower and financial resources. But the end result was always the same – Mason got away.

But this time, he slipped out of their grasp with one of the gold animals which Maria had hoped to hide from Mason forever.

Mason was not one to accept only partial success; he wanted the full magnitude of his endeavors. Maria was positive Mason wasn't going to stop now.

She needed to find a way to keep Jenna safe. Only Jenna knew where the other four treasure pieces were hidden. It wasn't going to be an easy task.

Jenna flat out refused the FBI's offer of protective custody. Maria couldn't blame her. Mason had been eluding the FBI for such a long time. Jenna had no desire to live her life under a rock.

She wanted to work with Maria to bring Mason down, but she wasn't going to hide from him.

Maria admired Jenna's resolve but it also scared her. Confident people didn't always win, and sometimes they ended up dead. Maria wracked her brain. She would have to be creative. She would have to do whatever it took to keep Jenna...and Jonathan safe.

Wherever Jenna happened to be, Jonathan would most likely follow. The mysterious bond tying him to Jenna was not about to be broken now.

Maria shook her head. Too much personal drama was starting to mask her ability to think clearly as a senior agent. Thoughts were wavering too much towards the people she cared about. She was becoming distracted. The reports were taking way too long to complete.

Maria's cell buzzed, interrupting her train of thought. She managed to smile for the first time that day.

"Hi, Damian."

"Hello, Sweetheart. I miss you. When are you coming home? The bed is getting cold."

"I miss you, too. I'm hoping to finish up today. The reports should take me another couple of hours then I have to give a final update to the Manhattan team."

Maria checked her watch. "If I catch a late afternoon train, I'll be home in time for dinner."

"Grilled salmon, roasted potatoes, chilled Chardonnay?"

Maria's mouth was watering.

"Perfect. Dessert in the hot tub?" She could tease just as well as her husband.

"Without a doubt. I can't wait to see you."

"Hold onto that thought. I'll be home in a few hours. I love you."

Before leaving New York, Damian tried again to convince Maria to give up on the Hamilton case. But she still wouldn't let go.

Maria couldn't break the promise she made to herself thirty years ago. In a hasty move, she started the fateful wheels in motion which had claimed so many innocent lives.

Maria owed it to each and every one of Mason's victims to finish this through to the end...*one way or another*.

Maybe she needed more caffeine. Coffee always pumped her up and gave her a boost to move a little faster, mentally and physically. She jumped up from the desk she was borrowing and inattentively collided with another agent.

"Oh, I'm sorry, Agent Turette."

"Not a problem, Agent..." Maria squinted to see the FBI badge clipped to his jacket.

"Agent Scott Michaelson, Ma'am. Again, I am sorry for knocking you down. I was asked to bring this to you."

Michaelson handed Maria a tan envelope with her name printed on the front in neat block letters.

"Thank you," Maria called as Michaelson departed.

When Maria turned to sit down, she noticed the stack of papers she had neatly compiled was tipped sideways, scattering reports everywhere.

"Well, that's just perfect."

At this rate, she'd be lucky to catch a late train unless a small miracle happened. Her romantic dinner on the patio with her handsome husband was looking more distant in the future.

Maria sank to her chair and unclasped the envelope, pulling out the one item it contained.

The small photograph made her gasp in horror.

Mason Hamilton was tormenting her again.

Chapter 38

Teresa welcomed Jenna back to Cape May with a big hug.

"I'm glad to see you. I made you some iced tea."

"That sounds good. I can't wait to relax for a few days."

Agents Jacoby and Thompson barged in the kitchen right behind Jenna.

"We'll take a quick look around," Jacoby said as he drew his weapon.

"No need; I've already done that!" Teresa called as the agents headed up the stairs. "I think I can handle a surveillance sweep by now!"

Teresa turned to face Jenna who was starting to laugh.

"Men!"

"I'm sure they're just doing their job."

"Oh, I'm sure that's what it is. But they're wasting their time." Teresa shrugged. "Oh well, let them get their jollies."

Teresa set two glasses of iced tea on the table.

"All clear," Thompson said as he joined them in the kitchen.

"Thank you *so much*," Teresa retorted. "If you two want to bunk at my house next door, I'll stay here with Jenna. There are two guest rooms on the upper level. Take your pick."

Jacoby nodded. "That works for us. Agent Turette suggested that as a possibility. Just let us know what your plans are so we can join the party. Here's one of my cards. Both of our cell numbers are listed on the back. Have a good evening."

After the agents left, Jenna took her glass to the living room. "Your tea and my favorite spot. I'm happy."

"Are you...*really*?"

Nothing got past Teresa.

Jenna glanced off in the distance. Her smile turned downward.

"I didn't mean to bring you down from your cloud."

"No, it's ok, Teresa. I have to talk about it eventually. I screwed up...*big time*."

"Well, you don't have to talk about it now. You need a change of pace. Do you feel like going down to the beach?"

"Sounds perfect. That's just what I need. I'll change in a few minutes after I'm done with my tea. Would you mind calling Jacoby?"

"Not at all. Might be fun to see them in their speedos."

Jenna made a face causing Teresa to roar with laughter.

The sun had begun its descent but the skyline was still fairly bright. Jenna and Teresa kicked off their flip flops and headed down from the wooden ramp separating the beach from the Promenade. Although the Cape May Beach Patrol had lowered their lifeguard chairs which signaled the end of their official day, a few families were still enjoying the least crowded time on the beach.

Teresa and Jenna planted their beach chairs just above the small rise in the sand while the agents sat farther back. They were far enough away from the rolling surf, but close enough to appreciate the gentle sea breezes.

Jenna dug her toes into the sand and sighed contently. Closing her eyes, she listened to the calming sounds of the ocean. A light breeze blew her hair away from her face, almost lulling her to sleep.

Teresa hated to break Jenna's relaxation, but it was time. Jenna deserved to learn the truth.

"I have something to tell you," Teresa began. "This will be a lot for you to take in after everything else you've lived through this summer. But it's time you know...*about your mother*."

Jenna's eyes flew wide open.

"What else is there, Teresa? Mom helped conceal Jonathan's existence, and she hid the treasure pieces in our beach house. What else can you possibly tell me?"

The look on Teresa's face made Jenna grip the arms of her chair.

"There's a lot more, Jenna. But for starters, your mother was CIA... like we all were. Maria, Candace, Gail, Lois and I."

Teresa paused, knowing this was the biggest shock of all.

"My God, Teresa, I can't believe this."

"It's true, Jenna. One day this will all make sense. We were all recruited by the CIA in our junior year of college at Syracuse. We trained together at Langley, and became part of a mission called "The Circle." We were assigned various tasks to take down

Mason Hamilton, *Senior* and his son. Your mother was an integral part of the mission. She tracked illegal transports of priceless artifacts all over the world. Museums reported missing artwork from their inventories, only to have them re-surface at a later time. By then, most were fakes returned to the original owners, while the authentic pieces were sold on the black market."

My mother...working for the CIA? Jenna was numb from the shocking news.

This was way too hard to comprehend. Lois Green...who baked cookies for PTA fundraisers, who organized the annual holiday greens sale at school, the Sunday School teacher who helped third-graders learn their bible verses...*living a double-life as a CIA agent?* This was too absurd.

But not totally...inconceivable.

Jenna blankly stared at some seagulls flying above the water's edge. Memories sifted into her mind about her mother's occasional absences.

Business trips on the spur of the moment. Last minute appointments Lois couldn't reschedule. Relatives needing help who lived in other states. Girlfriend weekends not listed on the family calendar she always kept in the kitchen.

All lies? Lois had been so convincing...Jenna never once questioned her mother's motives. Why would she?

Teresa continued as Jenna sat spellbound.

"We had to shift gears in 1980 unexpectedly, when Maria...I'll just call her Sylvia now. Anyway...Sylvia suddenly found out she was pregnant. This threw our mission off-course. We all banded together. We came up with a plan to keep the baby safe so we could continue our investigation. We all thought...God, we were all so stupid back then. We actually thought we were getting close enough to taking the Hamiltons down. How wrong that was!"

Teresa paused, closing her eyes briefly.

"This is incredible," Jenna commented as the truth began to sink in.

"Maria didn't abandon Jonathan. She stayed in touch with all of us to make sure he was ok. We took care of him while she underwent a complete transformation. She cut and dyed her hair, she lost weight and trained; she became someone totally *new*. The next time we saw her, she re-emerged as Special Agent Maria

Turette. She's been after Mason Hamilton ever since, trying to find a way to make him pay for all the hurt he's caused. Unfortunately, Maria hasn't been able to pin a single charge on him. He's too clever for that. One day, he'll slip up and there won't be anyone around to save his sorry ass. Maria will never stop trying."

"I don't know how she does it, Teresa. How does Maria stay sane? Mason Hamilton is the most evil person I have ever met."

"You don't have to worry about Maria, Jenna. She is totally driven. She believes Hamilton will get what he deserves."

Jenna nodded as she mindlessly picked up a clump of sand then let it fall through her fingers.

"I admire her, Teresa. Maria did her best to coordinate the museum raid. I don't blame her for what happened to me. I hope she knows that."

"Maria thinks very highly of you, too. She told me so. She wants to protect you, Jenna. She made a promise to your mother when you were very young. Maria told Lois she would always look after you and Austin if...anything happened."

Teresa reached for Jenna's arm.

"Last November, a strange man came to your parents' house when your father was out running errands. He accused your mother of hiding the treasure pieces. She was completely thrown off-guard. No one had mentioned the treasure pieces in such a long time. He threatened her. Your mother slammed the door in his face and set off her car alarm. The man fled and didn't return, but he scared the hell out of Lois. She called me immediately, and we contacted Maria."

Jenna recalled how agitated her mother seemed the weeks right before Christmas. Lois had been withholding her fear and didn't want to involve her family. Her mother was taking a risk to save the most precious people in her life, but none of them knew anything about it.

"Maria wanted to assign a few agents to keep an eye on Lois, but she was afraid your father, you, or Austin would be suspicious. Then she would have no choice but to explain her involvement. So against Maria's suggestion, Lois only allowed the agents to make drive-bys. Your mother was always worrying about everyone else, when she should have been worrying about herself."

Jenna swallowed hard.

Why couldn't you have told me, Mom? Your secrets cost you your life.

"Now I'm worried about you. I may have done something to arouse Hamilton's suspicions."

"I don't understand, Teresa. I thought George was the one who told Hamilton about Candace's letter? Isn't that why he kidnapped me? To see if I knew my mother's secret? Hamilton made that assumption when I was tied up in his office."

Teresa wondered. Maybe Jenna was right. Could it be just a coincidence?

"At the beginning of the summer, I received an envelope with instructions from the CIA. Inside were two old newspaper clippings. One was an obituary for a man named Henry Stanick and the other was the article describing the apartment fire in which Sylvia Bernard reportedly had died. Someone else died in that fire, Jenna. It was a cover-up. After doing some research and calling Maria, we both think it was Henry Stanick's niece, Alina Catrall. When Maria left New York, she completely forgot Alina was coming over the next morning for breakfast. Maria thinks Mason's men surprised Alina and killed her before she had a change to explain who she was. Then when they realized their mistake, they set the apartment on fire to cover their tracks."

"And Mason didn't know his men killed the wrong person?"

"I'm not sure. Mason is very intimidating. Maybe his men were afraid to admit their failures."

"Wasn't the body identified?"

"Everyone assumed the body belonged to Sylvia Bernard. It was her apartment. She apparently matched the general physical description of the burned remains. DNA testing wasn't perfected back then. It was an open and shut case. Delving into Alina Catrall's death would only raise suspicions. The CIA didn't want to take a chance Hamilton would figure out Maria was still alive."

"So the CIA covered up Alina Catrall's death in order to save their undercover agent and their mission?"

Teresa nodded. "For the greater good, sometimes..."

Jenna was totally amazed. But she understood.

Teresa continued, "I was instructed to put the clippings and a note in a new envelope then mail it to a post office box in New York. Another agent would retrieve the package and deliver it to Mason Hamilton's office. This was a plan to flush out Mason hoping he would make a mistake. I prayed this was the last time I would be contacted and given orders from the Agency. But as you can see, once an agent, always an agent. You never retire from the CIA; you just go under the radar for awhile."

Teresa felt her shoulders sag.

"Saying I'm sorry now doesn't even begin to take the edge off, but I am sorry…if this chain of events has put you in danger."

Jenna clasped Teresa's hands.

"How could you possibly have known, Teresa? I don't blame you for what happened."

Jenna felt a mixture of emotions as she and Teresa sat silently watching the ocean crests roll in and out again. The truth felt so painful now.

But Jenna knew once the hurt subsided, she would have the courage she needed. To take Mason Hamilton down.

Epilogue

Jenna stepped off the plane squinting in the Jamaican sun, so appreciative for the absolutely beautiful day. In her haste to pack, she forgot her sunglasses which she sorely regretted now.

No worries, she thought to herself. *I'm on vacation.* Those words sounded so strange as they echoed in her head. This was actually a real *vacation.* Carefree, no schedule. Just a few days of relaxation before the new school year started and she was back in the classroom.

Walking across the carpet rolled out to welcome island guests, she inhaled a mixture of sweet, exotic scents from the tropical foliage. Inside, the airport was bustling as the first flights of the day were now arriving.

Jenna was greeted with a warm radiance as she headed for baggage pick-up. Every attendant offered a gracious smile. A nice way to start off the day after the early morning flight.

The invitation had arrived unexpectedly a couple of days after she returned to Cape May. She was so surprised to receive a hand-written note from Tumi Carile, who invited her to spend a few days in Jamaica visiting with his family. Tumi stopped by the hospital on the day she was discharged. They had struck up quite a conversation, talking for over two hours.

Tumi shared a few tales of growing up in Jamaica. His parents divorced when he was young; his mother leaving her homeland to live in the States with her new husband. Tumi stayed in Jamaica with his father, learning through a misdirected piece of mail several years later he now had a step-brother.

As an only child, Tumi was naturally curious about his stepbrother, just three years younger than himself. Tumi repeatedly begged his father to allow him to visit his mother, stepfather and stepbrother in the States, but his father flatly refused.

Tumi's father died suddenly of a heart attack the day after he graduated from high school. Feeling such loneliness, Tumi desperately wanted to reconnect with the rest of his family. He left for the States the same afternoon he buried his father.

It was a sad story, but Tumi told it with such passion Jenna couldn't help but feel he had overcome so much. The more she talked with Tumi, the more she liked him. Tumi's thick Jamaican accent and his undeniable polished manners added to his charm. Towering just over six-foot- seven, the soft-spoken man with graying temples, had befriended her. No wonder Chase had great admiration for his friend. She could see why.

But Chase never went into details about their association. Tumi was a mystery that didn't need to be explained, Chase had told Jenna. He left it at that and she didn't pry. Anyone who wanted to keep an eye on her back was ok in her book. But one day, Jenna promised herself, she would find out more about Tumi Carile.

Too many mysteries had already started a whirlwind of danger.

Tumi assured Jenna he would keep her safe in Jamaica if she would consider a visit to his homeland.

Teresa wasn't so sure. She cautioned Jenna about leaving the States right now. The FBI had no jurisdiction in Jamaica. Mason Hamilton was still in Venice according to the latest news tabloids, but he had connections all over the world. It was risky, but Teresa also knew Jenna needed to get away for her own sanity.

Jenna waited for her suitcase at the baggage carousel.

A man approached her holding a sign with her name on it. He was wearing a silver Rolex with a small chain dangling from the side. Tumi had worn a similar one at the hospital. Tumi specifically told Jenna only his trusted allies wore the same watch. It would be a sign to know she was in good hands.

"Greetings, Miss Jenna. I am Markus. Tumi Carile has asked me to drive you to your hotel."

"Thank you," Jenna said as she handed Markus her suitcase.

Markus was one of the largest men Jenna had ever seen. With huge, thick arms and an enormous physique, Jenna thought he could probably wrestle a bear and win. Markus wore a brightly-colored shirt decorated with orange and white flowers, which complimented his rich, chocolate skin. She doubted anyone ever poked fun at him for fear of his intimidating stature.

The car Markus drove was as big and bright as he was – a yellow Hummer with huge wheels about four feet tall. Jenna had no idea how in the hell she was going to hoist herself up. Her injuries hadn't healed completely. Pulling stitches was not the way she wanted to start her vacation.

"I might need some help," Jenna hinted as Markus deposited her suitcase in the back seat.

Markus grinned. He quickly circled the car and easily lifted Jenna into the front seat like she weighed nothing.

"Thank you, Markus."

"My pleasure. The hotel is just a short drive. Tumi reserved a room for you at The Royal Palm. It's one of the nicest hotels in the area. You will like it."

Arriving at the circular driveway in front of the hotel, Markus bounded from the Hummer and handed Jenna's suitcase to the valet.

"Take care of her, Gerald," Markus chimed as he helped Jenna to her feet. "Miss Jenna is Tumi Carile's guest."

"Ah, Markus, my good friend. You have brought a beautiful young woman to our wonderful hotel. Of course, we will take exceptional care of her. Anything for Mr. Carile."

Gerald bowed slightly to Jenna, and then extended his hand.

"Gerald LaTrobe at your service, Miss Jenna. If I can do anything to make your stay at The Royal Palm a delightful experience, I hope you will not hesitate to ask."

Jenna blushed. She had never stayed at such an elaborate hotel, nor had a valet ever addressed her with such formalities and courtesy. She was extremely impressed.

"Thank you...*very much*."

Markus handed Jenna his card.

"Call me, Miss Jenna, if you need a ride or anything else. I'd be happy to take you on a tour of the island. I have all kinds of trivia to share with you."

Jenna smiled and nodded. "About Tumi Carile?"

Markus laughed causing his entire body to shake.

"Ah, Tumi. He must remain a mystery, I am afraid. You will not get any secrets out of me."

Jenna frowned slightly but she took it in stride.

"Well, thank you anyway for picking me up at the airport. When will I see Tumi?"

"Tumi will be in touch with you shortly. I will let him know you have arrived. Please enjoy the amenities of the hotel. Enjoy your stay, Miss Jenna."

Jenna waved as Markus rolled the Hummer out of the hotel's main entrance. She followed Gerald into the lobby as he led her to the registration desk.

"Miss Reed, welcome to The Royal Palm," the desk clerk said as he laid a key on the marble counter.

Jenna was in a daze and didn't immediately respond. She was too busy staring at the ornately adorned lobby. Antique chandeliers dangled from the tall ceiling. Various tapestries in mosaic designs lined one wall. The furniture was modern in contrast, but blended well as the hotel theme presented her with a mix of Old World charm and modern affluence.

"Miss Reed?"

Jenna turned back to the front desk, embarrassed she hadn't paid attention the first time.

"I'm so sorry. Thank you."

"Room 115, Miss Reed. Follow me, I will show you the way," Gerald said as he wheeled Jenna's suitcase through the lobby and down the first corridor.

"You have a ground floor suite with a view of the ocean on one side, and our pool on the other. Mr. Carile requested you receive one of the best suites we can offer."

"Unbelievable," Jenna remarked as Gerald opened the door to her suite.

"Indeed...he is."

Jenna glanced around the huge suite. She was excited! From the sliding glass doors off the patio, she could walk a short distance to the glistening fountain pool. The beach was a little further beyond the pool and visible from the bedroom. She could sit up in bed and look at the ocean. Life was definitely getting a little better!

"Enjoy your stay, Miss Reed."

"Only if you promise to call me Jenna."

Gerald bowed.

"Jenna. A graceful name. If you require anything, please call the front desk and ask for me."

Gerald turned to leave.

"Oh, wait, Gerald."

Jenna opened her purse intending to provide a tip, but Gerald shook his head.

"No, Jenna, it is not necessary. We do not accept gratuities at The Royal Palm. It is our pleasure to make your stay most enjoyable. You will reward us greatly if you leave with a smile and you promise to return. Then we know we have exceeded your expectations."

"I'll remember that, Gerald. Thank you again."

Jenna didn't waste any time. She quickly changed into her black-and-gold striped bikini and a t-shirt. Her scars had not completely healed, and she was still self-conscious about how she looked. Even though she didn't know a soul in Jamaica, she couldn't stand the idea of people staring at her.

She rolled her t-shirt sleeves up and over her shoulder, baring her arms as much as possible. It would have to do. She hadn't come down here to impress anyone.

Just to relax.

Jenna closed her eyes and laid her head back against the chaise. The peacefulness felt so good.

Two hours baking at poolside was quite enough for her first day in the hot Jamaican sun. Jenna wiped away a bead of sweat which had rolled down her face. She needed a cold bottle of water.

As she closed the door to her suite, Jenna stopped abruptly. A small white envelope had been slipped under the door. A sense of dread immediately sent a chill through her body. Both hands trembled as she fumbled with the back flap of the envelope.

As soon as she saw Tumi's signature, Jenna was able to exhale.

Dearest Jenna,

My apologies for not greeting you in person. I was detained, and could not get to the airport in time. I trust Markus was an able and entertaining guide. This evening my family and I invite you to be our guest at a reception at the Island Palace Hotel, just a short walk down the street from your hotel. I will meet you in the lobby of The Royal Palm at seven-thirty. Please accept the enclosed certificate to Moni-

*que's dress shop on behalf of my forgetfulness. I should
have mentioned the reception in my earlier correspondence.
I look forward to seeing you this evening.*

                                                    Tumi Carile

"Ok, Tumi, you're on," Jenna said to herself as she tossed
her towel across the wicker chair just inside the door.

"Why the hell not? I deserve a fun evening out!"

After a quick shower, Jenna was pumped up for her shopping adventure.

Monique's was located within the hotel's lobby. Adele
Louise, the store's manager, greeted Jenna as soon as she stepped
inside.

"Ms. Reed, I am pleased to meet you. I am Adele Louise.
Mr. Carile speaks very highly of you. He told me to expect you. I
will be very happy to show you our lovely dresses."

A petite woman in her early forties, Ms. Louise commanded
a presence in the way she walked and talked. Sophisticated, yet
full of charm, she made Jenna feel very welcome in just a few
short minutes.

"We have some new arrivals you must see!"

Jenna followed Ms. Louise to the far end of the store. Several racks of gowns lined one wall, all in deep colors and patterns.
Jenna was encouraged to try on as many as she liked in front of the
full-length mirror in the middle of the store.

"You look...*stunning*," Ms. Louise said as she clasped her
hands.

Jenna admired herself in the mirror, turning from side to
side. The floor-length, silk gown she had chosen was an intense
shade of jade. It was high enough in the front to hide her scars,
yet low cut in the back, flowing into a cascading drape which
ended just above her hips.

Jenna turned, allowing the flare of the long gown to swing
across the floor. At Ms. Louise's suggestion, she also chose a pair
of four-inch silver heels.

Jenna was ecstatic. The gown complimented her features so
well, clinging in just the right places. The silkiness felt cool
against her skin, making her feel totally sexy.

But for a moment her heart sank. She had no one to feel
sexy for...she had pushed away Chase...and Jonathan.

Jenna's face showed her sadness until Ms. Louise stood beside her.

"Sometimes we make the effort...*just for ourselves.*"

Ms. Louise lightly tapped Jenna on the elbow.

"You look exquisite. Feel good about yourself. I will have the gown and shoes delivered to your room."

"Thank you...for everything."

Ms. Louise's words of encouragement were just what Jenna needed.

Tonight she was going to dress up and turn a few heads. If not for anyone, but herself.

The afternoon passed quickly. Jenna took a walk down to the beach and marveled at the beautiful landscaped areas surrounding the hotel. Soon it was time to get ready for the reception.

Jenna waited in the lobby until ten of eight. Was Tumi standing her up...again? Tumi wasn't starting out with a good track record. She decided to wait in her suite.

As she turned to leave, Jenna was stopped by Albert, the hotel's concierge.

"Miss Reed, I have a note for you from Mr. Carile."

"Thank you," Jenna said as she opened the envelope.

Dearest Jenna,

> *You must forgive me once again. I am unable to escort you to the Island Palace Hotel this evening as yet another matter requires my utmost attention. Please proceed to the reception and I shall join you shortly. I promise you, this will be the last time I will send correspondence instead of meeting you in person.*

> *Tumi Carile*

"Mr. Carile, you are the mystery man," Jenna said quietly to herself as she made her way to the front of the hotel. Glancing to her right, she saw the large sign for the Island Palace Hotel at the end of the block.

Gerald, the valet who greeted her earlier, was still on duty. When he saw Jenna coming out of the lobby, he bowed to her and smiled.

"Miss Reed, you look...*dazzling.*"

Jenna blushed at his compliment.

"Thank you, Gerald."

So what if Tumi hadn't been able to accompany her? She was a big girl. She could certainly walk to the reception by herself. She was feeling good.

Jenna arrived at the Island Palace Hotel at exactly eight. She was so proud of herself. For once, she was actually on time for a party.

The lobby wasn't quite as lavish as The Royal Palm, but still exuded a welcoming aura. Soft hues of peach and moss green adorned the lobby catching Jenna's eyes.

A few hotel guests were reading newspapers and working on laptops. There were no signs directing guests to a reception, no music filtering in from an adjacent room, and no one was dressed in suits or in cocktail dresses. Jenna felt a little over-dressed.

Jenna soon caught the attention of the front desk clerk whose eyes seemed to linger longer than necessary.

"Can you please direct me to the reception?"

"The reception?" The clerk gave Jenna a puzzled look. "I am sorry, Miss. I am not aware of a reception this evening. I will check with the manager. One moment, please."

Jenna gazed around the lobby once again as an uneasy feeling swept over her.

Stop it, she told herself.

She couldn't help it. Her senses were starting to tingle. Something wasn't right. The hotel was almost deserted.

The desk clerk returned with the manager at his heels.

"Miss, there is no reception scheduled for this evening, or the rest of the month. I am sorry you are mistaken."

Jenna shrugged. She couldn't believe this. Somewhere she had gotten her signals crossed. Perhaps in her haste she hadn't read Tumi's note completely.

"Thank you for checking." Jenna turned to leave.

"It is a lovely evening, Miss. You should take a stroll along the walkway behind the hotel. It connects all the hotels along the shoreline. It is well-lit. Allow me to show you."

The manager walked Jenna to the side entrance which led to the stone walkway, now glistening under the moonlight. Tall gas lamp-posts were positioned along the perimeter of each hotel property.

The muted lighting created such a romantic ambience with the ocean as a backdrop. Jenna couldn't resist. She kicked off her shoes and walked barefoot along the weathered stone tiles.

Too bad she didn't have someone to hold her hand.

Stop wishing for someone...you wanted to swear off men for the summer, didn't you?

The little voice in Jenna's head was saying *I told you so* loud and clear, but it didn't make her feel any better.

Loneliness captured her mood. A couple at the water's edge caught her eyes. They were engaged in a passionate kiss. She remembered how that felt. The intensity. The heat. The powerful desire between two people...wanting nothing more than...

Jenna just shook her head as she continued on her way. She had all that...and she let it go. There was no one to blame...but herself.

Footsteps sounded on the tiles behind her. They were getting closer. Jenna's skin froze; the balminess of the breezes instantly sent a chill over her entire body.

Can't I have one night when I don't have to look over my shoulder?

At first she was afraid to turn around, too scared to see who was following.

But fear had made her stronger. Jenna grabbed the side of her dress, and turned quickly to her left with as much courage as she could gather.

It couldn't be...

Jenna was mesmerized. Her feet sunk in the sand as she skidded off the stone tiles. She couldn't believe her eyes.

Was she dreaming?

There in the moonlight, a man stood before her, handsomely dressed in a black tuxedo. He stretched out his hand and held her gaze.

She couldn't help but stare into the familiar eyes of the one man she had ever wanted to see and be with on this Jamaican beach. At that moment, she completely forgot her lecture about needing space and time. Was this her destiny, or a set-up by Tumi Carile?

It really didn't matter...because within seconds she was falling in slow motion into the arms of...

Chase Garrett.

"Jenna!"

Chase didn't give Jenna a chance to berate him for following her, or even a chance to speak. He found her lips and took complete control. Folding Jenna's body close to his own, Chase felt his body shudder as he laid his hands across Jenna's bare back.

"You look so...sexy. You feel...," Chase said, his breath ragged after such a long, passionate kiss.

"Don't talk to me, just kiss me," Jenna drew Chase's mouth back down to her lips. This wasn't just a reunion between two former lovers; it was a reconciliation of two hearts that refused to let go.

Jenna pulled Chase in the direction of her hotel. Unspoken words of forgiveness and undying devotion were resonating louder than either could comprehend at the moment. All they both desired was a chance to demonstrate the passion which had ignited the first time they had been together.

At the door to her suite, Jenna gave Chase her key. Agonizing moments gripped them both until the door clicked opened. They reached for each other again as their eyes locked, the suspense of their passion ready to explode.

Chase prolonged their kiss as he slipped his fingers under the straps of Jenna's dress lowering them to her shoulders. As his lips grazed her neck, Chase felt an uncomfortable rush of air roll over them.

In his haste to get Jenna into her room, Chase hadn't completely shut the door.

Two seconds later, the door was suddenly slammed behind them.

Jenna and Chase were now staring into the barrel of a gun held by someone in the shadows, his face invisible in the dark. Only the light from the moon sneaking in through the blinds of the windows illuminated the tip of the weapon.

As the unknown invader stepped closer, Chase stepped protectively in front of Jenna.

"Who the hell are you?" Chase defensively held Jenna back with his arm.

"Ms. Reed? Are you...Jenna Reed?"

The voice belonging to the man who now held them captive was firm, but not threatening. The pointed gun was enough of a deterrent.

"Yes," Jenna answered as she pushed up her dress straps. "Who wants to know?" An air of defiance emanated from the stance she had taken.

The man stepped from the shadows and quickly lowered the gun.

"I apologize for the intrusion. I'm Damian Pierce. My wife is Maria Turette. She's *missing*...and I need your help."

Jenna stepped out from behind Chase.

"What? Maria...! What happened?"

"We have good reason to believe she's been abducted...on the orders of Mason Hamilton," another familiar voice answered.

Jenna turned in the direction of the voice she knew so well...and held her breath.

Jonathan Knox stepped into Jenna's view, his silhouette making an ominous presence in the dimly-lit room. Finally getting a view of Jenna in her long sensuous gown, Jonathan inhaled sharply before he was able to continue.

"We believe my father....has taken my mother hostage and only you can help us," Jonathan added.

Damian interceded. "I received a ransom request. Whoever has Maria doesn't want money... just the four gold animal figurines...sound familiar?"

"Yes..."

Jenna was cut off by the appearance of yet another man stepping out of the shadows.

Tumi Carile bowed slightly as he joined the others. "It appears I must apologize...*once again*."

Jenna stared in unbelief at the men assembled in her room.

"My brother's idea," Tumi said as he gestured towards Damian. "I assure you, Jenna, it was not my intention to lure you to my country under the guise of a vacation. I truly did want you to visit Jamaica. However, the timing of Maria's disappearance required creative actions."

"And I was just starting to enjoy myself. I should have known better."

Jenna put her hands on her hips and stared at each man who was surrounding her, three of whom were pleading for her help and one, no doubt, would try to convince her to turn around and get the hell out of here.

"There is…another piece of…disturbing news," Damian said as he looked directly at Jenna. "This morning, I received Intel from my sources in D.C. There's been another murder you need to know about."

"Who?" Jenna asked, feeling the rigidness of her body start to wane.

Damian hesitated before continuing. The impact of the news would most likely send Jenna over the edge, but he couldn't keep it from her. She would learn soon enough.

"Teresa Maylor was found dead in your beach house. She was stabbed using the same method of a contract killer we've been tracking for quite some time."

Jenna could barely utter a sound. "The Closer?"

Damian nodded. "We lost his trail shortly after the take-down in New York, but apparently he didn't go far. I'm sorry I had to be the one to tell you."

Damian let the words sink in as he watched Jenna's body slowly lean against Chase.

"Why?" Jenna tried to scream, but the blood was rushing to her face far too quickly. She felt so hot; her throat was constricting. She was grateful, once again, for Chase's supportive arms wrapping around her at the moment she needed them the most.

Jenna was too despondent to notice Jonathan's reaction. He was crumbling inside, but for once, he held his ground and tried to remain calm. This wasn't the time to deal with his jealousy as he watched Jenna being comforted by Garrett. There were other important issues to deal with first.

"Tell her the rest, Damian," Jonathan said emphatically.

"Do you think that is wise?" Tumi interjected. "Jenna has suffered several shocks this evening. Perhaps additional details will only cause…"

"What else, Damian?" Jenna managed to say.

"Intel indicates Mason Hamilton has bragged about closing "The Circle" by executing Teresa Maylor. In his sadistic mind, he has now fulfilled his father's dying wish. You know about The Circle, right?"

"But Hamilton is wrong. Maria is the only survivor now," Jenna said in a hushed tone.

Damian nodded. "I hope to hell he hasn't figured out who she really is, or she may be dead already."

Damian looked away and Jenna immediately felt his pain. She remembered her anguish vividly when she first learned of Austin's kidnapping.

"What do you need me to do?" Jenna asked, knowing the answer already.

"No way." Chase's arms tightened around Jenna's waist. "You are not going to risk your life again!"

Placing a hand on his chest, Jenna looked deeply into Chase's eyes. The same passionate eyes which attracted her the first time they met in Cape May. Once full of excitement and wonder at the start of their relationship, were now filled with tender affection coupled with deep-rooted fear.

"Maria's life is in danger. She didn't give up on me, and I can't just stand by and let anything happen to her…especially if I have a way to prevent it."

Chase laid his hand against Jenna's cheek. Her mind was made up. He didn't stand a chance of changing it. Jenna Reed was the most determined and amazing woman he had ever met. But he knew the ground rules now and he had a decision to make.

Chase released Jenna from his arms. He picked up her purse she had tossed on the dresser beside the door. Finding her cell phone inside, he placed it in Jenna's hand.

"Go ahead, make the call."

His arm returned to Jenna's waist, giving it a firm squeeze.

"I don't think you're going to make it back to school in time. *We* have work to do."

Keep your chin up…

The Jenna Reed story continues in *Counteract*…

About the Author

S.A.Van lives in Wilmington, Delaware with her husband, daughter, two cats and two dogs. Her love of suspense novels complex with interwoven stories and memorable characters, led her to pursue her passion for creative writing.

After earning her Bachelor's Degree in Criminal Justice, she spent several years working in the fields of finance and law. Currently, she divides her time working in an administrative capacity at an independent school and creating future installments of The Counter Series.

Please visit her website at:
www.sa-van.com

About Cape May

Author S.A.Van's favorite vacation spot!

For more information about visiting Cape May, please contact:

The Mid-Atlantic Center for the Arts & Humanities
P.O. Box 340
1048 Washington Street
Cape May, NJ 08201
www.capemaymac.org